The Tree of
Lost Dreams

THE TREE OF
LOST DREAMS

Frank Sousa

Library of Congress Control Number:		2014911987
ISBN:	Hardcover	978-1-4990-4583-3
	Softcover	978-1-4990-4584-0
	eBook	978-1-4990-4582-6

Rev. date: 11/14/2014

To order additional copies of this book, contact:
Xlibris LLC
1-888-795-4274
www.Xlibris.com
Orders@Xlibris.com
541452

CONTENTS

This book is dedicated
to my family that I love so,
and stands by me no matter what.

Special thanks go to fantastic friend
Maureen Mo Bail and wife Char for their
hours of transposing my words into a
language known as American, whether right
or wrong.

PROLOGUE

This book, the Tree of Lost Dreams is the second part of a trilogy, with each book having the ability to stand on its own.

The Tree of Young Dreamers was the initial presentation and we hope you enjoyed it.

The final book, The Tree of New Roots is presently being written. And if anyone can guess the direction it is taking you can join the rest of us vagabonds with runaway imaginations.

"Young Dreamers" followed the dreams of Johnny DaSilva whose diverse chromosomes left him on a teeterboard of life that could change with the wind. He led a gang of friends who lived out their dreams on The Big Tree, where on its limbs they rode as in the days of the Crusades knights; on a spaceship of Buck Rodgers or high in the crows nest of a pirate ship.

And of course the girls hid nearby, wanting to join in their adventures. Nothing doing.

Yet each had the urge to 'learn' what a girl was made of, what a boy was glued together with.

Too young to serve in WWII, the friends tried every method imaginable to get into the service and fight as gloriously as they did on the wings of the Big Tree.

They felt cheated when the war ended and their tum on the hero's podium was lost, seemingly forever. But not so.

It was only months after graduation that the Korean War broke out, leading Johnny to say, "Now we have our war!"

The Big Tree boys, now men, swiftly discovered there were no giant mobs of well wishers seeing them off to the sound of a Sousa March.

If they thought their bon voyage was quiet, their return home was so silent that time stood still.

Johnny's family of his Ma, sister Roma and brother Jazz wrote to him- "Say your Prayers." "Write and tell Jazz to stop scaring my boyfriends away" and "Get one of those bad guys for me."

Yelena's letter was one of exuberant adoration and plans of a story book marriage and fame with Johnny.

Bernadette's heart had to be hidden in the shadows of underserved shame.

It did not take the Big Tree gang of brothers long to realize that war face-to-face was down and dirty; not exactly like towering above your enemy from the softly swaying limbs of the Big Tree.

CHAPTER 1

JUNE 25, 1950

Yelena Smoltz had no sooner finished her Rockledge High presidential graduation speech about the everlasting peace of the present time with "World War II was the war to end all wars. Thus, this means we go forth and seek our future in peace," when the world erupted again.

A lovely thought in a lovely speech. The problem is that war in a little-known place on earth, Korea, broke out. The Big Tree Gang's worry that their chance for glory was lost forever with the end of World War II was needless.

When World War II had broken out, the Big Tree Gang ran around, yelling, "The Japs have invaded Pearl Harbor!" then asked each other, "Who is Pearl Harbor?"

Soupy Campbell, then a pipsqueak, said, "I think she is the Jewish lady on Franklin Street who sews fancy clothes."

When the radios blared and the paper headlines roared, "North Korea Communists Have Invaded South Korea!" Johnny and the gang were teenagers, no longer little rascals, and told each other, "The Communists have invaded South Korea!" and then asked, "What is Korea?"

No matter, they now had their very own war.

The thirty-eighth degree of north latitude was better known as the 38th parallel in Korea.

It meant war if either South or North Korea crossed it. The North crossed it.

The boys of the Big Tree were about to have their own war. Some felt the pangs of patriotism they felt during World War II being fanned—that this perhaps was what they had been waiting for without even realizing it.

They had no more idea where Korea was than the young knew where Pearl Harbor was on December 7, 1941.

The 38th parallel was a line set at the end of World War II by the victorious allies.

When Japan surrendered, many of its troops occupied the peninsula. Americans started the roundup of those troops in the south.

Meanwhile, Russia, intent on a foothold in Korea, started a similar mop-up of Japanese troops.

A compromise was believed needed, and anxious to get its troops home, "Why not here?" an American officer had asked, pointing to the 38th parallel, which divided the country nearly perfectly in half.

The division was so close, one had to think of how a wise parent taught their children to share equally. One cuts the cupcake in half; the other has first choice.

And thus, Communism in the North and Democracy in the South operated on the opposite sides of the fence in plain view of each other.

A setup that apparently pissed off the have-nots of the North like flies on the toilet seat.

This was the report according to the *Boston Globe*, utilizing slightly different phrases, in an in-depth report after the dirt-poor North Korean invasion of the wealthy South Korea.

"Hey, we've only been out of school and out of work for five days, and some nice people go out and find us a job," Scoff Burns said as the gang sat around in the Big Woods, the dark broken by the small fire they had lit from dry branches snapped from the crowded pines there.

Johnny read haltingly, his ability added to or subtracted from by the flickering flames and the returning nightmare that his mother had died. But she was very much alive, as it turned out.

"We're gonna have to kick the Japs' asses again?" Soupy questioned.

"Ain't the Japs," Scoff said. "They're too busy taking jobs away from our parents selling all that crap over here."

"Who then?" Soupy asked.

"The Chinks?" Rhesus ventured.

"Nah, they own half the laundry starch and all the Chinese restaurants in San Francisco," Scoff said, adding, "It's the North Koreans."

"Actually, it's the Communists," Tim said, drawing everyone's attention, as they had not gotten used to the fact he was part of their night wanderers, having missed them once they graduated.

"Who in hell are the Communists? Do they commute someplace?" Righty asked.

"They're trying to take over the world," Tim said, his dark face setting a superserious tone as the firelight flickered on his features like an old-fashioned, herky-jerky silent movie. "The Communists."

"Who the hell do they think they are—Adolf Hitler or something?" Johnny asked.

"Hey, we stopped them in Berlin, and now the red buggers are trying to sneak in the back door," Bird said.

"So what?" Soupy said. "What the hell do they have over there besides rice paddies and water buffalo?"

"Yah, why should we give a good hooty owl shit what happens over there?—wherever in hell 'over there' is. Hey, their slits grow' sideways, a guy has to lie flat on a table while the Chinky, Chinky China woman stands up to get drilled," Skinny Potts added.

"What do you know about getting laid?" Rhesus mocked. "You're still dating your old high-school girlfriend, Merry Palm."

"Palm this."

"Produce it."

"You're missing the point," Tim said. "We've got to stop the spread of Communism."

"Why? Why in good flying fuck at a rolling doughnut do we have to stop them?" Rhesus asked.

"Hey, if we don't stop the donkey fucks there, we'll have to fight 'em here," Johnny said . . . *wonder where . . . those donkey fucks . . . came from . . .*

"Why can't we just send the Commies a note telling 'em we'll kick ass again if they don't cut the crap?" Rhesus said.

"Who the hell are the Communists—just the North Corinthians or whoever in hell they are?" Skinny asked.

"It's not just them. It's the Chinese and the Russians who are Communists and want to make everyone Communists," Tim said.

"Yes, and the first thing they do if they conquer our country is trade Ted Williams to the Yankees, close all our Italian restaurants, and replace 'em with Chinese restaurants. Instead of trying to get us to do that goose step like Hitler tried, they get us squatting on our haunches, arms crossed in front of our chests, and kicking our legs out in front of us the way those Cossacks in the movies kick all the horse shit away from them and into some innocent person's lap—probably on someone wearing brand-new white ducks," Johnny said. "We've got to fight them there."

"Fight who?" Boattail asked.

"The bad guys," Righty said, nodding at Johnny.

"The rat Commies," Scoff said.

"We missed the last war," Johnny said, "but this one isn't getting away from us."

"Holy mackerel," Tim said, "we have our own Audie Murphy here."

"Sergeant York," Pointer said. "Sergeant York was a better shot than Audie Murphy."

"Rat's ass, he was, ask the pope," Soupy Campbell said.

"All I know," Johnny said, "is we lucked out. We got our own war now."

CHAPTER 2

ONE BY ONE

They showed up one by one at the Big Tree.

The word was that Johnny DaSilva was calling a powwow on who wanted to fight the nutso Communist North Koreans and some of their Russian sponsors.

He had bought the government gumdrop. "If we don't fight them there, we will have to fight them here."

The recent graduates of Rockledge High and their friends who flew the Big Tree twin fuselage P-38 Lightnings and F42 Gull wing Corsairs were appearing out of the dark like Dante's shades.

They were greeted by the usual war party campfire, a fire kept low so as not to attract the local volunteer fire department.

There were semi-bare-ass buddies dancing around the flames, with war-whooping secret cries that only the chanter knew. Some chants were without imagination—"Ugh, ugh, ugh."

Others were imaginative—"Ke wah zay, bi chy kerokai ne kaywah," which also meant nothing.

Ah, but some reeked with nonsense—"Ke hay mohegana—walla walla bing bang."

Then some dripped with teenage double entendres—"Ohwowi, hornyboy adinkydo on shore-ah titty wawa."

Yet their war dance lacked the wild vim and vigor of past powwows. When Skinny, the final missing member of the Big Woods Gang, showed up, everyone became as quiet as a mouse hiding under a leaf being sniffed by a cat.

The reason for the lack of ass-slapping and dick-pulling was that a vote was to come before their council, one they did not want to take—a vote on whether to go to a real war, their own war, in Korea.

They were now silent, heads bowed, none singing, "Start me with ten who are stouthearted men, and I'll soon give you ten thousand more."

They had sat shoulder to shoulder, hoping the closeness would make them bolder and bolder. It didn't work.

They weren't stouthearted men but rather were boys of sixteen, seventeen, and eighteen. They were silent young war party braves whose kid dreams of war had, up until this point, involved cowboys shooting make-believe Indians and Indians scalping make-believe cowboys galloping off into the sunset on make-believe horses to chase girls—well, actually to ogle them or to see who made the top smart-ass remark to have a girl scold them.

There had been no tom-toms to spread the word around town that a powwow was to be held at the Big Woods.

There was no word of mouth—just a blank stare, a tilted head, just a frown followed by the look being turned away.

They knew something was up.

But not only weren't they stout hearted men, but also they weren't even men—only kids who really didn't know what the hell they were doing, what they were getting into. Kids who not only didn't have the time of day but also didn't really care what time it was.

But seventeen-, eighteen, and nineteen-year-olds are easy pickings in wartime. They truly believed they could not die—that like John Wayne, they would all be heroes. The girls would take numbers like they were at the supermarket meat counter, just for a chance to swoon at their feet, to remove their high-school bras that had been starched to points.

Tim Yanders and Johnny had talked things over before the powwow. They were first there, greeting each member of their Big Woods Gang with a nod, wondering, "Who's going? Who's staying?"

And "Why?"

Dink and Pointer appeared first. They had traveled the furthest, from Chelmsford, on the 1929 suicide clutch Indian motorcycle they had bought along with Johnny for $75. When they bought it, it still had the slipstream of blood along the back fender from a foot of the former owner ripped off at the ankle boot.

The three of them had just come out of the old Rialto Theater in Lowell. They had watched a double feature, *Pathé News,* several shorts including Laurel and Hardy, an ongoing Batman series, a dancing ball sing-along with the great majority of kids inserting their own substitute words, such as the Eskimo Song where "Muck-a-luck" came out "Fuck a duck."

All the way home, they sang out, "Hush, hush, you mucken fuskies!"

Oh, yes, they also had a magician, complete with an assistant that, according to Dink, "If she wore her skirt any higher, she would have two more cheeks to powder and another head of hair to comb."

They discussed the assistant all the way home, comparing her to everything from a battleship with all the turrets in the right place to a fruit tree full of ripe plums, all ready for pickin'.

Of course, their very favorite of all time, one that would last forever was "Ain't a fit night for man nor beast," or something like that, as they weren't into quoting verbatim. To better imitate the bulbous-nosed W. C. Fields, they would stick their forefingers in their nostrils to flare them out. This also helped their W. C. tonality.

Their favorite movie on the day of the motorcycle purchase was the showing of *Jungle Book*, not only because it was full of wild animals but also because they started an innocent riot during its showing.

They didn't get to view the entire movie, as they were invited by the ushers and manager, quite nicely, to leave, "or have their asses kicked so hard, they would be wearing their assholes as necklaces."

Sabu, the Jungle Boy, had just been presented his first knife and had proudly proclaimed, "I have a tooth."

And Dink had called out, "So what? I have thirty-two."

That alone wasn't enough to get the exit invitation.

At that point, all they got was a flashlight beam in the face and the usher's warning, "Shhhh."

Some guy three rows back yelled out from a throat lubricated from a bottle of Three Roses, "So what, I have eleven toofs in my head."

"I've got a partial plate" came the cry from the front row.

"Shut up, asshole" came a sweet female voice from the rear.

"I've got a full plate," a toothless old lady answered.

A little old man nearby with a roar of a whisper, "I don't have a plate, but I have a knife and fork if you want to get together and share our tools, little lady." Then realizing he had yelled out in public, he stuck his head in his bag of popcorn, his face entering the bag much like a Boston Commons pigeon would on discovering a discarded bag of goodies.

The little old lady, quite smitten by the little old man's ardent attention, plopped her teeth back into her mouth, not without some difficulty, as her mouth still housed a goodly supply of popcorn. She smiled a come-hither smile, complete with dribbles of butter from her mouth that gave her the appearance of a salivating salamander.

She tried again to return his words of offered intrigue but only came up with a "Pee yooo. Later, alligator, afta da shoe."

Many laughed. Many booed. One middle-aged woman of the streets with hair so frizzy, it looked like she had stuck her finger in a live electrical socket, yelled to her, "Go gettem, Tiger!"

Others, the Sabu admirers, didn't see the humor and told them to shut up.

The frizzy-haired lady of the streets, whose mouth was a red smear like it was painted on by highway department painting center strips on town roads, yelled again to the old lady, "I wear falsies too. No shame in that. But the rest of me is real," and she tossed her frizzy-haired head and shoulders backward over the seat, "except false teeth, that is," and she thrust her breasts skyward, giving the appearance of two baldheaded men suddenly appearing from out of nowhere.

"A cheer for Tilly. A cheer for Tilly," a rather well-dressed dandy sang out. The gentleman had on occasion utilized the lady's services.

"A cheer for Tilly . . . and her tits!" came from an innocent voice of a thirteen-year-old boy who had once given Tilly his candy money to grant him a quick squeeze of what she termed her hummers. She had named her breasts herself, as she got no greater pleasure than having a gentleman friend hum a favorite tune on them.

A voice from a gentleman, who ducked his head from view, shouted, "Tit-tit, hurray!"

She didn't want the cheering to stop and encouraged others to join in by waving her hands like the conductor of the Boston Symphony Orchestra.

She was so happy, she wanted to break her solemn vow right there in the movies to "never give no freebies," although she had given the lad there in the movies back his movie money a year after his sweet little squeeze and hum.

She told the boy, "You must-ent tell no one."

He had said, "Man, that's a double negative." She had smiled, though, not knowing what a double negative was, although she thought that perhaps it was a double exposure of a photo.

"I won't tell no one I felt your jubie doos," he had solemnly sworn.

"No, no, you can tell about your grabby—you just can't tell no one you got a freebie."

At this point, the movie crowd's battle lines were drawn.

One group chanted, "Tit-tit hurray!" and the other, "Shut the ferk up!" Even the crudest, unless crocked, would yell, "Shut the fuck up" in a movie theater with thirteen-year-olds in it.

The situation was getting mean.

Dink, Pointer, and Johnny were hurting so much with laughter, they couldn't join either group.

"Here they are!" A flashlight beam hit them. Then another and another, until the beams of all the ushers were on them.

"Hey, turn out the searchlights. I feel like a flying fortress over Berlin," Johnny said.

"These are the wise guys that started it," the smallest usher said.

"Out!" the manager screamed, failing completely to be the cool dude he envisioned himself to be.

"Bottoms up!" Johnny said, ducking down and crawling under the seats until he got to a row free of ushers. His cousins followed suit.

"Bad luck," Pointer said, as the three walked along the street, picking up discarded cigarette packages and stripping the tinfoil off the inside wrapper and adding it to a ball congregating in Pointer's pocket. Early on, he was named keeper of the tinfoil by his brother and his cousin. Later, it would be added to the soccer ball–sized roll of tinfoil kept in the closet, beside the giant ball of string they had collected. The string was big enough to break an arm.

Pointer's first broken arm was the result of a fall from an oak tree he was shimmying up to get a high-hanging Baltimore oriole's nest from which long lengths of string were hanging.

Dink had also wanted to start a hair ball but lost the argument despite his saying there was plenty of old horse, dog, and hare hair hanging around that they could work with.

Johnny had soothed his feelings by naming his cousin keeper of the belly button lint ball. Not only did the cousins and Johnny collect their own belly button lint, but also a goodly number of the gang also gathered lint for the ball, a team effort that amounted to a softball-size presentation.

Dink, in the infinite wisdom that he attributed to the fact he was a year older than his brother and a month older than his cousin, had started the belly button ball off with a mothball center and the words, "There's gonna be plenty of wool in this thing, and we ain't letting no moths murder our effort. This is just the start. Someday I'm gonna have a belly button collection of lint only handpicked by yours truly from the navel of those wonders of the world, the opposite sex."

Johnny felt pretty good that Dink was no longer sulking after the sinking of his idea to start a hair ball and congratulated his cousin with "Today, one piece of belly button lint, tomorrow the world."

Dink was joyous and yelled out to the world, "Someday a pillow filled with public hair from da girls."

"Pubic," Johnny corrected.

"Wattaya, can't spell?"

"Dink, your carnal knowledge is limited."

"You talking about me only collecting publics from carnival women? Forget it. You've never even been laid, Mama Cuz. Marmalade, get it?"

"Jeez," Johnny moaned, "the corn is as high as an elephant's eye."

"What are these public hairs?" Pointer asked.

"Pubic, Phew-bic, dummy," his brother said.

"Wasn't that riot the funniest we ever started? What good luck. 'I have a tooth,'" Johnny said.

"Yah, but we never got to see the second movie, nor the funnies. The manager couldn't have been any angrier if he had a bee up his butt. That was bad luck."

They all agreed that not seeing the rest of the show was bad luck.

But their bad luck didn't last long.

Their luck changed to good the moment bad luck entered the life of a passing motorcyclist and he had his leg torn from its knee socket.

The twenty-two-year-old rider was checking out a fancy lady standing on the street corner when he should have been checking out traffic at the intersection he was rapidly approaching, and he arrived in a tie with a bread truck, claiming the intersection only moments before he was to claim it, and his only choice was to lay his bike on its side. Except the cycle's two wheels and one of his legs, his left, ended up under the truck wheels, which screeched "black, black, no takesy back," and the leg was gone.

He was hauled off to the Lowell General, and his old Indian was hauled off to Lengieza's Garage. Joe Lengieza was the owner of a contract with the city to haul off and store a variety of vehicles—wrecked, stolen, illegally parked, or abandoned.

Johnny, Dink, and Pointer followed the tow truck by hopping onto the running board of a passing '34 Hudson and ordering the driver, "Follow that truck!"

The old gent was caught up in the excitement of what he believed was a police chase yet wondered, looking at the three boys, how the city hired police officers so young.

At the garage, Dink and Pointer got into a shoving and shouting match, which the garage manager attempted to break up via negotiations, as both kicking a kid who wasn't a relative or kids getting away with guff were no-no's in a place of business.

While everyone was thus involved, Johnny checked out the registration, which was attached to the neck of the Indian's handlebar by two small coil springs holding a plastic container.

The ownership papers read "Maura J. O'Connor, 229 Lyman St,

Lowell, MA.," despite the fact the name Jackie "Black Jack" O'Connor was scrolled across the tank within the body of an eagle airbrushed onto it and surrounded by pinstriping, that alternately was broken by tiny replicas of the jack of spades.

At seven thirty the next morning, a young and tearful Maureen O'Connor, with twin two-year-old girls, holding on to her apron strings, answered the doorbell, a cigarette dangling from her mouth.

"Yah?"

Before Johnny could speak, one of the twins said, "Hungry, Mommy."

"Hold off, Maura Junior, your mommy needs cigs, and she ain't moo mooing, so ya gotta wait for your moo-moo milk." She readjusted her breasts inside a too-small nursing bra, "Yah!"

"We're awfully sorry about your husband, "Johnny said, looking at what he believed was the queen of milkers then, taking his eyes off her breast, stared down at his feet, as if the most important happening in the world was taking place on the toe of his Keds. The Keds had seen better days, as the tip of a sock was peeking out through a worn area in the sneaker toe, looking like the tongue of a frog that had been stepped on.

"A horrible thing," Dink said, "and we're not here to take advantage of . . ."

"Yah, sure. You got a cig?"

"No, I . . ."

"Yah, then waddayagut? Waddayawont?"

"We want to buy your motorcycle," Pointer blurted out.

"How much ya gut?"

"Seventy-five bucks," Johnny said.

"Ya crazy."

"Hungry, mommy."

"Shut up, Maura Junior. I asked youse guys, ya crazy or somethin'?"

"I'm sorry, ma'am, that's all we have," Johnny said.

"You seem like a nice kid," she said. "Ya gut a cig?"

"I don't smoke."

"Look, I don't give two good shits about the story of your life. If I take the $75, will one of you run down and get me a package of butts?"

"I'll go," Dink said.

"Let me give you the change for the cigs."

"Old Houdini-hand doesn't need no money. The hand's quicker than the eye."

"Yah," Johnny said, "but a kick is faster than your ass."

"What? Me worry?" and he was off.

"Here's the money, ma'am, but I'll need some papers."

"Give me the money, and you'll get the papers when I get my cigarettes."

"Hungry, mommy."

"Don't say it again."

Johnny reached in his pocket, remembering he had stuck his Baby Ruth candy bar there during the movie with the thoughts of eating it torturously slow in front of his cousins, approximately forty-five minutes after they had gobbled theirs down like ten little piglets on an eight-titted sow.

He had secreted the candy bar against his thigh, where it burned with an almost erotic "Here I am, big boy."

Once or twice during the movie, he had moaned, "Oh, baby."

And Dink had poked him in the ribs and asked, "What ya got? A hard-on for Sabu?"

"OK if I give the kids some Baby Ruth?"

Maura O'Connor, biting her lip and looking past Johnny for Dink and her cigs, said, "Yah, sure, whatever. Let them have a bite of your candy, but you gotta pay the dentist."

Johnny ripped the wrapper off and broke the bar in two, handing the halves to the twins, who gobbled the chocolate in such fashion that there was as much on their cheeks and fingers as in their mouths.

Looking at the sacrificed chocolate, Johnny was nearly overwhelmed with the desire to lick the twin's fingers.

Dink arrived moments later out of breath. "Here's the cigarettes. We've gotta leave and pick up our bike now."

"Why are you so pooped?" Pointer asked his brother.

"Whoever thought some bowlegged old man could run that fast. And for a lousy pack of butts. I'm glad I didn't take a carton."

"We'll drop off the money for the cigs when we get it someday," Johnny said.

"Are you for real, Goody-Two shoes? The old goat probably steals pennies from kids," Dink said.

Maura took the cigarettes out of Dink's hands, "Ya shoulda got a carton. The old fart probably steals pennies from kids."

"Yah, sure. Over here. You can sign the papers over here," Dink said, leading the woman to a coffee table, "and here's a piece of paper," he said, pulling the bill of sales the three of them had written up that morning, complete with serial and model numbers. "Just sign this."

She puffed on the cigarette as she tried to read their handwriting.

Dink lit up a second cigarette and handed it to her when the first burned her fingertips, "Here. Now please sign."

She took the offered cigarette, looked at the bill of sale in front of her, looked at the three youths, Pointer squeezing the package of cigarettes in his hand, and signed, while looking up at them with a sly smile. "I would have given the damned bike away. What did it ever do for me but give me a pogo stick for a husband. Although I think I loved him."

Johnny handed her the money, all ones, and she grabbed the package of cigarettes out of Pointer's hands, slamming the door in their faces.

Pointer whispered to Dink, "Ask her if we can have her husband's leg?"

Johnny immediately pounded on the door.

The door opened, "Yah? What the hell now? I only had one bike."

"Your daughters. You forgot your daughters. You better buy them some milk, or else."

"I didn't forget no daughters. They'll get their milk. Don't you go telling no social workers no lies. I need the money. I got enough troubles. When my Pegleg Pete comes home from the hospital and finds out I sold the Indian, tough shit. What's another black eye."

Johnny looked at her closely . . . She will have . . . three eyes . . . as, for the first time, he saw the heavy powder she used to cover up a matched pair of blackened eyes.

She saw him staring. "Yah. So what if I can outfit a whole city of raccoons with masks?"

They had turns pushing the motorcycle the nine miles back to Chelmsford, petting it as times like it was a new puppy.

It took time, but back at the farm, they squared their new bike away. There were foxtails from Reynard reds they had shot with their single-shot .22 as they checked out the farm's chicken coop contents. The coup de grâce was the airbrushing of "Dink, Johnny, and Pointer, one for all, all for one" on the bike's tank where once had been the name Black Jack O'Connor. The painting of their names was the entire ten yards, a first down!

The only mishap once it was on the road, sans number plate, was when Johnny ended up doing a half gainer, ass over tea kettle and landed over the handlebars. This landing, a one-pointer, pretty much turned his right knee into garbage. The knee injury gave him a matched pair. His left knee wasn't much more than broken glass, a gift from a 250-pound linebacker from Winchester, who took it personally that a 142-pound running guard from Rockledge would dare try to sneak a halfback through his turf.

That was pretty much the history of the bike the brothers showed up on at the Big Woods powwow, a powwow geared to making that new Korean War old news by ending it immediately.

"Those Japs!"

"Koreans, Johnny," Dink corrected.

"Those Koreans aren't going to wipe their asses in my country."

"Oh, wow," Dink said, striking up a Sousa march. "Three cheers for the red, white, and blue."

"Well, we're here in the Big Woods not to bullshit but to kick ass," Skinny Potts said. "So I figure seeing that today's June 27 . . ."

"Jesus, a genius," Soupy Campbell said, "knows today's date. Want to try to guess the year, Einstein?"

"As I said, before I was so rudely interrupted," Skinny said, "today's June 27, 1950, and if we train this weekend . . ."

"Yes," Tim said, enjoying playing the set-up man at his first Big Woods powwow.

"Yes, by God, we can end it all on July 3 and march through Rockledge Square on the Fourth of July with the good old Rockledge high-school band playing 'Hail to the . . . Us'—yes, hail to us!"

"And the cheerleaders would be peeling grapes and feeding us as we lounge across the backs of a dozen pink Caddy convertibles."

"And I'll have a life-sized picture of Big Lefty with me," Righty said, ducking, as Johnny gave him an "I'm with you all the way, all the time" punch to the biceps and a "Sounds good to me."

"Wonder if I can get a special molded helmet," Scoff Burns said, pushing the long hair on the side of his head back until both sides met in the rear, and taking his right hand, made a part where the wings met in the back. Satisfied with the tonsorial efforts, he then ran his hand over the flat top of his butch haircut, sort of like an F4U making a smooth landing on an aircraft carrier.

"Enjoy, buddy boy, the marines don't allow no duck's asses on top their grunts," Johnny said.

"Who said anything about the marines?" Soupy said. "I was thinking about joining the BAMs."

"What the hell is a BAM?" Dink asked.

"Broad-assed marine," Soupy said, lauding this inside knowledge over his friend.

"They'd take you," Righty said, wetting down his eyebrows with his finger.

"Oh, yah. You're the one who squats to pee, Righty," Soupy said.

"Oh, go pee, Soup. Pea soup," Righty said. "Get it? Pea soup?"

"Spare me," Scoff Burns said.

"Yup, Scoff's gonna be spared. You bet. You scoff something up that isn't yours in the Marine Corps, even a pencil, and you go in the brig. My cousin said so," Skinny Potts said.

"What do you know?" Fats said. "The only uniform they'll get to cover you will be a pup tent."

"Hey, Fats, don't go calling my pot black when your kettle spout is so small. You won't even get issued a raincoat. They'll just cut neck and arm holes in a condom for you," Skinny said, attempting to suck in a stomach that looked like someone had tossed a giant doughnut over him and it got stuck at his navel.

"Anyway, who said anything about joining the marines? This needs some thought. Let me scratch my fat ass on that one for a while," Skinny said, scratching his huge buttocks, like a bear pawing for ants in a rotting stump.

"The marines are the ones who will end it, fast. And that's where to be if you want to fight," Tim said. "But of course, your chances of getting killed are better."

"Yah, but in those dress blues, your chances of getting laid are better," Dink said.

"Nooky is nice," Soupy said, "but is it worth getting killed for?"

"Yup," Skinny said, shifting his scratching paw from his butt to the half moon of stomach that hung over his belt then, with fake surreptitiousness, sneaking his hand to his crotch, adding, "and big guy says 'yup' too."

"With your fat arse and luck, you'd get your private shot off the first day," Scoff interjected.

"General. General. Not private. And he can take care of himself. General Dork always could. Always will. And by the way, Mr. Scoff, who are you to comment on one's makeup? You, being the only baseball player in the history of the Middlesex League, arrested for really stealing second base. And home, first, and third."

"There was a market," Scoff said, "and it's not my fault the stupid Lexington manager forgot to collect the bases after our game. He should have taken the heat."

"Oh, sure. Give me a break. You believe your own stuff. Get your feet stuck in your own bullshit," Soupy said.

"I believe that the dress blues will get you into something pink worn over something pink," Skinny said. "Have you ever seen the dress blues? Dark-blue jacket with red piping all around. Gold buttons. A white belt with a gold bucket with the Marine Corps emblem. Royal-blue trousers with a blood-red stripe up the side. A white cap with another gold emblem."

"Yah," Dink said, "the girls line up to sign your dance card."

"To get laid," Pointer said.

"And the corps issues you an extra dick," Rhesus said, "'cause there's no way you can get away with a single dork."

"I can live with that—two dicks," his brother said.

"Is getting a little nooky worth getting killed for?" Soupy asked, giving Rhesus a shoulder shove.

"No way," Rhesus said.

"But a lot of nooky, yes," his brother said.

"We're acting like kids," Tim said.

"This is no kid scat," Johnny agreed. "We've got a job to do."

"Hey, I didn't go to school all my life to learn to get killed," Soupy said.

"You didn't learn nothin'—what are you talking about?" Righty said. "You know less than I know."

"Cheez, I can't be that stupid."

"You can if you study," Righty said.

"Let's knock off the poo-poo platter. If we're gonna get into this before it's over, we've gotta get serious. We've got to stop them there. We don't want no wars in our country," Johnny said.

"Yah, they would fuck up our football fields with those split-toe sneakers," Skinny Potts said, adding, "My cousin is over there, and he says they wear sneakers."

"Maybe we can play them in a pickup basketball game—winner gets Korea," Righty said.

"Well, I'm joining up," Boattail said, "as long as I get the dress blues, don't have to get shot at, and can sleep in my own bed."

"I agree," Rhesus said, crossing his eyes, tilting his head, and sticking his tongue out the side of his head. "Our maw didn't born no idjits."

"Christ, keep that up, they'll make you an officer," Johnny said.

"Let's sign up tomorrow," Tim said. "Communism needs to be stopped now."

"What's Communism?" Fats asked.

"They want to conquer the world," Johnny said.

"So what! You always won at Monopoly and didn't want to share Boardwalk, Park Place, Pennsylvania Avenue, or anything," Pointer said.

"Stalin and the Russians killed more of their own people than the Nazis killed Jews and Gypsies," Tim said.

"Forget Tim. Boattail too. You guys aren't joining up. You're going to college. We need someone with brains to run things in our country after we kick ass," Johnny said. "You make us proud learning, and we'll make you proud fighting.'

"Bullshit," Skinny said, "this is all bullshit. Let them kill each other. Johnny, you've been beating up bullies all your life, and there's now more than when you started."

"You let someone piss on you once, next time they shit on you, and then they rub not only your nose in it but also your sister's and mother's and little brudders', ah, brothers'," Johnny said.

"You've been seeing too many John Wayne movies. Anyway, who died and made you president?" Skinny said.

Righty put his arm around Johnny and said, "I did."

"Jeepers, did a mouse sneeze?" Skinny said, smiling at Righty.

"Hey, I've got big *cojones*, paisan," Righty said, placing his left hand in the elbow of his bent right arm, extending his middle finger up in salute.

"Big balls, you say," Skinny said, walking toward the tiny Righty, smiling, his legs wide apart, throwing first one shoulder forward, then the other, singing, "Do your balls hang low . . ."

"Do they dra-ag in the snow," Soupy sang.

"And jiggle to and fro," Scoff put in.

"Look, I liked Johnny's speech, seconded by Tim," Skinny said. "And I go along with his being elected president, but who died and made him pope?" He again finished by blessing the Big Woods Gang.

"I kiss your ring," Boattail said.

"Kiss my thing."

"I'd have to find the string first."

"Nice talk about my finest possession."

"I say Johnny for pope," Boattail said. "He could push his Grandfather Shiverick's paint cart around, singing onward Christian soldiers. And we'd have to buy one less tank."

"Kiss my ass," Righty said.

"It would be like kissing a sparrow's," Boattail said.

They all laughed.

"Then kiss my ass," Skinny said.

"I wouldn't know where to start," Boattail grinned.

"You're all ass," Rhesus said, making brownie points with his brother. He remembered his brother had taken all the brown Necco Wafers from the package and put them in his pocket for later, declaring, "They're too good for the proletariat."

"Leave Protestants out of this," Fats said.

"Let's talk about tomorrow," Tim said. "This signing up isn't kid stuff."

"Let's talk about girls, not war," Scoff said.

"OK," Fats said, "I love the girls, and the girls love me. Actually, I love pu-pu . . . ah, pus-pussy. I get so excited, I salivate and stu-stu-stutter."

"There's more to a girl than her snatch," Boattail grinned, setting his little brother for the punch line.

"Yes, there's tits," Rhesus said.

"I agree, that's why I call myself Tat," Soupy said, "you know, tit for tat."

"You take the top, but I like the fire down below," Boattail said, changing over to singing the Wheaties song, with a slight change in words, "Have you tried pussy? The best breakfast food in the land."

"That reminds me, I forgot to feed the cat," Scoff said. "My mother will kill me."

"Your mother's been dead for years," Rhesus said.

"Why didn't no one tell me? I've been feeding the stupid cat for ten years."

"Boy, what an outfit we're gonna be. I can hear the platoon leader counting cadence," Johnny said. "Left, left, left-left-left. Let's roll up the sidewalks. Tomorrow. At high noon. We all meet at the top of the Big Tree."

"In the Big Woods?" Pointer asked.

"Yah, unless they moved the Big Tree to Florida," Skinny said.

"We march to the federal building in Boston and sign up," Johnny said. "That way, we can all stay together."

"Nothin' doin'," Soupy said. "Remember the Sullivan Brothers? All five went together."

"That was a movie," Dink said.

"Oh, yah, then why did they name a ship after them then?"

"I can't imagine losing five brothers," Rhesus said, "unless one was named Boattail and hoarded all the chocolate Necco Wafers."

Johnny put his arm around Righty.

"Any questions?" Johnny asked.

"I'm an inch too short," Righty said.

"I won't be eighteen until next February," Pointer said.

"I think I'm too skinny," Fats said. "Maybe they'll take me in the marine band, and they can play my ribs rather than a xylophone."

"Why don't you three guys stay a minute and let me think?" Johnny said.

The rest disappeared into the dark silently, which had been the tradition since they started playing cowboys and Indians in the Big Woods a decade before.

"I'll meet you at the Indian," Pointer yelled to Dink hidden in the dark woods.

Dink's muffled owl call returned through the black meant "OK, little brother."

"Pointer, bring your birth certificate a good hour before the other guys get here, and we hop off to Boston. Now beat it. And take good care of our Indian. The bike's got my name on it too."

"Fats, you have to go to the drugstore. Pick up three sets of Dr. Scholl's shoe inserts, and if you don't have any money, have Scoff do the shopping. See you later, alligator."

"In a while, crocodile."

"Yo, fasta da feasta," Righty tossed in.

"Yah, kiss my keesta," Fats said, signing off and disappearing in the black.

"Let's head down to capture a little light," Johnny said, and the two of them moved softly through the darkened woods.

"What's that?" Johnny asked.

"What's what?" Righty said, standing still.

"That snap."

"I stepped on a twig."

"You'd never surprise a big ten-point buck when you're still-hunting."

"So?"

"But you would get the attention of some enemy out there in no man's land on listening post."

"Yah. So what? I'm not going to pass, with my bad eye and all," Righty said.

"We can get you past that eye test in Boston tomorrow, but you don't have to go. You already lost Big Lefty."

"That was a long time ago," Righty said.

"Yah. Sure. Like it was yesterday."

"Like two seconds ago, but a million years ago." Righty said, a tear forming in his blind eye only.

"I know. I think I understand. A little bit."

"It's just a different set of bullies, and I want a piece of them like Big Lefty wanted the Nazi murderers," Righty said.

"That's pretty corny."

"Sure. But not as corny as your flag waving."

"OK," Johnny said, sharply cutting off the conversation as if he remembered something very important. Turning, he tried to make out the shape of the Big Tree in the dark. The thick trunk they had shimmied the bark nearly smooth on, could only be seen in his mind's memory, but the strong upper branches where they sat like magpies for years could be made out as could the branch tips that spider-webbed in the dark sky.

Righty followed his friend's look toward the tree, where their eyes rested, hoping its shape would clear up.

But it didn't; the darkness got deeper.

The Big Tree and the Big Woods were already disappearing from their life.

Then without a word, they headed down.

Righty didn't snap another twig, but he did let fly with a snapper of a fart.

"Hey, some North Korean on listening post would hear that, and your ass would be tattooed by a burp gun."

"Maybe not. How would a North Korean know what language it was in?"

"True. Garlic is spoken throughout the world."

They trotted through the smaller tree line at the bottom of the hill. They spotted the rock near the road that was partially lit by a nearby streetlight and headed toward it.

"Over here," Johnny said, leading the way to the rock.

"It's your left eye, right?"

"Yah," Righty said. "I can't see nuttin' out of it."

"OK, watch me and practice this tonight and tomorrow morning."

"Yah."

"When the doc is checking your right eye, you hold your left hand over your left eye." Johnny demonstrated as he spoke.

"Yah."

"Then when he says, 'Your other eye,' you do this." Johnny dropped the left hand covering his left eye and raised his right hand, which he covered his left eye with.

"So I still can't see out of my left eye to read the chart."

"You didn't catch it." He repeated the process, dropping his left hand from covering his left eye and then covering the same eye with his opposite hand. "You're reading both times with your good eye, just changing hands."

"I'll be hot damned."

"Let's scoot. And get some sleep, or else it will be noon, and all the guys will all be at the Big Tree and ready to roll and us not there."

They both struck into song at the same moment, "As those Caissons go rolling along. For it's high, high hee, in the field artillery. Anchors away, my boys! Semper Paratus is our guide. From the Halls of Montezuma to the shores of Tripoli."

"Where's Tripoli, Johnny?"

"Hey, I'm not sure where Korea is."

CHAPTER 3

4F TO 1A

"John, you don't have to go," his Uncle Luke Shiverick told him.

"I have to, Uncle Luke."

"We won the Big One, World War II. The war to end all wars. The bullies were beaten. Unconditionally."

"There's a new set out there."

"John, listen to your old Uncle. This is different. The last one, the Krauts attacked the world. The Japs sucker punched Pearl Harbor. English-speaking people were killed. This Korean thing is halfway around the world. We don't speak Korean. We speak American here."

"This war is to keep it that way."

"Come on. Give me a break."

"Uncle Luke, excuse my English, but me and the Big Woods Gang got screwed out of fighting in your World War II, but this time, we don't get shortchanged—we have our own war."

His Uncle put his arm around his nephew. "Look, I told Sis that I'd have a talk with you. You tell your mother I almost talked you out of it. Don't tell her I'm proud of you."

"You'll keep an eye out for Mum, huh?"

"Sure," his Uncle said, pretending to unscrew his right eye and cup it in his hand. "See?"

"Maybe I should ask an adult to watch out for her," Johnny said, smiling.

"Nice shot. Your first shot at your old Uncle. Maybe someday you will be a man. I'll take you for a roller coaster ride on the Hurricane down Revere Beach."

"I don't think so." It was only the past weekend that he saw his Uncle's picture posted inside the ticket booth of the Nantasket roller coaster with the words "Watch for Loony Luke—this nut cake takes the front seat of the coaster, and when it speeds down the steepest incline, he stands up."

Johnny had been proud of his Uncle when he spotted the poster. He heard Uncle Luke's picture was posted on all coasters throughout the northeast, but he'd never had the privilege to spot one. He wanted to point it out to his friends but didn't. He also hoped he didn't look enough like his Uncle so he'd be grounded.

"OK, here's the deal"—it was his Uncle's voice—"I'll let you go, but you have to use both your brain and common sense combined."

"Agreed," then thought . . . *I won't stand up in the front of the landing barge like a cutter's bowsprit . . . and I won't paint a bull's-eye on the chest of my uniform . . . and if the corps has roller coasters, I won't stand up on those perpendicular drops . . . When I was young and not particular, I'd line up the girls and do them perpendicular . . . My sweet hey-suzi me could die a cherry . . .* "I've gotta go. I'm meeting my fellow marines in the Big Woods."

"You know, when I was a kid a million years ago, we used to call it the Big Woods too."

Johnny tried to imagine his Uncle up the Big Tree. "Bet you got to the top of the Big Tree by scotch taping a pair of pigeons to your feet and flying up."

"Nice shot. Strike two. But your Uncle's not going to be whiffed by some young punk," he said, reaching out and grabbing Johnny by the sideburns and lifting up, until Johnny was on his tiptoes, his temples on fire with the pain . . . *I know you're waiting for me to cry out . . . ain't gonna be . . .* "Who do you think you are, Miss Kelly?"

"You mean that old maid sideburns lifter was still there when you were in the sixth grade?" his Uncle marveled. "Good Lord, she was a hundred years old when I was there. She probably still trims her nostril hair."

"That was nostril hair? We thought it was living, breathing dragon flames."

His Uncle swung him around and gave him a loving boot in the can, "Git. I don't want you around when your mother finds out you're joining. Sis will murder my reputation, as well as me. Git and don't look back."

Johnny trotted off; it was nearly eleven. The first of the guys would be showing up.

He was sitting on the highest limb when he heard the old Indian's throaty roar far below; then the motorcycle's last gasp as the throttle was cut, turned off far below.

Johnny knew it was the cousins down from the farm. "I knew the two shits would show."

He peered down into the treetops of the lesser oaks and pines, willows and birch, looking for the movement of his two cousins coming upward.

The smaller trees swayed slightly in the breeze. He could see the stand of young maples and birch where they played tree tag. Everyone except the one who was "it" climbed a tree as "it" counted to sixty-nine, a number they had carefully selected at the time because they had heard the older boys laughing about the number over the years. They thought they knew why the number was special, yet they could not figure out why. Back a couple of years, one of the older boys had tried to explain that girls down there looked like tacos, but none of the Big Woods Gang liked Mexican food.

At the end of the count to sixty-nine, the action started with the kid who was "it" climbing after a fellow monkey, preferably a heavyweight like Skinny Potts or someone who couldn't swing from tree to tree with the greatest of ease.

Skinny was an easy catch, sort of like a hungry bluegill on a warm day.

To escape, those who didn't want to be "it" would swing their tree from side to side until it had enough sway so they could transfer to another tree.

The game had a lot of interesting byplay.

Soupy was the best in the treetops. He swung with the abandon of one without fear, a free spirit who perhaps could drop a large rock on a sleeping skunk, which he had done.

Johnny smiled to himself.

He held the smile; it widened when he spotted movement in the slight openings of treetops and trees below.

He did not see the trees, for if you saw the trees, you wouldn't see the individuals moving through their openings, his father had told him as they roamed the dark forest shadows searching for the gray ghost, the white-tailed buck.

The first time his father told him this was on his first deer hunt. It was on Legate Hill in Charlemont . . . Look at the openings for movement there . . . Look for a horizontal line . . . the buck's back . . . not many things are horizontal in the woods . . . Don't look for the entire animal . . . an ear twitch . . . a tail flick . . . maybe a small patch of white on its chest . . .

Johnny spotted the first figure, moving upward, close to the ground; not a twig snapped. He looked for the second figure. But Dink never appeared.

I knew Pointer couldn't do it . . . No matter . . . we're all different . . . He always pointed at someone else . . . Let Dink do it . . . Johnny did it . . .

Dink and I will do it for him there in Korea . . . wherever . . . and whatever Korea was . . .

The figure was closer now, waving, "Johnny, Johnny, it's me—Pointer."

Johnny watched as his younger cousin started shimmying up the tree, got to the top limb, and crawled out, hugging the branch. He was the only one in the gang who was afraid of heights thus had to go straight up to the top.

"See," Fats said, "it is as easy to sit on top as up the first limb some four feet up."

Pointer's answer was "Sure, but the fall is eighty feet rather than four. It's not the fall—it's the sudden stop that hurts."

But there he was, up eighty feet, sneakers dangling in space, sitting beside Johnny, but with both hands clamped like eagle talons on the branch.

Johnny balanced a large piece of bark on his lap, along with a variety of pens, small bottles of black, blue and white ink, razor blades, and pencils. "Let's have your birth certificates."

Pointer doubled the power of the grip of his left hand on the limb as he reached in the top pocket of his polo shirt and took out the certificate. He had put it there specifically so he wouldn't have to move and groove trying to get it out of a tight pants pocket while on the limb.

Pointer watched as his cousin worked over the certificate, carefully scraping out the year of his birth with the razor blade and whitening out the smudge to the side of the scratch marks.

Suddenly, Pointer was a year older, as Johnny, picking up a pen, wrote a new birth date in the blank area. "There you are, old man."

"Where's brother Dink?"

"Dink's not here," Pointer said, taking the certificate and tucking it back in his shirt pocket.

"I noticed."

"He's decided to go to college."

"Good. We can all use a little smarts."

"Course he quit high school a couple of years ago, so it will be sort of tough getting into, ah, Yale—yah, he said he's going to go to Yale."

"Of course. Then he can be an officer and boss us dummies around," Johnny said.

"Yah."

"Yah," Johnny said, agreeing with his cousin's "yah," "Sure."

"You and me know he's scared of nothing on this earth."

"I know."

"Johnny, I'll tell you somethin' if you promise not to tell anyone else."

"You know better than that."

"I'm scared. Big time."

"We're all born scared or stupid."

"Yah, if you say so."

"I say so. Let's head down. I spotted a skinny scarecrow through the trees. Gotta be Fats."

They both started back along the limb, Pointer hugging the limb as he crept, and Johnny, who always walked the limb upright, following his cousin's lead.

"I ain't never seen you do that before, crawling the limb."

"We can't all be Soupy. Even if we practice being stupid. Can you imagine what a shitter it would be to die by being stupid—like in a car accident or at work? I wanna die in the saddle."

"You ain't never been laid," Pointer said.

"I mean like John Wayne always dies, on a stallion during a charge. Not like Errol Flynn in a woman's saddle."

"Yah. You sure you saw Fats, Johnny? I didn't see nothin'."

Johnny talked as they shimmied downward. "You better practice seeing things starting now. Don't look at the trees. Look at the openings."

"I'm glad you didn't want anyone to pound spikes into the Big Tree to make climbing easier. Can you imagine heading downward, backward like this, and looking up and seeing your cojones stuck on a nail like Christmas bulbs on a fir? Not me."

"Me neither."

They dropped the final few feet to the ground, seeing Fats.

"Fats, how's it going? Still pulling your skinny pud?" Pointer said, making a fake pass at the thin boy's crotch.

"I've cut back. I only yank it before and after sex."

"During your prayers," Pointer said.

"Nah, I'm afraid God will get me. During supper, I give it a few extra twiddles."

"Twiddle Dee, Twiddle Dumb. But good for you, Fats. Confession cleanses the soul, and your chances of getting into Irish heaven are greatly enhanced," Johnny said, slapping his friend on the back.

"Careful, you'll break his body," Pointer said.

"What's Irish heaven?" Fats asked.

"It's where everything that is illegal or fattening on earth, such as eating two desserts or having three girlfriends, as required. Whiskey on your Quaker Puffed Wheat, green beer, a girl with four-leaf clovers rather than pubic hair. You know," Johnny said.

"Think I'll change my name from Gouveira to O'Gouveira," Pointer said.

"Fats, I spotted you coming up. You went along the ridge," Johnny said.

"What's that got to do with the price of tea in China?"

"You'd be a silhouette in combat. What the gooks can't see, they can't shoot. What the gooks see, they shoot."

"Good. What's a gook?" Fats asked.

"Gooks have peckers shaped like baseball cards," Pointer said.

"Whahh?"

"Yah. The gook women have pussies that grow sideways, not up and down, so the guy's willy whacker needs to be shaped like a baseball card."

"You're sounding more like an eighteen-year-old every day, little cousin," Johnny said, "but not a nice one." Johnny gave Pointer a gentle bear cuff beside the head. "Fats, you get the Scholl's?"

"Yup, but what are they for? My feet don't hurt. You're the one whose knees go click clack."

"Yah, sure, click, clack, Paddy whack, give the dog a bone."

"How are you going to get by that doctor with football knees that sound like a one-lung John Deere?" Pointer asked.

"No sweat. You got the Scholl's or not, Fats?"

"Do bears go in the woods?"

"Not when they have a potty thunder pot taped to their tail."

Fats handed the shoe inserts to Johnny, who took them and slapped Fats across the cheek, in a cavalier fashion more suitable to challenging someone to a duel. "En garde! Peckerhead."

"What are they for? Ping-pong or swatting flies?"

"Thin Man, just watch," Johnny said.

"Call me by my proper name, Dick Powell, Myrna Loy."

"Can we get with the game plan?" Johnny said, sitting on a stump and pulling out his jackknife and a pencil, which he placed beside him. "A shoe, Fats."

Fats shrugged his thin shoulders, took off a shoe, set his feet like a quarterback, and tossed the shoe to Johnny in what would pass for a spiral if the laces didn't make it look like a Spalding reject.

"Who would have suspected that our friend had a foot fetish?" Soupy said, rolling his eyes then crossing them before getting them back to their regular socket assignment.

"Hey, we all have secrets, Skunk Killer," Johnny said, calling his friend by the name he carried when they were younger and played cowboys and Indians in the Big Woods.

"Thanks for the profundity, oh Great Chieftain Dipped in Dung."

Somehow, even at the tender age of ten, they had managed to come up with enough Indian names that involved some sort of scatology. Righty Minichelli was Fung Goo Dung; Boattail Eurashian was Feather Fecal; and Scoff was Human Swill Swiper.

An exception was Skinny Potts, who, while sitting around the powwow naming fire in the Big Woods years before, was dubbed by Dink as Potts to Piss In. Skinny was later rebaptized by Rhesus to name their big-bellied friend He Who No Seeum Prick; the vote was unanimous for the second offering—unanimous except for Dink.

Those were the days that, those friends thought, would never end. The biggest worry was searching for bird feathers for headdresses, chestnuts for tossing at each other to carve into peace pipes, or roasts to go with ears of corn, swiped from a farmer's field.

The roast, which nearly always followed a bare-ass swim at Buckman's Pond, also included crayfish they collected. The big discussion was whether to cook 'em or cast 'em, as the crawdads were also excellent bass bait.

Buckman's Big Boulder was not only the sunning area for the gang but also the diving platform off which they could do jackknives, gainers, frog dives, swan dives, and an occasional, on purpose, when someone felt bonzo, a belly flop with its resulting pink belly.

Reports had it, according to unofficial historian Dick Tracy, who claimed the job because his Uncle was a copy reader on the local weekly, that Buckman's Big Boulder led to both the catch of the year, Yelena Smoltz falling big time for Johnny, and one hell of a beating from Johnny's mother.

Actually, it wasn't a beating as much as it was her bayonet practice on him, thrust, butt, slash, with the broom.

The Yellow Peril would make its way from Rockledge through the Fellsway to its switch-over point in Malden where riders would change over from the electric trolley to the electric trains that made up the perimeter of the Boston "El" Elevator System. It passed close enough so Peril riders could see the Big Rock and its inhabitants.

The bare-ass sun worshippers always made it a point to dive into the water when the Yellow Peril was heard "bebopping through the distant woods," as Dick Tracy reported in his oral history.

"On this one day, Johnny was crapped out, sleeping like a bear in January and was late getting up to dive," the tale teller continued.

"It was at the point where the trolley was alongside the boulder that a surprised Johnny got up and prepared to dive."

"Here's Rockledge's finest moment—Ms. Yelena Smoltz was on that trolley, and like a little girl in a candy store on seeing Johnny completely unclothed, in the buff, in the altogether, his doer of deeds waving in the wind . . ."

"Perhaps she saw John's dirty-deed doer," Soupy cut in, "and was smitten."

"Please," Dick Tracy said, holding up his hand for silence, "seeing Johnny's doer of deeds, it was reported that she said, 'That Tootsie Roll is for this sweets lover.'"

"Tell us more," Righty said, serving as straight man.

"That's not the end of the saga of In the Buff on Big Boulder," Dick Tracy said.

"It seems that another viewer from the El was John DaSilva's mother, who also bore witness to his swan dive, a perfect thirteen on a scale of one to ten."

"Yes?"

"And she later will punish her little boy's pee-pee with a broom."

His tale was greeted by applause.

"Thank you," Dick Tracy said, with a sweeping bow.

"Ego maniac," Righty said, "my applause was for the unsung hero, Johnny's pee-pee."

"Here-here."

"Where-where?"

"Three cheers for Johnny! The unhung hero."

"Our leader who hasn't been laid."

The talk ended when Johnny picked his jackknife off the stump beside him and bared the blade menacingly and then picked up one of the Dr. Scholl's shoe inserts.

"Don't do it! We were just kids kidding," Dick Tracy said before falling silent.

The silence was a dual tribute to their curiosity as to what Johnny was doing with the knife and the Scholl's sole, as well as the fact that they had played themselves out ragging him.

"Let's have your foot, Fats," Johnny said, "here, on the sole."

"You're not gonna cut off my foot, are you? I'm a terrible limper."

"I once knew a man with a wooden leg named Pete," Rhesus said, as he had a hundred times before.

"What was the name of his other leg?" Boattail asked, as he had also asked a hundred times before.

"Spare me. Don't make me notch three," Fats said, staring at the two notches on Johnny's knife.

Johnny looked at the notches on the handle and remembered the hunts with his dad . . . *Those were two great bucks . . . those legate hill rackers . . . They just should have stayed home . . . in their swamp . . . or on their high hill . . . I never would have shot 'em if they weren't there . . .*

"Hey, you there, Johnny?"

Johnny's thoughts strayed far away . . . *The next notches . . . will mark my gooks . . . They should have stayed home too . . . Don't tread on me . . .*

"Hello?" Fats said, placing his skinny foot down on the sole.

Johnny traced the foot outline with the pencil and then commenced to cut a quarter inch inside the drawn perimeter with the jackknife, which he couldn't stop staring at . . . *Human notches . . . I'm not sure I can . . . I know I can . . .*

He traced and cut the second insert. This done, he used them to cut six more soles.

Johnny set up two piles of soles, four in each, and had Fats stand up straight. He pulled a cloth tape measure that his mother used in sewing from his pocket, "Stand up straight," and he measured his friend.

"Stand on the soles."

"What?"

"Stand on the soles."

"I'm only doing this because I think you're crazy and I'm scared shitless of you."

"Smart lad," Johnny said, measuring Fats a second time. "Good, you're an inch taller."

Johnny glued the two sets of soles together.

"They won't fit in my shoes."

"They'll fit in these," Johnny said, taking a pair of very large sneakers from a baby bag, "Scoff commandeered them off a clothesline last night."

"Yah," Scoff said, "serves 'em right. You don't wash sneakers. In fact, they ain't no good until they're ripe. That's the way to get girls—ripe sneakers. You hear, Johnny?"

"Gee, thanks. I hope I can handle all the girls signing my dance card when I put your stinky 'clean sneaker, stinky sneaker' theory into practice."

"Up ya giggy."

Johnny put the inserts in the sneakers. "See if you can get your feet in."

"They're OK, but what are they for?"

"You're gonna be tall enough to pass the physical. All you have to do is glue them to the bottom of your feet." . . . *Seems like a lot of work . . . just to take a chance . . . on getting killed . . . Cut the unhappy horse shit, Johnny . . . Yes, sir . . . President Pope . . .*

"Are you saluting yourself, Johnny? Have you slipped off the dark side?"

"Remember," Johnny said, "when Fats goes up to get measured, Pointer will try grabbing imaginary flies. They'll get distracted and not look at Fats. As Pointer grabs flies . . ."

"Can I eat them?"

"Hey, have sex with them if you want, but be careful. We don't want you rejected or 4F cuz they think you're crazy. Just a wise guy will be good enough."

"Hey, this is the marines," Rhesus said. "If they think he's crazy, they'll make him general."

Only Johnny spotted the nearby movement in the woods . . . *Was it a white tail? . . . I'm the deer hunter . . .* Then he saw a section of blackness move. "OK, Righty, come on out with your drawers up."

Righty appeared from behind a nearby bush, a shadow.

"Not bad," Johnny said. "I didn't see you coming."

"Good," Righty said, who had deer hunted with Johnny and his father in the rolling hills adjacent to the off-limits Quabbin Reservoir.

"Except for your white socks."

"So?" Skinny Potts said.

"Two sos. If the wrong guy sees you, you're dead. And the second so, sew buttons on your fly."

"What makes you resident expert?"

"Nothing," . . . *except I know . . . just a tiny bit more about seeing in the woods . . . in the dark . . . All an expert is . . . is one who knows a little bit more than you . . .* "I used to talk with my Shiverick and DaSilva uncles after World War II, the big one, the second big one, if you count World War I, the big war to end all wars. They told me, to have a chance to stay alive, you need a lot of skill," . . . *and all the luck in the world . . . but the very best way to stay alive in war . . . is be 4F . . . If they believe this, how in hell did they join up . . . thinking this shit . . . Maybe they thought 4F after they fought . . . Thinking this shit makes me dizzy . . .*

"Hey, Daffy Don Dilly, what gives?" Soupy asked, checking Johnny's lost-in-space look.

Johnny stayed in his trance.

"What are you thinking, Johnny?" Righty asked.

Hearing his best friend's words, Johnny said, "I was thinking we all better get rid of all our white clothing. A buck's white tail sure draws fire."

"Do we get paid for this boot training?" Boattail asked, flapping his red eyebrows like flying cardinals. "I can use a couple of bucks for a brew."

"Nah, nope, the eagle doesn't shit until we sign on the dotted line. So away we go, Boston bound."

"Last stop—Korea!" Pointer said with enthusiasm.

"I don't like the sounds of that 'last stop' crap," Boattail said.

"I've got the squeaking shits," Rhesus said, disappearing into the woods.

They sat around, waiting for Rhesus's return and killing time by tossing the bull around by the tail.

Finally, Boattail said, "Big brother must have shit his brains out and forgot how to get 'em back. Let's go. He'll catch up. If I know my slick big brother, he'll beat us there. It's a long jog if we don't hitch a ride."

The band that started toward the federal building in Boston was made up of Johnny, Righty, Pointer, Rhesus, Fats, Skinny, Tim, Soupy, and Scoff.

They divided up into twos—better for thumbing.

They would do the Boy Scout run—fifty-walk-fifty, thumbing while walking.

"Whoa up," Pointer said, "who's gonna watch the Indian?"

"Jesus wept. We forgot," Scoff said.

"The bike. What idiots we are," Johnny said.

"Comes the dawn over Marblehead," Pointer said. "Me and Johnny can have turns giving rides."

The first trip with Pointer and Johnny kicking the old bike home with Fats aboard went without incident.

The final trip involving Johnny, Skinny, and Righty proved most interesting.

Skinny took up two spaces on the wide, fringed Indian seat, but they figured that if Righty rode tail gunner, he could sit on the back fender, feet resting on the rear axle, and hang on for dear life, as Righty couldn't get his arms around their hefty friend.

"Be careful back there, Righty," Johnny said, cranking up the old horse until it gave its throaty war cry. "You'd look funny with six-foot-long legs shaped like wheels."

Righty sang, "As those caissons go rolling along," his blue and white Rockledge High letterman's jacket tied around his waist, flapping in the breeze.

"For it's high, high, hee in the Field Artillery!" Skinny sang, and they were off, and running.

"Keep your legs away from that muffler," Johnny yelled back to Righty. "It's hot, hot, hot."

"Don't worry."

"Why should I worry? You're the one who would have a hot foot all the way up to your ass."

They buzzed up to Pond Street, leaned into the corner at Pine, and did a wheelie, with the help of Skinny's extra tonnage, as they swung into Main.

They swung past the S/Sgt. George Hall Congressional Medal of Honor Winner Swimming Pool, past Duck Pond, the Fellsway, through Malden without incident, until they hit Somerville, where a cop doing traffic near Dilboy Field yelled, "Hey, no three guys on a bike! You clowns think you got a Volkswagen bug there or something? Hold up. I said *stop!*"

"I'm only one guy," Skinny yelled. "Give it a goose, Johnny."

Johnny did, causing Skinny, who was waving his cap at the cop to try and follow us, to lose the cap.

The officer picked it up and wiped his ass with it. "How do you like that, you wise-ass little peckerheads."

Johnny opened the cycle up as the chubby cop appeared to actually be closing the distance between them, but swung into a stretch of open highway and was away.

The Big Tree riders spun past the mud flats that led into Boston, smelling heavy with salt and low-tide leavings.

The wind whipping through Johnny's hair turned him into a World War I fighter ace, wingman to Eddie Rickenbacker, the youngest among the Yanks to fly the open cockpit fighters . . . *Where you could look the enemy right in the eye . . . before you shot him down . . . then flew over the downed craft . . . and both the victor and the vanquished . . . waved . . . mutual respect . . .*

He wished he had a bright-green scarf so it would whip behind him as he revved the bike another notch. He could visualize Denny O'Toole breaking out a green scarf in the Greater Boston Hockey League, the oldest high-school hockey league in the country, when Rockledge scored its third goal to lead Arlington three to zip with only five minutes to play.

Denny cut a grand figure. The only thing that took away from the moment was the fact that the Spy Ponders were so enraged they kicked keister, scoring four quick goals. They not only took home the GBI Cup but also took home Denny's cup, which he had pulled out of his cup holder, and scaled across the ice. To this day, O'Toole's cup rests inside the GBI Cup, which rests in the trophy display case at Arlington High School.

Denny's father appeared before the school board the following Wednesday, demanding his son receive his letter for playing varsity hockey, and threatened to sue the town.

This was a hollow threat, as it would have been brought out in court that the two black eyes his son wore were the result of his pummeling his son for pulling "the damned fool stunt that pissed off the Arlington players like a fly on a toilet seat."

The Rockledge coach told the school board he would award a hockey letter to Denny "only over my dead body."

Then the coach later got in trouble with the board when he was quoted in the Rockledge weekly that "if Denny O'Toole's brains were dynamite, he wouldn't have enough to blow his nose."

One board member, also a poor loser, said the school committee should consider firing the coach for allowing the boy to wear the flowing green scarf, thus igniting the Arlington team.

Then the coach not only dug his hole deeper but also commenced to step into it and shovel pig manure on top of himself after he again was quoted in the weekly, "Everyone here knows full well that all hockey players are particularly feisty individuals. If hockey players weren't so crazy about cracking each other skulls, they would have taken up basketball."

Another result was that the quotes blindsided the coach and ended his twenty-nine-year career. Johnny thought a lot about the title game, the end of Coachie's career.

Johnny, his motorcycle roaring, thought . . . *Never enrage the enemy . . . You never know who the enemy is . . . Yesterday's good works are today's. You should have known better . . .*

Johnny sped the bike into Scollay Square and a street construction site, where he was flagged down by a duty officer. Johnny turned backward and blew a kiss.

"Watch out! Don't hit the cop!" Skinny yelled, as a second officer stepped into the street.

The day dreaming Johnny hadn't seen the Scollay Square cop, who did not enjoy any motorcycle, bicycle, unicycle, or anything that came close to his white gloves. "You little touch hole!"

His hand was the side of a ham, and in its white glove, it looked like a giant Mickey Mouse fist.

Johnny smiled.

"I'll wipe that shit-eating grin off your face," the cop said, reaching for Johnny's neck, just missing.

Johnny goosed the Indian to escape harm's way . . . *Jeez . . . if I had a scarf . . . the bastard would have had me . . .*

"You're all assholes!"

Skinny spit toward the cop, who was now shaking his fist, but only managed to decorate Righty's face with spittle.

"Thanks. I was afraid I was going to go all day without anyone spitting in my face."

Johnny had to brake down to a stop as he spotted the construction workers the policeman was protecting, giving the officer a chance to close the space, rather quickly, between him and the bike riders.

He had been activated when he spotted Skinny's lips purse in a spit presentation.

The policeman was shaking his fist as he ran.

Skinny was prepared to beg for mercy as the chasing officer quickly closed the distance. Johnny gave the bike full throttle, and Skinny changed his mercy pleas to a shake of his clenched fist and the challenge, "You wanna fight!"

"Then join the marines," Johnny said, pumping his arm up and down.

"Like we are," Righty yelled.

"The marines would use you cock knockers as toilet paper. You can kiss my arse and go to hell," the beer bellied officer yelled, coming to a halt out of breath.

He would have found enough breath to reinvigorate his charge of the heavy brigade if he had heard Skinny's parting shot, "Wouldn't know where to start kissing—you're all ass."

Righty's jacket slid downward from where it was tied around his waist until it came to rest against the muffler.

A cop two blocks away on the other end of the construction site witnessed the taunting of his fellow finest and stepped into the only opening the motorcycle, now under full power, could come through, a sort of a blockade but without a cruiser.

And he would have stayed right there, forcing Johnny to drive the bike into a gaping construction hole. But when Righty's jacket resting on the hot muffler burst into flames, the officer, who had been cited twice for heroism, stepped out of the way as the Indian looked like a fire-breathing dragon.

Righty slapped out the flames before they ignited the entire jacket and his clothing.

A third officer, just coming on duty, enjoyed immediate and blinding anger at spotting their action and stepped out in front of them.

What followed left the officer mad as a wet hornet.

As the bike and occupants approached the officer, Johnny put on the right-hand blinker. The man in blue stepped in that direction, his extralong Billy Club held two handed to the side like a batter waiting for the pitch, glaring under his arms, looking for the ball, which, in this case, was in the Indian occupants' hands.

The officer's problem was that he wasn't a switch hitter, as, despite the directions and hand signals that indicated a right turn, at the last moment, Johnny laid the bike over and hung a left. Besides evading the would-be batter, the move caused Righty's foot to hit the hot top, bouncing his leg into the air and catching him in the teeth with his knee, chipping a near-perfect V out of his front teeth.

The first sign that greeted them said, "Revere," the exact opposite of the direction they wanted to go.

"We're heading to Revere," Skinny yelled into the wind.

"Yes, I know. That's where my Uncle Luke's picture is, by the ticket booth at the Hurricane. His picture is posted at every roller coaster up and down the East Coast and as far West as St. Louis so no one will let him get on a roller coaster."

"What the hell is that all about?"

"He gets in the front seat, and when it starts to head down the steepest free fall, he locks his knees and then stands straight up, as it plunges straight down."

"What a way to get your jollies," Skinny said. "I'd rather kiss a rattlesnake. But why are we headed to Revere Beach?"

"I want to see if he's still posted on the wall at the Hurricane. And I want to have a word with his 'wanted' poster."

"What the heck are you talking about?" Righty asked. "You can't talk to a poster."

"I know. That's why anything the poster of Uncle Luke might have to say could be real interesting. I can talk to him. Get some good advice."

"I hope you've got fifty-two jokers in your deck and are really heading to the federal building," Skinny said.

"Johnny's pulling your dickie bird," Righty said. "We had to cut this way to avoid that cop with the club."

"Sweet Jesus, I forgot we're joining up. The marines will be a cinch after this," Righty said.

"You bet your old oaken bucket," Skinny said, "we're tough."

Righty reached around his rotund friend and squeezed his nipple through his shirt, "Tough titty."

"You touch my breasts again," Skinny said, faking anger, "without saying you love me, you'll get your ass kicked royally."

"Funny about your Uncle Luke," Righty yelled up to Johnny.

"What about him?"

"It would be funny if he died in bed."

"He's a wild and wonderful whacko," Skinny said, rolling his eyes then crossing them, which went unappreciated, as it went unseen. Johnny was in front of him, and Righty in back.

"Uncle Luke has had lots of good advice," Johnny said. "He stopped us from smoking when we were six years old. We had swiped a package of Wings and were smoking when my aunts caught us, and we were going to get a good whipping. He came along, put his arms around us, telling our aunts to 'mind' their own beeswax. He put his arms around Righty and me and led us up into the Big Woods. He lit up a Parodi for each of us—you know, those crooked little black cigars that would make a maggot gag."

"When we were done, we never touched another smoke, and when I told him back then that I was going to join up when I got out of school, he gave me my first sex talk."

"Watch the road!" Skinny yelled. "Or we'll be painting that dotted white line down the middle of the highway a solid red."

"Anyway, Uncle Luke said there were lots of ladies of the night as you traveled around the world. Real tempting. But that if you indulged your pecker, it could fall off, or at least end up looking like a lawn sprinkler system."

"What he did was whenever he went out on liberty, he'd drink a few beers," Johnny added.

"So?" Skinny asked.

"Well, Uncle Luke said that all men, even the great ones like himself, had great sexual fantasies when they drank, but the booze kept them from performing. He said it was sort of like trying to put a marshmallow in a keyhole."

"A truly great American," Righty said.

"Nothing would stop me from having sex," Skinny said, groping his crotch; but unable to find it, he declared to his friends, "My god, someone swiped my Jolly Mean Giant."

"You mean Tiny Tim," Righty said.

Skinny gave him an elbow, adding, "Up your bony butt."

"Cheez, you should have played basketball. Whatta you do, sharpen your elbows?" Righty asked.

"He played basketball but gave it up after he swallowed the basketball," Johnny said, reaching behind and pinching Skinny's ample midsection.

"We're getting close. There it is, the federal building and our guys," Righty said.

Meanwhile, back at the cycle's muffler, Righty's jacket, which had been smoldering, ignited again and burst into flames, which spread to the grease and oil collection on the rear wheel and chain sprocket, just as Johnny pulled the bike up to the front of the federal building.

Righty jumped off the bike and was grabbed by Johnny, who threw him on the ground and rolled him until the clothing fire was out.

The bike fire burned itself out within moments, having not reached the gas tank.

They checked the bike, and Johnny put it up on the kickstand, as

Pointer, Scoff, Fats, Rhesus, and Tim, who had been resting on the steps, bounded down to them.

"Nice entry," Rhesus said.

"Wot 'appened, old chap?" Fats asked in his best English accent, his skinny body racked with laughter, as he ran toward them with his giant sneakers, complete with three layers of Dr. Scholl's height-enhancing inner soles that slapped like an angry beaver's tail.

"Cheez, Fats," Righty said, "you look like a seal flapping that way."

"Arf, arf," Fats said, slapping his bony hands together in front of him, flicking his head in the air like a trained seal tossing a beach ball.

"Toss him a fish," Scoff said.

"Don't need one, wise ass. I'll just sniff your girlfriend."

"Not nice," Scoff said, punching his skinny friend in the shoulder. "Best be nice or I'll stop dating your sister."

"No one talks about Sis that way," Fats said, getting ready to throw a hay maker that was stopped by Righty, giving the appearance of two flyweight boxers clinching.

"You don't have a sister, nitwit," Rhesus said.

"Now you tell me. I could have killed the swine, my mistake."

Scoff gave Skinny a big kiss on the cheek with a resounding "smack," and the words, "I just love you, big boy. You're so violent."

That set them all off. They all started giving each other punches with the fore and middle fingers leasing the attack, as they yelled "Noogie!" with each connection.

They tumbled up the stairs like a waterfall going upstream, yelling and giving noogies.

"You fiddle fuckers best knock it off and get up here!" a navy corpsman who gave potential marines their physicals yelled.

They took two and three steps at a time and entered a room outfitted with scales and eye charts from which the yelling head had appeared.

There were two long lines of young men.

One line was made up of bare-ass young men. The other line was more modest, outfitted in their football, baseball, soccer, and other varsity letter award jackets, T-shirts, cardigans, and pullovers, worn over their skivvy shorts. One individual wore a suit and tie. No one stood near him, knowing the marine standing in the corner, his head shaved to the bone, would soon be upon him.

Johnny and his friends were pointed to the line that appeared to be heading toward the marine, where they waited and kidded each other, until a voice, similar to the one that had yelled out the door earlier, said, "Knock it off, you're not here for tea."

Their line ended at a desk where the marine now sat ramrod straight, bedecked in dress uniform, the dark-blue jacket with the bright-red piping, a white belt with a gold buckle of eagle, anchor, and a ball, representing the world they were to defend. His blue trousers sported a blood-red strip down the side. The jacket arms were bedecked with gold chevrons and hash marks piped with red.

All this was set off with a chest full of ribbons, which were very colorful and would attract girls—make that women, according to the thinking of the young prospective marines.

To the practiced eye, they wore a Purple Heart for taking a Japanese sniper bullet in the shoulder on Saipan, a Silver Star for getting a flame thrower under control that threatened everyone around as it seared a 360-degree circle as its carrier was shot down on Iwo with his finger clamped on the trigger, plus a Bronze Star for crawling into the black of a jungle night among the Japanese, who were also out there executing wounded marines. There was a variety of unit citations and theater ribbons, including the Bataan ribbon. Missing was any sign of a good conduct medal, thus explaining the corporal stripes despite the five hash marks that denoted four years' service each.

"Look at that," Rhesus said, poking Pointer, "if that doesn't get you laid, nothing will."

"Hey, give me two uniforms."

The recruiting corporal looked directly at Pointer, who looked directly at the floor.

"Birth certificates, gentlemen," the recruiter said, with an extremely friendly appearing smile, "and please fill these papers out."

"Seems like a pretty nice guy," Scoff said.

They filled out their forms and got into the second line.

"Clothes," a navy corpsman in a white T-shirt, white ducks, and a navy-issue cap pushed far back on his head, Leo Gorcey–style, said in a voice that threatened to fall asleep before the entire sentence was out, "Clothes off, buck naked."

They all undressed, leaving their shorts and T-shirts on.

"Buck ass naked," the corpsman said.

Within moments, they stood there, outfitted only in their penny loafers, sneakers, white bucks, and brown-and-white saddle shoes.

Nervous, their privates retracted like frightened box turtles. A few secreted tugs were given in an attempt not to look too tiny down below.

Pointer sneaked in a tug but was caught by Rhesus, "Hey, no hard-ons in line."

"You don't have to worry, grape nuts."

The line ended at a chair where a second corpsman, cap low against his eyebrows and much more attentive, wielded a flashlight, like the maestro who headed up the Boston Pops at the Shell on the Charles wielded his baton.

At first, back in the line, they didn't know what the corpsman's drone "skin it back, turn around, bend down, spread 'em, shove off" meant.

As they got closer, they saw the flashlight beam play on the inspected one's private parts and then his rear end.

"My god," Skinny said, "he's looking up guys' assholes."

"Just feel glad he's not humming 'Chattanooga choo-choo,'" Johnny said.

"He looks too much like that guy that helps the kids into the swan boats on Boston Common," Rhesus said.

Skinny covered his butt and genitals, saying, "He doesn't get to do that stuff with me unless he says 'I love you.'"

"Don't worry about no love affair," Scoff said. "When he sees your fat arse, he'll toss that penlight away and bring in a searchlight to check your Callahan Tunnel. And he'll probably have a corkscrew needle, a foot long, for you."

"Ah, come on, cut the caca," Skinny said, "that's not funny."

Scoff, flexing his thumb and forefinger like a doctor checking out a syringe, said, "Say ah."

"Come on, cut the crap, pretty please. I'll clamp down on the needle," Pointer said.

"Hey, this place is scary, people looking up your arse with a flashlight and under your foreskin. What are they looking for, spy messages?" Fats said.

"Yah, yah. Pretty please, Scoff, knock off that corkscrew needle stuff. Hey, pretty please with sugar on it. These guys are scary enough without you coming on like Dr. Ghoul."

Skinny spent more time under the flashlight than his friends. He couldn't spread his chubby cheeks far enough for a good bird's-eye view.

The flashlight maestro corpsman said, "Pudge, I've been checking taillights for nine years now, and your cheeks are the first ones I've seen that come complete with a double chin. If old toothless there swallows my flashlight before I'm done, you'll owe the government of the United States $8. Next."

Johnny whispered to Skinny, "You'll get even the next time he looks up your ass—we'll put a glass eye up your tail, and won't he be surprised to see someone checking him out."

Scoff was next.

"Skin it back, turn around, bend over, spread 'em. Where'd you get a pucker hole like that, son? No one ever tell you about avoiding Greeks bearing grease?"

"I got hemorrhoids."

"Sure is a mean-looking tail. Glad it doesn't have teeth. Shove off."

But each made it past the flashlight wielder with the same butt and balls they started out with. Their papers were signed, and they were directed back into the line where the marine recruiter still sat, his back straight as a ramrod.

Rhesus nodded toward the corporal and whispered to Scoff, "Wonder if they pull the corncob out of his ass at five."

"Not until six," the recruiter said, giving a friendly misleading smile. "Papers, birth certificate."

After checking the corpsman's short arm and tail inspections, he checked the individual birth certificates, waving each one in turn.

"Whoa up, whoa up, young sir," he said to Pointer, looking closely at the birth certificate Johnny had doctored up that very morning in the Big Tree.

Pointer turned, walked back toward the desk, sweat suddenly breaking out on his forehead, leaving him feeling it was setting off some sort of "look at me" alarm.

"Uh, oh," Johnny whispered to Righty . . . *Come on, Pointer . . . swagger back . . . wrinkle your forehead . . . look old . . . Where did I foul up on the birth certificate? . . . Oh my god . . . he's gonna pass out . . . or shit his pants . . . I'll spend four years in jail rather than the marines.*

"Yes, sir," Pointer said, panicking, wanting to salute, but his hands flapped by his side like a beached seal's flippers.

"Your birth certificate . . ."

"I can explain, sir."

The recruiting sergeant looked Pointer directly in the eye, and the boy could feel himself coming apart at the seams like a Raggedy Ann doll in the mouth of a "bad dog."

"How in hell can you explain that your birthday falls on the same date as mine—November 10, the Marine Corps' birthday. Happy birthday to all three of us in a few weeks. Move on."

The recruiter looked at the altered birth certificate . . . *Good job . . . Better than I did twenty-two years ago . . . God . . . I was a porgy bait fifteen . . .*

"Gentlemen," he said, "follow the yellow brick road," and he nodded to yet another room, where another corpsman said, "Get your banty rooster asses over here."

The Big Tree Gang moved as a clutch of bantys, no longer roosters but hens, toward a weight and height measuring scale.

"Strip down."

The clutch looked at each other. All were stark naked.

"We're naked, mister sir," Righty said,

"You guys with the hard-ons, get rid of 'em. We need your true weight."

The friends checked each other. Who could get an erection while frightened out of their hides?

"Hey, you," the corpsman said to Skinny.

"Who, me?"

"Yes, you, Butterball. Jesus, I oughtta stick a turkey feather up your ass and take you home to my mummy to serve on Thanksgiving. You're guilty."

"I didn't do nothin'."

"Then do something. And your little buddy behind you, take those sneakers, or snowshoes or whatever they are, off your feet. You won't make the height even with elevator shoes on."

Righty carefully removed the sneakers so as to not knock off the three layers of Dr. Scholl's Inner Soles glued to his feet to pass height requirements.

Johnny started humming as Righty did a skinny man's waddle and shuffle to the scales, making it difficult not to lose his soles.

His friends sang, "Be kind to your webbed-footed friends, for that duck might be somebody's mother," drawing the corpsman's attention away from Righty.

"Cheez," Rhesus whispered, "he walks like he's got a load of shit in his underwear yet no skivvies on."

"You guys like to sing?" the corpsman said. "I'll send you back for another short arm inspection, with special orders that they not return you here until you hum two octaves higher."

Righty was now on the scales.

"Don't go standing on no tiptoes, shorty," the corpsman said, adjusting the height-measuring arm. "You better hope you got a wart on top your head, otherwise, you ain't gonna be tall enough."

Johnny looked at Righty then the corpsman . . . *Don't press down too hard with that arm, sailor . . . Breathe deep . . . It will make you taller . . . Pretend you're being stretched and tortured on the rack . . .*

"You're lucky you didn't fart, you wouldn't have made it. Actually, you're an inch over the minimum. Next," the corpsman said . . . *If the short shit wants to fight so bad . . . I'll make him taller . . . Where do the marines find these? . . . I wanna get shot and kill idjits . . .*

Johnny whispered to Righty, "I can't figure it out. I measured you with the Scholl's, and you only made it by a quarter inch, and this guy has you an inch over."

"I cut out a patch of hair then made some flesh-colored papier-mâché and glued it to my squash, combed the hair over the area, and then used that spray stuff women use to make their hair stiff as the town drunk."

"You, William Powell, Thin Man," a second corpsman said, "get your skinny tail on the scales so I can send you home. You sure you didn't escape from no concentration camp or something?"

As Fats stepped up to the scales, Johnny stepped forward with him as he signaled to Righty.

Righty started talking to himself, "High diddle, diddle, I gotta piddle, so where is the potty, Scotty. So the cow jumped, and I gave it a moon." On announcing the word "moon," he turned his back on the corpsman, bent over, and slapped his butt.

"Don't waste your time, son," the corpsman said. "I'm not in charge of giving Section Eights. Besides, I'm married. Save that for the doctors," the corpsman said, not noticing that as Fats stepped on the scales Johnny stepped up right behind, as the others gathered in a tight circle, pretending great interest in their skinny friend's weight, and placed his toe against the back of the scale.

The corpsman read the scales several times, "I would have guessed he was closer to thirty-five pounds than 135. Must be a full moon. This scale is acting loony. First, the midget makes the grade by nearly an inch, and then bones here makes the weight by seven pounds." . . . *That Portagee kid was pretty good with the toe . . . This is the craziest critter group ever . . . and just kids . . . with proper training . . . They can go from crazy to insane . . . They'll make fantastic marines . . . even without eyes and ears . . . and being midgets . . .*

"Hey, you," the corpsman yelled to Johnny, "why are you limping? Did you stub your toe on a rock?"

"There was a cockroach on the floor, and I stomped it," Johnny said.

"You screwed up, son. The US Navy of the United States of America has to account for all those little buggers. But I'll let you go this time, but don't go killing no sand fleas where you're going, or your ass will be ashes."

"How in hell can killing a flea get you into trouble?" Skinny asked Johnny.

"Don't know, unless it's one of those highly trained ones that star in a flea circus."

"Ask a silly question, get a silly answer, my ma always says."

A chubby civilian doctor was sitting on a stool like a punished schoolboy. His stomach rested on his thighs, his clipboard used the top of his tummy as a table, and he didn't look up as he ordered Johnny to "sit."

Johnny sat on the stool beside the doctor, who appeared to have fallen asleep. In reality, he was just thinking of what would be in the refrigerator tonight, if the day ever ended.

During the lull, Johnny used the time to admire the top of the doctor's stomach, now that the clipboard was by his side.

There was a small sliver of onion, a small piece of potato chip, and something that Johnny at first thought was a fingernail but on closer inspection determined was a piece of garlic that had fallen from the Italian grinder he had ordered so he wouldn't have to get off the stool at lunchtime.

The first time that Johnny realized the doctor was awake again was when he reached down, plucked the garlic from his stomach, and rechanneled it into his mouth, an eating action consummated with all the reverence of someone taking Holy Communion.

"How's your hearing, son?"

"I can hear a feather falling."

"Don't go telling no windies. Now face the other way and repeat what I whisper," the doctor said. Then he whispered, "Sally sells silver seashells by the seashore."

"I think you mean Sally picks silver seashells by the seashore," Johnny said.

"You know, you kids know how to ruin someone's day. Nest—I mean, next."

Each of the friends repeated the doctor's secret whispering.

The doctor was elated over the fact that while signing their hearing charts, he discovered a piece of pepperoni that had hidden from his hungry maw by secreting itself between the pages on his clipboard.

"You didn't test my ears," Soupy said, figuring the doctor already knew he had trouble hearing and had flunked him without the test.

"Oh, yes. You must be Campbell," the doctor said. "I nearly missed your papers. They were hidden under a piece of pepperoni. Ha-ha, joshing, of course."

Soupy's chance of passing the silver shells hearing test were relatively slight, the result of a mother who boxed his ears every time he stepped out of line, which was as often as an alley cat scratches fleas. Although Rhesus hadn't helped Soupy's hearing when he dared him to stick a firecracker in his ear and light it. It was only a little ladyfinger, but it collided with his cochlea at a proximity that even ladyfingers weren't made for.

Soupy stepped forward . . . *When in doubt . . . step out . . . Johnny said fake it . . . and they'll take it . . .* "No sweat, Doc, I can hear a guppy burp during a thunderstorm."

And he immediately repeated the words Johnny had whispered to him,

"Sally sells . . ." giving the doctor's version of having Sally selling seashells rather than picking them.

What made his hearing test different from his friends is the fact the doctor hadn't started his whispering when Soupy repeated the saying.

"Yes, yes, your hearing is the very best of all," the doctor said, scratching his head . . . *I don't remember whispering to him . . . No matter . . . you don t have to hear to become cannon fodder . . .* "Let's dot the eyes now—dot the *eyes,* get it? We're going to read the eye charts."

He scribbled his signature on their hearing charts, leaving a scratching similar to what a chicken leaves on a barnyard floor.

He motioned them to the eye charts with "Don't try any cute stuff like having memorized the eye chart," he said . . . *You've got to see . . . so you can tell who's killing you . . . so you can't hear the ocean even in a seashell . . . After the hand grenade range, you'll hear more bells than the hunchback of Notre Dame . . . Damned kids . . . want to get killed . . . Glad I never had any . . .*

He flicked the room lights off and the eye chart projector on, beaming the various-sized lines of letters against the wall.

Johnny stepped up first. The doctor handed him a patch to cover his entire eye and said, "No guessing. When they repeat the eye test at Parris Island, they use the latest in machinery, which we'll be getting shortly. I take a very dim view when they flunk one of my patients down there after I pass 'em up here. OK. You're all warned. Cover your left eye."

Johnny raised his left hand and covered the left eye and read the chart two lines lower than most recruits.

"Ted Williams's eyes," the doctor said, "a natural sniper and point man. Better go to the barnyard, son, and learn that bobbing motion ducks have because you're going to have to learn how to duck. Next."

The buddies worked their way through the charts without incident, until it was Righty's turn. All their chattering ended. The silence was as thick and cold as a block of ice. Righty's very bad eye, his right one, was watering like a salivating dog getting its first real meal in a week at the pound.

The more he thought "right over right, right over left," the thicker the stream of tears.

"OK, cover your right eye. Right over right with that patch. No trying to peek. All you'll read then is the ceiling and floor."

Righty covered his right eye and commenced to read the chart as low as Johnny had.

"Now the other."

Instead of covering his left eye with his left hand, he used his left hand to cover his right eye. The doctor scratched his head with a . . . *Wot the . . .*

Righty read the chart a second time with his left eye.

"You pass, I guess. Now get out of here," he said, rubbing his cheeks with his hand . . . Guess I'm just tired . . .

"You all pass. Let me sign your charts. Take your papers to the recruiting sergeant.

The recruiter looked each set over carefully . . . *Seven of them from the same town . . . except that little Portagee kid . . . Happy birthday, kid . . . Hope you get to see your real eighteenth birthday . . . I hate this job . . . sending them off . . . They don t have the slightest idea what war is . . . shitting your pants with fear . . . twenty-four hours a day . . . Well . . . being there is better than sitting here, twiddling your thumbs . . . pulling your pud to the Marine Corps hymn . . .* "Must be good air, there, in Rockledge. Sign these papers, and you're almost there."

They all wondered where "there" was.

"Good." The recruiter picked up the phone and hit an extension. "All ready."

Within moments, a marine captain appeared.

"Line up, gentlemen," the sergeant said, saluting the officer.

They started to form up in a ragged line.

"Side by side please, gentlemen."

The sergeant read their names off.

Each answered yes.

"Shortly, gentlemen, instead of 'yes,' it will be 'aye-aye, sir.'"

Turning to the officer, the sergeant said, "All present and accounted for, sir."

The officer nodded. "Raise your right hand. Repeat after me."

They looked at each other then forward and raised their right hands. There would be no looking backward.

They repeated the swearing-in oath.

"You are now part of the United States of America Marine Corps."

The sergeant saluted the captain, who pivoted on his heels with the sharpness of a figure skater, and disappeared.

"Captain O'Hare said you are part of the US Marine Corps, not Marines. It will be a long haul before you are marines. Some of you will never make it, but meanwhile, you are porgy bait. Your dog shit asses no longer belong to you. Your drill instructors will furnish your toilet paper, a mixture of sandpaper and barbed wire."

The friends looked at each other, both questions and doubts in their minds. Only good friends talked to each other the way the sergeant was talking to them.

"Hey, you, fat ass," the recruiter said to Skinny, nodding to Fats, "you'd better cut some of that lard off and stick it on your buddy."

"Sergeant," Skinny started to stutter.

"Shut up, elephant ass, or I'll tie your trunk to your balls. Don't ever talk to a marine without first being addressed. And then it's 'sir.'"

"Yes, sir!"

"Didn't I tell you to shut up? If I want any shit out of you, I'll kick it out."

The recruiter caught Fats rolling his eyes, "Look, fly spec, don't roll those big blue eyes at me, or I'll run your skinny ass down an M1 barrel as a cleaning rag. Now listen up. You dicks be here June 27, 0700. One second late, and this little old Georgia boy will be using your Bars-ton arses as tank tread. Dismissed."

They stood frozen on the spot. The man who, only moments before, calmly called them "gentlemen" was insane.

"Out! Before I puke," the sergeant said.

They scurried away, holding close together like a school of little fish fleeing a predator, fearful that the one broken away from the school would be destroyed.

As soon as they hit the stairs and were out of earshot, they all started talking at once.

"They must have cut his hair so close, they must have shaved off his brain," Johnny said.

"I ain't takin' that shit from no one," Rhesus said.

"Pretty tough," Tim said. "I can't figure what the thinking behind it is."

"We got crapola and no dress blues," Scoff said.

"We better get them at Parris Island, or I head back home," Pointer said.

"Wanna bet?" Righty said.

"I'll write my congressman," Rhesus said.

"Yah, sure," Righty said.

"If we all stick together, we'll be all right," Tim said.

"We've got three days before we shove," Scoff said. "I wanted the dress blues to get a little going-away poo tang."

"Yah," Skinny said. "There's this little girl in Woburn whose heels are rounded for anything in uniform."

"Where's your old Cub Scout uniform?" Johnny asked, giving the Cub Scout two-finger salute.

They all gave the salute and sang the song they had sung around the old Panther Patrol campfire in the Fellsway.

They each sang their variation of the song grammar school music teacher Ms. Whister had taught them, "We're all pals together, birds of a feather, you are not alone when you belong to the Lone Star Rangers, Panther Patrol Man to man."

They all exchanged knuckle noogies to the shoulder, a little harder than usual. The noogies became even harder as each took umbrage to the increased whack, insuring that the corpsmen who gave them their shots on Parris Island had good black and blue marks to sink their darts into.

They were strutting and marching when they arrived at the charred Indian cycle.

Charred or not, the motorcycle cranked over on the first kick.

"Pointer, you've got to hightail it all the way to Chelmsford. Why don't you take a couple of guys, drop 'em off in Rockledge, and then head home?" Johnny said.

"Nah, Cuz. We're gang. I walk to Rockledge with you guys first. We can all have turns pushing War Whoop."

It was well after dark when they hit Rockledge Square.

The center was quiet.

"No band," Rhesus said.

"I noticed," Johnny said.

CHAPTER 4

YELENA

"You should be signing up for college, not the army."

"Marine Corps."

"It's all the same. Fighting instead of working it out like a philosopher or poet doesn't make sense, Johnny. You could be a poet-physician, anything you want to be," Yelena said.

"As a senior in high school, I had math. Arithmetic. Two plus two is four. Not Algebra. Geometry. Trig. Your dreams are higher than my sky," Johnny said.

Johnny tried to see her irises as they walked in the dark in the stillness of the Sheepfold grounds, that only short hours before had resounded with the voices of happy children and their folks that watched them. But despite the full moon, her gray eyes absorbed the available colors during the day and reflected the hues of the earth around her (her irises could not be seen), and her eyes only reflected the silver-white of the moon.

The first time he realized Yelena's eyes changing colors was on the dunes of Cranes Beach. They turned hazel beneath a wind dwarfed evergreen, on fire as she looked skyward at the weather warming sun, blue when she rested them against open hues between scudding clouds, then salt and pepper as they walked between the sun and salt bleached sands on that day last summer.

Then into the pounding surf that vibrated against their bodies bringing them to life with a frightening power.

He remembered back when he and his father had trekked from their parked car to the surf, rods in hand, and then the striped bass hitting as they rode to shore on an incoming wave. The bass's eyes had been bright silver, reflecting the moon, as they breathed their last breath there on the sand. Only moments before, they had powered their way beneath the waves, panicking the mooneyes and silversides before their open maws.

When Yelena looked directly at the moon, her eyes were the shining reflections of the lovely doe caught in a flashlight beam at night or the sad reflection of the breath-dragging bass.

"You were the one, Johnny, who laughingly told me your mother had put the little sign over your toilet, 'Aim high, there is plenty of room.'"

"I think she was talking about something else."

"I don't think so. Poets take many forms and beget other poets. Your defense of that poor Bernadette girl against that foul bully in your own football huddle was an action dictated by fate many years ago. Your mother's broom beating of the would-be thief, her whisk against his knife, is an example. There is no cause bigger than a small one."

"Yelena, no pedestals for me."

"I wouldn't put one there if I didn't think you could climb it."

She no longer was glancing up at the moon. Her eyes changed from those brilliant reflections of the frightened doe to the salt-sun bleached crags, colors that could not be duplicated on a palette.

Johnny drifted back to the night and previous dawn with his father and Jazz. The sun glaring over the sea's far horizon and bouncing off the sand had nearly blinded them. Johnny almost missed the little shack, a squatter's shack, built of driftwood by an artist who would never try to sell a painting or become a poet-physician.

Johnny wondered how he could attempt to paint a sunrise he couldn't look into, yet was content to imagine his own sunrise.

The sun had tanned the artist on the beach to a dark brown, much darker than Tim's cocoa color, a color Johnny had tried to copy under the sun once he realized girls liked muscles and tans. He had sat in the sun for hours, lifting a rock shaped like a bowling ball, hoping to build a biceps on his immature arm.

The artist had gotten out of his chair, a piece of artwork in itself, made out of twisted driftwood, and walked off several paces, paintbrush in one hand, private in the other, and kicked away the sand like a cat in a sandbox and relieved himself in it. His sand-kicking accuracy was that of the average cat, very low efficiency.

Watching the man pee, Johnny thought him as free as the breeze . . . *Hi diddle-diddle . . . the cat had to piddle . . . The artist jumped over the moon . . .*

Johnny wanted to be that free someday. He thought that someday such a shack would be his, off Wellfleet where the sand dunes were even higher—Wellfleet, where Marconi sent that first message across the ocean on the waves of the air.

Off Wellfleet, tales of the sea had it that a pirate ship, the *Widah*, had gone down, crew and gold; someday he would return, paint, write, although he knew how to do neither. He would someday look for pirate's gold pieces and dream.

There was plenty of room in his mind and imagination, but when others tried to set his sights, it left him unsure of what he wanted, if anything.

Without a word, Yelena and Johnny lay down on the warm sand, looking skyward, their thoughts carried by the wind.

It was years before that his father and he had actually been heading for the tip of the Cape, Race Point, where the fall migration brought the bass closest to the Race Point shore. They had run out of gas. It was 5:00 a.m.

Johnny's father had a bucket of live eels, with a few dying porgies mixed in, in one hand, and Johnny's hand in the other. The rods Johnny carried, their butts dragging in the sand, were ones they made in the cellar. His little brother Jazz, barely four years old at the time, held on to Johnny's belt.

Whenever Johnny turned to make sure he was OK, Jazz would give him that bucktoothed smile that made Johnny want to either laugh or cry. Sometimes he did both when he looked at his little brother.

Johnny often thought about saving for his sister Romala's wardrobe. He didn't exactly understand why his mother needed his help to buy food. He thought her a money-grubber despite the fact that friends described her as someone who would give you the shirt off her back and then her skin.

After all, didn't his father work way down in Pennsylvania in that Sun Ship Yard building those huge Liberty ships faster than the German U-boats could sink them? That was before the newspaper reporters had come to his house in the dark and stole Jazz's, Romola's, and his pictures to put in the newspaper, on the front page—the papers he had to deliver.

The liar-thief reporters made the judge send their father to the war to end all wars, to have large hunks shot out of his body just because women wouldn't leave him alone.

Now he was going to finish the job. There would be no more wars when Johnny and his friends headed over there . . . *Over there . . . over there . . . the yanks are coming, and we won t be back . . . till it's over, over there . . .*

His father's second family of three children had died in that fire in Pennsylvania. The pictures of Johnny, his sister, and brother were presented as if they had been the ones burned to death, and he had to deliver these papers.

"A penny for your thoughts. What are you thinking?" Yelena's soft voice brought him back to the evening that had sneaked in on them. "Johnny?"

She was bathed completely in the moonlight, the same blinding sand silver of the artist's shack of years before, the most beautiful, elegant, unreachable woman in the world.

He understood that she believed he was special, and in much the same manner humans questioned the gods in the mountains, in the heavens, as to their bad luck, he questioned his good luck . . . *Why me . . . ?*

"Why me?" Yelena asked.

Johnny jumped, startled, her words the same as those in his mind.

"Why me? Why me, Johnny? Why did you take me to your Big Woods?"

"It's just—"

"Say it. Say it, please."

"It's just—"

"Yes?"

"I—"

She waited, her eyes wide, her pupils, drinking in all available light, nearly rippled out to the perimeter of her irises, picking up the full reflection of the moon, causing her eyes to quiver as their rods and cones fought for domination yet confused by darkness and moonlight. "Yes?" she pleaded.

"Might not come back."

"You wanted to share this moment with your Juliet?" Her bottom lip pouted and quivered, but to a different drummer than her eyes, causing her entire face to shimmer before him.

He breathed deeply, trying to catch his breath, choked on the air as it wouldn't go down, and started to panic and thought . . . *Where is a paper bag . . . to breathe into . . . when you need one . . . ?*

"Come here, my prince."

Coming from anyone else in the world, the words would have set off a length of laughter that would have ended with the words "cornball, cornball," but he said nothing. His eyes did the speaking, declaring he not only was not a prince but also wasn't even a prize, and he looked down at his feet. They looked as big and even a bit bowlegged—bowlegged feet, like the clown in the Shriner's Circus he had seen looking under the flap of the tent. The Shriner, who spotted him, took him into custody, brought him to a front-row seat inside, and handed him the thing he had dreamed most of in life—that blue, fluffy taffy on a cardboard cone. The man in the red fez with all the gold print on it had one of the clowns sit on his lap and kiss Johnny on the cheek. Everyone laughed, except Johnny, although it was sort of fun, except he worried someone would see that his white shirt was definitely grayish.

Yelena's slender hands drew him back into reality as she pulled him toward her then freed themselves from his fingers and ran them up his arms to his shoulders and pulled him close.

"Speak softly, speak gently," she said, taking his chin in her hand, trying to get him to look at her.

"I . . . I . . ." he stuttered and thought . . . *What type of daffy don dilly . . . piece of silly bat scat . . . am I? . . . Look up . . . into her eyes . . . She wants you to . . . Look up, last of the Mohicans . . . Look up, last American hero . . . Look up, the one chosen to save a people . . . that may no longer exist without him . . . Look up . . . dimmest of all dipsticks . . .*

He slowly raised his eyes, his pupils widened in the great circle of a great horned owl, and looked into Yelena's. He was terrified for a split second. Her pupils appeared as tiny bright dots. It was the moon reflecting in them as her eyes looked into his and past into the moon as she pulled him into her breast. Her touch was as timid as a baby touching a puppy's nose, but as powerful as the thrust of a sounding whale.

He found himself being drawn downward, not into her blouse, but into her naked breasts. She had somehow freed them from her blouse without him knowing it.

"My bosom freed from its earthly bounds draws you near to what will be our earth heaven."

"I . . ."

"Yours," she murmured, words nearly lost in the wind whispering in the leaves of the Big Tree, directing a nipple with all the subdued holy fanfare of a Communion wafer to his lips. "Yours."

Johnny needed time to think. He had almost questioned, "Mine?" and thought . . . *What a double clutching klutz . . . Shouldn't I kiss her first? . . . What if we bump noses . . . and it's a standoff . . . and I can't even reach her lips for a kiss? . . . What if I stall minuscule inches from her . . . from her . . . breast? . . . It can happen . . .*

He remembered the junior high baseball game against Lexington. Coachie, that week, had just finished teaching the younger players to start their slides into the bag early. "You break an ankle sliding late. You'll never get under the tag sliding late."

He had started his slide too early, way too early, and stalled in the dirt nearly two feet from second base. The second baseman had not only tagged him out, not only tee-heed and told him "You can get unstuck now,

You can head to the bench," but also added a coup de grâce and tagged Johnny on the fly, leaving a dirty circle "there" on the crotch of his white baseball pants.

What if he stalled, frozen, paralyzed, just short of this beautiful girl, this beautiful breast? . . . *Oh my god . . . help me . . .*

His cock had been electrified immediately, like lightning hitting a lightning rod, on realizing her breast was nearing his mouth, but then quivered and finally lost its vibrations, like a spent tuning fork, as he asked himself . . . *Why me . . . ?*

She gently settled his head between her breasts, breasts as soft as the downy feathers beneath a hawk's wings.

He breathed the sweet odors carried to him as the heat of her body wafted them upward.

His eyes turned first to one nipple then the other. He felt greedier than any of the hogs on the farm, Bog included. He giggled and felt an almost insane urge to nose like a porker seeking truffles in Mother Earth.

He had to put the ribald song the gang sang on seeing the bouncing Bettys of girls jogging in the early dark, "The moonlight lit on the nipple of her tit, as I . . ." out of his mind.

Johnny told himself . . . *Concentrate . . . Johnny . . . concentrate . . .*

He tried to turn both eyes outward at the same time, to watch both nipples at the same time, but couldn't.

He always had had the ability to cross his eyes, which will make his little brother laugh and get his mother angry and declare, "Young man, your eyes will freeze that way someday, and then who'll be sorry?"

Pain streaked through his head as he attempted to look sideways in two different directions.

"Are you all right?" Yelena asked, seeing his eyes cross.

"Yes, yes. Ah, I . . ." *Oh . . . shit . . . Shut up, Johnny . . .*

"Just rest, my darling. They—we are not going anywhere."

He closed his eyes and thought . . . *Uncle Manny was wrong . . .* Johnny remembered standing outside the door, listening to him speaking to his brothers in a low voice so the kids wouldn't overhear, "Let's talk tits. I'll tell you this, no big deal. Once you've seen one set of boobs, you—want to see them all."

The brothers had laughed; Manny in the contentment of "Wasn't that a great line?" Francisco in his roar of the bear, and Johnny's father in that soft chuckle.

Uncle Manny was wrong . . . I only want to see Yelena's . . .

He tried to work up the courage to open his eyes . . . *Only Yelena's . . .*

He had forgotten the time he had seen his first bare breasts. Scoff was in the car with some girl from Everett, and he had thrown open the car door, and the interior light went on. The girl was sitting on his lap, her breasts out and being firmly massaged by Scoff who appeared to want to purloin them, and Johnny had suffered what he remembered as his "first instant stiffy."

Johnny slowly opened his eyes, peering through his eyelashes in an attempt to hide the fact he was staring into Yelena's nipple, afraid she would think him "dirty" and push him away.

A single moonbeam had found its way through the leaves, and like a spotlight on an actress on stage, it held on her tiny pink star of night.

Johnny could feel himself swelling down there, and he slowly worked his body away from her.

A breeze so soft, it almost wasn't, stirred the leaves above ever so gently. The single beam remained on the young girl's breast, yet a falling leaf touched softly on her nipple appeared to be flicking its tongue on her, licking, licking.

"Yours," she signed again, so low that her voice appeared to come from beneath one of the fallen leaves at their feet.

His eyes were melted into her nipples that appeared to be whispering in his ears, "Yours, yours."

He was positive his long eyelashes fluttered against her breasts. Johnny wanted to lick them so bad that he was dizzy, in deep pain. He licked the inside of his mouth, his lips, instead. His mouth, his lips struggled, laden with the salivation of a pack of bell-struck Pavlovian hounds struggling against restraining muzzles.

"Take me."

On hearing Yelena's words, Johnny's erection, which had been thumping against his trousers was like a Little League baseball player's pounding the plate with his bat, anxious to belt the next one into space, withered on the vine.

She let herself onto the ground, and as he watched, she gently pulled her skirt above her waist, splaying her legs as she did so.

"Be gentle."

She hooked her thumbs into the top of her panties and rolled them below her knees and then gently hooked her toes, first into one side and then the other, and pushed them off.

"Be gentle, my hero. I have never given this gift to anyone. Never."

Her legs were now spread-eagled like the frontiersmen captured by the Indians and tied naked in the high noon sun.

He thought about that day, when he had made that hit during a football game, knocking him unconscious . . . *Which team was it? . . . Cheez . . . what team was it? . . . What a question . . . you simple spastic . . .*

He was on the turf, just out of bounds. Yelena had just ended a "fight, team, fight" cheer, leaped into the air, and landed in a perfect split, inches from his face, her hidden tuft kissing the very turf he was a warrior on.

She had smiled down on him, a smile of concern and pride.

And there was Yelena, in that blue-and-white cheerleading uniform, declaring to this strange boy, "You have sacrificed your very body, your very soul, for your team, for us. Up, wounded warrior."

He wondered whatever happened to "fight, team, fight, sis boom bah" and felt like a dog doll made out of rags being commanded, "Up! Sit!"

How many times, late at night, long after going to bed, had he found himself with his hand down there, on himself, soaked with his own wetness dreaming of such a sight.

The first time, he had wiped his hand off in the bathroom, checking his palm for hair, feeling unbearably stupid—that crap his buddies fed to each other, "You pull your pud, your mother will find out, cuz you'll grow hair in your palm." . . . Stupid . . . stupid . . . stupid . . .

And now, on this night, on the beach, a hair's breadth away, was the most beautiful girl in the world.

This beautiful girl was made even more beautiful by her "Save the seals," "Save the butterflies," "Save the dormitories," "Save the world," . . . *Please . . . not . . . save Johnny . . .*

She always did the impossible—got the kids to still cheer when the team was getting its ass booted unmercifully, got the arthritic grandparents to stand and cheer, even sing "Boola, boolah, boola, boolah, that's the war cry of Rockledge High School. We will down them, we will crown them, until they holler, boola boo! Rah, rah, rah."

Later, in the huddle, he had tried not to peek at her, hoped that the opponents would run a play along the sidelines so he could knock their halfback into the stands—knock himself out. She would give him mouth-to-mouth resuscitation. She would breathe too much sweet air into him. They would float off on a cloud. He would turn back and tell Coachie that when he returned, he should have inserted a play where the guard carried the football.

One time, as they were lined up for the play, a pass, Johnny had glanced to the sidelines, looking for Yelena—Was she talking to another boy?—as the quarterback called the signals, "Hut one, hut two."

The quarterback was decked by the defensive tackle Johnny was supposed to block before he even got back into passing position.

As Johnny came back to the huddle, head on his chest, the quarterback said, "What's cooking, Johnny? Did you take out a million-dollar policy on me before the game and name yourself beneficiary?"

The next play, Johnny nearly decapitated the Howe High tackle, driving him into a linebacker and then headed at the defensive halfback, snorting like a bull and throwing a cross-body block that had the effect of a scythe on wheat.

The halfback had looked up from the ground, feeling his ribs, "Whattaya, bonko, you cockroach fucker."

The night, after he had nearly crippled half the Howe football team on one play, he dreamed of Yelena. At first, it was in the most tender fashion—as tender as two babies touching fingertips for the first time in their new lives. Johnny's imagination drifted from the pacific to the Sahara, and every place in between.

Yelena and Johnny were tiny Lilliputians sitting on a leaf on high. It was separated from its limb by the breeze of a hummingbird's wings. They held their tiny hands as they wished their magic carpet on, on, until it settled on a tiny pond in nowhere land, where a loon sang in the distance. Their hands now entwined with the nearly desperate need of the tendrils of the climbing ivy up a red brick wall.

For eternity, they would hold hands and gently press their lips together, only to return to looking into each other's eyes, speaking only with their eyes, and the slight squeezing of their hands.

Then a breeze stirred; their leaf was moved about on the waters, shifting them beneath the leaf's gunnels as one end, then the other dipped, lifted, and it yawed. They were tossed about. Johnny found his face in the area where Yelena's cheerleading split had left her touching the turf on that football field. Again, he was inches away. Before he could flick out like an archer fish, the leaf shifted. And now they were face-to-face. He wanted to enter her.

But the fates of the wind decided otherwise, and he was thrown onto his back. His turgid tool now appeared as a mast on their tiny vessel.

The sweet song of the distant loon had turned into the roar of an injured lion within his very head.

He looked around on the leaf. She was no longer there. Perhaps she had been swept off. Or perhaps his love had not waited. He had wanted to wake up from his dream, racked with feeling nothing. Could it be more painful than wondering whether the one you loved would wait?

He had looked down. It was still there, his stiffy, which to him was a terrible swift sword ready to do battle, to impale, and to create a glorious agony. One plunge of his terrible swift sword would leave them wet from navel to knee, quivering on the ground like a live wire torn from its lofty post, a spark spitting serpent dying from its own anger.

The night after the football game, the moon was benignly smiling at them they shared a blanket beneath the big tree, laughing at his ludicrousness as its beams did a bacchanalian dance. The breeze stirred the massive hulk of the Big Tree, causing a movement of the root system beneath, its oaken groans urging them to complete nature's calling, exciting them into an undulating eroticism, and inviting the young couple to join in.

"I am too," Johnny said.

"You are what, my love?"

This time, instead of staring down, he looked directly into her eyes, "A virgin."

"Then up there. Up there!" she pointed at the loftiest limb of the great oak, a giant branch that belied nature's order, as such grandness belongs to the lower limb.

"What, what?"

"We must climb to the highest point, to the precipice, together, to give our God-given gifts to each other."

Johnny did not know how to return romantics to her. He dipped into his memory for a helpful hint from Peter the Great and Catherine, Romeo and Juliet, Mickey and Minnie.

The only romantic vision was the statue of Juliet in Verona. One copper breast was shiny from thousands of hands cupping it, while tourists, proud of being so humorous and daring, posed for pictures.

He was saved from the "thee" and "thou" speech as Yelena stood to climb upward. She managed to get her dress down, her blouse closed, but through mistake or design, one breast peeked out between unbuttoned buttons like a baby bird thrusting out of its nest.

"I'm afraid it's a pretty scary climb," he said, which meant his knees were putty weak from having the shiny breast even brighter in the moonlight.

Johnny had seen many bunnies, both domestic and wild, noses twitching nervously, but never, never ever, had one made him . . . hot . . .

"We must climb upward, always."

She took his hand and cupped it on her breast.

"It's a high tough climb," . . . *and I'm not sure . . . I can make it . . . in this condition* . . . He tried to work what could only be described as the fiercest of all erections down into his pant leg.

"What are you doing?" she asked.

"Nothing! Honest."

He tried to think of church music, his pastor's face in prayer, as he attempted to kill the first phenomenon of an erection for a real-live girl.

Then suddenly, the struggle ended, and he felt the unnatural destruction between his legs.

He wondered about its death. It was like running a one-hundred-mile marathon—no, a lifetime race, only to stall, quit, inches from the finish line.

The vision in his mind was of Aunt Hope at his christening, as she whispered in a roar to a giggling friend . . . *I pity poor Johnny . . . English conscience . . . Portuguese genitalia . . .*

"The loftiest limb for the loftiest gift woman can give." Her words brought his thoughts back to hers. She was glancing heavenward.

He stood frozen for a moment as she started climbing upward as in a trance.

Johnny, worried that she would bruise or cut the bare breast that scraped along the bark as she climbed, followed as if to offer her help.

As he climbed and looked under her billowing skirt, he could see that her panties were still on the ground, having deserted their Swiss Guard duty to her basilica. Suddenly, he ceased worrying about her bare breast being bruised and worried about himself. His cock, like a phoenix, arose from its own ashes like a yo-yo in love and made his climb a doubly painful one.

He did not want to look up; she was so vulnerable. He closed his eyes, squeezed them tight . . . *Grandfather . . . Grandfather Shiverick . . . please help . . .*

He partially opened his eyes and squeezed them tight again . . . *for I cherish the old . . . rugged cock . . . shit . . . I mean cross . . .*

His eyes were wide now, accustomed to the dark . . . *It . . . it is underneath . . .* As she climbed, the secret area between her legs took on all the athletic movements of the rest of her body. Her body spoke to him, and pleaded with him. His own grandfather's mouth appeared and mouthed the words he had so long considered, but only to himself, that he become a man of the cloth, of God.

His eyes burned, with tears, and his stomach roiled and turned sour with his own disappointment in himself. Yet the ache and fire down below was fanned and flamed even hotter. Then only to be doused in a sizzle as the blackness of Yelena's pubic hair assumed a doppelganger, a ghostly counterpart in a living person, as his battle went on. It exchanged with an alter ego, his grandfather's huge white eyebrows, chanting . . . *No matter what . . . you always have to answer to yourself . . . Gifts can only be given in love . . . Anything less is not only digging your own grave . . . but also throwing the dirt on top yourself as well . . .*

He stopped his climb . . . *Oh . . . why . . . why can't I stop thinking . . . thinking . . . Please . . . someone . . . help . . .*

He could hear his grandfather DaSilva, *Go fuccum get it . . . Go fuccum catch it . . .*

He didn't stop thinking. He heard his grandfather Shiverick singing, *For I cherish . . . the old rugged cross . . .*

"My god," he said aloud, and thought . . . *It's exactly a year ago . . . It couldn't be . . . That Grandfather Shiverick . . . he had never been sick a day in his life . . . had gone to bed . . . never to wake up . . .*

The mortician that came to the house had so much difficulty in trying to get his rigor mortis frozen hands out of the praying position that he left the old man thus.

His grandfather was laid out in his bedroom for three days, Johnny not leaving his side.

His first remembrance of him was his trotting alongside his walking grandfather, his little hand trying to push on the handle that propelled the giant wooden cart that held the paints, the brushes, the oils, the lead, the chippers, and the giant wooden extension ladders needed for house painting that clacked along the side with all the romance of a fire wagon. He especially liked it when the wooden wheels with the tin treads hit the cobblestone streets, as not only were they sounds like the beatings of holy drums, but also, at this point, his grandfather always smiled down on him. His lips never moved, his teeth never flashed. Only his great white eyebrows frowned deeper, and the smile was in the direct look his grandfather gave him, not only into his eyes but also into his heart.

Johnny became more and more proud as additional kids joined in the great gaggle, forming a great tail and an always changing leader. The faster runners tried to keep ahead of the cart propelled by the old man, but they could not and fell back, like the giant honkers in a majestic V of Canada geese, charged with breaking the buffeting headwinds on high for the flocks, only to fall back and be replaced by another great bird, which in turn swerved and had to fall away.

Some kids beat their tin can drums; others banged metal garbage bucket covers together. And the cymbals clanged, while the dogs were a great bass chorus of red tick hounds and the tenor of Boston terriers.

It was a charge of the light brigade, kids waving their reed swords as they sang, "He has loosed the faithful lightning of his terrible swift sword," in a number of different versions.

When they arrived at the house to be painted, his Uncles Matthew and Luke would always be waiting.

And the kids, although kindly shooed off by the Uncles so they wouldn't be around, Lord forbid, if a bucket of paint fell three stories, remained. But as much as they wanted to obey, they pleaded with Uncle Luke, the great roller coaster legend, to show them how he could run up and down the four-story ladder backward, no hands.

Which he would eventually do, but only after exacting a promise that none of them would try such a foolish stunt.

When the kids drifted off, Uncle Luke became Loony Luke, as he need not have worried about their running up and down ladders backward or standing up in the front of roller coasters. Each kid realized they were from a different gene pool, except Johnny.

He was nearly as proud of his Uncle, or at least loved him enough to be proud regardless, and defended him to the hilt. Kids only had one swing at calling him Loony Luke and then were "out," as Johnny took a variety of actions to redirect their thinking.

When his aunts pointed out their brother could not hold a job as he marched to a different drummer, Johnny endorsed his Uncle by giving him an impish smile.

Aunt Hope, who had little hope for her favorite brother, countered that he "marched to a different bummer."

It was Uncle Luke that got Johnny his first praise as a house painter.

His grandfathers and Uncles had just completed painting a four-story-high house, involving multiple extension ladders. They were packing the paint cart and hanging the ladder on its side when Grandfather Shiverick discovered a small section at the very peak that they had missed.

Dismayed at anything less than perfect, he said they would come back the next day when the paint was dry, and cover the missed area.

It was Uncle Luke who said the three adults could hold the thirty-foot ladder straight up in the air, inches from touching the house and wet paint, and balance it there, while Johnny climbed upward and dabbed the area.

At first, Uncle Matt was big time against it, his grandfather was undecided, and Luke was big time to committing the boy. After all, Johnny was eight years old at the time, but Luke could already visualize the boy as his replacement as the royalty of the roller coasters. He saw Johnny's mug shot beside his at the Cyclone, the Double Crop, warning that the above should not be allowed to ride the wild ones.

His grandfather soaked the paintbrush and handed it to his grandson as if passing the torch of life.

Johnny took the brush and climbed swiftly. *The big ladder . . . is the Big Tree . . . The Big Tree and I are one . . .*

As he neared the top, a slight wind made balancing of the heavy ladder very difficult. The trees in the distance signaled an even stronger wind was coming their way.

"Best you come down," his grandfather said.

Johnny climbed the last few feet, trying to balance the swaying ladder with his feet to help those below who strained with the effort.

He reached out and, with unhurried strokes, calmly licked the paint into the old clapboards and watched as the dry wood supped, and he was satisfied.

Before he could start down, the wind that had warned them earlier said, "Times up!" and now the ladder swung in ever-widening circles, and Johnny tried to make his way down.

"We can't hold it!" Mark said to his father and brother in a voice kept under control by a supreme effort.

They were going to lose the boy.

"We can," his grandfather said in a low voice whose very power cut through the wind.

But dust devils surrounded the ladder and presented its opinion, "No, you can't," as the three men struggled, as the boy tried to gain a step downward without being thrown to his death.

Johnny could feel his sphincter flexing and unflexing, the speed of the closing and opening repetition increasing every moment, and he feared he would go in his pants and fall to his death . . . *covered with my own shit . . . What will they say . . .*

He wanted to leap down to the safety of his grandfather's arms, but they were helping hold the very ladder that was leading him swiftly to panic.

The three powerful men's arms and backs and legs strained in what appeared to be a losing cause.

Until.

Johnny was on the ground.

Then the wind thrashed the now-empty ladder against the house, shattering it into a game of pickup sticks.

As quickly as the small twister had whipped up, it disappeared.

The relief on the three Shiverick men's faces could not be hidden.

"Lad, did you not hear my 'best ye come down'?" his grandfather said, not in an "I told you so" manner but addressing someone who disobeyed an order from a person no one disobeyed.

Johnny barely heard his Uncle Mark's words, "You did not hear him, boy."

"Yes, Grandfather, I heard."

The boy and his Uncles waited for Grandfather Shiverick's terrible swift sword to fall with Marie Antoinette finality.

"Well, your action certainly bought you a wild ride on the wind," the old man said, as Johnny neared the ground.

His Uncle Luke wrapped his arm around his shoulder and whispered, "Now you understand my stand-up roller coaster rides."

"Yes."

All four looked up. The splintering ladder had not damaged the paint job. The job was complete.

Uncle Mark looked at the boy and applauded softly.

"No need to applaud work well done," the old man said.

The four walked in silence, their hands touching on the handle of the cart.

Three different generations understanding the need of meeting obligations in life. But now he was back.

"Are you all right?" Yelena called down from the Big Tree.

"Yes."

"Then upward. Always upward."

The branches had thinned out as she approached the top, allowing the full power of the moon to catch her.

Both her breasts were now out, and as the Big Tree rocked slightly, she appeared to Johnny as the most beautiful bowsprit ever to seduce the seas.

She was at the giant swaying topsail.

"Hold tight," Johnny called up.

She climbed out on the limb, got to her feet, and walked slowly out on it.

A bolt of heat lightning lit the sky, blinding him momentarily as he looked up. When he opened his eyes, he expected she would be gone, disappeared forever, had never existed.

Except she did. Yelena was no longer standing. She was on her back on the giant limb, one arm extended skyward, inviting a second lightning bolt, the other lowered, beckoning him upward.

Had the lightning been that of his grandfather Shiverick's terrible swift sword, or was it the bolt as he climbed the stairs that day toward Pie's bedroom? That of his other grandfather Antonio DaSilva at the farm. He saw the feet, the male feet pointing down, inside the soft feet of the woman, their owner's out of sight.

Then seeing the woman's feet fire into the air. Now her entire legs could be seen. There was a frantic, powerful bouncing on the bed that repeatedly sent the feet upward, as if trying to embed them in the ceiling.

"Upward," Yelena's voice chanted.

"Only to bring you back to earth."

Without a word, Yelena stood again, returning to the trunk of the Big Tree, sleepwalker, placing her breasts back into her dress, keeping her hands there for a moment, then removing them.

She kissed her hands and then blew two kisses to Johnny below, spread her arms in preparation for a swan dive that would dash her beautiful face into the earth.

And then climbed down to safety.

Taking his hand, she led him out of the Big Woods. "I did not want to give myself until marriage."

It wasn't the heat lightning that lighted the entire Big Woods around them for a brief moment and made them shiver; not unlike animals coming out of the water, but rather like archangels attempting to shake off demons that had alighted on their backs and sunk fangs into them, fangs that left feelings they did not understand.

Demons that whispered in their ears secrets they had never heard, providing promises so lustful even their youthful imaginations could not comprehend.

They shook several times, looking at each other apologetically, unable to explain what they were apologizing about.

Her smoky gray eyes, wide as if in great mortal fear, probed deep into his emerald eyes, seemingly drowned in their sea foam. And he feared turning into ashes as he saw the gray smoldering turning to platinum, to mercury.

The streak of lightning that slashed through the sky was no longer the simple announcement of torpid weather by shimmering heat lightning. It was a bolt that smelled of cordite, whose very power had climbed down a tree, shattered in the distance and set their very feet afire with fear.

They ran, holding each other close, through the rain that had followed until they got to her home.

Without a word, they parted.

Did Grandfather Shiverick . . . somehow . . . cause the terrible bolt . . . no . . . no way . . . Jose . . .

That night, it wasn't the face of his grandfather Shiverick on the opposite end of the teeter board from him, that teeter board that balances dreams on one end and nightmares on the other.

And it wasn't the childhood chant of his grandfather Shiverick who sang softly, as the board lifted little Johnny skyward, "Teeter, teeter, lifted upward to Saint Peter. Down, down, to touch the ground, and worship where he walked."

It was his grandfather Pie on the other end of the board, the end of his belt hanging in front of him like the hot tongue of a lizard, chanting, "First time, Pie Pay. Second time for narda, nothing. Third time, she pay."

The dream was real. Too real. He saw his grandfather Pie, not like he was looking into a crystal ball; but terrifying enough, he saw him as a reflection, as he, Johnny, looked into a mirror.

Then as if someone had changed the station on the television set, he saw the old man's feet.

And once again, Johnny crept up the stairwell at the farm, stopping just short of the landing.

He had seen the fancy lady from Lowell go into the house moments before he started his crawl up the stairs.

Johnny heard her high heels, patent leather red, as they clicked on the worn wooden stairs, each click setting up a clog dance that sent sexual shocks through his loins as if the spike heels were indeed a molten nail that stabbed him repeatedly, so very painfully, he could not understand why it felt so good. It was the same reaction he got when he got poison ivy on his feet, between his toes, joining the athlete's feet there. And he had scratched and scratched. It felt so gloriously good. Until he became raw, and it was as if someone had poured kerosene into an open wound.

She had stopped on the front stairs of the farm, bent over, her short skirt riding high on thigh, and wrapped the red ribbons that fed from the top of the shoes around her ankles, tying them where they met at the bottom of one calf.

Then he saw the flash of red between her legs as she pivoted to tie the other shoe's ribbons. Was it her panties?

Or was it more? . . . *It could be . . . why not . . . ?* The hair on her head was nearly as bright as the ribbon she tied it back with, a loose bondage that left little ringlets below her ears.

She entered the house and walked up the final stairs to Pie's bedroom.

Johnny followed and stopped just short of the landing. He spotted his grandfather's feet, pointing downward, almost hanging off the edge of the bed.

Then another pair of feet appeared, pointing upward. Actually, it was the pair of shoes he saw first, red ones, with ribbons dangling from their top—ribbons that had been tied moments before, below, as he had watched.

Then the shoes were kicked off.

One landed to the right, by the legs that supported his grandfather's pinball machine. He could see the bottom of the metal clothes hanger that his grandfather had straightened out and inserted into one end of the pinball machine so he could activate the scoring bumpers to pile up the free games.

The other shoe flew to the right and settled against the legs that supported the keg of dandelion lion wine that fermented there, the flying shoe had activated the tiny black fruit flies that had gathered around the cask. Some were sodden and had trouble flying.

Now the legs of the cask, the pinball machine, and the bed were part of a chorus line that witnessed in stillness the dance of the two humans, but humans without legs or bodies, for only the feet told the story of the dance.

Feet that danced in the air as if on a puppeteer's strings.

The toes facing up, those that had been home to a pair of fancy red leather shoes, that drew circles in the air. The tiny feet drew soft circles, like a child with a stick in the sand, but then the toes flexed and unflexed, and the centrifugal force became faster, more demanding, demanding the pile driver increase its force, enough to pulverize.

The huge soil-darkened feet of the old man dug deep into the mattress, like oxen at a county fair attempting to pull the extra weight on the drag sled, which would make them winners.

The bottom of the old man's feet was stained from the soil and the grapes. The fancy lady's feet were as pink as her hair.

Then they shot into the air, followed by her calves, her thighs. The dark area. The red had had to be her panties. The hair was black, black, a black sheen, as that of a panther and appeared to undulate like seaweed worked to and fro by a changing ocean tide.

His grandfather was there. Jungle boy. Saber. With his tooth.

He was like Bog the hog, who, when enraged with Johnny on his back and Pointer swatting its curly tail with a plank, attempted to buck him off, arching its back and grunting like a constipated elephant.

Then so swiftly, he was not sure it happened, the feet had changed. Now hers faced down. Suddenly, her back appeared. Her red hair dancing back and forth on it, as her head first swayed from side to side like a mare under a loose rein, but then suddenly snapping forward and backward as if a bee had stung its under belly.

With a whinny, the fancy lady tossed her head backward until her hair touched the upper cleavage of her buttocks; and eyes wide open, she stared into Johnny's as they peered over the top of the landing.

And she smiled.

Opened her mouth wide. Then formed a tight circle. A volcano.

That night, he closed his eyes and conjured up the lady in red, her volcano mouth.

Except the lava erupted in Johnny's hand, scalded it.

He cried Yelena's name, fought his way out of bed, a fire down below, and into the bathroom where he sat in the sink and turned on the cold water full blast.

Despite the cold water, his hand still burned with shame.

The hot pain was much like the first time he and his father had found the honey tree.

They had captured a small bee in a box, put rouge on its rear end, and released it, taking a compass reading on the insect that made a bee line to its honey home.

His father had lit a piece of newspaper to smoke the bees out of the honey storage hollow. He told Johnny, who was suffering the hungry horrors to wait until all the bees had fled before reaching in.

He hadn't waited and reached into the honey hole and was rewarded with a burning fist full of bee bites.

He did a painful dance of a wild man, while a slow and haunting voice, Yelena's, filtered through his mind, "Is this all there is to love, then keep on dancing . . ."

CHAPTER 5

HELLO, GOOD-BYE

During the days between their signing up and when they were to arrive at the Marine Corps Recruit Depot on Parris Island, the friends came together, drawing strength and solace in greater numbers, as like the schools of mooneyes whose pods swam the waters off Plymouth.

The boys would drift apart, as the school of little food fish shredded by the predators—wolf fish, mackerel, bluefish, striped bass, like the friends, wished to be away from the schools under attack, each screaming out in silence, "You want him! Not me!"

By not coming together, they indulged in the denial that they had really signed up.

Those who had not signed up with their friends drifted away not only from those who had hitched up but also from each other.

Nothing was ever said about the no-shows. The original philosophy that had brought them together was transferred over—companionship without demands, like the soft breeze and the butterfly.

But with the friends, new and stronger one-on-one relationships sprung up. It was easier to confess to one buddy than a group. For one thing, in one on one, if a confidence was betrayed, you could deny it.

"I'm not afraid, Johnny," Righty said. "If I make it back, I'll spend the rest of my life raising hell with you and all my Lefty brothers. If I don't, me and Big Lefty get to explore the Big Woods again, but from up above. Big Lefty let me tag along everywhere."

"Did he take you, or did you follow him?" Johnny said, poking his friend in the ribs.

"Same-ee, same-ee."

"Yah. Jazz has followed me here and told his buddies I'd take him. It kinda keeps things continuous."

Johnny and Righty had bumped into each other, completely unplanned, after midnight, at Spot Pond. Each couldn't sleep.

Righty had tried counting stars.

Johnny had played a boys' game of kadiddle. When playing with a girl, whoever spotted a car with only one headlight working, got to get a kiss from the other. There were no losers. But Johnny did not have a girl to play kadiddle with, at least in purely a playful manner.

With Johnny and his little brother, "kadiddle" gave a point to Jazz every time a passing car's left headlight was out, and one to Johnny when the right one wasn't working. They would watch out the window from the foot of their bed, heads propped up on hands and elbows. This was a spring, summer, fall game they used to conk out on nights that sleep came tough.

The winter go-to-sleep substitute meant watching the distant trees as a new blast of wind caught their tips, and each quickly giving an estimate of how many counts it would take before the distant wind rattled the loose, frost-covered panes of their window. One, two, three—then four, the really noisy pain in the butt.

Counting stars or headlights hadn't worked for either that night, and Johnny found himself sitting on a smooth round boulder with his feet in the town drinking water when he heard the soft rustle in the woods nearby, He said too aloud, "You're not a deer."

But he wasn't surprised when Righty's shape appeared from out of the pines and scrub oak. "Nice try, maybe I'll make a hunter out of you yet."

"Why do I have the feeling that we might end up the hunted?"

"Come on, with God on our side, who can set us asunder?"

"Whew, deep stuff, John. Or is it Matthew, Mark, or Luke?"

"Hey, they teach you cat-licks that good religious stuff we Protestants get."

"Hey, you E-piss-in-the-pail-agains are almost samee-samee as us."

"Oh, sure, but the Episcopal bishop doesn't have a nose shaped like a crooked potato like the pope."

"You know what the pope is saying when he's up on the balcony in the Vatican talking to the throng, and everyone thinks he's giving a blessing, bringing his hand downward, then sideways?" Righty makes the blessing sign of the cross, chanting, "Will all you goddamned ginnies get off the grass?"

"Forgive him, Father, for he knows not what he does," Johnny said, "and don't stand beside me during the next lightning storm, just in case the pope has any pull with God." Johnny blessed himself, with his fingers stopped at major points, "Nipple, nipple, throat, belly button."

"You are one religious sucker, Brother John. What's that lipstick you've got on?"

"All bull tickie aside," Johnny said, "I believe that this can't be the final answer to the story of life. I'm not sure if I could live without knowing that someday when Grandmother Shiverick and Grandmother Mine and I cash in the chips that we'll meet in heaven or whatever passes for that fresh baked, big apple pie in the sky."

"Wow! But you know full ass well that no one is more God fearing than a Catholic unless it's an Italian Catholic."

"Amen, brother."

"You believe too?"

"You betcha bippy. I believe in everyone's God. When I go into combat, I'm gonna be wearing a little gold cross, just like the one you've got around your neck, and even rosary beads. And I'm gonna wear one of those Star of Davids. And I'm gonna wear whatever us Protestants wear around their neck."

"And what's that?"

"A four-leaf clover and a rabbit's foot, I guess. I'm going to carry one of those small Armed Forces bibles in my shirt pocket."

"I heard that every ounce counts when you're in combat—that guys toss away their gas masks, mess kits, ammo, to lighten up. So why carry a Bible?" Righty asked.

"Don't laugh."

"Nah."

"I remember my Uncle Manny DaSilva—"

"He's the one that got wounded five times?"

"A trillion times. Got shot in the stomach, the brain, the eyeball, but no fatal shot to the balls, which, according to him, would have made him die of a broken heart."

"You going to stop interrupting?"

"Yah," Righty said.

"You going to stop interrupting?"

"Yah, I said."

"You're not shitting me, are you?"

"Couldn't shit you, Johnny, you're too big a turd."

"God, that saying was old when Methuselah was a pup. Anyway," Johnny said, continuing, "Uncle Manny told me about this guy that got shot by a Nazi sniper right in the heart and didn't die."

"How come?"

"'Cause the bullet hit the Bible he had in his breast pocket."

"Hey, watch your language."

"What language?"

"Don't play innocent. Pocket. Pocket?"

"Pocket, what?"

"Pocket, breast pocket. Breast."

"You're a sick salamander, good buddy. Anyway, I'm carrying a Bible over my heart."

"Yah, yah."

"It works. Hey, my Uncle Manny carried a Bible in his skivvy shorts all through Sicily and Normandy. And he never died of a bullet-hit heart, or no broken heart despite getting hit everywhere from the tip of his toe to the top of his head."

"Boy, I hope someone's secretly taping this conversation and leaving it to Harvard, MIT, or Oxford for posterity," Righty said, sitting on the boulder beside Johnny.

"Talking about leaving things, if I buy it in Korea, I'm leaving my brain to Harvard and my dick to Smith."

"Who is Smith?"

"Smith is a girls' college, dummy."

"Cheez, I might go there. Can you imagine sitting in a biology class with a bunch of girls all looking at your pickle dick? I'd become big man on campus with the simple words: 'That's my dearest buddy Johnny's dick.'"

"Talking about that, remember Anna Mae Burbot's English class?"

"Do I? One tough lady. You had to hold your breath for the entire fifty minutes of her class. They say she was a full colonel in the WACs, Women's Army Corps, during World War II."

"Anyway, remember Tinny Timkins, the new kid, was giving an oral topic in Ms. Burbot's class, and I whispered something to him?"

"Do I!"

"And Ms. Burbot said to me, 'Mr. DaSilva, would you like to tell the class what you just whispered to Mr. Timkins?'

"'No thank you, Ms. Burbot."

"'Well, let me put it a little more pointedly. Tell the class what you just whispered to Mr. Timkins."

"'Yes, Ms. Burbot."

"'Tell it.

"'Well, I whispered it because only Tinny, Mr. Timkins, and you were the only ones who didn't know."

"'Didn't know what? What did you whisper?'"

"'Tinny, your barn door is wide open, and one wrong move, and your horse will escape the barn.'"

"And she started screaming and screaming that you were talking about Tinny's genitalia in front of her class."

"And the principal thought someone had set a fire in the chem lab."

"He called the police and fire department, and everyone rushed to our room."

"And the principal got Ms. Burbot calmed down, sent the police and fire away with a thank-you, and then turned to Tinny and said, 'Young man, do you realize your fly is wide open?'"

"Ms. Burbot started screaming all over again."

The two friends had to catch their breath as the pain in their stomach increased as they relived the day.

"Remember," Righty said, "the firemen and police came running back into the room? They thought some sort of fire alarm had gone off."

The tears rolled down their faces, a few of the more ambitious streams settling on their aching stomachs.

"Stop," Johnny said, "I'm peeing my pants."

"And the principal whispered to Ms. Burbot that she should take a day, a week off."

Johnny tried to wipe his eyes and hold his stomach.

Couldn't do both and slipped off the boulder into the lake.

"And he forgot to suspend you!"

Righty climbed up on the boulder and jumped high into the air, his cannonball exploding beside Johnny, filling his mouth with the good drinking water of Rockledge.

Johnny spat out the water. "I'll beat you to the Big Tree. We'll dry up there."

"Sounds pretty good. Can you wait a sec? I want to let one more leak 'cause I know our dear old history teacher, Mr. Dalone, will be taking his drink from the tap early tomorrow morning."

"Ah, he wasn't such a bad shit," Johnny said. "Most of what we got is what we asked for. He just wanted to learn us something."

"Yah, I know. I'll hold it till we get out of the water."

"Just as well, we don't want this reservoir overflowing. Beat you to the Big Tree, the best drying tree in the entire world."

They gathered their clothes and trotted the mile to the Big Woods and ran upward through the dark, naked as jaybirds.

"Hey," Righty said.

"Hey, what?"

"I just got a switch on the dick."

"Didn't know they made switches that small."

"Funny, donkey donk."

The Big Tree was still there. It didn't appear to be the giant it was when they were little kids, but its importance was just as great.

"Hey," Righty said, as they climbed.

"Hey what?"

"This is bad luck night for my private."

"How come?"

"The damn tree bark hurts."

"Hey, be happy its bark's not as bad as its bite."

Righty rolled his eyes skyward. "What did I ever do to you, Lord?"

They reached the top and shimmied out on that big limb that had no right to be that size that high up, at least according to botany books, books the Big Tree apparently hadn't read.

The top limb swayed in the breeze, drying them.

Johnny and Righty, swaying to and fro, did not look unlike corn-stealing raccoons late at night, swinging in the stalks having a ball.

The moonlight at times caught their eyes, making them shine, not unlike raccoons looking down a flashlight beam, not understanding the farmer's words, "You've ruined your last corn, you thieving bastards," then pulling the trigger, sending their brains exploding.

"Yah, I'm not afraid. Going way 'over there,'" Righty said.

"Me either."

"Perhaps we should be."

"Nah," Johnny said.

"Perhaps a little bit."

"Well, maybe a little bit, but it's a little tough to be afraid of anything when you're sitting on top of the Big Tree."

It was the next afternoon when Johnny was walking the woods between his house and the old East School he remembered spotting Soupy Campbell by the old stone wall and slowly sneaking up on him.

The old stone wall was a hundred years old—no, two hundred. Some farmer had cut down all the trees, dug the knifelike rocks out of the soil, and then used oxen dragging a thick oak branch with forged hooks on the bottom to drag the bigger boulders off to the side, where they served as the base to the wall.

Word was that the farmer was attacked by Indians, scalped, and his family killed. While they were killing his family, scalp missing and all, the farmer had crawled to a hollowed-out section of a giant dying oak and hidden there. So the story went, although some claimed this event happened in Deerfield and not Rockledge. The farmer had lived to finish the stone wall.

Johnny had searched the wall many times for arrowheads and without telling his friends, looking for the long-ago farmer's scalp. Wasn't the hair the last to disintegrate on a corpse?

Often he wondered whether one of his friends, Johnny Brown, had manufactured the arrowhead he had shown Johnny. Come to think of it, it was the same friend Johnny Brown who made up the story of the Indians scalping the old farmer. Johnny Brown had offered to sell Johnny DaSilva an arrowhead for three cents. Johnny wanted to find his own. It just wouldn't be the same to buy one. He would find one.

Johnny found himself searching among the moss-covered rocks. Surely, there was one there, perhaps with part of a farmer's young son's heart still stuck to it. The real thing had to be there.

He thought . . . *Perhaps . . . but what was that song we sang to him . . . Johnny Brown . . . you're a clown . . .*

Johnny Brown had contacted polio and died. His mother, who had lived alone with her only son, had put a black crepe on the door of his house. All the windows shades were drawn, the curtains closed. Johnny Brown's mother wouldn't let anyone in to see her only son's body.

Johnny had walked by the house that night, alone, singing to himself, "Johnny Brown, you're a clown."

And now his favorite clown was sitting a short distance away, staring into the distance. Johnny wondered whether he was thinking of the day they had discovered the skunk sleeping on the flat rock, the one Soupy now sat on.

After a while, Righty got slowly to his feet, walked off, still looking into the distance, and said, without looking back, "Thanks, Johnny, for sitting with me."

Johnny stood on the high rock overlooking Buckman's Pond.

The pond was so profuse with pond lilys, it was nearly impossible to spot a patch of water.

A lone swimmer made a path, a single water lily stem in his mouth, the slower on one side and the long trailer of the stem on the other, creating a wake outside the wake made by his body.

"What are you doing here?" Rhesus yelled up to Johnny.

"What are you doing here?"

"I asked you first."

"Nothin'. Just visiting some of the old spots we might not see for a while."

"You answered your own question."

"I mean, Korea is a long way away," Johnny said.

"Yah, I looked at a globe. It's shaped like a dog's head."

"Your ass is shaped like a dog's head. That's Australia."

"Look, Mr. F in History 1, Australia is in Europe. That's where the guy with a mustache like a broken comb lived."

"That's Hitler," Johnny said.

"That's where Hitler chased that singing family, the Trapps, out of."

"So, Rhesus, what are you now, Mr. A in History 1?"

"Hey, Einstein, it wasn't me that spelled his own name wrong on the top of his exam."

"Yah, but everything else was right."

"You're as dumb as Soupy," Rhesus called up, rolling over on his back. "Remember Hoppalong?"

"Yah."

"Yah, until he ate that live grasshopper on a dare, we all thought he had a great brain. He was dumber than Soupy," Rhesus said.

"Well, OK, you're as dumb as Hoppalong, but I always thought it would be a toss-up between grinding a grasshopper between your teeth and dropping a rock on a sleeping skunk."

"OK, OK, I take it back. You're not as dumb as Soupy."

"Thanks, Rhesus. You're sweet. But dumb as a cow flop."

"You wanna buy a couple of pounds of ant hair yet to be harvested?"

"Sure. But first you have to buy the eyeball of a star-nosed mole I dug up so I'll have money to buy your ant hair," Johnny said.

"Sold. You take checks?"

"No, but I take Slovakians."

"You're as funny as a rubber crotch."

"Bouncy, bouncy bally, I lost the head of my dolly," Johnny said, pulling a water snake that was sunning on the lily pads and tossing it through the air at Rhesus. "A tie to wear with your Sunday go-to-church suit."

"You bum! You're not smart enough to be stupid. The Marine Corps will take your smart-ass and diaper it with barbed wire," Rhesus said.

"Me ass will chew it up, and I'll spit it out at the gooks."

Rhesus sang, "We're the boys of Rockledge High, when we get there, the Japs will die."

"We're not fighting the Japs. They're one of our best friends. That's what happens when you treat the defeated good, I guess. We're fighting Koreans."

"Who in hell are the Koreans?"

"Just some front guys for the Commies. We gotta kick their asses over there so we don't have to kick 'em here and mess up our beautiful country. That's what our president said."

"My beautiful country is Buckman's Pond."

"Yah, I know. Me too. And the Big Woods too."

The two friends saw something move.

"It's a bear!" Rhesus said.

"Nah, it's Timmy, picking blackberries."

"John, you're harder to find than a tiny star in a crowded constellation," Tim said, working a picker branch off his shirt.

"Why didn't you give me a call, Tim?"

"It would have been easier than trying to track you down these last few days. Of course, it would really be difficult to call you, seeing you don't have a telephone."

"You could have called Righty, and he would have come over and told me. Anyway, I've been trying to find you. We've only got a few days left," Johnny said.

"A few days left in Rockledge. A few days left here. We've got an entire lifetime ahead."

"Yah, I know."

"Remember our tin can telephones when we were kids? We tied a piece of wire between the cans and had turns holding a can up to an ear while the other spoke into his can. The tomato juice cans worked best. They were biggest."

"The cans were also ribbed," Johnny said, "and we could really hear each other."

"Yes, when we yelled into the can loud enough—loud enough so we didn't need the cans."

"Yah, Tim, you and me always had to work overtime to get to each other. We usually had to send smoke signals."

"John, remember when we got that first paper route together? What were we, in the third grade?"

"And when I collected the money that first Saturday and put it in the paper bag."

"And when we got back to the store, there was no money in the bag. It had all leaked out through a hole."

"And you were so damned good about it, Tim."

"Yes, and you wanted to belt me."

"It would have been a lot easier if you'd been a king-size bonzo, and I could have belted you. And you could have whacked me. And we could have forgotten the money."

"Remember we had to sweep out the paper store for two months to pay for that week's papers? Those were the good old days."

"I'll let Mr. and Mrs. Remember dredge up the old days. I'm heading home," Rhesus said. He ran a few feet away, tossed a handful of acorns at Tim and Johnny, and with a "Hi, ho Silver-ware, Hitler lost his underwear," he was gone.

"You didn't have an alarm clock when we got that first paper route. You used to tie a string to your toe and hang it out the window. When I woke up, I would go to your house and pull on the string."

They walked slowly toward the library. The gang wasn't at their in-town meeting spot, the library brick wall.

They walked inside and sat in a dark area. The library was empty, except for the old librarian.

Johnny whispered, "It was the first grade when you moved from South Boston to here. Remember, Tim?"

"How can I forget? I felt like an outsider until you saved the day and gave me a shove at lunchtime. And we wrestled. And got kind of worked up. And then you said, 'The only reason I wrestled you was because your tan is better than mine.'"

"I knew I could never fight you for real, Tim. That first time, when we were wrestling, you smiled, and your smile, a three-lane highway, swallowed your ears."

"No easy task," Tim said.

"Yes, first time you came into class, I didn't even know you were a kid. With those ears, I thought you were some sort of handles on a loving cup, or something."

"No loving cup here. Rumor has it, John, that you and I are the only virgins in the town over fifteen years old."

"Not by choice."

"I disagree, John," Tim said, whispering even lower. "My parents always said, 'You must give respect to get respect.'"

"Heavy-duty stuff, Tim. I don't think I can lug anything as heavy as virginity on my back."

Dark was setting in fast.

Tim sat down on the trunk of a fallen tree. "Draco," he said.

"Leo," Johnny said, sitting beside him.

"Orion."

"A giant hunter, slain by Artemis."

"Residing east of Taurus."

They lay back in the grass, hands folded behind their necks.

"Tim, you shouldn't go."

"You know, John, it's the first time I've laid back on the grass here. I always said hi to the gang, went inside, and hit the books."

"That's why you shouldn't go."

"And when I talked about our gang, my mother would say, 'Tim, your father and I didn't move lock, stock, and barrel out of South Boston to the suburbs for you to be in a gang.'"

"Some gang. Raiding cherry trees. Tying a chicken to a teacher's front door on Halloween and ringing the doorbell."

"Putting marbles inside the hubcaps of a teacher's car after he tried to make one of our friends look dumb."

"Yes, regular Machine Gun Kellys."

"Instead of calling us a gang, perhaps a different title—'an all together.'"

"Yah, I like that. An all together."

"We weren't Mugsy, Bugsy."

"Nah. We were more like Spanky, Spot, Alfalfa," Johnny said.

"Remember, in grade school, everyone had a jackknife? You were special if you had the high leather boots with the knife case sewed just above the ankle. And there wasn't even a nicked finger when we played Around the World flicking the knife from fingertip, elbow, shin, nose, forehead, spinning to the ground to claim a section of the world we drew there. You always tried to claim Portugal and England. I wasn't sure where or what to claim. You were good with the knife and gave me half the countries you won."

"I can see the day kids will be frisked for knives. The world is getting crazy. You have to pay a nickel to use a public toilet now," Johnny said.

"You couldn't wait until the third or fourth grade, when your parents determined you were ready to get your first jackknife, and if you were real lucky, you got the boot and knife combo."

"You entered manhood with the responsibility of your own knife. It was like when my sister Romy got her first bra. It was about the size of a tiny titmouse nest. It took three handkerchiefs, two balloons, and a partridge in a pear tree to fill it. But Ma presented it to her, not because she needed it but because she 'needed' it. And she was an immediate woman. She even got the talk about the birds and the bees, you know. Bees bite you. Birds shit on your head. And the responsibilities of getting a bra. That it was a fortress. And one had to fight all invaders. The reason I know this is my Ma told me I had to help defend that fortress. 'Let it be known Romy is your little sister. That you will kick the tail of any boys that come around. Even the big guys. Even if you have to use a two-by-four or a red Mickey brick. This is your sister. Protect her.' Boy, I got a long way from our first jackknives, huh?"

"Yes, I know," Tim said, "I have four sisters. My mother told me I had to watch over them. The problem is that Teah and Tatiana can kick my butt."

"Yah, didn't they take that jujitsu stuff where they break rocks with their heads?"

"I don't know about rocks, but they sure could make a board into toothpicks with a cry and a stiff hand."

"And we carried our jackknives only after learning to close them by pushing on the back of the blade," Johnny said.

"I never got to carry a jackknife," Tim said, "because my Ma said everyone would think I was dangerous. What did a knife have to do with making you dangerous?"

"I don't know how it made us dangerous when we were young," Johnny said, "but it will make us dangerous shortly, when we get issued a KA-BAR knife and a bayonet. You'd better believe it."

"I'm not even sure I can shoot at someone, let alone plunge a knife into a human."

"It's going to be you or him, him or me."

"What about what you said your dad said to you when he handed you that first jackknife," Tim asked, "and told you, 'You are now a responsible human being'?"

"I just thought he meant that he worked hard to buy it, and if I lost it, I was tossing away his work. But I remember I went from five feet ten inches to ten feet tall."

"I read someplace that some grammar schools in New York won't let kids bring their jackknives to school anymore. Makes no sense," Tim said.

"How can you carve your initials in a desk?" Johnny asked.

"The desks aren't wood anymore."

"What are they made of, steel?"

"Fabricated stuff."

"I wonder if my old desk with 'JD and YS' carved in it is still used?" Johnny asked. "I know that big smooth bark beechnut tree still has the initials on it and is still standing. I visited it the other day and made the initials deeper. Carved in an infinity sign."

"I saw it. I buried Bugs nearby."

"I didn't know your rabbit died. I would have gone to Bugs's funeral."

"I know."

"You had him a long time."

"Yes." Tim gave a quick glance at Johnny then looked down and fell silent.

"OK. What's bothering you? I know you know rabbits, even Bugs, don't live forever."

"I know."

"So?"

"Johnny, nearby yours and Yelena's initials on that beech, someone had carved in—'What about Bernadette?'"

"What guy would do that?"

"Who says it had to be a guy?"

"The letters were similar to the ones you blocked out declaring "JD and YS."

"What are you saying, Tim?"

"Humans can't make humans an afterthought. Can't make a human a 'PS.'"

"Tim, if kids can't bring jackknives to school, how do they play mumbly peg, baseball territory?"

"I told you I didn't have a jackknife. What games are they?"

"You had to at least watch the games."

"Nah. I used recess and lunch to bone up on the sciences."

"Sure. What can you get higher than an A-plus?" Johnny said, punching his friend in the arm.

"Well, you know, my education is far from complete. What is this 'own the world' and 'baseball territory' knife-tossing thing?"

"Well 'own the world' was when you drew a picture of the world and tried to carve it up for yourself."

"That's what the Communists are doing in Korea—tossing the knife, trying to own the world, and claiming the humans that live there."

"Yah. Baseball was when we drew a ballfield in the dirt and had circles that were marked HR, single, out, double play. Your knife toss got you hits and scores. Everyone wanted to be the Sox, or the Brooklyn Dodgers."

"The beloved Bums. If they ever moved the Bums from Brooklyn, the world would end," Tim said.

"You'd better believe it."

"Mumbly peg? A knife on your nose. Too tender to think about."

"Sure was. Heard that Hoppalong once played with his dick head as part of the game. With Soupy, of all guys. But then again, who else would play such a stupid risk game except a guy that swallowed a grasshopper and a guy that dropped a big rock on a sleeping skunk?"

"You have to love them."

"Yes," Johnny said, "but you sure don't have to kiss them."

They both laughed as they punched each other in the shoulder.

"He really put the tip of the knife on his private?" Tim asked, his face serious.

"Hey," Johnny said, "you look as serious as a Jewish doctor circumcising his nephew."

"Yup."

"Yes," Johnny said, "the only look more serious in the medical profession is a veterinarian docking a Weimaraner's tail as its mistress looks on."

"So what's next? Will Scout Masters collect the knives from the troop each time they finish carving their fuzz sticks?" Tim asked.

"Someday they'll have metal detectors at kindergarten classes or before you can go into your DeMolay or CYO class."

"You are kidding, right, Johnny?"

"Yes, but my Ma does say all the time, 'The world is going to hell in a hand basket,'" Johnny said.

"Yes, but we can save it," Tim said, looking directly into Johnny's eyes, challenging, and questioning.

"Yes, we can, but we can't tell others we're doing it. They'll think we're crazy. They already thing we're nuts for going into the marines. More and more guys are saying to let the other guy do it."

"And we're the other guy," Tim said.

"Yes. But it was by choice. That's what makes us different."

"A lot of other guys are going with us."

"Did we do wrong, taking them with us? You and I joined up for different reasons," Johnny said, looking at his feet. The toes of his socks were showing through the tip of the worn-out sneakers.

"I know," Tim said, shifting his feet. "We joined to help make a better world."

Johnny stared at his friend's face. It glistened with a fine sheen of sweat in the moonlight despite the fact the night was cool.

"That's awful heavy stuff, Tim. We're still just kids. Partly."

"I want to stay a kid, at least a short while longer. I want to get my ashes hauled. I want Tonto Steinberg to strike again."

"You mean strike for a first time."

"You too?"

"You and I have always told the truth to each other, Johnny, or not said anything."

"It hurts to break out in a sweat, start stuttering, and get gas when you try to tell someone a windy. Everything happens, stopping just short of my nose growing longer with twigs sprouting out of it, but the truth is, I just want to get laid."

"Why is that so important?" Tim asked, tilting his head to the side as he fought the darkness for Johnny's eyes.

"The actual act doesn't mean diddly beans. I just don't want to die a virgin. Jesus, when I meet up with our friends in heaven or hell, I don't want them laughing and pointing out that Tonto Steinberg is still a virgin."

"John, do me a favor, just don't die," Tim said, punching his friend in the shoulder, an action he had seen other members of the gang do continuously but which he had never participated in until this night.

"I won't. You promise you too won't die there, Timmy, in Korea, wherever in unholy Hannah it is."

"I promise I won't die. It would really fuck up all my plans."

"What's with the 'fuck' bit? I've never heard you swear. Don't do it for me."

"It's not for you. I'm just practicing for the marines. We're going to be in the corps shortly, very shortly."

"Yes. I wish they'd check us out our dress blues before we head to Parris Island. It sure would help Tonto Steinberg here fire that old love arrow and allay my greatest fear. I might carry two bibles into combat, one over my heart, the other over my pecker."

"I'm worried that when I get frightened in boot camp or combat, someone will catch me rolling my eyes like Step and Fetch It."

"He's a stereotype of a race, always frightened."

"What kind or race? Hundred-yard dash? Marathon? You've never been frightened in your life."

"Yes, I have."

"When? When, Tim?"

"Try all the time."

Johnny searched for his friend's eyes in the dark but could only find their whites. He started to punch at his shoulder but instead put his arm around his friend and drew him close for the briefest of seconds. "Me too."

"Especially about not getting it before I die."

"Are you sure you want to persist? Yelena has a reputation of giving only a giant-size no, even to the polite ones that say 'May I?' even they have to go all the way back. Why is it so important?"

"I guess it would allow me to go on to the next step in life. Whatever that is."

"You try it with Yelena, and you could lose her. Maybe Bernadette, Bernadette Clarkson. She's struck on you, big time. Ever since you slugged that jerko bonzo in the huddle. They say she has changed from Madame Bovary yeses to nunlike nos. John?"

"Yes?

"I've never talked to no one like this before."

"Me neither. Thanks."

"I don't think you could take advantage of her feelings. You're not made that way. To use my mother's cliché—'You're not cut from the same bolt of cloth as others.'"

"Just call me the ragman."

"Call me the sandman. It's getting late, Johnny."

"Yes. Color me gone."

"See you on the train, John."

"Yes, see you on the train, Tim."

"Pardon me, boy, is that the Chattanooga choo-choo?"

"On Track 29."

"I'm gonna give you a shine. A shine. I'm giving myself," Tim said, his brow furrowing, "a shine."

Spotting the frown in the usually smooth brow, Johnny said, "We had it easy, being the poorest family in town, because we never knew we were poor."

"It was easy for us too, Johnny, being the only family in town nervous about carrying a jackknife."

"Tim, cut the poo-poo. You and your sisters are the best athletes, best students, and best looking in the town."

"Sometimes that isn't enough, sometimes it's too much."

"Hey, poo on you, 90 percent of the girls and guys in the town spend hours in the sun, spend big bucks on lotion, and suffer burns trying to get that coco Ovaltine look you get for nothing."

"I'll swap."

"OK," Johnny said, "as long as I don't have to throw in my long john—Mr. Stalwart, the unused super stiffy."

"I'd have to take up weight lifting to take on that big a responsibility."

Johnny belted Tim in the arm. "You're gonna be one of the boys if you're not careful."

"Will you always be a friend?"

"Not just a friend, a best friend. You're right up there with Righty, Soupy, and my dumb cousins. No matter that Righty's nose is bigger than his wanger. No matter that Pointer squeals on Dink and me when the thumb squeeze is on. No matter that Soupy is playing with a fifty-eight-card deck, all jokers. No matter that my donk swings to and fro, drags in the snow. What's on the outside is pigeon shit that washes away in the snow. It's what's inside."

"OK. Kiss me good night so I can beat it."

"Only if we forget the Chattanooga choo-choo and rumble on home on the Wabash Cannonball."

"Just don't put me on that train to Parris Island too fast. I have to let a few dozen mosquitoes land on my arm and watch them fill up with my blood," said Tim.

"What the hell's that all about?"

"My cousin who joined the corps last month wrote that we stop in Washington, Yamasee, then Beaufort, home of the South Carolina State Bird, the sand flea. If you kill one, you have to bury it in a full-size grave, four feet by seven feet by six feet deep."

"Sounds great. Think I'll go right to Korea."

"No can do. First, they make you forget all that safety stuff, you know, when you got that first jackknife. You have to sharpen that KA-BAR until just looking at its edge makes your eyes bleed."

"Holy shit," Johnny said.

"Amen."

"And then some."

It was a week later. Johnny was jogging the eighteen miles to Chelmsford to the farm, cutting through woods, hopping fences, getting back on the road, when he heard the old Indian motorcycle behind him. It sounded like an Indian war drum, not like the throaty roar of a ruptured lion grunted out by a Harley.

"Hey, cousin, what's buzzin'?" It was Dink. "How come you didn't tell us you were coming?"

Dink braked to a stop, slipped the Indian's kickstand down, jumped from the motorcycle, and rushed at his cousin, arms open. He had spotted Johnny jogging down the distant hill into the giant raspberry patch, the hog pens, the apple orchard, through next spring's potato fields, now planted with soil-saving timothy, clover, and other oxygen donors and honeybee enhancers. Territory was too rough even for the fearless Indian.

Johnny liked to jog the last distance through the woods, cutting off Riverneck Road and through the farm's acreage, allowing himself to sneak up on the country cousins.

"Pointer and I spotted you. We were bombing after a woodchuck with the Indian. Why didn't you call? Too good for the cousins?"

"Nah. This was just gonna be a quickie visit. I was just gonna ask Mine to keep a candle lit for Pointer and Me."

"You're too late. She has more candles lit for you two than a hog has warts on its balls. Not scared, are you, cuz?" Dink asked, tossing a punch into Johnny's arm.

"Nah, I'm not scared. After riding Bog and swiping old Osterhouse's underwear off the line and all that, nothin' can scare me."

"What then with the candle?"

"Korea's a long way away, and I just wanna make sure I can find my way back. Sometimes it takes only one little light."

"Maybe there's no such place as Korea," Dink said, giving Johnny a noogie in the arm. "Maybe the politicians made it up—made up the war—so their cousins can sell some tanks to the government and perhaps slip them a couple of bucks, just enough so they can buy their way out of purgatory. 'Cause rumor has it, the pols won't be able to bullshit their way out. One of these days, they'll choke to death on their own puke. That's why I'm not going. I want to be here to witness it. Besides, someone has to be here to screw all the girls, all the ones you didn't tag, and that's all of them. You might be the only eighteen-year-old Portagee virgin in the whole damned world. Johnny?"

"It is as simple as 'someone's got to do it.'"

Dink said, "How could you buy into all that crap they dish out? Since when do we have to fight other people's battles? Sure, I can see kicking the weenie off someone that leans on your sister. But why in hell should we go over there and save the Chinks? For crise sakes, they soak their noodles in the toilet bowl before they feed them to us fluckin 'mel-lick-cans.' And after they take your best clothes, they say 'no tickee, no laundree.' And the Southerners feed us that crap 'cause they send all their kids to the Citadel and other military schools and can only get jobs if there's a war."

"Dink, don't do that to me."

"I can't help it. I don't want to see my little brother and favorite asshole cousin killed to save a bunch of people whose women's pussies grow sideways. For crise sakes, you'll have to stand up while she lies on a table for you to get laid over there."

"It isn't your philosophy that I want you to stop talking about. It's the soaking-the-noodles-in-the-toilet-bowl bit. You know I love Chinese food."

"Too much. Too much. I'm trying to be serious."

"OK. See this." Johnny drew a line in the gravel at his feet. "You know that asshole Harrison who set the cat on fire, and you said you'd poke out his eyes and tear off his balls and stick them in the sockets if he ever came within a thousand miles of you?"

"Yah. Let's go find the asshole."

"Anyway, the Russians and Chinese want Communism to take over the world, when one guy works his butt off and the guy who does nothing gets to share it. That means the people have no say. So in Korea, we drew a line and told those assholes that if they come within a thousand miles of crossing over it, we poke out their eyes, tear off their balls, and stick them in their ears."

"Eye sockets. The eight ball in the corner pocket."

"Anyway, these cats want to set the world on fire."

"Let them burn everyone, I don't care. Well, don't let them burn Nookie—she's got those great giant tits."

Johnny winced.

"Ya got gas? Johnny, they fed you so much of this shit, your eyes are turning brown, and it's coming out your ears."

"They're slaughtering innocent people. The newspapers say so. If you believe in God, we stood around for years, while Hitler slaughtered innocents."

"Why did you drag my little brother in? If anything happens to Pointer, anything."

"We've always taken care of Pointer."

"Yah, but 'we're' not going there. Only you."

Dink stepped toward his cousin.

Johnny drew a second line in the gravel.

Dink spat on it.

"Hey, cut the talking shit, you guys." It was Pointer. "I found a great high bush blueberry patch. What's with the war line? We'll get enough fighting in pretty soon."

"Why, cousin Pointer, you sound like a diplomat."

"Why, cousin John, I'd rather make a burp sound like a dipsomaniac."

"You're both politicians," Dink said, cracking their heads together.

Johnny jumped up on a tomato crate, "Ladies," he bowed to Dink, "gentlemen," he bowed to Pointer, "if elected president, I will not send your boys abroad. Let them find their own broads."

The brothers tipped their cousin off his soap box.

"You always wanted to do good, Johnny," Dink said. "That's what always got you in so much trouble."

"Yah, who do you think you are, that young nun down in the islands, Sister Terry?"

"Sister Teresa," Johnny said. "No one could ever be that great. Can you imagine having so much love, so much dedication that you could hug a leper?"

"You could be hugging one, and a nose could fall off and go down the neck of your shirt or something," Dink said.

"Gross," Pointer said, making gagging sounds with his throat and holding his hand over his mouth as if to prevent barfing.

Johnny rubbed his stomach. "My tum-tum. Let's mosey on down to moo town and get some warm milk." He bowled his legs and sauntered off.

As they approached an old milk ladder cow, Dink started kicking cow flops. "Come on, let's see who can kick a field goal."

They spent the next five minutes trying to kick a buffalo chip over the goal posts beyond the unperturbed cow's back.

"Hey, I'm working up a sweat," Johnny said, going to his knees and rolling over on his back and then shoving himself beneath the cow like a mechanic rolling under a car chassis.

Within moments, all three were beneath the cow, yanking on her spigots. Actually, each was involved in an experienced finger squeeze that started between forefinger and thumb and worked down the digit scale, setting up a steady stream of warm milk.

A curious farm cat investigated and, on finding the action, opened its mouth and was greeted by three steady streams.

Using a little ingenuity, they soon had the cat looking like the inside of an udder.

Satisfied with their work, they got into a milk war that left them laughing.

"Remember the firefights in the goat shed and then downing the flies? The first to get five was an ace," Johnny said.

"Yah, and the time the goat shit in your milk bucket," Dink said, "and we had to empty out all the milk, wash the bucket, and then fill the bottom with stones and put clean milk in to make it look full. When we had to pass Pie's inspection, I almost filled the bucket with shit right before his eyes."

"Instead, you filled your pants," his brother said.

They stayed beneath the cow slinging the bull.

Dink said, "Remember the time you brought your city slicker buddy Righty to the farm? He didn't know what an electric fence was, and while we were watching the cows, he whips out his wand and starts to let a leak."

"And the stream hit the electric fence," Pointer said.

"And the electricity climbed up that stream into his pud," Pointer added with glee.

The three of them grabbed their stomachs and held tight to cut down on the pain, as Johnny added, "It's the only time in my life I ever saw a man's dick jump higher than his head."

"I hope she doesn't crap on me," Dink said, trying to reposition himself a greater distance from the rear seat of the cow than he found himself in.

"Remember the time we were playing baseball in the cow pasture with the Henergen brothers and you slid into second base, Johnny?" Pointer said. "You actually slid past second base as you landed on one truly slimy slippery cow turd."

"Yah, and you got up and ran like hell," Dink said. "We thought you were scared of cow shit or somethin'."

"But you were frightened by no cow flop," Pointer said, puffing out his chest with pride in his cousin. "Nah, you just got stung by all those bees that were feeding in that flop slop."

"You hear the one about the farmer's daughter that fell asleep in the cow pasture, and when she woke up there was a cow standing over her? And she said, 'One at a time, boys.'"

"Heard it! You dipstick, I heard it more times than Mine repeats her rosary," Johnny said. "Let's pick some wild strawberries. I can still taste the cream in my mouth."

"Bullshit," Dink said. "Don't change the subject 'cause you know I love strawberries. What's the idea getting my little brother signed up with the Marines? I'm gonna kick the shit out of you."

"You and whose army?"

"Look," Pointer said, "I've got some real fun, concerns real shit." He pointed to the old two-seater outhouse, the one on the main drag in front of the farm. The fruit and vegetable stand was long gone, and the two-seater outhouse stood alone, making travelers of Boston Road wonder who and why anyone would build an outhouse beside a highway.

The three of them had often discussed this question as to what people driving by thought.

Dink had said, "People probably thought there was roadwork going on, and they built it so the workers could take a crap."

"Nah, no conscientious city or state workers would ever take a crap on company time," Johnny had volunteered.

"Why would they ever need a toilet on a job? Especially when there are woods nearby."

"Let's torch it. Let's burn it to the ground. A celebration of us going away," Pointer said.

"Let's tie Pie to the seat first," Dink said.

They stared down at the old backhouse, which was out front. It was so tipped, it made the Leaning Tower of Pisa look like an upstanding citizen of architecture.

"It would be too much like burning an old friend," Johnny said.

"Yah," Pointer said, "it's where Johnny almost saw his first and only pussy. He still thinks it's hidden under the woman's armpit."

"Let's dig up the tunnel and crawl down to it," Dink said.

Pointer, undoing his belt so its tongue flapped in the breeze like a lizard's, said in his best imitation of Pie, "Sumna-a-bitch, you go-um in that tunnel, and I'll set it fuckum-on-fire."

"Remember the smoke driving us down the tunnel until we were up to our chins in shit?" Pointer said, laughing. Johnny's line and his spit long forgotten.

"And Johnny chanting, 'Don't make a wave,'" Dink said.

They looked at each other and stood silently for a moment.

Then Johnny broke off three hollow reeds, tossed one each to his cousins, and held his high overhead. "The Musketeers!"

"All for one, one for all!" Dink yelled.

"Till hell freezes over!" Pointer said.

They walked slowly from the field, picking up Devil's Paintbrushes, Queen Anne's lace and buttercups, which they held under their chins to determine whether they liked butter or not, a decision made when and if the bottom of a chin turned yellow with the reflection.

They picked daisies, plucking the leaves one by one.

"She loves me, she loves me not. She loves me, she loves me not," Pointer chanted.

"She loves me, she loves me. She loves me, she loves me," Johnny echoed.

Dink added, "She wants my hot body, she wants my hot toddy. She wants my hot body, she wants my . . ."

Pointer tried to stab his brother in the private with his reed sword.

The rest of the trip out of the field was spent trying to impale each other's penises on reed swords.

As they neared the edge of the field, Johnny said, "Just a few more days, and we're off to war."

"I ought to kick the living piss out of you," Dink said.

"We're almost to the boundary of the farm. Maybe we should hold hands the last few feet," Pointer said.

"I don't need that chicken shit," Dink said.

Johnny reached out and took Pointer's out-held hand and then grabbed Dink's hand fiercely, but he didn't have to as the hand was willing and ready but just couldn't say so.

They reached the road.

Johnny was back at the farm.

"One for all," Pointer yelled.

"And all for one," Dink echoed.

"Till hell freezes over," Johnny said.

Little did he know that hell would freeze over.

CHAPTER 6

BERNADETTE

Bernadette spotted Johnny walking down Main Street toward the Fellsway.

She followed, staying far enough behind so that even if he looked back, he wouldn't know who it was before she disappeared into the dark.

But he didn't look back.

His shoulders slumped, he stared at the ground as he walked, his brain and imagination a three-headed monster that kept biting each other's face.

A night crawler that had come out during an early morning drizzle but was caught by a surprisingly hot sun that morning was baked to the pavement. His mind skipped back to a Pathé News shot of World War II where marines had flushed out the contents of a Japanese cave. The flushing vehicle was a flamethrower.

The contents were the Japanese soldiers that did not know the meaning of the word "surrender."

Despite the fact the film was in black and white, viewers had little difficulty visualizing in color that the still-alive, burning enemy were a strange mixture of color and black and white. The color being the yellow of their skin, that section not on fire; the red, "make it rare"; pink, "make mine medium rare"; and charred, "well done please." . . . Jap rats . . . then . . .

But as he prepared to leave, to fight, it was different. He wondered . . . *Did they have a mother . . . a girlfriend . . . crazy cousins . . . ones that flicked rice at each other . . . from chopsticks . . . rather than mashed potatoes . . . flipped with a spoon . . . shit . . . double shit . . . double shit . . . with whipped cream on it . . . think about Yelena . . .*

Bernadette kept to the shadows behind him, on the edge of woods.

Unlike Johnny, she didn't look down. If she had, she would have realized her bare ankles were being brushed by poison ivy leaves ripe with their venom that turned their tips red.

Johnny saw little honeybees drinking of the clover. *Nice little guys... We should never have shot at them ... with our BB guns ... Boy, we used to break our butt ... nailing the spring that propelled those little BBs to the goat shed wall ... stretching them ... forcing the spring back in ... so now that shot that would barely break a pane of glass ... could now shoot completely through the thickest of cans ... the Carnation evaporated milk can ... the tests ... shot sweat BBs with that power ... hunting mice with an elephant gun ... Righty's brother ... Big Lefty ... could have been sent home in a tea bag ... Timmy Sullivan's brother ... who had been in his outfit ... told Uncle Matt Big Lefty had been evaporated when an artillery round landed on top of them ... killing mice with elephant guns ...*

A medium-sized red ant, the middle of its body a darker red than its ends, carried off the body of a black ant twice its size.

Other red ants carried off body parts.

A cottontail scurried out of the clover, stopping a short distance away, eyeing Johnny, its nose sending signals like the key he used in sending Morse code at those troop meetings, where the old scoutmaster gave them messages like "SOS, dit-dit-dit, da-da-da, dit-dit-dit, save our ship."

The practice signal he liked best was the one with rhythm—"Best Bent Wire"—da dit dit dit, dit, dit dit dit-da; da dit dit dit, dit, da dit-da; dit da da, dit dit, dit da dit-dit.

His father used to write from Italy in Morse code, but he couldn't decipher it because the censors cut out large strips, but he did learn from his father that it was "dit" instead of "dot," like he had learned in Scouts, and "dah," instead of "dash." God, he was proud to give this information to his troop mates who were dot-dashing.

A grasshopper teetered on the tippity top of a strand of grass, and Johnny wondered how it maintained its balance, how the stalk kept from bending back to earth.

Then a second grasshopper appeared on the scene and jumped on the back of the first. They appeared to be humping ... doggy-style ... *Wonder if they get hung up ... like dogs do ...* He had heard his Uncle Manny DaSilva tell his girlfriend years before that when the male dog reached the point of no return, a great knot appeared in its throbber so it couldn't get it out, and that this nuptial tying of the knot ensured continuance of the species—that most of the time, the male at this moment of truth would do a 360, God bless him, tossing a hind leg over the female's back so they ended up dancing cheek to cheek.

Johnny had seen this many times, two dogs hung up butt to butt, and was always surprised at the reaction of adults.

Some tossed buckets of cold water on them, calling them "public pigs" . . . as if they had the dough to go . . . to a motel . . . and even if they did . . . would they be accepted?

His sympathy was with the dogs, thinking . . . *God . . . if I ever got to do it . . . and someone tossed cold water on me . . . I'd kill 'em . . . or worse, I'd wait till they did it . . . and toss ice water on them . . .*

Others, discovering nothing but hound dogs dancing tail to tail, cheered.

Watching, Johnny wondered . . . *Would it be possible for humans to do it . . . do it while on all fours . . . each facing the other way? . . . God . . . what am I thinking? . . . I haven't even done it the straightway yet . . .*

The grasshoppers were becoming more and more active . . . *You talk about bebopping . . . baby . . .*

Then suddenly, they both sprung high into the air, and Johnny felt that hot wet heat on his thighs . . . *Oh, Johnny . . . you sick puppy . . .*

Bernadette saw Johnny put his hands to his temples and stagger, and wanted to go to him . . . *Stay away . . . He doesn't want you . . . Why would he want you when all the town's girls want him? . . . Yelena has him . . .*

The tracks for the Yellow Peril swung into the woods. He now walked the tracks, not sure whether to take half steps to every tie, or giant steps to every other one. He repeated after each step, "May I?" Not wanting to be sent back.

Bernadette, from the angle she was on, could partially see the movement of his lips. *Were they forming Yelena's name? . . . Let it be my name . . . I'll be the goodest woman in the world for him . . . if you will . . .*

Johnny heard a twig snap. Bernadette stepped back into the dark shadows, her hands to her lips.

She saw his lips move, full face, and believed . . . *He said my name . . . Bernadette . . .*

As Johnny had turned to the sound of the cracking twig, he had continued his steps and formed the words . . . "May I" . . .

His may I's ended, and he stepped onto a track, placing one foot behind the other, awkward at first, then picking up the rhythm; and suddenly, he was high overhead in the big top, defying death on the high wire, as thousands of people looked up, all of them Yelena's, beautiful and smiling. There was only one face in the crowd that wasn't hers. It was blurry. Out of focus. Swaying. There appeared to be tears on the cheeks. It looked somewhat like Bernadette, but not really. What would she be doing there? He closed his eyes but still couldn't see who it was, and squeezed them until it hurt. The face was coming into focus, but at the last moment, he only saw the tears. He could feel their warmth. Taste their saltiness. But then the glisten of the tears turned to the smile of Yelena.

He opened his eyes and looked straight ahead. He was still on the track, but now his feet didn't have to send messages to his brain. They thought for themselves.

And the track was predictable. Always there. Parallel. Yet in the distance, they came to a point. The tip of an arrow . . . You say, LaRue, Lilly Bolero . . . and then like that . . . quick as an arrow . . .

While the tracks were predictable, not so the large chips of granite set between the tracks and on the shoulders.

Bernadette, keeping on the shoulders so as to be able to make a quick escape to the shadows, had fallen twice, cutting her knee the first time, exposing a small piece of bloody cartilage that poked through her oozing blood like a vulture feeding from the inside out on the piece of pulpy flesh that rimmed the wound like the crater edge of a volcano.

On her second fall, she realized she had been walking through the poison ivy that had not only rimmed the edge of the woods but also worked its vines into the granite chips.

She knew that she should wash the poisonous dust of the leaves off her ankles and cleanse the filth out of the cut; she knew that the rust from the railroad ties that was scattered in small flakes on the granite chips could mean tetanus, or the painful tetanus shots to prevent the spasms, lockjaw, and even death.

Duck Pond was to her left, and while she couldn't see it, she could smell its coolness and believed she could hear the slight tumble of the small spring fed brook there, to wash out her wound, to wash off the poison ivy juices.

She kept going . . . What if he turns off? . . . Oh . . . Johnny . . .

She did not look down, but she knew the blood was still there, her own cartilage the very vulture's beak that ate her alive.

Bernadette remembered the last time she couldn't look at her own blood. She was eleven.

Yes . . . eleven . . . my birthday . . . I was so happy . . . Friends . . . loads of them . . . My parents . . . my father beamed again . . . Presents . . . a cake . . . punch for everyone . . . My father beamed at me . . . gave me a special glass . . . I got so dizzy . . . and then he told everyone . . . "Thanks for coming . . . Come again sometime" . . . but I would never want them to again . . . and he beamed at me . . .

Bernadette looked pleadingly at the sky. "Please, no."

But her plea did not work . . . "Drink up . . . my princess . . ."

"No . . . please, Daddy . . . I'm so dizzy . . ."

"This will make you all better . . . and your daddy . . . who loves his little princess . . . Daddy's little cupcake is now a woman . . . a little princess cupcake who is now a full-blown angel cake . . . Drink up . . . you will feel so good . . . and your daddy, who loves his angel cake will feel so good too . . ."

He took her pudgy soft hands in his giant hands, which turned to coarse sandpaper from twenty years in the mills.

I love my daddy so . . .

She had taken her tiny hands out of his, placed them around the large hands, and told him . . . "I will always love you, Daddy . . . always protect you . . . Daddy . . ."

And daddy said . . . "Sometimes little princesses have to make their big daddies happy."

He slipped his hands out of hers, cupped them within his, and moved one of her hands toward the slight swell of her breast, a swell as slight as a becalmed ocean.

She had only noticed that swelling that very morning as she tried on her birthday dress.

She had also noticed the slight hint of a shadow, down there, where she had never touched. She couldn't make out what it was.

She had taken the magnifying glass from her stamp collection. She loved her stamps. The colors. The flowers. The presidents. Someday she would be a painter. A president.

She sat on the edge of her bed and held the magnifying glass near the shadow. It was some kind of fuzz, like hair. She wondered whether she was turning into some kind of monster, covered with hair. Would it cover her shoulders, her forehead? Her lips?

She threw the magnifying glass to the floor. The hair disappeared. She looked close and touched herself there. It was like the down on the baby duck her father had given her on Easter with the words "It's like you, my duckling, first down, then thick feathers, then you fly, and your daddy will fly with his little baby duckling." That moment, it was all too beautiful.

Then his look changed, and she had asked him, "Did I do something wrong?"

"No, little darlin', you can never do anything wrong to your daddy."

And she knew he would forgive her for anything she did wrong because he loved her so.

He hadn't eaten any of the birthday cake she had cut. Yet when he came close, after her friends had left, he appeared to have some sort of white frosting in the corners of his mouth.

He squeezed her little hands then softly squeezed her tiny breast.

She giggled when he did this, but stopped, confused as he worked his hand slowly downward.

"You have a little angel cake down there," he said in a voice that wasn't his. "You must never touch down there. It would make you a very, very bad girl. If you itch there, Daddy will scratch. If you hurt there, Daddy will kiss it and make it better. Make it purr."

Her hand, guided by his, slipped into her panties, the ones with the smiling mother duck and her laughing ducklings on them. Then he released her hand and said, "We won't tell anyone what a naughty girl you were down there. Will we? Of course, we won't. People will say 'shame-shame' to you."

She remembered his exact words from seven years before, "Daddy will pet the nice little kitty. Make it all better."

He had taken her other hand and guided it to the crotch of his work pants. "Now you pat the nice little puppy."

But I knew puppies were soft . . . not hard . . .

She had drawn her hand back, confused, frightened.

His words were now crooned, "Now don't be a naughty baby. Come to Papa. Come to Papa-do."

He gave her another glass of that special punch. She held her lips tight, but he stuck his thumb in her mouth, pushing down on her lower teeth with the middle of his thumb as he pushed upward with the end of his thumb. And he poured the rest of the punch down her throat.

Then his words came through her blur . . . "Such a good little girl . . . loves her daddy . . . Don't ever be a naughty girl again . . . who would hurt her daddy . . . who loves her . . . Don't ever be bad again . . ."

Although she could not remember having been bad . . . *I would never hurt my daddy . . .*

She stumbled on another granite chip and looked down. The blood still oozed from her knee. She was covered with blood, then . . . like now . . .

She wanted to turn back. Johnny was swiftly disappearing. She looked down again and forced herself to look at her bleeding knee. The white sliver of cartilage poking out of her was still an evil beak, eating her from the inside out. She was bleeding more profusely.

What a good little girl . . . Daddy's little girl is . . . The blood means you love your daddy . . . like he loves you . . .

She felt like throwing up, so dirty, so filthy, everything behind her.

After her birthday party, the bleeding, she wasn't naughty to any of the boys. She let them all play doctor, then more, time and time again. They were a blur of faces, nonfaces, until she saw Johnny's.

She followed him, lurching, as her body racked with the pain of heaving. Until there was nothing left to heave. But she heaved regardless until a thin pink line hung from her mouth. She had retched up a piece of her stomach lining.

A tear streamed down her face, caught the corner of her mouth, and worked its way down the thin pink of flesh that hung from her mouth.

She had cried and thrown up every time a strange boy did her. They talked about Bernadette from all the towns around—"You want to try something good? Give it to that beautiful babe from Rockledge. The lightest blue eyes in the world. And all the time you're screwing her, she's crying, 'Oh Daddy.' She loves it so much."

Of course, they didn't know about her "no" to Johnny and her "you're a nice boy."

Of course, there was no fight to get her. She cried while they did her, but they didn't give a good crapola.

All the fight had been slapped out of her, or so she thought. Yet she staggered along the railroad tracks, following the boy.

Her father had slapped her face and punched her tits. In fact, during one joyous drunk, he had punched her breasts to the same rhythm as a boxer working on a speed bag, complete with the footwork.

Despite the pain, she did not cry.

Nor did she cry when she walked by the older men sitting around outside the fire station when they stopped talking about former Red Sox third baseman Jim Tabor throwing the ball so hard from the bag to first that the first basemen complained. They talked about Cousy, how the Couz could fake a magician out of his jockstrap and actually toss a pass from behind his back. They never ceased to talk about their big, bad Brooo-ins and how no defenseman could hit like old Eddie Shore—that is, until heavyweight champ Rocky Marciano, the Brockton Blockbuster, came along. They would forget wondering aloud how long Eddie Kelly could keep running the Boston Marathon, not knowing he'd be doing it long after some of them were on their way to Dante's Inferno or Mic-Heaven, the haven of Irish only, where Communion was a beer and pretzel.

No, she didn't cry when she heard their whispers, "A single blooming flower so very often picked."

Nor did her tears come when she walked past the groups of gossiping women who ceased their chatter to look down their noses at her and clear their throats as if to sit.

The boys were more direct; no whispers as she passed by. No. They were more direct. "Hey, Nookie, I'm in the army now. I really need a plow!" "How about a private from a private, Nookie?"

It was as if her father was punching her breasts each time she heard it. "Didn't I tell you guys she's like two of those Mount Sugarloafs up in Sunderland?"

"Bull. Try Mount Suribachi. The five of us could raise the flag there."

"Hell no, them hummers are big enough to be snow-capped Kilimanjaros."

"The Matterhorn. Man would risk his life to climb . . ."

"Those Grand Tetons."

"Twin Peaks."

"Jesus, I swear I saw Washington, Lincoln, and that old Rough Rider Teddy Roosevelt peeking out from between 'em."

"All I know, just a peek at them, and ba-*boom!* Mount Vesuvius, move over."

She didn't cry.

Well, just once.

As she walked by the spa, she saw the reflection in the window. Johnny had grabbed a boy she didn't know, the one who said, "I did her from behind. I can't stand to see her cry." Johnny had hooked his fore and middle fingers into the collar bone of the boy who couldn't stand to see her cry and pulled down. Until she heard the pained "Enough already. What do you want, an 'Uncle'? Uncle then. Uncle."

Most of the talk, at least the loud talk from the boys, had died down since that day.

She thought that if Yelena was a boy, she would have done the same thing. But Yelena silenced the girls with a silent look, one in which her friends could see their own reflections in her clear gray eyes, a picture they did not particularly enjoy.

Their faces appeared in the same big-nosed, chinless shape that reflected back from a shiny Christmas bulb or in a photograph shot through a fish-eye lens.

The cartilage beak coming through Bernadette's knee looked like a piece of human gristle. She was chewed by a vulture without being given the dignity of dying first.

It wasn't that it was so bad being eaten alive, human carrion being fed on by all, or nearly all. What was bad was that Johnny saw this feeding.

A single tear started down her cheek but stalled. What she believed was a bottomless well was dried out.

She turned to return home, but something caught her attention from out of the corner of her eye.

Johnny had slipped from the track he was walking on. His sneaker caught on a railroad spike that had heaved up from its iron harness and tripped him.

The fall was a good one with centrifugal force providing speed, and he went down without even having a chance to yell "Timber!"

His forehead thumped into the granite, a sound like a Halloween pumpkin being dropped from a great height onto the hot top.

The side of his head hit the track, and it felt not only like his ear had been torn off but also like someone had poured kerosene into the hole where his ear had been and set a match to it.

When he hit, he not only bounced but also bounced several times, like a dribbled basketball.

Then he was still.

Bernadette rushed down the tracks, never quite getting the correct sequence of landing squarely on the ties, and several times she fell, opening her knee wider. The added blood left the piece of white cartilage looking like a rooster in a cockfight, the loser, its eyes ripped out, its beak torn off, but its nerves still fighting, a small part of her body reenacting what her entire body was going through.

She fell again, this time avoiding landing on her knee, but banging her hip into a railroad spike that jutted several inches out of the earth and into the air.

It slammed into her like a hot rivet, and she floundered on the tracks like a squirrel whose hind section was run over by a car.

She remained silent, despite the pain, but Johnny's word reached her as he stirred, "Shit. What a thump."

He doesn't need me . . .

He was doubled over again.

He does . . .

Then she heard the thump, thump, thump. He was pounding in the spike that had tripped him up.

Bernadette got up on all fours, crawled into the shadows, fell prostrate onto a bed of moss there, buried her cheek into it, and felt her tears puddle up. She lifted her face and saw Johnny disappearing around the distant corner.

She tried to get up, but the sliver of cartilage had bent like a bow and now stuck into the very wound it came from.

She made it to her feet and leaned against a large pine whose lower limbs were removed to prevent them from reaching out and beating against trolley cars.

The pitch oozed from the tree's wounds, stuck to her shoulder . . . sap against sap . . .

She wrapped her arms around the tree . . . *Oh, Johnny . . .*

She didn't know how long her arms were around the tree, but the pitch that smeared her inner arms held her a bit in its lock. She panicked. Large hands had held her small ones in their grip, directed them, downward . . . *No, Daddy . . . please . . .*

"No!"

Her own voice startled her. She looked around. Not sure where she was. How much time passed.

She heard the *ka-plunk!* like a large bullfrog, then heard Johnny's voice, "One, two, three, four, five."

She walked slowly toward his voice, keeping in the shadows.

"One, two, three, four, five, six, seven!"

She saw him skipping flat stones across the surface of Duck Pond, counting its hits.

A raft of curious black ducks joined the audience of nosey mallards already riding out the ripples.

Johnny stopped scaling the stones.

The mallards came closer then retreated slightly as Johnny reached into his back pocket. They changed their tact and swam at him, stopping just a few feet from him.

He was peeling a flattened peanut butter and jelly sandwich. He took one bite but gave in to the mallards, tearing off small pieces and tossing it to them, until it was finished.

When it was all gone, they gave him hell, as only ducks out of the mating season can do.

"Hey, give me a break. I'm hungrier than you guys, and I don't see you tossing me anything."

He watched as a blob of duck shit bobbed to the surface near the tail section of the nearest drake.

"Thanks. Thanks a lot. Do I get any toast with the poached egg?"

He laughed, but it made his empty stomach hurt, and its growls were that of a bear who had set its bare butt on a red anthill.

Wonder if . . . I could scale a stone . . . and clock . . . ten of them . . .

His stone performed so many surface skips, he couldn't count fast enough to record them.

Bernadette wanted to cheer . . . *A new world's record . . . Great . . .* but she had to be silent, or he would discover her . . . *Oh, Johnny . . .*

She stepped deeper into the shadows as Johnny turned from the water and walked into a nearby beech grove, stopping at a giant whose smooth silver bark was a beckoning canvas to the jackknife Johnny drew from his pocket.

He had carved "JD" and the year into hundreds of similar trees over the years while hunting or hiking. He had carved his initials on high in the August heat while backpacking and low in the January snow as he hunted hare.

In the snow, he often had to push the tip of his knife with both hands as the cold made them stiff, cold as the winter-kissed bark itself.

The high winds on the hilltops caused the trees to swing and sway with Sammy Kay as he attempted to carve his initials accompanied by the clack, clack of the treetops with their frigid whippings.

More than once, a big rack buck ghosted by without him spotting it. He was so caught up in writing his name into a book of bark two hundred or more years old. It was his identity with the wilderness.

Once, an elderly woman had heard him telling Righty about carving his name in trees wherever he believed that no man had ever walked before.

"If I find any tree that you've defaced, I'm going right to the police."

Johnny had watched as she limped off, so frail that the flatness of the sidewalk proved almost too much. He wished for her . . . *May your legs become as strong . . . as your mutterings . . .*

"You better never let me find a helpless tree that you've scarred for life."

"Yes, ma'am."

"Don't you go getting snotty nosed to me, young man, or I'll nail your ear to the tree, when I find it. I love trees."

I do too . . .

He felt contrite, knowing that even if at one time she had entered the wilds that she would never do so again.

Her baying in the distance was the voice of Uncle Manny's dog, which is a combination of beagle and blue tick hound, "Sam What Am What Am."

A strange dog; he wouldn't come when you called "Sam."

He wanted the works, mustard, relish, chopped onions—"Sam What Am What Am."

Although the floppy-eared hound made some exceptions, like if you were offering the leavings from a steak barbecue, which took place on the farm whenever a cow was slaughtered.

Then not even a simple Sam was needed. Just a "come and get it" sufficed.

Some of his scraps weren't completed as the hound picked up the scent of a varying hare and went howling up and down the bunny trail.

When Johnny heard the baying it also sounded somewhat like the pastor at a cathedral he had visited with his grandfather Shiverick, haranguing the cheapskates that dared think they could come out of the cold and sit in a warm church every Sunday and only put fifty cents in the collection plate.

Uncle Manny had told him that when he heard "*the* dog"—that's the way he described his hound when it was out of earshot, with big time emphasis on the word "the," and Sam What Am What Am, sounded like he hooked his balls into a barbed wire fences that he was "on rabbit" and would bring the bunny full circle.

When the hound's howl got close, Manny would take the .22 bullet out of his pocket and put it in the chamber.

He rarely missed. The brothers were to take a single bullet or shell with them because of the cost of ammunition. Later, when times were a little better and a whole box of bullets could be afforded, still only a single shell was carried—a sort of macho thing he had learned from Uncle Manny, who would hide an extra shell or two in his boot top.

Often, the hare would stop its bounding when it sensed someone was there.

His Uncle told him, "That's when most guys blow it. They swing that gun to their shoulder too suddenly, and the jack bounds off. It's slow and easy bringing it up. Let it think it's hidden from you. That white fur on snow gives them that feeling. They think they're invisible."

They weren't. Its quivering nose was even more of a giveaway than its black eyes that showed.

Now the frightened hare did the spying. Bernadette watched him carve . . . *What* . . .

He would carve then stop. It appeared each time he stopped, he gently rubbed that spot down below . . . *Oh* . . .

She had never felt this way about a boy. She had never wanted a single one of the many, many that had marched over her body, rejoicing in what they believed were her tears of joy.

Johnny was remembering one cold, windy winter hunt that he carved, carved in pain with frozen fingers. He had warmed his hand repeatedly inside his wool trousers.

Then he spotted the doe. It was close enough that he could see her eyes glistening, the thick curling eyelashes that protected her large eyes.

Then suddenly, he believed she spotted him, as she folded her front legs so that her shoulders were close to the ground. She lifted her tail, displaying a giant large flag, a beware warning, and then thrust her rear end high in the air, white tail skyward. It was the type of warning deer gave to others of the herd hidden nearby. But it wasn't a warning. Rather it was a "come and get it" act.

A buck with a ten-point rack appeared out of the shadows, grunting like a constipated water buffalo. It steamed directly to the doe and then went up on its back legs, pawing the air as if trying to claw the clouds out the sky.

A risky action, because if the doe was completely in estrus, she could kick out the very teeth needed by the buck to survive.

She didn't kick. Instead, she elevated her hips even higher, splayed her legs, and thrust backward into him, causing the buck to explode in midair like a severed power line.

Despite the warmth of this August day, Johnny shivered, picked up the pace of his carving, no easy task, and he repeatedly reached to move his penis to a different position in his underwear as the available space shrunk as his size increased.

Bernadette hugged her face tighter to the tree, not quite understanding what she was seeing but feeling the new beads of sweat along her hair line, on her upper lip, and along the bottom of her bra.

Little did she know that Johnny was thinking of two does at that time.

Yelena . . . a beautiful doe . . . proud . . . a leader . . . brave and smart . . . He conjured up a picture of the doe lifting her hips for the buck to enter her.

But wait, there was a second doe, frightened, injured, and keeping to the shadows. But it too was beautiful . . . *No . . . go away . . . go away . . . Bernadette . . .*

But the second doe didn't go away. He moaned, "Yelena. Bernadette."

Bernadette thought she heard the wind whispering her name . . . *My imagination* . . . thought she smelled blackberries . . . *crazy . . .*

But there they were . . . *Why didn't I see them earlier? . . . So very close . . . so very far . . .*

Johnny had stopped carving, put his hand down into his trousers, and closed his eyes.

Bernadette scooped up a handful of the ripe wild berries with one hand and undid her blouse top with the other. She removed a single breast from its cup, and soon it felt the slight breeze its freedom introduced it to. Her nipple, always prominent and pointed, now quivered like the nose of a buck rabbit with high expectations. She crushed the berries on her nipple, felt the sting on its tenderness, as she saw Johnny's eyes flutter and heard his soft "ahhhh-g."

Johnny had slowly brought his shotgun up and found the "boiler house," as his dad called it, behind the front shoulder, always a quick kill.

He had wondered whether it would be cricket to shoot anyone or anything, getting a little . . . *What if it had never gotten laid before . . . What if I got killed, never having got it? . . . But there isn't all that much food hanging around the house . . . Old Mother Hubbard went to the cupboard . . . to get her poor daughter a dress . . . When she got there . . . the cupboard was bare . . . and so was her daughter . . . I guess . . .*

He had to take the buck . . . meat in the icebox . . . But he had waited too long. The doe peaked and, with a powerful twist of her body, sent the off-balanced buck piss pot over teakettle and left it partially camouflaged in a stand of young maples and alders, leaving a questionable shot for the deer slug.

Johnny could just make out the white triangular patch of the buck's throat. At least it looked like the white neck spot nearly every whitetail had. And that sure looked like the shiny black nose of a deer.

He slowly brought the single shot Savage up again . . . *Remember, son . . . we don't shoot to wound . . . We're never that hungry . . . If you don't respect the game, why hunt it? . . . Besides . . . I wouldn't want no animal walking around, bawling . . . with my bullet . . . or arrow burning its guts out . . .*

He walked slowly toward the stand of young trees, his gun at high port, ready.

But the tracks in the snow showed the buck had backed up, keeping its eyes on Johnny, until it reached safety, and then bounded off.

He turned. The doe was still standing where it had thrown off the buck, licking herself.

Normally, his father and Uncles didn't shoot does. "Don't want to go killing no golden goose. No seeds, no plants."

Of course, there were exceptions, like when you were hungry, and this was one of those "Old Mother Hubbard, cupboard is bare" times. Whenever he brought home a ruffed grouse or deer he had harvested, his mother told him not to tell his sister. "Say you bought a chicken or a steak instead of putting your money in the collection plate." She'd believe that. This would have worked out fine each time, except his mother forgot to tell his little brother and Jazz loved to tell Romy, "It's one of those soft-eyed deer that Johnny killed. And it bled."

Roma would say, "Ugh. Horrible," which led Jazz to dozens of "it bled, and it bled, and it bled," until their mother said, "That's enough, young man. Just enough."

And Jazz, as young as he was, knew about his mother's terrible swift broom, as he had seen his hero, Johnny, dance and duck, curtsy and cower, as she worked her wonders. Thrust, butt, slash, performing with precision without having a Marine Corps piss pot on her head.

He started his trigger squeeze on the doe. His father's words always came to him at this time. *Breathe in deep but quietly. Let half of it out and then squeeze the trigger, like it was a rubber ball in the palm of your hand.*

As he squeezed, the doe again spread her legs wide, and Johnny thought that perhaps the young buck, or a big one for that matter, might be coming back for seconds.

He held off.

But she was not being receptive. She plain had to relieve herself.

Johnny watched as the heavy yellow stream flew through the air with the greatest of ease.

He held off his squeeze, thinking, *No real gentleman, including a Yankee, could shoot a lady letting a piss.*

But he should have. When her steady stream of hot water hit the snow, it set up a veil of steam that allowed her to disappear.

When the steam dissipated, the doe wasn't there.

Johnny wondered just where in hell she had disappeared to . . . *Hu-hu-hu . . . only the shadow knows . . .*

"Ah, shit!" . . . Wild goose . . . brother goose . . . which is best . . . a wandering fool . . . or a heart at rest . . .

He walked over to the yellow snow. It was quickly freezing. He wondered if he could get some sort of transparent case that you could keep ice in so it stayed frozen. And when people came into his house and asked, "What did ya get?" he could answer, "Over there."

After all, hadn't his Uncle Manny missed a rack buck when his shot had hit a tree limb? And didn't he cut down the limb and put it up over the fireplace? When people asked, "What the hell is that?" he'd say, "What are ya, blind? You don't know a giant buck when you see one."

When people would ask Johnny about the snow riddled with doe urine, he could say, "What are ya, stupid? Don't you know a big pisser of a doe when you see one?"

He had carved a strange message even he wasn't sure of in the big birch that day.

Bernadette watched as Johnny started carving again but much slower this time. The urgency was gone, replaced by slow, almost indolent carving that sounded much like a lazy cat sharpening its nails on a bedpost.

Johnny was swaying slightly as he carved. The silence of the coming night was setting in. The active chirping of the wood thrushes and cardinals was replaced by single chirps, more subdued, accompanied by the tree frogs that started their trilling monotone song, a night version of the cicadas, the heat bug.

A metallic sound broke the rhythm of nature, followed by Johnny's soft "Bat shit," not quite a curse but rather a commentary.

She watched as he folded the broken blade of his knife and put it into his pocket and sensed he would look in her direction and worked herself into the long shadows cast by the trees as the last of the sun went down.

She held her breath for a moment, an hour, until she heard his soft footfalls on the forest floor. They were so quiet, Bernadette couldn't determine whether they were coming in her direction.

It was then she realized she still cupped her breast in her hand. She released it with a start, afraid he would catch her and know what she had done to herself but not know she had done it for him, with him. The single tear that had trickled down her cheek was of happiness she had never known.

The twig snap was in the distance. She looked out just in time to see him leave the woods and step onto the tracks. He didn't walk the rail or the ties, but instead, head down, disappeared in the shadows, appeared again, disappeared, and then was gone.

When she could no longer see him, she stepped from behind her tree and walked slowly toward Johnny's carving tree, feeling as guilty as if she had opened and read his diary.

Darkness fell quickly now, but rather than heading to the last daylight of the tracks, she continued toward his tree.

Each closing step became slower as it darkened until she forced each step as if working with seriously injured legs. The dark terrified her.

It has, even since that night, after her birthday party, when her father had come into her room.

After that, he always came in the dark, checking her two younger sisters first to ensure they were asleep . . . "Bernadette . . . my little lady . . ."

When she had cried, he had whispered in her ear, the sourness of his breath, gagging her, gags he mistook for sobs . . . "Don't you fret . . . my little Bernadette . . . that loves her old daddy . . . and when my little Bernadette's daddy loves her . . . you can pretend your old daddy . . . is just some boy . . . you like . . . extra special . . . and you want to make this boy . . . ahhh . . . very happy . . ."

The first time he came to her bedroom, two days after her birthday party, she had pretended she was asleep, and he went away.

The next time she pretended she was asleep, he tried to press his hardness into her hand and tried to pry her fingers apart. He put it between her breasts . . . "Oh, my little baby . . . with such a tiny back . . . tiny waist . . . has such big . . . no huge . . . set of tits . . . Daddy just wants you to feel happy . . ."

She tried to turn over, as if she was moving in her sleep, but he took her shoulder and turned her back.

Then she felt it against her cheek. He squeezed her breasts, then came the sticky wetness.

The moment he left her room she, moved quietly to the bathroom, where she threw up. She scrubbed her breasts and her cheeks until they were raw.

She had tried one last time to fight him off the only way she knew how—to pretend she was asleep. But this time, she felt his hardness against her lips. She clamped her mouth shut, flexing her jaw muscles until the pain shot into her temples, across her forehead, seared her brain, broke her very heart, but he pressed his strong forefingers into her cheeks until the pain forced her to open her mouth.

She later went to the kitchen and washed the inside of her mouth with the homemade lye soap, scrubbing the inside of her mouth and cheeks with a toothbrush until thin orange streams of blood came down the corners of her mouth.

She removed a butcher knife from a drawer, put it to her wrist, but could not do it.

The next morning, at breakfast, she had stared hopelessly at him and then at the floor, wondering whether he would again come to her room in the dark.

She spent the day in her room, trying to cry but unable to. Finally, exhausted, she fell asleep. How long she had slept, she wasn't sure, but it was her father's voice that woke her up.

But he wasn't hovering over her in the dark. He wasn't even in her room.

His raspy voice came from her sister's room; burned into her. "Wake up, little Kelly. Be quiet. We don't want to wake up your sister, do we? Time to stop being a little girl. Time to be a big girl for your daddy."

Terror struck Bernadette. She lay frozen, staring upward in the pitch dark.

Then she whispered, "I'm awake, Daddy. You're in the wrong room."

"What a good big sister," he whispered as he entered her room. "What a good big sister you are, you really are, and a good daughter who doesn't want to hurt her daddy by crying anymore."

She never cried again when he entered her room. The weeping after that went to the boys she gave her . . . disgusting . . . self to. That is, until the day Johnny had hit his teammate after he had said those things about her.

She stopped being available to the boys from Rockledge and surrounding towns, but she didn't stop being afraid of the dark.

Yet she didn't make a swift run to the final day's light of the tracks. Instead, she continued toward Johnny's carving tree.

The branches reached out and scratched her arms and legs, her face, and combed her hair into a witches' brew.

Then she was at the tree. She couldn't make out the carvings, only see the broken tip of Johnny's knife wedged in the final letter.

She felt the carved letters with her fingers, trying to decode them in the dark. She put her face within inches of the tree. She almost could see, but couldn't.

She made out the heart with her fingertips. The "JD."

It was some time before she deciphered "loves."

"JD loves . . ."

She tried to make out the initials, but her fingertips couldn't react . . . *Let it be me . . . Let it be me . . . Fool . . . fool . . . I hate me . . . Fool . . . pig . . . No . . . No . . .*

She squeezed her eyes tight. A pitch black, darker than the night enveloped her. She wanted to run. Run. But didn't. She squeezed her eyes tighter.

When she finally opened them, the carving was clear—"YS."

"Yelena."

She rested her head against the smooth bark, the carving . . . The knife hadn't broken off . . . in the *S.*

There was another letter. She found the spot where she had removed the tip of the knife from and traced backward.

It appeared to be a *P*, not quite completed when the knife snapped.

Could it have been? . . . No . . . fool . . . pig fool . . . The start of a B . . . B . . . as in Bernadette . . .

She put her head against the carving. The tear that fell along her cheek changed path and dripped into the *B.*

Her fingertip traced the letter one last time.

That's how Johnny found her, her head against the tree. He had returned with a sharp-edged rock to dig his knife tip out. Perhaps his Uncle Manny could weld it back on. After all, hadn't he always claimed he could weld the assholes of two skunks together and not spill a drop? And Uncles don't lie . . . except to save their ass . . .

Johnny's night vision was exceptional, a skill perfected by nights of catfishing and following Sam What Am What Am and others in the pack made up of friends' dogs, chasing raccoons and bobcats from the dark mountains.

When he first saw her, head against the carvings, he told himself . . . *Go to her . . .*

He held back, watching her sob . . . *Tell her . . . the knife broke . . . while carving a B . . . B . . . as in Bernadette . . .*

Suddenly, there was a strong beam.

The full moon had come over the tall, heavy pines, with a spotlight.

His feeling that he wanted to console her became one of confusion.

The moonlight on the top of Bernadette's breasts was too much.

She changed from a sad girl, sorely needing consoling, to the doe, the doe in estrus, that hunkered its shoulders close to the ground, elevating its hips high, offering a pinkness, a wetness he had never seen. The frantic pawing of the air, the tearing up of the earth. The snorting. Mewing . . . *She'd been following me . . . It must be . . . now . . . I'm not going to die a stupid . . . virgin . . .*

He wanted her. She was special. In many ways. So frail, unprotected, helpless. Her voluptuousness was a paradox, he thought. *She was like . . . a nun . . . with huge tits . . . Cut the shit, John . . . you worthless bastard . . . Just go to her . . . hold her close . . . nothing else . . .*

He felt spent. *Which is it? . . . Tonto Goldberg . . . or the white knight . . . I'm so spent . . . spent . . . How many boys . . . spent inside her? . . . How many boys . . . had called her a douche bag . . . a walking used condom . . . ?*

He backtracked into the dark of the thick low pines, toward the rail tracks.

Go back . . . you fool . . . No . . . Yelena's the one . . . No . . . Bernadette . . . Go back . . . She's a pig . . .

He was on the tracks now, running, his eyes closed.

Then he heard it. The Yellow Peril. In the distance.

He could feel the ties beneath his feet vibrating, slightly at first, then more so.

Its single giant headlight appeared in the distance though the trees, like a stick being clacked against a picket fence.

Now the light made the corner, Johnny figured, less than a half mile away. Approaching in slow motion, its light loose from so many Rockledge boys, Johnny included, having swiped rides on the Peril, perched on the light.

He sat on the track and watched the approaching trolley, its overhead live line sending out sparks like the devil himself sharpening his spear on a grindstone.

Now it was the hulking fullback of Reedmont, in his rotten banana-yellow uniform, charging down on him.

"Fuck you! I ain't moving."

But he did, only after he gave the conductor a fright that would lead to an early retirement.

Hey . . . we all need a cheap thrill . . . Here's a freebie . . .

Johnny looked after the passing train as it disappeared in the dark . . . Bernadette . . .

Would she panic? Freeze?

It was too late.

She fled.

Bernadette had felt a presence in the dark, despite not seeing Johnny hidden there, and believed she saw a moving shadow heading away. Toward her sisters? . . . *I'm awake, Daddy* . . .

It was then she heard the Yellow Peril and realized the only way she would find her way out of the woods and back to the tracks would be to spot its light approaching in the distance and quickly make her way toward it.

Then it was there, and she was running toward the tracks. If she timed it right, she would get to the clearing as the trolley did.

Luckily, she got to the tracks after the Peril passed, as she tripped on a ground vine and fell forward onto the tracks.

Unluckily, she ripped open the knee again, flogging pain into her body almost as intense as that in her heart.

Later, when the wound healed, she would wonder whether that *P* was meant to be a *B*.

She never caught up to Johnny, nor did he wait for her.

Chapter 7

BIG LITTLE MAN

"Hey, little buddy, you're the big man now."

"Nah, Johnny, you'll always be the big man. I'm just like a patch you put on my bike tire just to keep it going," Jazz said, looking up at his big brother.

"Nope, you're *the* man—that is, *the* man, the big little man. Hey, you're not a kid anymore. You're in the sixth grade. Why, when I was in the sixth grade, I was chasing girls and . . ."

"I heard Righty tell you one day you'd never get laid if you lived to be a million."

"He meant I'd never be an egg. You know, an egg. I mean, what's an egg? Something that comes out of a chicken's rumpus room. If city people knew that their egg came out of a chicken's rumpus room, they'd gag. When he said I never would get laid, he meant I'd never be an egg, something that comes out of a chicken's patouchee."

"Oh."

The two sat on the porch looking at each other, sort of smiling. It was evening. Johnny would be leaving for boot camp the next day.

"Do you think I can wear your Marine Corps suit, the one that is all red, white, and blue? There's this little girl in my grade. I think she really likes me. I tugged her pigtail, and she said she'd kill me if I did it again. She wouldn't have said that if she didn't like me."

"I'd think not," the big brother said, punching little brother in the shoulder.

"You're gonna be careful in that place, Go-rear."

"Korea."

117

"Yes. Ma told me you'd be careful, but I want to hear it from you."

"You better believe it. I just want to get over there, kick ass, like Pa kicked the Krauts' asses in World War II, and I want to get home by Christmas."

"Yah. You can do it. Kick ass. And get home before Christmas," Jazz said, smiling that bucktoothed smile that looked like a stack of dominoes attacking.

"You have to be the big guy while I'm gone. And take care of Ma."

"You bet. You bet your bottom dollar I'll kick ass here."

"Don't swear."

"Right. I'll take care of Ma. Can you bring me a gun from that island you're going to? Hawaii?"

"Parris Island. You don't need a gun. Just use a two-by-four or watch Ma the next time she does the bayonet drill on you. The tip of the broom in the gut. Swing the whisk part up and clop the chin. Then butt end in the back, with the whisk. Then slash down with the handle, and for good measure, a whack with the handle in the Cajuns will take anyone up a couple of clicks."

"No one goes near Ma."

"And no one touches Roma."

"I'm not protecting no sister."

"Yah, you are," Johnny said, pulling Jazz into his chest, knotting his hand so the fore and middle fingers formed a knuckle sandwich, which he rubbed into Jazz's head. "Noogie. And if you don't listen, you get an Indian burn." Johnny gave little brother a preview of a burn by rubbing fast and hard until Jazz's scalp seemed to catch fire.

"Uncle!"

"You never cry Uncle. Ever. No matter how bad you're hurt. No DaSilva says 'Uncle.' No American says 'Uncle' to anyone, except maybe ourselves. Can you take more Indian burn without crying out 'Uncle'?"

"You bet your ass."

"Don't swear."

"Why?"

"'Cause it hurts Ma," Johnny said.

"Then why do you swear—to hurt Ma?"

"Because I'm stupid. That's what big brothers are for. So you're going to protect Roma? Beat the snot out of anyone that, ah, touches her, ah, anyway."

"You mean if some guy cops a feel?"

"Where'd you learn that stuff? Huh? Where'd you learn that stuff?"

"I think I heard Leo Gorcey say it," Jazz said, protecting his head from a noogie or Indian burn.

"I'll kill this Gorcey guy, whoever this piece of shit is, that talks that way in front of a little kid."

"Don't swear, it hurts Ma."

"Don't be a wise ass, little man. I just wanted you to say it hurts Ma when you swear."

"You said I was to be the big little man. Leo Gorcey was one of the Dead End Kids, with Crazy Shak and those other guys. I don't know why I have to protect Roma. All the guys in the ninth grade are afraid of her."

"Yah, yah. Just do it. You want to wear my dress blues, don't you?"

"Sure. There's this little girl . . ."

"You getting sin-nilly at age eleven, forgetting what you already said."

Johnny looked skyward, pleadingly, "Lord, what did I ever do to you to deserve a little brudder like this?"

"You musta been a good boy," Jazz said, smiling, slanting his eyes to make himself Oriental, forcing his buckteeth further forward by pulling his bottom jaw back.

Johnny grabbed him and pulled him toward him.

Jazz put his hands over his head. "No Indian burn, I'm not saying 'Uncle,' even if my head catches fire."

Johnny kissed his little brother tenderly on the forehead.

"I'd rather a noogie."

"Look, King Brayer of the smart-asses, it just doesn't end with protecting Romola and Ma. Like there's the Christmas thing. You know, you go into the woods and carve down a small Christmas tree." Johnny handed his brother his jackknife, which Jazz took in his palm and stared at in disbelief, dropping his low jaw, jutting it out, making his buckteeth appear normal size for a moment.

"Look, the dentist doc has got an envelope full of money. I've been saving for three years. And I'm sending my first check from Parris Island to Ma, half for her and half to go with the envelope to get your teeth fixed."

"Will I be as pretty as you?"

Jazz ducked the slow-motion roundhouse Johnny aimed over his head.

"No one's that pretty. Ma likes that crazy yellow and gold berry vine at Christmas, bittersweet. Cut some of that. You'll find some in the Big Woods, right behind the Big Tree. It's strangling an elm tree there."

"I'll give you your knife back when you come home," Jazz said, looking up from the jackknife in his palm.

"If the stupid Elks try to give Ma one of those poor people baskets at

Christmas or Thanksgiving, you kick it off the porch. Ma hurt her foot the last time she did it."

"After I kick it, can I sneak an apple or a banana if I eat it behind the house?"

"No way, Jose. You take something like that, you'll ruin your life, Ma said so. You take something like that, and I'll give you an Indian burn until your pecker catches fire."

"Don't swear."

"Look, pipsqueak, you can take one apple, but when you grow up, you have to go by the Elks Lodge, where they have the big metal elk inside the fence, and toss a crummy quarter on their porch. Let them know we aren't poor. A deal?"

"A deal. I'll toss a half buck," Jazz said. "And, Johnny, just because you speak correct English to me, like Ma always asks, doesn't mean I'm gonna talk that way too. Maybe I'll toss a dollar with a note to 'stick it, we ain't poor, you Elk's arse.' I didn't say 'ass,' Johnny."

"You don't have to do that. The Elks mean good. They just don't understand that some of those they think are poor—aren't."

"I'll still tell them to stick it, for their good work, and maybe punch that metal elk in the snot locker and dent it. Just for a warm up in case anyone gives ma or Romola a hard time. They're tough, but I'm tougher. Tougher than even you, Johnny. Nah, we're both as tough as each other."

"You little dork. I guess Ma and Romola will be safe big little man. Just in case I don't make it back."

Jazz grabbed his big brother, pulled his head down to his tiny chest, and gave him a noogie.

"Don't say that, Johnny."

Johnny saw Jazz's eyes start to fill up.

"I'm just kidding. No Chinky, Chinky Chinaman, one hung low is going to starch my shirt."

"Are Koreans Chinamen?"

"No. Well, sort of. I guess. I don't know. Why do you ask so many questions?"

"'Cause I don't want to be stupid like you."

"I never would die and hurt Ma on purpose. But I'm going there to fight, and sometimes she sort of got in the way. All mothers sort of do that."

"Then don't get dead over in Gonorrhea, it would really hurt Ma."

"Never mind that crap. Get the tree and the bittersweet for Ma. Maybe carve her a little wooden whistle too."

"Why a whistle?"

"I don't know. Kids always make things for their mothers at

Christmastime. Things they can't use. Maybe she can direct traffic or something."

"Why would she want to do that?"

"Cheez. Why couldn't God have invented little kids . . ."

"Big little men."

"Why couldn't God have built some sort of invention into little kids that would eliminate their questions?"

"You mean like tape over the mouth?"

"Jazz, listen up. I don't have forever. I have to talk with Romola and Ma tonight too. You remember what we did last Christmas—when there was no money to get Roma all the stuff she wanted. The dolls. The little rocking chair?"

"Yah, I mean, yes, we sure scared the crap out of that guy in the store."

"Don't swear! We didn't scare no one. We just protected Romola while she sat in the store's rocking chair and rocked that doll she liked. And no one bothered her. Remember?"

"Yah, because we scared the sh . . . we scared the bewilligers out of him."

"I think he understood why you and I stood there, on each side of Romola, while she rocked and combed the doll's hair. He was a pretty big guy, and he sort of kept the other customers moving by, no stopping and staring. But you did good."

"You did good too."

"Yah. Thanks. Anyway, you have to do things like that. That's what big brothers do."

"But I'm her little brother."

"Not anymore."

"Now go in and go to bed."

"I'll stand by the rocking chair in the store. Don't worry. Can I wear your dress blues when I do it?"

"Yah, yah. Just don't go potty in them."

"Come on, Johnny."

"Just being horribly funny, Big Little Man."

"You're the best brother I have."

"That's one of the benefits of being the only brother."

"You want to come up to the bedroom and scare the shi . . . scare the *sheet* out of me—I mean, scare the sheet off me?"

"God, I had to do something awful wrong for this type of punishment."

Jazz ran at Johnny, gave him a noogie to the biceps, and was in the house so fast, he would have beaten Flash Gordon and Mercury in a foot race, flat out.

Johnny caught him on the stairs.

Jazz forgot to count and was lodged in the hole where the stair tread should have been.

"You hit me, I'll kill you, dead," Jazz said to his brother, "kill you more deader than yesterday's fart."

Johnny grabbed Jazz, placed his head in a headlock, and started giving him an Indian burn. "You're going to be the man, but the man doesn't have to talk dirty."

Johnny increased the speed and pressure of the Indian burn to his little brother's head and could feel the heat building up. Johnny expected his brother's hair to burst into flame like so much tinder. "Give up."

"Sure, when shit turns to sugar."

"Good on the not giving up, bad on the word selection."

Johnny pulled down his brother's pants—the family couldn't afford skivvies—and swatted Jazz's bare ass with a whack that sounded like the Red Sox giant first baseman Rudy York belting a long ball.

Then he gave his brother a kiss on the cheek.

Jazz belted Johnny's stomach. "That's for the smooch stuff, sissy."

Johnny laughed and sat his little brother down on the steps.

"Ya think that whack on your tail section sounded a little like York hitting the Green Monster?"

"Yah," Jazz smiled his "eating corn through a picket fence" smile.

"'Member the time York grabbed Johnny Pesky before the game started—stuffed him in a baby carriage and pushed him around the base paths?"

"Yah, I 'member."

"You remember I told you that Pesky and Ted Williams flew Marine Corps planes during World War II?"

"Yah, I 'member they flew. What was World War II?"

"You were too young."

"I never was young," Jazz said.

"Good. You have to take care of your sister, as well as Ma, you know."

"I don't gotta take care of Romola. She's a girl. Plus she's tougher than you and me."

"I don't think so. What makes you think so?"

"Last summer, up at York Beach with Nanna Shiverick, Romy stepped on some guy's white shoes, and he told her to 'watch it!' and she said, 'Watch this,' and stepped on the other one, after first dipping her shoe into a mud puddle."

"I didn't know that."

"That's not all. One guy called her toothpick, told her to 'grow some tits,' and then went into the men's toilet."

"So?"

"Sew buttons on your old man's fly. Anyway, she finds a piece of rope and ties it just outside the men's toilet door, about eight inches off the ground. Then she went in to the men's room."

"My god, Ma will kill you and me, Roma and Rags if she finds out."

"Romy finds the stall the guy is sitting in, his pants around his ankles. She yanked them off and ran with them."

"No."

"Yes!" Jazz said, building up enthusiasm, enjoying the full attention of Big Marine Brother. "The guy without the pants comes running after her, hits the rope, flies through the air, and not with the greatest of ease."

"Yah."

"He's lying there flat on his stomach, his butt looking like two half moons coming up. Romy then tossed the guy's pants high up a thorn bush and tells him, 'Grow some pants.'"

"Holy mother of god."

"Yah. So I'll just have to look after Ma, Johnny."

"And she can look after you. Maybe the wrong DaSilva joined the Marine Corps."

"That's not the end," Jazz said and started laughing. "The guy headed for a tree to escape her, and when the ballicky bare-ass guy gets about ten feet up the tree, Romola yells up. 'I'm sending my pet squirrels up the tree. Better watch out!'"

"Sweet Jesus, and I drew paper dolls and all their clothing for her, a born killer."

Chapter 8

BIG LITTLE WOMAN

"Roma?"

"Yes?"

She was sitting on the couch, playing with the *Gone with the Wind* cardboard dolls Johnny had drawn for her, Clark "Rhett Butler" Gable and Vivian "Scarlett O'Hara" Leigh. Johnny had been careful to make the swell of Scarlett's bosom as gentle as a calm lake.

Johnny had designed, cut out, and colored the civil war uniforms, the flowing dresses the color of wild flowers.

One fantastic brother?

Not really. The cardboard dolls and their clothing, the horses they rode, the cricket set, Scarlett's fancy shawls, and Rhett's hunting hounds were part of a swap system. Romola, in exchange, made fudge for Johnny from the sugar he had collected on a lend lease program, similar to the one he had read about between this country and its allies during World War II. There was no intention to pay back the various restaurants he collected the sugar from.

She also made him french fries with potatoes he saved from the potato fights the guys had in a Concord potato patch they visited. Several of the hand grenade spuds tossed at him were caught in midair and pocketed.

The cooking, of course, was done when their mother was at the box factory.

Johnny looked at his sister. "How about a similar deal with Jazz when I'm gone? You make him french fries and fudge."

"What do I get out of it? He couldn't draw a straight line or color between the lines if his life depended on it."

"He agrees not to be a pain in the ass to you."

"That sounds more than fair, but impossible, for him."

"He'll protect you."

"Ha! Protect me! I can take the twerp ten out of ten any day of the week and twice on Sunday."

"I know, but Jazz doesn't know. And he'll be the only brother you got for a while. And take care of Ma too."

"Yah, yah, yah. I already plan to get a job after school, right at the box factory with Ma, and I'll give her the money."

"Forget it, the money for Ma. I'm sending her my check. I don't need money while fighting a war."

"You're going to need money to get laid. According to the guys, you couldn't get laid in a whorehouse with a fist full of twenties."

Johnny reached out and grabbed her skinny arm and twisted, "Where did you learn to talk like that?"

He stepped back to cool off, got angrier, and stepped toward her threateningly.

She stepped toward him, her jaw in the air, her lower lip puckered out, and then without warning—wrapped her arms around his waist and cried. "I hate you. You don't have to go to that Korea place to fight. I'll fight you. Or you and me and Jazz will go to South Boston. The Paddywhacks there will fight anyone that ain't one of 'em."

"Who taught you to talk that ethnic poo-poo? Paddywhacks. Some of our best friends are Catholic."

"Yes, but you wouldn't marry one, would you?"

"Where'd the ethnic stuff come from?"

"I have ears," she said, looking up at him, searching his eyes. "If you get killed, if you get killed"—her lower lip, still puckered out, started quivering—"I'll . . . I'll . . . I'll kill you! I'll kill you."

"Will you take care of Ma? Don't work. Enjoy school and learn something so you don't ever have to work in a box factory. I'm going to be a doctor or a poet. Yelena told me so. You can be something too. Maybe drive a train or become president."

"Maybe I can learn to do hair. Or nails."

"Yah. You remember that sign that Ma hung in the toilet, over the john—'Aim High, There is Plenty of Room'? The sign was saying you can be anything if you aim high. Maybe you can be a beautician. Or do nails. Or do both."

"Johnny?"

"Yah?"

"Ma put that sign up so you and Jazz wouldn't piss on the seat, or the floor."

"Can't you say 'leak,' like a lady?"

"Leak, like a lady."

Johnny looked skyward. "Lord, what did I do wrong to deserve a sister like this?"

"I'll watch out for Ma, Johnny. You watch out for yourself."

"Don't get soupy with me, Roma. This kid was born to take care of himself. I heard Aunt Hope tell Aunt Faith I came out of the womb like a windmill."

"Oooh la-la, my big brudder is Don Quixote. He howls like a coyote and duels with an imaginary windmill, finishing its bay at the moon! I'll take care of Ma."

"Another thing."

"Watch it, brother, I've already let you sign my dance card once."

"Jazz."

"OK, OK. I'll kill him for you."

"When the Elks deliver that poor folks' basket at Thanksgiving . . ."

"Yah?"

"Jazz is going to kick it off the porch, into the street, so Ma won't hurt her foot again."

"So?"

"Well, your sneaky little brother is going to grab off an apple and a banana and sneak them behind the house. Find him and kick his sweet little tail."

"With pleasure . . . snitch."

"God, am I glad I'm leaving you behind!"

"Johnny, I'm not getting out of bed just to see you go fight a war tomorrow morning. You're not worth it."

"I know, tough guy."

"Johnny?"

"Yah?"

"Can I have a sort of, sort of . . . a hug?"

"Sure, as long as you don't grope me."

"Lord-dee! Where did you learn those worrisome words, boy?"

"Right here."

"What about the hug?"

"Grope-free?"

"I'm not going to grope a boy, a man, who has never made love."

"You can't speak that way to Tonto Goldberg."

"You ain't no Tonto Goldberg."

They hugged.

Their eyes closed.

"Roma?"

"Yes?"

"Jazz is going to watch over you while you hug that doll in the rocking chair next Christmas. Let him."

"It's your nickel."

The two of them headed up to their bedrooms, chanting, "I wish I had a nickel. To buy a pickle."

It was much later that Johnny went downstairs again. Jazz had finally fallen asleep after two hours of kadiddle, which Jazz won, spotting seven cars before big brother, who claimed first sighting of six before little brother.

Just before he fell asleep, Jazz asked big brother, "You didn't just let me win, did ya?"

"Did *you.*"

"No, I didn't."

"I'm not asking you, Jazz, if you let me win. I'm correcting you, it's did 'you,' not did 'ya.'"

"You say 'ya.'"

"Well, yah, I'm sort of stupid, aren't I?"

"Yah, sort of."

CHAPTER 9

MA

"Ma?"

"I thought you went to bed."

"Just wanted to tell Jazz he was the man of the family now."

"Good."

Johnny stood in silence as his mother crocheted. She had crocheted shawls for every female member of the Shiverick clan and was on her second time around. She had taken up the hobby after the kids' father had come back from the war and left home.

"Anything more, son?"

After a while, "Yes."

"What would that be?"

"I love you."

"I know."

"I'm not saying that because I'm a-scared."

"You're not afraid, son."

"I know."

"Not a-scared."

"I know," he answered.

"I mean, that's poor people's talk. Frightened. Scared. No such thing as a-scared. We've never been poor."

"I know," he answered.

"Thank God you and your brother and sister know you've never been poor."

"Ma, I have a confession to make."

"See your parish priest."

"We're not Catholics, Ma."

"Pretend, for one visit."

"You're a clown."

"Paint the town brown."

"You are the laughter."

"Tumbling after."

They looked at each other, smiled, and tilted their heads.

"Ma?"

"Yes?"

"I told Jazz to kick over the Elks' Thanksgiving basket so you wouldn't hurt your foot again."

"That's nice."

"And told him he could sneak an apple and banana."

"That's not nice."

"But I told Roma what he was going to do."

"Snitch."

"Told her to kick the bejeezus out of him."

"Watch your language, young man. You are not in the marines yet."

"Anyhow."

"Yes?"

"If he's hungry, don't let her do it."

"Of course not."

"Of course not," Johnny echoed.

"John?"

"Yes, Ma?"

"Your great-Uncle Henry Hennergar was in the Marine Corps, World War I."

"I saw the painting beside Grandma Shiverick's bed one time."

"In his dress blues. He was so proud."

"The dress blues are different than the ones I'll get."

"How so?"

"Great Uncle Shiverick's blues had a leather collar," Johnny said, "so when someone hit them there with a sword, it wouldn't completely cut your head off. And you had a chance to kill the one who killed you."

"Don't talk that way. Your great Uncle was a tiny man, tiny like your grandmother Shiverick. Maybe even as tiny as your grandmother DaSilva."

His mother paused then continued. "All through school, he had to fight. Mother told me he always lost, badly, but never quit. The fact that he fought never won him any respect, but it was different when he came home that last time, she said. Mother told me that it was 'Hi, Hank, go get 'em.' In the Marine Corps, and war, in general, there's no rich, no poor, no short, no tall. From the day you signed up, you started getting respect."

"Yah, I know, Ma."

"Even your sister Romola was impressed."

"Make sure she kicks his bony butt until it flames if he tries to eat that Elks' basket. Unless he is hungry. Then let him eat a couple of pieces of fruit."

"Of course."

"And then she can double dribble his fanny with her foot, like a basketball, have her make Jazz's butt bounce. We all need respect."

CHAPTER 10

HEY, LOOK AT ME! YAMASEE

"What the hell did it mean, Tim, that crap back in Washington, in the Capitol—'black only'? Are they trying to tell me where I can't shit? That I can't crap, and pull down my fucken' drawers in there even if it's rolling out of me like I was a Tootsie Roll factory?"

"I didn't see anything," Tim said, not looking Johnny in the eye. "Let's look for Yamasee, we pull in there next. Then Parris Island."

"What do you mean 'I didn't see'?" Johnny said. "Then that sign on the shit house door that said 'white only,' are they telling me I have to crap there? That's bullshit."

"Let's call it human shit and let it go."

"What's cooking here?" Pointer said, kissing Johnny on the back of the neck.

Johnny gave his cousin a shove. "Is this love, or are you just fooling around?"

"Just fooling around, but by that mean look on your face, it looks like you need some lovin', cousin."

"Hey, we're pulling into Yamasee," Skinny Potts said. "I thought they were kidding. There is such a place, whatever it is?"

"Roll call," Johnny said. "Scoff?"

"Yo."

"Fat?"

"Yo."

"Tim?"

"Present and accounted for."

"Rhesus?"

"Hey, tally mon, tally me banana."

"Soup?"

"I wanna go home. Show me the way to go home. I'm tired, and I wanna go to bed."

"This isn't going to be as easy as I thought to kick those gook butts," Johnny said, giving Soupy a sideways boot.

"Righty?"

"I had a good home, and I left, I left. Left, right, left."

"My god, I thought I had one sane one here."

"Pointer?"

"I can't think of anything funny to say."

"Just let us get a peek at your face," Rhesus said.

"Hey, listen to the guy who takes an ugly pill with every meal. And then has seconds on the pill."

They all stood in the aisle, and when the train ground to a stop, they all pitched forward into a heap, except Johnny, who yelled, "Fumble," and Fats, who yelled, "Pig pile."

It was while they were floundering about like flopping fish that the giant red-faced marine buck sergeant stepped into their car. "What's this, some type of Yankee turkey fuck! Get your bald asses out there and line up."

They climbed over each other to get out, a game of leapfrog, with a lot of the leaps going incomplete.

Finally, they were all lined up and giggling like children, which, for the most part, was what they were.

"Well, aren't we the cute little ones?" the sergeant said in a sweet tone that would provide enough syrup for a church pancake breakfast.

"Seems like a nice-enough guy," Johnny whispered to his cousin, who, to put it mildly, appeared to be shitting his pants with fright.

Johnny had barely uttered the word "guy" when the "guy" was in his face, big time, so close that a strange marriage of the fresh smell of aftershave lotion and the stale odor of cigarette butts made Johnny's nose want to punt.

The buck sergeant looked down, saw Johnny smiling in complete confusion and again, ever so sweetly, and declared, "Well, aren't we the sweet, gentle, still-tied-to-his-mother's-apron, smiling-pussy lad that we've been looking for to wash the BAM sanitary napkins? And BAM stands for our 'broad-assed marines,' whose asses are narrower than your tubs of shit and who, if given the chance, could kick your ass."

Still inches from Johnny's face, the sergeant said, "And where are you from, lady?"

"The town's so small, you wouldn't know the name. It's about ten miles north of Boston."

"My good aching holy ass, I ask a simple question, and I get a fucken' geography lesson. I'm afraid to ask how old you are—I'd probably get the Einstein theory. And how did you say 'Baar-ston.' Did you paaark the kaaar? Listen here, boy, you ever talk without being asked to talk, I'll tie your tongue to your testicles."

Johnny didn't know what he was supposed to do. He thought . . . *This guy thinks . . . he's the pope . . . I wish this sergeant was the pope . . . and I was a catholic . . . then I could kiss . . . the cock knockers . . . ring . . .*

"You understand, boy! You understand!"

"Yes."

"Yes, what, ant turd!"

"Yes, I understand."

"Shut the fuck up. Who do you think you are talking to? Why you talking at all? You think that you was some kind of human being? Do you think you're some sort of human being, boy?"

"Yes, I . . ."

"Shut the fuck up, boy. I won't say it again. You speak when I tell you to. Do you understand that?"

"Yes."

"Who told you could speak, boy! You see all those other citizen assholes lined up side my train, boy?"

Johnny looked down the line where other marine sergeants looking surprisingly, like they only had one face between them, were also holding discussions with the new recruits.

"Who told you to look away from me, boy? You know what you are, boy?"

Johnny didn't say a word.

"I asked you a question, boy. Are you too good to speak to a lowly old buck sergeant? Well, I tell you what you are. You're a shit bird, a shit bird from Yamasee. And you know what, boy? I'll tell you what. You see every one of those little old Yankee boys lined up, coming down here to my home that I love, and want to pretend they can become marines?"

Johnny kept his eyes on the sergeants.

"I'll tell you what you're gonna do, boy. You gonna tell each and every one of them, louder than the bang of an Eleventh Marines artillery piece, you're going to tell each one, 'Hey, look at me, I'm a shit bird from

Yamasee.' And, boy, you're in luck. So you won't forget what you have to say, I have something here for you to wear around your scrawny neck."

A corporal, with the same face as all the sergeants, handed Johnny a sign that read "Hey, look at me. I'm a shit bird from Yamasee," and handed him the sign with the words. "You gonna wear this, boy, for your entire four years in this man's Marine Corps. Boy, when I said 'Marine Corps,' you didn't salute. Unless you got a spare ass, you're gonna have to shit through your ears, 'cause the next time you don't salute when you hear those words, I'm gonna kick your ass over the moon. And I don't care whether you bump into the cow that's jumpin' over that moon or not."

Johnny looked at the sergeant and remained silent . . . *Cheez . . . this idiot once read a book . . . Hi diddle, diddle . . . the cat and the fiddle . . . the corporal jumped over the moon . . . and all over the buck ass private . . . me . . .*

"Boy, I hope you ain't doing no thinking," the sergeant said. "I catch you thinking, you better have ten asses, cuz I'm kicking nine over the moon, moo cows or not."

Cheez . . . they must have read to each other . . .

"Now git, you baar-ston baars-tard. Now take off like a big-assed bird."

Johnny took off like a big-assed bird, and his voice could be heard repeatedly up and down the line, "Hey! Look at me! I'm a shit bird from Yamasee" . . . *So much for . . . respect . . .*

CHAPTER 11

AN ISLAND VACATION

"Gentlemen," the tall blond marine said, although there was a feeling he didn't truly feel they were gentlemen, or anything for that matter.

What made his salutation appear insincere was the lack of stripes on the top of his sleeve, yet there were three hash marks on the sleeve bottom, indicating he had a minimum of twelve years in the corps.

He was going to be their DI.

While most of the drill instructors wore buck, staff, or gunny sergeant chevrons, his only indication of rank was unfaded areas where once stripes had been sewn, only to later be cut off. It appeared he had held noncom stripes of several levels at one time.

Boot camp on Parris Island had been a sixteen-week sojourn; that was prior to the need for fresh bodies in Korea, so everything was abbreviated.

The majority of recruits presently standing before him would be private first class in less than two months and would outrank him, as his sleeves were devoid of a single stripe; he was a buck-ass private.

"Gentlemen, I am Pvt. Seabag Calhoon. My real name is Ahab Calhoon, Seabag being a loving moniker stuck on me by gentlemen such as yourselves—a loving moniker given to a loving person. You may call me Sir. Big *S*."

"This might not be so bad," Soupy whispered to Johnny.

"I don't know."

"I was named Seabag by a variety of dog shits, such as yourselves who, for a variety of dog shit reasons, found themselves emptying their seabags of gear and refilling them with sand for the reason of making your exercise more meaningful. Might I add that I best not find a single spec of sand on any of your class A uniforms.

"You will also learn to do the Manual of Arms with your seabags. Recruits of the past were so joyous about the use of said sand-filled seabags used in lieu of Charles Atlas weights and rifles while marching, they named me Seabag. I love the name. But hopefully, I will never find the shit sucker who first tagged me with it. It makes me sound like some sort of sailor's whore. Best you not call me Seabag. Sir, capital *S*, will do just fine."

A recruit with the unlucky draw of the straw in the name department by the name of William X. Balls snickered.

"Well, well, what do we have here, the pitter-patter of a pussy," the DI said, smiling at Balls. "What's your name, son? It appears we will be friends. You enjoy my jokes."

"Yes, sir," Balls said.

"Mr. Seabag," interrupted a tall thin recruit from Pennsylvania with posture so poor, he appeared to be a scarecrow with a potbelly.

Seabag turned his gaze from Balls to the new voice. "And what would you like, boy? Don't answer. A brain transplant. That's it. We'll upgrade your cerebellum and sweep it out with our cerebrum. We'll get you the brain of a newt. What in holy good fuck do you want? A toilet pass so you can travel down the yellow brick road and squat in the little girls' room? Scarecrow, if you only had a brain, you'd realize you do not speak until spoken to in this man's corps."

"Mr. Seabag, I was in the National Guard and know that only officers are addressed as 'sir.'"

"Oh, isn't that interesting, dear? Could you tell me your name? Or do you have to look in your wallet to figure out what it is? Do you have it tattooed on your dick, you piece of ultimate perfection as far as the asshole of a hog is concerned?"

"I don't have to look in my wallet. Ah, sir, my name is Matthews Shleisslinger, but my friends call me Slinger."

"Well, I certainly want to be considered a friend, Mr. Shit Slinger."

"I'd rather be called Private Shleisslinger."

"Shut up! And you, Balls, you've got to be pulling my dick. Balls? As far as I'm concerned, your name is Shit Minus One, Squared to Infinity. And when I ask your name, you will answer Pvt. Shit Minus One, Squared to Infinity, Balls. And if that isn't a stupid enough name for you, tell me now, and I'll sleep on it."

"Yes, sir. My name is Private Balls."

"Balls?"

"Yes, sir."

"Balls!" the DI cursed.

Private Balls didn't answer.

"Don't you know your name, boy?"

"I thought you were swearing."

"I think this platoon best call me 'Sir,' big *S*."

"Yes! Sir!" the platoon answered as one.

"Even when you think I'm not around, don't even think the name 'Seabag.' You who would call me Seabag when you believed I wasn't about. Be it known that I am always about, in person and in bad spirit. I'll know what you are doing and thinking at all times. And not through some rat ass tattletale. I don't use finks. I do not use spies. I'm God, goddamn it. In fact, anyone who would rat on you—well, I kill rats. You never tell on a fellow marine.

"If you're ever taken prisoner, and you better not be unless you are out cold, you give name, rank, and serial number only. If someone is fucken' up your 'toon, don't tell on him. Fix his ass till he breathes to the same cadence you do."

"Your 'toon is everything. Its moving parts are your fire team. There are four men to a team. A fire team leader, his assistant, a BAR man— Browning automatic rifle, that is. Twenty-one pounds, seven ounces when loaded. The magazine—it's not a clip like in your M1—holds twenty shots plus one in the chamber, weighs twenty-one pounds, seven ounces. It can fire five hundred rounds a minute if the assistant BAR man can feed its maw fast enough to turn the barrel red hot. You can always tell if the person carrying the BAR is the real BAR man or just someone who picked it up from someone who went down. If he isn't the real thing, his left hand is burned and scarred for life. If fed fast, the barrel will melt and hang there like a droopy dick. The boiling barrel, if grabbed instead of the forearm, can burn you so badly, you can't thumb rides, pick your nose, or scratch your ass. You will be shooting the BAR when we hit the range. So you better listen. All the time. You, tall in the saddle, what's a BAR?"

Tim looked at Johnny, back at the DI, "A BAR is a Browning automatic rifle. Twenty-one pounds, seven ounces loaded. It can fire five hundred rounds a minute if the magazine is fed in fast enough. The magazines are self-contained, not clips as in the M1 rifle. Sir!"

Tim was on the verge of a good sweat.

"One thing I won't tolerate is uppity, boy. You understand uppity? Just give the answers to the question. No one asked you to sweat."

Tim's sweat turned into rivulets that streamed into his eyes.

"You going to cry, boy?" Seabag lowered his eyebrows, glared at the tall dark recruit, took a step forward, and stuck his nose against Tim's. "You understand 'uppity,' boy?"

Johnny started to take a step toward the drill instructor but was stopped short by Righty, who grabbed the back of his jacket.

Spotting Johnny's step forward, the DI, his eyes lost in the shadow of his campaign hat, said, "Well, well, what do we have here? This 'toon could be fun," the DI said.

"I pushed him out of line, sir," Righty said.

Seabag changed his gaze to Righty. "Boy, if someone wants to challenge someone, don't you ever stop 'em. The corps is taking kick-ass orders to challenge. You understand, you sandbox cat shit?"

"I . . ."

"Boy, you shut your puss or feel my boots. You want to end up with a boondocker in your kisser? You understand? I'll kick you in the face. If I want any shit out of you, boy, I'll kick it out."

"Yes, sir!" Righty said.

"Shut your flappin' asshole, boy."

"Yes! Sir!"

"Jesus Christ! I'm gonna make duck shit soup out of you if you don't shut up. Don't even think a word, let alone say one, even a small word. And I won't just be making it out of just your bung—I'll make duck soup out of the entire 'toon 'cause you and the 'toon are one. The plat-toon is not everything like I said. No. It's more than everything. It is the Marine Corps infantry fighting machine. And each and every one of you, when you leave here, if you leave here, will be an infantryman whether you go into the Air Wing or are assigned to a ship. If you are a cook or clerk. Or draw a navy yard or embassy, peel spuds, or end up underwater with a demolition team, you are first, last, and always a marine infantryman. A marine is first, last and always an infantryman. A marine is an M1. Although you are not marines, you dog shit fuckers might possibly be one someday. If I have a say. You understand?."

Platoon 127 answered as one, "Yes, sir!"

"You are one. *One!* You fight like hell as one. You don't rat. I don't care what type of pain someone inflicts on you trying to get the inside scoop on your 'toon, either here or in combat, or in Timbuktu. You never tell anyone anything except your name, rank, and serial number. Although you can toss in an 'up yours,' if you don't like your front teeth. Or your nuts. They like to slowly pull out your front teeth or cut off your balls when they take you prisoner. Now you will all have the same middle name for the following sixteen weeks of boot camp. Your name is 'toon 127—wait, no, make that the next seven weeks. The length of time of your training has been cut. I've only got seven weeks to form you pieces of diarrhea into a muscle."

The DI looked skyward. "Oh lord, what did I ever do to you?"

He looked back at the young faces, many who had just finished high school or were pumping gas down at Jake's or Frank's or where they worked on hot rods or station-sponsored oval track race cars, which left everyone broke and discouraged.

They were part of that old gang down on the corner that, up until the North Koreans invaded South Korea, was only broken up by wedding bells.

The DI's smile was so malevolent that Soupy that night in the tent swore, "Sure as shit, I shit thee not, I saw little red devils appear in Seabag's pupils. And the evil little Hades bastards had the same smile he had."

Many of the boots, but only in their mind's eye, looked skyward and wondered, *Oh Lord, what did I ever do to you?* They forgot, under the twenty-four-hour-a-day hounding and harassment they were getting, of their visions of walking down the Main Street of their hometown in dress blues, warriors! Ready to go to war. To fight for right and freedom, after first fighting off the women who burst their bras trying to attract one of these ramrods dressed in the colors of the flag, with a little gold thrown in for good measure.

And here they were—only dog shit—ground under the heels of a man who didn't have a single stripe on the top of his sleeve, only three on the bottom that pointed out that in twelve years in the corps that he hadn't graduated from kindergarten.

The DI's voice cut through the hatred and hurt they were building up for this stranger standing in front of them—"When I question you, your name will be John 'Dog Shit' Doe, or Jack 'Dog Shit' Smith. I better not hear anyone using the name used to sign into motels with your girlfriends. Yes, I'll be there with them while you're on fire watch or peeling ten million potatoes. You aren't even good enough to be the worms in fresh dog shit, so why would you deserve a woman?"

He looked up and down each line slowly. Every set of eyes stared stunned, into nothing. Nowhere.

"No. Not one of you bat shit bastards better sign or call out the name of Gen. George Armstrong Custer, my hotel, motel moniker. And don't even think 'Seabag.' Because I can read your minds. I can read small print. Just call me 'sir.' Got it? Yes, of course you have. Regardless of what Private and friend Matt Asshole Slinger Shleisslinger says, despite the fact he is my friend, like Private Balls is my friend."

"Sir?" It was Shleisslinger.

The drill instructor looked in disbelief at the skinny recruit who was built in the shape of a question mark, shook his head, and cursed, "Balls!"

"Yes, sir." It was Private Balls.

"Oh good mother of Jesus," Seabag moaned and turned his attention from Shleisslinger to Balls. "What in unholy Hanna type of name is Balls, boy?"

"Balls is an Irish name, sir. Some have shortened it to Ball. Somewhat like a person of Polish persuasion shortening his name from Poppowidski to Popp."

"Jesus wept, now a history lesson, and I've only got seven weeks." Seabag shook his head, looked at the ground, then at the recruit. "Balls, I've never had a recruit as a friend, nor a teacher. Thousands have passed through my hands, but you, Balls, are about to become my first mentor and friend ever, in the world."

"Thank you, sir."

"Balls!"

"Yes?"

"You donkey's asshole, Balls, I'm cursing, not calling you. I give nightmares, Balls, not receive them. You forgot to say 'sir,' Balls, and that could be a bad thing for you and everyone else. When I want you, Balls, I will be calling out in a big *B*. When I'm cursing you, it will be in a small *b*—that is, unless I'm more pissed off than the fly on the toilet seat, then it will be 'Balls' with a big, big *B*."

"Yes, ah, yes, sir."

"Balls!"

Silence.

"Balls, when I call your name, your name with a big *B*, you'd better answer. Or you won't have any."

"I thought you were swearing, sir."

"Balls, big *B*, for now and forever more, you will shut the unholy fuck up. Forever. If you are bayoneted in the heart, or worse, in the balls, you are not to cry out. You understand?" The DI stared into the recruit's eyes.

No answer.

"Good. All of you, including my friends Shit Slinger and Balls, as a collective pod of pussies, are Platoon 127. There are eighty of you. If I can come up with one single marine in the next two months, I will be amazed. You understand! You're all going to flunk out. Here. Right here. Not one of you tit sucks can make it. You're not going to war and flunk out in combat, costing the lives of real marines. I'll break you here. Now who is the one son of a whore who is going to make it?"

The platoon answered as one—"*Me!*" in eighty different voices, although there were a few unconvincing ones included.

"I want you ladies to take off your granny rags and not only answer 'me,' but 'me, sir!' and in one voice, or by hot goddamned, there won't be a voice left here by midnight.

"And when I tell you to do something, you run. You do not walk. You do not jog. You run as if the devil was breathing fire on your bony asses. 'Cause that's where he will be.

"And if I say 'double time,' you better take off so fast, your uniform and skivvies will still be standing at attention on the spot you took off from. You understand!"

"Yes, sir."

"You understand!"

"Yes, sir!"

"I have a few questions for you. Do you love me?"

"Yes, sir!"

"More than your mother!"

"Yes, sir."

"Who do you love more than your mother?"

"You, sir."

"Who do you love more than me?"

"No one, sir."

"You dog shit squirms! You love your rifle more than anything in this world. Except the corps. You love your M1 more than your mother. You love your M1 even more than you love beloved me. Your rifle will save your life. It won't bake you cookies, but a cookie won't save your life.

"If I ever catch you not loving your M1, not cleaning your M1, not telling it you love it—not kissing it, feeling it up, cuming while you do it—if I find you not putting it together in seconds while blindfolded, with extra parts sort of snuck in, you dog anal retentives won't be able to find a hole deep enough in hell to hide from me.

"And if you don't dig your foxhole deep, no matter how tired you think your sing-along bouncing ball of an ass might be, no matter how many rocks are in the ground, you're gonna wish someone killed your sorry ass before I catch up to your scraggly butt. You understand the King's English?"

"Yes, sir!"

"Now you go in that door and check out your gear and come out that door on the other side faster than a fart travels in a gale. On the double, you triple assholes."

The recruits broke ranks and headed in the door. Within moments, they had basketed and marked their civilian clothes and were issued dungarees and dress greens, canvas leggings, and ankle-high boots, with the words from the supply sergeant, "These boondockers only run forward, boys. If you have a problem, shift your panties into reverse and head home."

Skinny Potts looked at the ankle-high boonies and whispered to Johnny, "They don't look nothing like those shiny, fancy, white-laced, crisscrossed, calf-high ones my sister's paratrooper boyfriend wore home on leave."

"I didn't get my dress blues," Pointer whispered. "How am I gonna get laid?"

Actually, Pointer thought he whispered.

The supply sergeant said, "You anus, a set of dress blues would take one glance at you and puke. Get out of my sight, you mammy jamming turd."

Another supply sergeant shouted, "Put on your dungarees and stow the rest of your gear in your seabag. You lose a single piece of gear in the next seven weeks, and you end up in the brig until your ass mildews."

The eighty recruits were issued their gear and within minutes were standing at what passed for attention outside the supply building. The glare of their drill instructor was hotter than the August sun that pounded down on them.

"OK, girls, over there, hairstyling. Tell the barber the type of cut you want. Tell them 'Seabag' demands they do as you request. You'll see results when you say the Seabag sent you."

Soupy moved into the first chair. He pushed back the wings of his duck's ass, made a little anal two-fingered part in the back, and told the barber, "Just trim the top flat. Seabag told me it would be OK."

"Why, yes, young sir," the barber said with a little curtsy, and then turning to the other barbers, who all bowed to him, declared, "Mr. Seabag wants them to receive special haircuts. Ain't that nice?"

"It certainly is," the other barbers echoed.

And they commenced to shave every hair off every head as the recruits looked on in shock. It was the same look that someone who expected to be served banana splits by a beautiful, full-busted waitress had, but instead suddenly found himself before a firing squad.

Later that night, at the slop shoot, Seabag and the barbers described the looks of the recruits when the hair hit the fan. It was something they never tired of reporting, the boots' expressions to each other. It was a bonus in a relatively low-paying job.

One barber that night in the slop shoot asked Seabag whether he got the message from the kid from "Joissey," who told him to cut his hair in his desired fashion, as directed by his drill instructor. The barber told the

"Joissey" kid, "Please, young sir, tell your DI, Gen. Custer Seabag, to stick his KA-BAR where the sun doesn't shine, except when he smiles."

Seabag told the barber, after ordering him another beer, "Must have slipped the kid's mind. He was so busy reporting what a king-size roach's asshole you are."

Their DI was waiting for them, checking his watch, as they barreled out of the barbershop like the bulls being released at Pamplona.

"Well, you silly snatches are going to be up a little late tonight for being a lot late coming out of that barbershop. You should have realized it would take time to get all those special haircuts you ordered. Talking about orders, I am going to explain one order I will not give you the next seven weeks."

There was a small sigh of relief that at least one order would not be given during their boot camp stay. It was a small sigh, as only a few remaining recruits believed something good could happen.

"The order 'at ease' involves spreading your feet, grasping your hands behind your back, and relaxing a bit.

"No, you will not hear 'at ease.' It would make me happy if you count sheep doing double time and sleep at attention. Because you will learn to move out many miles while marching at break step while sound asleep. Also the smoking lamp will never be lit. It takes big lungs to run up a mountain with a mortar base plate on your chest and an Anglar Nine radio on your back while lugging a box of ammo. That's all you pack mules will be good for."

The platoon did not answer, as they all had learned that their leader answered his own questions.

"Now when I say 'forward harch,' you start to harch, and when I call 'he-left,' your left heel better be thudding into that deck as one. And I'll check your heels every week. And lo and behold, if they ain't worn down, my patience will be. And you will become patients.

"And when I say 'rye,' your right boondocker better be clicking into the deck. And when I say 'halt,' you don't just slam on the brakes and fall on fat faces. No. It's 'halt' one, two, with that second step after the 'halt' seeing your heels click together. You got it!"

"Yes, sir!"

"I can't hear you."

"Yes, sir!"

"All-wart, harch!"

"What the fuck did he just say?" Skinny Potts asked Johnny.

"Forward march."

"Why didn't he say 'forward march'?"

"Because he said 'all-wart, harch,' touch hole."

"Hey, who died and made you King Seabag? Don't 'touch hole' me."

They were marching. Or they thought they were.

The DI's voice did a singsong, "He-left, rye, leff, hoo-do-ya, leff. He-leff, he-leff, he leff, rye, leff, hoodoya leff. Rye, leff, rye."

Johnny whispered to Righty, "I think he asked who left their ham on rye."

"Company, halt, one-two. Balls!"

Silence.

"Balls, big *B*, I'm calling you."

"Sorry, sir."

"Come here."

Private Balls burst from the line and stood at attention in front of his DI.

"Balls, Platoon 127 is going to be the best platoon in this man's Marine Corps. Ain't it, Balls?"

"Yes, sir."

"Ain't it, Platoon 127!"

"Yes, sir."

"When I ask you if Platoon 127 is going to be the best platoon in the Marine Corps, you say, 'Yes, fucken' A, sir. 'Toon 127 is gonna be the best platoon in the corps.'"

"Yes! Fucken' A! Sir!"

"Now, Balls apparently doesn't want 127 to be the best. Otherwise, he would be in step. Know his rye from his leff. Well, I will help Mr. Balls—where in fuck did you get a name like that? I will help my first and only friend ever, Mr. Balls, and anyone else who doesn't know his left from his right to remember which is which. And you don't know your left from your right if your heel hits a mini-millisecond after that of the entire 'toon. You understand, 'toon?"

"Yes, sir."

"I can't hear you."

"Yes, sir!"

"So, Mr. Balls, do you want me to help you remember your left from your right?"

"Yes, sir."

The DI kicked the recruit so hard in the shin that it sounded like a rifle shot. "Now, Balls, all you have to do is remember, the one you limp on is your right. Do you have anything to say, Balls?"

"No, sir!"

"Not even 'thank you'?"

"Thank you, sir!"

"I told you, Balls, you're going to be my friend. Now we turn our mutual friendships to love. The entire 'toon is in love, a love affair that started when you check out your M1. You will carry this rifle through your entire Marine Corps career. You will remember it better than your own name. If you ever lose it, or let someone steal it, or take it away from you—I will find it, and then I will use it to kill you. What court in the world would find your best friend, using your very best friend, your M1, to kill you, guilty of anything? Now you wouldn't want your lovable old Seabag getting a medal for killing a piece of shiftless donkey shit like you, would you? Of course not. So I guess you'd better believe you love your rifle more than your mother. Your mother can't kill no one for you. Your rifle has a better chance to make you up a batch of cookies than your mother has of helping you kill someone."

Johnny tried to suppress a smile and thought . . . *You ain't ever seen my ma . . . with her bayonet broom . . . and where in hell . . . is the Eiffel Tower Uncle Matt said was here . . . in Paris . . . Eiffel in Paris . . . April in Paris . . . Who can I run to?* . . . Johnny looked around for the famous tower he had first seen in *National Geographic* many years before. The corner of his mouth turned up in the slightest hint of a smile.

Seabag caught the small smile. "Did you smile, boy? Or are you upside down and your ass is happy? You smile in this man's boot camp, and it means this man isn't doing his job. Are you a cat? Some sort of Cheshire cat? You'd better have those nine lives, plus, if you're gonna smile. Lovable Seabag don't take kindly to no smiling. 'Cause if you smile, you're telling God, Col. Chesty Puller, that lovable Seabag, isn't doing his job. You don't want Chesty unhappy, do you, boy? Of course not. I want Chesty to be happy when he sees Seabag's boys. Did I see you smile, boy?"

The DI's face was so close to Johnny's, he could smell his toothpaste and the onion-and-cheese omelet he had for breakfast, sort of like reading the necktie of a sloppy eater late in the day.

"No, sir, I didn't smi . . ."

"Boy! If I want any shit out of you, I'll squeeze your ass till it pops out your ears. Now do you want old Seabag here to send Colonel Chesty a pussy? Do you think this here boot camp and your beloved Seabag are spending all the taxpayers' hard-earned money to send a pod of pouting pussies over there? To Korea. Where they eat dogs and carry twenty-gallon pots of human shit on their head. Do you think this is like a game of pin the tail on the donkey? If I sent Colonel Chesty a pussy, he'll say, 'Pvt. Seabag, you are now a minus buck-ass private,' which would mean that when the eagle shits, I would have fewer beer buying bucks in my pay. I don't want him reducing my pay."

Johnny stared at his drill instructor and bit his tongue until it bled to prevent a smile . . . *The corps doesn't have a rank . . . lower than buck private . . . this guy is . . .*

"You! Royal cunt!" The drill instructor was looking directly at Johnny yet was looking through him. "Are you biting your tongue? You know and I know that biting your tongue is the same as smiling. You are stealing from my beer money because Mr. Col. Chesty Puller is everywhere, all the time. If you ever, ever smile again, or bite your tongue so you can't smile, as long as you are in this man's platoon, I will hit you so hard, it will knock your teeth into your asshole, and you'll be able to eat corn on the cob with your tail. You understand, boy!"

"Yes, sir!"

"You shut the holy fuck up. I wasn't asking you no question. That was a statement. You understand, boy? You just shut your mouth. Or else I'll play ostrich with your head and your ass."

The DI pulled Johnny up against his chest, reached in his dungaree jacket, and pulled out Johnny's dog tags.

"DaSilva, John, 1137825, USMC. A pirate. That's what you are. Long John Silva. You're smiling because you got pirate gold. I think I can wipe that smile off your face. Do you, citizen DaSilva, think I can wipe that smile off your face and off the faces of all the other citizen puss in boots here who do not seem to understand your soul may belong to God but your ass is mine? And I'll make it shine."

Turning to face the entire platoon, the DI called, "Ten-hut! Or-ward, harch!"

Platoon 127 marched to the weapons building, filled out the paperwork, and was issued their best friend.

Johnny's best friend was 119782513 and appeared even more lethal than the old Stevens arms .410 shotgun with a .22-caliber mounted under it, a prelude to the over and under shotguns of the future.

"Why did they cover these things with molasses?" Soupy Campbell asked no one in particular.

"Idiots. Full grade. Yes, you are the dumbest I've ever seen. Your attention, please," the ordinance sergeant called out. "Your rifles are protected by Cosmoline, a grease made up of a mixture of whale shit, cement, and bubble gum.

"Course, you ig-rants didn't know that perfume is made from whale shit or puke, or both. I read it somewhere. Called ambergris or somethin'. There are buckets of kerosene outside. Brushes. I'd get them rifles so clean, they whistle 'Dixie.' Same as pigs do. You know pigs like to whistle 'Dixie' when they're clean? Of course, you know. You know 'cause you're smart-asses. Smart enough to learn your M1's names. Not your pigs. Then I'd put my rifle sling on. After I soaked my sling in neat's-foot oil. And then I'd tighten that sling as tight as a banjo string so you can play 'Dixie' on it. Now get out of here!"

Platoon 127 was only a memory as 128 recruits came through the door.

Johnny heard the ordinance sergeant's voice just before the door closed behind them. "Idiots. Full grade. Yes, you are the dumbest I've ever seen. Your attention . . ."

Platoon 127 fell in, dressed right, and stood at parade rest before their drill instructor. He held his cupped hand to his ear for some time before speaking, "I don't hear no 'Dixie' being whistled by your pieces. Is it 'cause they're not clean? Or is your sling so loose, you can't banjo string strum it? Break 'em down and clean 'em before my eyes. Tighten those slings like you were tightening your girlfriend's chastity belt before coming to this island to vacation."

He spoke as the platoon spread their shelter halves on the deck, dismantling their weapons and listening to their DI. "Remember how you took them apart, girls. I'll call down the heavens on the heads of anyone with a part left out. And before I go any further, I want you gooney birds to know that after the Marine Corps hymn, 'Dixie' is the song we love the most, the very most. In fact, we love everything in this man's Marine Corps. 'Dixie' is my personal favorite, but we especially love our rifles. We keep them with us at all times. In our hearts and minds, when we go to the head to shit, when we sleep with one hand on our pud and the other on our M1s. We don't take them into Tijuana whorehouses cuz you trade your life if you trade your rifle for a piece of pussy. And sure as God made big rebel watermelons, you don't want your piece to get a dose of clap. Any questions, bug burps?"

"Yes, sir." It was Scoff Burns. He raised his hand in the rear rank, despite a nudge in the ribs by Johnny. "Do we take our guns home with us when we go on leave?"

"What did you say?"

"Do we take our guns home with us when we go on leave, sir?"

"First, fairy godmother, you go on liberty. Leave is for pussy dog faces and swab jockeys that can't walk on or under water like us Jarheads can. But most important—that is a rifle! Not a gun. Now, boy, come forward."

Scoff moved forward slowly, looking over his shoulder at Johnny.

The DI tilted his head until his entire face was in shadow, yet the white of his eyes glared out at Johnny. "Do you think you would like to step into me, Pirate Long John DaSilva, in place of Fruit Fairy Burns? No, I don't think you do."

Johnny looked straight ahead . . . *Don't call me . . . yellow . . .*

"You," the DI said, changing his glance to Scoff, "come here. Breathe my words. Take your rifle in your right hand. That's a good boy. Now you hold your pecker in your left."

Scoff looked at his DI, positive he was kidding.

Seabag wasn't kidding.

Scoff slowly groped himself through his dungarees.

"Careful reaching into that pecker holster, boy. You lose one of those tie-ties on your skivvies, and the fan gonna hit the shit."

The strings on the side of their green skivvies served a dual purpose the boots knew nothing about. But the corps, in its wisdom, knew that the recruits would lose their baby fat, even if they didn't have any, and the tie-ties could tighten up the waistband.

Second, after they washed their skivvies, clean skivvies being third in importance behind clean dry socks and good boondockers in combat, they could use the tie-ties to tie the underwear to a clothesline or branch to dry.

"What's your name, boy?"

"Burns, sir!"

"Burns Sir. Is Burns your first name, Burns, and Sir your last name, boy?"

"No, sir."

"Are you trying to tell me, Mr. Burns Sir, that I'm some sort of relative, that I'm No Sir? You better not be saying you are related to me, you worthless ant turd. Now try again. What's your name, salamander shit?"

"Scoff Burns, Sir."

"Scott Burns? Your real name?"

"No, sir. Scoff is my nickname."

"Scoff?"

"Yes, sir. Because I used to swipe things."

"Used to. Better remember how. If you can steal, well, maybe this man's corps can use you. Used to swipe, huh? You always need a tire off an army jeep or a nice air force sleeping bag. Or one of those swab jockey filet mignons the cooks hide for themselves. They don't need that stuff ten miles behind our lines, but could I possibly have your real name, Mr. Burns?"

"Theodore Burns."

"Well, well, Theodore. Who in hell would name their kid Theodore?"

"I was named after Ted Williams, sir, the last man to hit more than

.400. My name was Joseph Burns, but I was renamed when Ted Williams came along and . . ."

"Shut! You sick donkey scat hole and listen. You now have your pecker in your left hand, or did you forget, and your rifle in your right. I now want you to take a little double time around the parade grounds, and everyone you see, you show them your rifle first, your pecker second, and you sing to them, 'This is my rifle, this is my gun. This is for fighting, this is for fun.'"

Scoff rolled his eyes.

"Oh, boy, you done wrong. Rolling your eyes. You better flee the scene before I feed them snake eyes to some grape-eating ape. You better take off like a big ass bird or—"

Scoff didn't hesitate, burning rubber as he fled to the parade grounds, where his revelation was heard, many times, "This is my rifle, this is my gun. This is for fighting, this is for fun," marking an estimated 1,298 boots sent on such a mission over the years. This lesson on naming your piece was later dropped as some ladies back home got their US senators to end boot hazing, nearly ending the corps' successful "break them and remake them" philosophy. It is not an easy chore to get a vibrant young man to the point where he will run directly into gunfire for his country.

Scoff drew a number of interesting comments in his rifle-gun jaunt, including "I don't see no serial number on that pecker, boy" and "Mighty fine-looking handgun, boy. Any chances of borrowing it for a Saturday night date with a little Beauford woman whose health card has been punched OK?'"

The one that got Johnny smiling and biting his tongue (so as to go unbeknownst to his DI) was the comment from the parade grounds on Scoff's smaller of his two weapons presentation: "If I had such a homely, snub-nosed, small-caliber weapon, boy, I wouldn't go flashing it around none."

When Johnny heard that, he felt his first full twinge of homesickness. He remembered the story about his mother, who was a passenger in the Model A Ford Flivver her sister Hope owned.

While passing a group of teenagers standing on a Somerville street corner near the Ford plant, one of the youths exposed himself.

"Stop the car," Johnny's mother commanded, according to Hope's tale that night.

"Now, Charity," Hope said, "don't go causing no incident. And you don't know if they're dangerous."

"Stop the car."

Hope told her brothers and sisters that night, after the kids had all gone to bed, so she thought, that Charity had walked up to the recalcitrant exposer and demanded, "Now just put that away. Just put that thing away. If I had something so small, so homely as that, I don't think I would go flaunting it in public."

She then pivoted and returned to the car, an avenging angel.

She did not hear the other youths ragging their friend, "Now put that away. Just put that away," "If I had one that small," "And homely. Don't forget homely," "If I had one that small and that homely, I don't think I would go about displaying myself in public." Their laughter came in gales.

If she had heard them, the car would have been stopped a second time, and the youths would have been lectured on the meanness of bullying.

After Scoff, his rifle, and groped goods returned to 127, the platoon proceeded to their new homes, pyramid tents, where they stowed their gear for four of the seven weeks. The other three weeks would be spent in tents on the firing range.

After the stowing, 127 was marched to a large corrugated metal building that contained numerous recruits from other platoons.

Platoon 127 stood at attention for nearly an hour, as the other platoons stood at ease, including some that received "at rest." Nowhere was the order "The smoking lamp is lit" heard during their hour of waiting.

Finally, an officer, a single gold bar on each shoulder, appeared.

His first words were "Step inside."

Once inside, the lieutenant lectured, "You men see why it's important being on time. There are other rules as well. Orders are never questioned. A request by an officer is the same as an order. Keep your nose clean. Keep out of trouble in boot camp and later. Save your trouble making for combat. Then raise unholy Hades. There are some that raise it at the wrong time." He glanced at 127's DI, devoid of rank, with three hash marks on the lower sleeve. Seabag stood at attention, like he was being awarded a medal. The recruits could see the old salt was giving a mental finger to the shave tail second lieutenant.

The lieutenant looked at his shoes then continued, never quite meeting the eyes of the boys eventually to be young men, and droned, "If you need help, you can always see your chaplain. Or notify the Red Cross. Sunday will be your day of rest, but don't bet on it. The only rest you can get will be to doze off in church. How many of you men are of Catholic upbringing? Stand up."

Nearly half the troops stood.

"OK. Your chaplain is Fr. Stryharzawicz. How many of you are of Protestant persuasion?"

What appeared to be the rest of the recruits stood.

"Reverend Goodall is your padre."

He looked around the room, was about to dismiss the troops, hesitated, and then asked, "Any Jews?"

A lone recruit in the middle of the room stood.

"Sorry, I didn't see your nose back there. When I say nose, it means 'I'm going to count noses, a nose check,' that's all."

The lone Jew was left standing as the officer looked around the room for anyone else he may have missed.

Johnny recognized platoon 127's only Jew. He was set back into 127 after flunking out of 119. Johnny searched his memory . . . *What was his name . . . Goldberg . . . Tonto Goldberg? . . . Nah . . . that s my name . . . Stein . . . that's his name . . . from New York . . . first name . . . Beer . . . Beer Stein . . . You're a clown . . . Johnny Brown . . .*

The officer looked at Stein, looked around the room slowly, checked again, left the recruit standing alone for what appeared to be an eternity, and asked, "Do we have anyone else of Jewish persuasion?"

Stein started to sway.

Johnny stood.

"What do you want?" the lieutenant demanded.

"You wanted all Jews or us of Jewish persuasion to stand up?"

"What's your name?"

Johnny almost answered, *Goldberg, Tonto Goldberg.* "DaSilva."

The lieutenant left Stein and Johnny standing.

"Any other late-blooming Jews?"

Righty stood up.

Pointer stood up, well, almost. He bent his over head against his chest, hoping the officer wouldn't recognize him in a later encounter.

Tim stood next.

"Jesus," the lieutenant said, "they're coming right from the Holy Land to Parris Island. You look more like an Arab."

Rhesus, Soupy, Skinny, Fats, and Scoff all stood, as did a few others.

"I think I had better talk with you—you, you . . . talk with all of you who appear to be new to the Jewish faith as soon as I dismiss this group," the lieutenant said.

"I'll talk with these pissants, Lieutenant, their asses are mine," Seabag said.

"You'd better talk with them, buck private. There are enough yard birds around here already without your adding more. You're answering for these yard birds? One foul up, and you'll all pay. Dismissed!"

Platoon 127 fell in outside.

The DI looked up and down the line. "Well, suddenly, 127 has sprouted a burning bush population. Funny, when I checked DaSilva's dog tags, they said *P*, as in Protestant, on 'em. I'm gonna talk to you like the nice officer wanted."

A collective shiver ran up and down the platoon, especially those of the late-blooming Jewish faith.

Righty blessed himself.

Seabag, even without wasps in his skivvies, was more than enough hell on earth. With the lieutenant's unveiled threat, they knew they were going to be stung dearly.

Seabag's first word, "When," was like an ice pick to the temple.

"When Stein stood up alone," he hesitated, "several of you assaholics pretend Jews stood up. Meaning, that you learned a basic of the Marine Corps, that you never leave your buddy's ass hanging alone, swinging in the breeze. You never leave our wounded or dead behind, no matter the price you pay.

"My only problem, what made me wonder," Seabag continued, "was why only ten went after the wounded, rather than an entire platoon. I want any of you who didn't stand to make up your mind—are you going to be marines or rat-shit coward? Rat shits can head home *now!* So 127 can go about being the best bad-assed platoon in the whole fucken' USMC, United States Marine Corps. No one heading home? Then answer one question—are we going to be the best!"

"Yes! Sir!"

"It's 'yes fucken' A, sir!'"

"Yes! Fucken' A, sir!"

"About-face. All-ward, harch!"

He marched them from the meeting building to the parade ground. "Company . . . *halt.* Do you love me?"

"Yes! Fucken' A! Sir!"

"You bet your hairless asses, ladies. Now twice around the parade grounds, except the ten who dared to stand up. You're special. Four times around. And don't try walking in the dark. I see in the dark. I catch anyone dogging it, I'll break their ass into so many pieces, we'll be able to box it and sell it as a thousand-piece puzzle. It's a mile around. By the time you're done your two miles, four for the tit-sucking ten, I'll have your fire watch and guard duties for the night setup. Fire watch does just that, watches the fire, and the guards guard while the rest sleep. "Not really, because tomorrow morning, each and every lard-assed one of you will know your Rocks and Shoals, that little booklet that tells you the million reasons the Marine Corps can lock up your ass and throw away the key. And of course, you'll know the General Orders. Rocks and Shoals. Rifle serial number. Your serial number. All the words to 'Dixie,' forward and backward.

"Reveille is at 0500. So I wouldn't spend a lot of time pulling the pud. Stack arms at the north end of your hut. Read your handbook on how to stack arms. In fact, I'd read the entire handbook tonight. I'd hate to be the elongated piece of giraffe shit that didn't have the answers tomorrow. Charge! Take off like big-ass birds!"

They were off and running into the dark parade grounds, their boondockers slapping the tarmac, barely drowning out their panting; but like all good things, bad things also have to come to an end.

They found themselves, tongues out like hot hounds in August, standing in front of their huts, their drill instructor in front of them. How in hell did he get there first? was the question in everyone's mind.

He wasn't panting. His tongue wasn't out. Yet during their run, he had passed each and every one of them.

"Let's get a few things straight here. There is no smoking unless I light the smoking lamp. And the smoking lamp is never lit, but your flashlights are. Snap 'em on. You ladies are going to go on a search for butts. When you find one, you field strip it. That means tear off the wrapper and spread the tobacco to the four winds. Fold the wrapper paper into something smaller than a sand flea. Dig your boondocker heel into the sand and give that spitball a proper burial. OK. I don't want to see nothing but assholes and elbows."

The platoon, flashlights on, became all assholes and elbows; no one was going to take the chance of standing up. They remembered too well that a kick in the shins, similar to a full swing with a board, was a reminder which was left and which was right, and found it easy to visualize what failing to transform into all assholes and elbows could entail.

In the dark, 127 members did not look unlike ostriches seeking a hiding hole or giant mushrooms that groaned.

A half hour later, they were standing at attention as their DI checked the area for a single butt.

Not only did he find it but he also found it lit, and in Skinny Potts's mouth, who was hiding behind his hut.

The DI looked down at Skinny, hidden in thought between the GI cans.

"Well, well, my fat fuck, what do we have here? If I was you, Potts, I do believe I would say my rosary, even if you aren't Catholic. Would you please follow me?"

Skinny followed the DI back to the platoon.

"My fat fellow saw fit to disobey orders. Did I light the smoking lamp?"

"No! Sir."

"Didn't I speak English, girls, when I told you how to address me?

I'm not just 'sir,' I'm something special, aren't I? What happened to my Christian name, Fucken'? Do you love me more than your mother, less than your M1?"

Some 127 members didn't know which answer their drill instructor wanted, but those who did were more than loud enough, "Yes! Fucken'! Sir!"

"Then did your dearly beloved light the smoking lamp!"

"No! Fucken'! Sir!"

"So lard ass disobeyed orders. Do you cunts understand that one man disobeying orders can cost the lives of his entire platoon! That is not a question."

"Potts, let me have your butts."

Skinny turned them over.

His DI stuck four in Skinny's mouth and lit them. "Now, boy, you climb to the top of that Quonset."

Skinny looked at the seemingly impossible task of climbing the tin rounded roof. "How?"

"Boy, yours is not to question why, yours is just to do or die. Shit wings. Stick bubblegum to your hands. Grab a fistful of tree toads. Make a giant pogo stick. Just haul your ass up there."

Skinny made several runs and jumps at the roof but slid back each time. As panic set in with each failure, he thought of sinking his teeth into the metal like a beaver into a tree. But instead, he opted to climb up the very edge of the roof, hand over hand, using the edge to pull himself along until he was crouched on the peak.

"Attention!"

Skinny stood up.

Seabag dragged one of the GI cans Skinny had been hiding behind to a spot directly below the terrified recruit.

"Now, boy, here's this can you liked so much. Let's hear a 'Geronimo' from you and then see your ass flying through the air. And I suggest you keep your feet together, your arms against your side, and suck in your balls, because I want you to land in that can."

"Go!"

"Geroni-mooooh!"

The amazing thing about his jump was that he made it into the GI can with everything intact, with his eyes closed so tight, they felt like they would pop out his ears.

Once in the can, Skinny took stock and was more surprised than anyone he hadn't lost a foot, arm, or ball, and started to get out of the barrel.

"I wouldn't do that, boy. You've haven't got yourself an order yet."

Turning to the four nearest recruits, "You four, get your wool blankets. Soak them down with warm water." All was quiet except for the cicadas singing their world's-on-fire dirge.

And it might as well have been, as the South Carolina heat drenched the platoon's body, already drenched from their sweaty parade ground run. The rivulets ran down their backs to the crack of their asses, which turned raw as if hit by a blowtorch.

The sweat streamed off their foreheads into their eyes.

"You there, boy, were you trying to keep that sweat out of your eyes by flicking your eyebrows into the air! I hope not. I don't think my weak heart could take two shit birds disobeying orders the same day."

The steaming blankets arrived just as the DI filled Skinny's mouth with cigarettes and lit them.

"Now, Mr. Potts, what in hell kind of name is that? Why don't you squat in that there barrel and start puffing while we make sure you don't freeze to death?"

Skinny hunkered down in the barrel as the wet blankets were put over him.

You could hear his choking through the heavy blankets.

"Any more of you shit birds once removed want to join in for a smoke while fat nuts here disobeyed an order and is being rewarded? It's your chance to enjoy a boon, a smoke."

One recruit suffering the smoker's jitters was about to step forward when he was nudged in the ribs by a buddy and immediately got the message. His smoking would be done in a trash can and under four soaked blankets.

"OK, fall out. Check the bulletin board for guard and fire watch duties. You, DaSilva, let that sorry piece of salamander shit out of the barrel."

Johnny rushed to the barrel, yanked the blankets off, and helped the choking Skinny out and was leading him away when Seabag's voice cut in, "DaSilva, tell Smoky Stover if he ever again disobeys an order in this man's Marine Corps, I could be inclined to forget my good nature."

Back at the hut, they laid Skinny on his rack.

"Are you OK?" Righty asked him.

Skinny looked up and then turned away when he felt the hot tears stream down his chubby cheeks.

Rhesus chipped in, "If that guy ever gets in front of me in combat, I'll shoot out the back of his brain."

"What brain?" Pointer asked.

"What did you draw for watch?" Righty whispered over to Johnny.

"I got the first two hours of fire watch and the last two guard duty. God, I'm more tired than a two-day old fart."

"Remember what Seabag said, you fall asleep on watch means a general court-martial. He said bad boys at Portsmouth like nothing better than have some hairless-assed little boys for a plaything."

"I want my momma," Soupy wailed.

"You horse's patootie of a skunk killer," Rhesus said, "get serious. We'll never make it out of here alive."

"I am serious. I'm making plans to get out of all this. There's a thing called a 'Section Eight,' means you're a little crazy, and they'll let you go home."

"You'll never get out on a Section Eight. You're a lot more than a little crazy," Johnny said.

"Hey, we all signed, so crazy is as crazy does," Soupy said, adding, "I'm so fucken' tired, I don't have the strength to close my eyes. I want out. I feel as crazy as a dog chasing its own tail."

"Soup, that was a good thing you did. Going in after that wounded Jewish boy, standing up with us for Stein," Johnny told him in an exhausted attempt to cheer him up.

"Don't butter me, I know when I'm chasing my own tail."

Johnny put his arm around Soupy's shoulder and sang, "Hey, the monkey wrapped his tail around the flagpole to smell his asshole. You did OK, Soup. I shit thee not."

"You couldn't shit me. I'm too big a turd."

"I know, but it took big cojones."

"You're the one that risked his ass, Johnny, with the cracker lieutenant," Tim said. "But, boy, did you see all the gang stand up?"

"What's with the swearing, Tim?" Johnny asked. "You never swore."

"You neither, John. Ho-ho."

"Yes. Well, I guess we have nothing better to do, but we all hung together, hung tough on standing for Stein. We didn't owe him nothing," Johnny said.

"Yes, we could have all hung from the same tree, our feet twisting in the wind. I was scared shitless," Pointer said. "How about you, Rhesus?"

"Not me. I'm too stupid to get scared. Hell, I'm so stupid, I volunteered for this crapola. I asked for it. Hey, over here. It's me. Rhesus Eurasian. Come put it in, sideways, with a hot poker. Then when I'm stuffed full of molten shit until my eyes turn red and brown, then turn on that giant blender. I earned a set of dress blues."

Scoff said, "I'm more stupid than you. I couldn't meet the mental requirements they set up at the test at the federal building in Boston. My

IQ was 80. So I went outside and had a guy hit me in the head with a baseball bat. I rushed in, took the test, and passed with a 68. I had made myself stupid enough to pass the requirements. But you, Rhesus scat, are lucky. You're a natural, a natural stupid. Is it possible for aches to ache? I sure would like to get hold of the big toe that was put on the scales in Boston and gave me the added pounds I needed to be here. To be here! Here, helping some guy from New York with a long, crooked nose that I don't even know."

"Treat your pecker like a sausage of baloney being run through a cutter," Pointer said. "And for what? I don't even know what a Jew is. I don't think we have any of them back home. Are they a rare species? What makes them so different?"

"They're all circumcised," Fats said.

"Hey, I'm a Jew," Rhesus said, hefting his private through his dungarees. "They did a snip on my tip."

"Why in hell does anyone want to cut the tip of his donk off for?" Fats whined.

"So they can give the tip to a Jewish girl."

"Why in hell would a Jewish girl want a foreskin for?" Fats asked.

"So they can put it under their pillow and wish for the rest of it."

Suddenly, each was too exhausted to talk.

"Listen to Skinny snore. He sounds like a Sherman tank," Righty said.

Their God sleep talk varied: "I'll be good if you let me out of here," "What did I do to deserve this God?" "Goddamned Seabag." But Rhesus's overstepped his future with "I'll get you for this, God."

He realized immediately he might have gone too far in threatening God and added a denouement, "I'm just kidding, God. I'm always clowning around. You gave me a great sense of humor. Thank you."

Johnny, who was standing fire watch, hearing Rhesus's expletive threat to God, said, "I don't know him, Lord," and added his own denouement, "and I sure as hell won't stand near him in a lightning storm. Amen."

And so ended the Big Tree Gang's first day on Parris Island.

Not exactly one they had anticipated.

When leave came, if it ever did, they would carry the word back home of the horrors of boot camp, not only to forewarn friends who might be considering signing up but to also bask in the glory of survival, although some would encourage kids they didn't like to join up, tell them that they would immediately be issued dress blues, and then set free in a horny Georgia city and be allowed to make their "pick of the peaches."

Not one of them the next day could think about that first day. The second day was too full to remember the first.

Platoon 127's first week of boot was what Tim called a Dostoyevsky novel—one of little crime and much punishment. Of course, Tim had to explain who and what Dostoyevsky and *Crime and Punishment* were after Fats said, "Knock off the heavy crap."

"Yah," Rhesus said. "How is it one of you college-course rich guys signed up with us general-course lowbrows anyhow?"

Tim just smiled that soft smile of his at his friend.

He was right about the crime and the punishment. The two did not fit, except in the Marine Corps, where they fit perfectly in the corps' attempt to break and then remake.

Righty Minichelli's punishment was the following day. He was the first to be fingerprinted, booked, and punished.

The platoon stood at attention in the stifling heat, sand fleas walking over their faces and their eyeballs, biting, knowing full well they were a protected species. Seabag had an M1 in his hands, demonstrating his words with action, as he went.

"You ladies will slam open your receivers. See that little arm that looks like a knife blade tip on your rifle bolt? Of course, you do. When the receiver opens, an old shell pops out and a new one in. For now, there are no shell games for you. It will be dry firing for a while."

He slammed the receiver with the butt of his hand. It flew open.

"Isn't that the way you're supposed to do it?" The drill instructor's questions were never questions. They were statements of fact.

"While you are at 'port arms' and hear 'inspection arms,' you hold your piece tight with your right hand. And whack that bolt with your left. I want to hear the metal moan like a happy tit. And that bolt better shoot open. And stay open. You do not—I repeat, do not—push it open with your thumb. Oh, no. And best you hit it hard because if it doesn't stay open, if it slams closed, oooh, dear."

Never did one little "oh dear" sound so ominous, terrifying to so many almost men.

And with pretty good reason as Righty found out.

During inspection arms, the bolts were slammed open with a revenge, leaving the flats of most hands involved feeling like a molten KA-BAR blade was slammed through the palm.

Johnny felt the lightning shoot through his hand . . . *Good Lord . . . now I know how Jesus felt . . . Jesus save me . . .*

The only consolation about Johnny's hand pain was the fact that it relieved him of the dog-tired thoughts of exhaustion of the previous day. The two watches of the night, especially the fire watch where he sat and watched the molten red top of the iron stove, left him lightheaded. He had feared falling asleep and falling face downward onto the stovetop. After his watch, he dreamed he had fallen and his face was seared to the stove, leaving him screaming and welded to it.

The molten stove watch was followed by his pulling guard duty.

Johnny erased the pain and exhaustion by remembering, when he was a young boy and his grandfather Shiverick sang him to sleep . . . *Yes, Jesus loves me . . . Yes, Jesus loves me . . . Yes, Jesus loves me . . . for the Bible tells me so . . .*

One pain rose above all the rest, thinking of Righty and the "inspection of arms" that day.

Seabag had ordered, "Hin-spection, harms!" Eighty M1 rifle bolts were struck as one. Seventy-nine remained open. One rifle bolt closed with the sickening rattle of a death row chamber being unlocked.

The unrequited bolt did not draw the stifled nervous giggles that flatulence flying in church invariably drew.

To the contrary, it drew a death rattle. No one wanted to glance down to see if it was their receiver that had slammed closed.

The one with the closed bolt knew only pure, unadulterated fear. It was Righty's.

Even Private Seabag, whatever his first name was, Calhoon was his last, was frozen in time.

Pointer's voice seeped through, "I didn't do it. It's not mine."

The drill instructor looked at Righty almost benevolently and uttered those most feared words, "You don't love me."

"I do, sir. Yes. Yes, I fucken' do, sir," Righty said.

Johnny closed his eyes and willed his friend to hang tough, although he himself could feel the fear in his spine . . . *Not in front of these Georgia crackers . . . and us . . .*

Twenty members of 127 who were part of an Augusta Marine Reserve unit activated in an attempt by the corps to bulk up its First Marine Division breathed a sigh of relief that it wasn't one of them whose bolt betrayed its owner.

Johnny didn't know what a "cracker" was until one of the Georgia boys, Lace, mentioned how he and his Rebel friends would "kick Yankee ass on the firing range the same way we kicked Yankee ass in the Civil War. Y'all don't even know Kentucky windage. We crackers can shoot the eye out of a snake at two hundred yards."

It was Josh van de Holden from Intercourse, Pennsylvania, who reacted. The Yankee boys loved the fact that good old Josh from Intercourse took umbrage to the statement "kicked Yankee ass."

Of course, the members of 127 didn't believe there was any such town until they saw the first postmarked letter Josh received.

When they did, they held a special ceremony, inducting old Balls as an honorary citizen of Intercourse.

Rhesus started a move to collect money to send Balls to Intercourse and have him elected mayor. Rhesus had no real thought of sending Balls to Intercourse, but he did see the potential to make a couple of bucks when his lily moneymaking memory clicked in.

John van de Holden's umbrage led to the polite, religious young man to offer the words, "I'll break your cracker ass Lace and stick it to one of your no-ass mules down there that you call girls if you don't be quiet."

The punishment was to be Righty's, not the threatened Georgians, but he would have to wonder and wait for it.

"Private Minichelli, you have committed a no-no," Seabag Calhoon said, sounding as if Righty had been a bad little boy and would receive a little boy punishment.

No such thing, but he would have to wait.

It was not until their first-aid class, the first chance to sneak a word in, that the incident was mentioned.

Johnny whispered to Righty, "I think maybe he forgot."

"I don't think so."

"You could be right," Johnny said, recognizing that Calhoon's little boy threat had the innocence of Pie's look just before beheading the worthless billy goats immediately after their birth.

"Gee, thanks for making me feel better," Righty said. "Cheee."

"I just don't think he forgot."

"I don't think so either."

Steak was served that evening, all you can eat. Johnny thought he had died and gone to heaven.

Chow call was also the time when boots could talk to each other. It was thirty minutes, three times a day, of trying to cram as much food into and cram as many words out of you as humanly possible.

One result was that it was relatively common, without trying or even wanting to, to spit mashed potato on your buddy when that rare laugh of the day was shared across the table.

It was then the choice of anyone who needed the release, to declare a potato war, one where the mashed spuds were flipped catapult-style off the end of your spoon. The idea was not to get caught.

While an occasional potato war was acceptable, not so for SOS (shit on a shingle) war.

It was one thing to have white potato on your face but another to have chipped beef death-gray on the skin.

SOS looked so bad, it was a constant subject as how to rid the world of it.

"Righty," Johnny said, "you took science. Matter cannot be created or destroyed, but we have to all work together. We've got to destroy this SOS shit before it gets us."

"Johnny, you're spitting on me."

"Yah, I know, but I still love ya."

"You spit on me too," Pointer said.

"I love you too, cousin."

Pointer blew him a kiss and smiled.

"You hear from Yelena much?" Righty asked.

"Like every day. She's been looking into Ivy League colleges, checking med schools, like Harvard, for me. How do you like them apples?"

"You know, Johnny," Righty said, "there was a guy who looked just like you in the general division with me. Our senior year, we had arithmetic, two plus two is three—that's how the rich cheat us. And we didn't have physics, chemistry, none of that stuff. Our own science was birds do it, bees do it, even little fleas do it."

The sound of the words "doing it" shook Rhesus out of his eating frenzy, and he started to sing, "My bonny lies over the ocean, my bonny lies over the sea, me mudder laid over me farter, and dat's how it came to be me."

"Johnny," Righty whispered, "Bernadette wrote me."

"Oh?"

"She wanted to know if she can write you."

"Hey, I'd like to hear from any of our classmates or buddies."

"I'm not sure whether she wants to write to you as a classmate or a buddy."

"Nookie wants to be your bosom buddy, Horny Johnny," Rhesus said, leering at Johnny.

"Fuck you," Righty said, "and the camel you rode in on."

"It'd be the best piece you ever had," Rhesus said.

"And the first," Skinny said, stuffing half a steak into his mouth.

"How in hell do you get to chew something that entirely fills your mouth?" Fats said.

"Shut your bony ass," Skinny said.

"Hey, bean bag brain," Fats said, "at the rate you're losing weight, they'll be calling you the thin man, not me."

"And at the rate you're gaining, we're going to pass on the calorie highway.

"Yes, I noticed that," Tim said. "The more opulent of us are getting more wiry, and those less ample are packing it on, and both ways, it's turning into muscle."

"What's this big word 'opulent' mean? Speak simple American," Pointer said. "Who could get fat with them working us harder than Rhesus works his too-little tool? I've been working so hard that I've got muscles in my shit. Everything is hard except my love muscle. We work so hard, we have no energy for a stiffy."

"They're putting saltpeter in our chow," Scoff said, swiping the pontificating Pointer's dessert.

"I don't salt my food, high blood pressure, my old man had it," Fats said, "and no one that I know of has stuck his peter in my chow. I haven't had a woodie either."

"That's not what they're putting in our food. They're introducing potassium nitrate and sodium nitrate," Tim said.

"Jesus, speak American," Pointer said. "Ya go to Yale or somethin'?"

Tim smiled at his friend. "One time, a bulldog named Eli growled at me."

"So? I don't get it."

"Hey, everyone is hauling ass. Let's git," Righty said, leading the charge of those who hadn't been watching the clock.

Johnny was still salivating when the platoon lined up after chow down for Seabag's critique of the evening's plan.

"'Toon 127, ten-*hut!* Dress right, *dress!*"

Although Calhoon hadn't mentioned Pointer's failure to slam his M1 bolt hard enough for it to remain open, Johnny felt uneasy for his cousin. He tried to put it out of his mind by turning his fear into hatred thinking . . . *I'll kill . . . that kook Calhoon . . . He's doin' nothin' but . . . tryin' to break people . . .*

They sweated while standing at stiff attention for what appeared to be a decade long.

But the steak still tasted good in their mouths. Scuttlebutt had rumored they would have steak that night as Calhoon had ordered, "Tuxedos and tutus for tonight's chow down, girls. Wear your khaki with field scarves."

Rhesus had asked, "What's with calling the neckties scarves?"

They had worn dungarees every day since arriving on the island.

"Don't think for one moment wearing dress khaki means you're marines. Oh, no. Oh, with a big *no*," Calhoon said. "The outfit is to be complete with cunt cap, that cap that looks somewhat like a miniature upside down canoe but looks more like a pussy, which is what you ladies are."

Johnny was thinking about Yelena. She already had him an internationally known surgeon and poet. Bernadette wanted to write to him. *Why?* He thought about the steaks he had just eaten and . . . *Why do I think . . . about the two of them . . . while I'm . . . salivating my steak . . .*

The only meat Johnny ever had seen was at Sunday dinner at home, and that was meatloaf with more than a liberal mix of bread.

The platters of steaks almost made Parris Island Paradise Island for Johnny, but not quite, but still caused him to smile.

"Pirate Don Dirk of Dow Dee DaSilva, is that a smile I detect?" the DI asked, almost lovingly.

"I was thinking of the loving name you gave our khaki caps, sir."

"Oh, isn't that sweet? The cunt cap is also called a piss cutter, DaSilva. And you do not have the slightest idea why. Please go to your seabag and secure your summer service khaki cap."

Johnny bolted from the formation and returned so swiftly, it was as if he hadn't left.

"Too slow, DaSilva."

"Yes, sir."

"Please place your piss cutter on your head."

"Yes, sir."

"'Toon, fall inside the head."

Platoon 127 broke ranks and ran into the head and lined up around the walls.

"DaSilva, you stand by that urinal. Gouveira, I heard that you're DaSilva's cousin. Come over here."

The DI pointed at the urinal. "Piss!"

"I can't, sir."

"Are you disobeying a direct order, Gouveira? Do I have to scare the piss out of you?"

"No, sir. I want to piss so bad, my eye teeth are floating. Please do not scare the piss out of me, sir, I will go oceans."

"I hope you are pissing cousins and not kissing cousins, you faggot maggot."

"Pissin' cousins, sir."

"OK, boy, roll out the howitzer."

Pointer unzipped his fly and took his tool out.

"Whoa up that horse, boy. Gouveira is the pee-yee here. Gouveira, in this man's Corps, we piss by the numbers. Ten *hut!* A rup, two, three—now you pee."

Johnny breathed a sigh of relief when his cousin's yellow stream shot forward.

"Now, DaSilva, as to the reason why this cap is called a piss cutter,"— the DI took the hat off Johnny's head and sliced through the yellow stream of his cousin—"so now, my dear friend, you understand how this great cap earned its name. Go get your dungaree cap. And by the way, having viewed your endowment plan, I will cease to call you the Pirate Don Dirk of Dow Dee and instead address you as Long John DaSilva. Also, I do not want to catch anyone smiling.

"The point I'm trying to make to all of you is we are not here to smile or to eat steaks at the taxpayers' expense. We are here to make you pussies into pricks, real pricks, killer pricks. And then, if that day arrives, if anyone makes it, you'll be marines. Now, which platoon is going to be the best collection of killer pricks on this wonderful island?"

"'Toon 127!"

"You're fucken' A, John! Now backpacks filled with sand, M1s, and twice around the area. Ho! Take off like big-ass birds!"

"And away we go," Righty said, giving Johnny a noogie on the shoulder.

John Joy, a big boy from Michigan, ran up beside Johnny and hissed at him, "Ho-hi, DaSilva. Thanks. This is just what we need, extra laps."

"Lap this," Pointer said.

"Sorry, I don't talk to midgets that have to tie a string to their cock so they can find it."

One by one, they pulled into 127's area exhausted.

Their combined breathing sounded like a giant exhausted dragon with some rasps sounding like a dragon's last burst of flame.

Calhoon looked over his platoon. Several were resting their heads on their chests; others stood straight, their eyes closed; some were sleeping while standing.

"I hope you ladies are tired."

"No, sir."

"I can't hear you."

"No, sir!"

Joy whispered to the recruit beside him, "I'm breathing so deep, I'm sucking air through my asshole."

"Well, well, someone did not run enough, has enough energy left over to make a speech. Off, you goony birds. Once around. They started the run, rifles clacking, packs slapping spines that were already screaming for mercy.

Joy ran the fastest.

He knew several members of the platoon were after his ass for making the run-causing speech.

The second time they completed their trek, there were no speeches.

It was long after the other platoons had called it a night. The couple of thousand of exhausted boots snored and farted, pissed and moaned in their sleep, setting up a rumble that sounded like Dante's shades' sufferings.

"There is one unattended matter before we go beddy-bye," the DI said.

Johnny heard Pointer's stomach rumble . . . *He can't be that nervous . . . the son of a . . . bitch . . . Calhoon . . . has terrified him . . . Pointer . . . take a couple of clicks up . . .*

Johnny, in a voice so low—he wasn't even sure he whispered to his cousin—said, "Take a couple of clicks up."

"Gouveira."

Pointer jumped when he heard the DI's voice.

Many in the platoon twitched like a live wire, with the majority hoping that any punishment meted out would be to Pointer alone.

The entire platoon could feel the boot's courage go down twenty clicks, a slight change on the M1 that would have him shooting himself in the foot.

"Yes, sir." Pointer's voice was the whisper of the doomed.

"What in unholy goat snot is a Gouveira? It sounds like some sticky shit syrup."

"I don't know, sir, but I am an American."

"Who in hell do you think you are, Kate Smith?"

"Yes, sir."

"What?"

"No, sir," Pointer said, his voice so low, those in the rear rank, half of whom were standing while asleep, wouldn't have heard if he had yelled it.

"You sorry piece of fried pussy, I can't hear you."

"Yes, sir! I said *I am an American!*" Pointer screamed at the top of his lungs, close to hysteria, tears.

"Gouveira? What kind of freak name is Goo aloe vera?"

"Partial Portuguese, sir!"

"Partial Portagee? What part is Portagee? You're not an American. Only marines are Americans, and those we fight for. Do you have a Portagee pecker. And if you do, do you lend it to the less blessed? I bet you couldn't wear short pants when you were in kindergarten. You're as endowed as your kissing cousin DaSilva. Is this a Portagee thing, cocks like stallions? Do you lend them out? You know you embarrassed your poor old drill instructor today when you purposely let your bolt slam closed? Do you know that?"

Pointer knew better than to answer.

Johnny looked at his cousin and pleaded in his brain . . . *Don't do it . . . Don't let this cocksucker . . . make you cry . . . Don't let 127 . . . see you . . . cry . . .*

"Oh, I get it. No words. You're deaf and dumb, with less emphasis on the 'deaf' and more emphasis on 'dumb.' I bet you couldn't even wear Bermuda shorts. Jesus, the girls must have trembled, and when your kindergarten teacher saw that you were the only one in the class wearing bell-bottom trousers rather than knickers, she kept you after school. Then she made you stand in the closet, with her. I bet she was as ugly as a pimple. I bet she told you that you were dumb. You are dumb, you know. Only someone very dumb would allow his receiver to clang closed when he knows that the person he loves most in life, his drill instructor, wouldn't allow anyone to do this, not even God, God being your M1. Why did you do this Mr. Gouveira to the person you love most, your DI?"

Pointer started to say something, but Calhoon cut in, "I'll tell you why you did this, because you don't obey orders. You want to be responsible for your fire team members to be killed, for your squad to be wiped out, for your platoon to die. For your company to be devastated. You want the battalion, the division, wiped out. That's why you did not hit your receiver arm hard enough to bang the chamber open. You did this because, heaven forbid, you do not love your DI. You did this, Mr. Gouveira, because you hate your rifle. Well, boy, let me tell you, absence doesn't make my heart grow fonder. And your brain is absent without leave. Am I right, Gouveira? Of course, I am. Even if I wasn't right, I'd still be right. Right, Gouveira!"

"Yes, sir!"

"You wart on a newt's dick! You don't even know when to shut up with a shoe in your mouth. Well, son," Calhoon's voice took on a fatherly tone, "togetherness is what a platoon is, a fighting unit, this is what it's all about. No one individual worries about hurting the flat of his hand whacking open his receiver. Therefore, I believe that your loving platoon members want to share something with you as a reminder that not even one of us is allowed to come up short. Please, gentlemen, one by one, go to Mr. Goo aloe Vera's rack and make him a mattress of your M1s. And please make sure the pointy part of the receiver is facing up, making it like one of those fucking fakirs that sleep on a bed of nails. Long John DaSilva, the pirate, and Mr. Lace, the gentleman from Georgia who hates your broad A paaark the kaaar Bostonians, will not place your pieces on Mr. Gouveira's sack. When Mr. Gouveira hits his rack, he will lie on his back, extend his arms to each side, thumbs down, and you two gentlemen will insert his thumbs in the receivers of your M1s. You will lock and load said thumbs, so he can get a nice night's sleep. And no one is to lay a hand on those two rifles hanging by their thumbs over the side of the bed. Not a hand. OK on the triple, break ranks, run your assholes past your head! Gouveira, DaSilva, Lace, ah-ten-*shun!* Stay fucken' put."

The rest of the platoon vaporized, and then one by one, the members reappeared and snapped to attention.

"Now, Mr. Gouveira, you can go to bed early. You have been a bad boy. You will lie on your back. Place your rifle in such a way you can kiss it all night and tell it how much you love it, despite the fact you failed it. It was made never to fail you. If you don't fail it, it is God. God never fails. Off! You sweat off a turd's balls!"

Pointer spun his wheels heading for his hut.

"Lace, DaSilva, do your duty and help our weak-palmed fairy friend finger fuck your receivers."

When the tall Georgian and the willowy Bay Stater entered the hut, Pointer was lying on top of the rifles, his arms extended, thumbs down, his rifle muzzle near his lips so he could kiss it during the night.

His thumbs were inserted in the receivers, which were gently closed by Lace and DaSilva.

"DaSilva, don't go letting your little Yankee sissy cousin cry, y'all hear?" Lace said to Johnny, "or he won't be part of 127 as far as this good ol' boy is concerned."

"Shut the fuck up, or I'll turn your arse to grits."

"Arse? Is that an ass, broad A Boston boy? Why don't you bring it on?"

"Taps" were more sorrowful than usual as the switches were thrown in the tents. Each boot spent a few moments wondering what it felt like sleeping like a "fucken' fakir," although most had no idea what a fakir was. They knew that a herd of M1 receiver bolts would feel like, but it was only a few moments of wonder as every second of sleep was needed if the next day was to be survived.

When Calhoon entered the "arsenal tent," as it would be called from this day forth until boot camp ended, it sounded like a firefight among the tents. There was so much snoring on so many levels, including Pointer, whose snoring sounded like a combination thunderstorm and sobbing.

Everyone was asleep, except the fire watch, Skinny Potts, who was so exhausted, he stood at attention despite the fact the fire watch, unlike those doing guard duty, was allowed to sit. To sleep on guard duty or fire watch, at any time, was like a death sentence. No, it would be worse; death would have been welcomed.

He stared stunned at the stovetop, which was a dull molten red. Every once in a while, drool fell from his lips and did a sizzling dance across the stove lid.

He had his hands folded so that his thumb pushed up on the bottom of his cheekbones and his forefingers pressed on the corners of his eyes to keep them open. His chubby back was to the door, and he didn't hear or see the DI enter.

Calhoon went to Pointer's rack.

Johnny was asleep on the floor on one side of his cousin's bed, having first established a way that the rifle Pointer's thumb was in, rested on Johnny, taking the painful pull off Pointer's thumb and arm.

The DI muttered to himself, "I'll be hot damned. He isn't laying a hand on the M1. I'll be damned, damn Yankee."

Calhoon went to the other side of the rack to see if the recruit's thumb was stretched like the neck of a fat horse thief that had swayed in the breeze a couple of days.

"I'll be double dirty damned."

The thumb wasn't stretched.

The rifle rested against Lace, who had taken apparent pains to work himself into a position where the rifle weight was taken on his back without touching the piece with his hands.

The DI muttered in a voice that would have awakened the average sleeper but not a chance with these exhausted boots, "A real Southern gentleman. Maybe the South will rise again. Maybe these pieces of shit can be molded into something after all."

On hearing the DI's voice, Skinny, his eyes still supported open with the finger-thumb coordination, turned and spotted Calhoon and thought to himself . . . *What a nightmare . . . I can't wait to wake up . . . and tell the guys . . . the nightmare I had . . . where Calhoon . . . actually smiled . . . a little one . . . but a smile . . . He must have just killed something very slowly . . .*

But Skinny was so exhausted at reveille and roll call that he couldn't remember anything, not even the fact that when his watch was up, he fell exhausted on his rack and slept, without removing his finger and thumb supports that kept his eyes open.

It seemed they had just closed their eyes when Calhoon's voice, sounding like an officer in the English army, cried out, "All right, all right, I say, old chaps, hands off your cocks, on with your socks, spirits, eh wot." His words were followed immediately by the painful sounds of reveille.

Johnny carefully lifted the rifle off his chest and freed his cousin's thumb from it and tried to wake him up. No luck as Pointer snored on. Johnny then cried out, "Calhoon killed Pointer."

Pointer, on hearing he was "killed," jolted awake, jerking Lace's rifle so as it hit the Georgian in the face.

"Asshole."

The boots had thirty minutes to relieve, shave, and shower each morning, but Calhoon cut it to fifteen minutes so they could enjoy fifteen minutes of extra exercise with full seabags.

Some of the boots ate with their eyes closed, while others ate while sound asleep. This was the beginning of the day, not the end. Those who were wide awake enough to think of what the day promised, shoveled the chow in like a coal man stoking a steam engine on the Santa Fe.

It was exercise, class, drill, class, hike, class.

Seabag's close order drill had a slightly different twist than that of other DI's.

It was with fixed bayonets, un-scabbarded, bare steel tips glistening in the first sun or day. The usual marching manual of arms was made even more interesting by putting in the "propeller" spin, whereby the right forefinger was inserted inside the trigger guide, the left hand grabbed the barrel, and the rifle was spun in a 360-degree circle, which, in effect, meant a bayonet sharpened to arm hair-shaving efficiency came whizzing past the boot to the your left and right.

Not only had the number of steps per marching minute be exact, but also each boondocker had to thud as one.

The routine varied little, although each day, there was a questionable betterment of some sort or another.

Such as "beach party" day.

It was a pleasant surprise to many of those of 127 when Calhoon, on a particularly blistering day of heat and training declared, "Beach party. Let's take a swim."

Of course, there were some of the more wary who cautioned fellow boots in low hisses, "Sure," "Clap trap," "Don't buy a single ounce of that royal crap. A swim, ha!"

"Ladies, let's fall out for five, fill a combat pack with sand, being careful not to entrap a single sand flea, hitch on your entrenching tool, and fix encased bayonet, and fall back in. Dismissed."

Calhoon was checking his watch as the last boot fell back in. "Dress right, dress!"

The entire platoon's left arms shot out as one and touched the shoulder of the boot beside them as they got the proper distances between each other.

"All ward, HARCH!"

Platoon 127 stepped out as one.

"A leff, a leff, a leff right leff, hoodoya leff, a reep, hare leff, hoodoya leff, reep, hare, leff. Hay leff shoulda, *harms!* Hay, right shoulda, *harms!*"

"To the winds, *ha!*"

The platoon smartly went to the four winds. The left squad marched off to the left, the right squad to the right. The second squad continued forward, while the third squad did a "to the rear."

It was a unanimous feeling of the platoon that this was their favorite command as they dreamed they would be allowed to just walk away, walk away from it all. But it didn't work that way.

The four squads marched off to the four different points of the compass, getting further and further apart, until the desire to keep on marching was overwhelming.

Just keep on marching to Augusta—as in Augusta, Maine, as well as Augusta, Georgia, then on to Intercourse, Pennsylvania, to Saint Albans, Vermont, the Loop in Chicago, to Washington DC to Washington State.

And not return from the four winds.

But all did return on order and marched to the beach party.

As 127 filed into the swimming pool area, 129 filed out in wet bathing suits.

Calhoon's voice sounded hollow in the large pool area, "If I may have your attention, Esther Williams clones. You will not be wading and invading on foreign lands in your bathing suits."

Apparently, all eighty recruits of 127 were indeed Esther Williams, as all gave their undivided attention.

And all realized that in reality, this was not going to be a beach party at all. The only party would be for Seabag.

"Now, ladies, your swimming apparel was selected by me as last night's locker box inspection turned up the fact that you all had left your two-piece bathing suits at home."

Johnny remembered the time the police had escorted his father off the beach at Revere because he took the top of his suit off. He remembered the exact words of the police: "The next time, it's the pokey."

The police had eyed his father earlier, as he was the only man whose top had an open back.

"The pokey. We don't need nudists here. With ladies about."

Calhoon's voice cut in, "Thus, your present bathing outfits will be your dungarees, boondockers, combat pack, entrenching tool, and your God, your M1. The same things you will wear when you step off your landing barge into the ocean. Now to complete your vacation here on this island, and get your merit badge, the corps believes you must be able to swim the length of this pool. While bathing suits are prescribed, they are not commanded. Now I don't know a single marine who stepped off a landing craft into the Okinawa or Iwo surf that was dressed in a bathing suit. They were outfitted as you are. Except those who carried the mortar base, Anglar nine radio and other sundry gear heavier than what will accompany your swim today."

Even to the good swimmers, the pool looked the width of the English Channel. To the weaker and nonswimmers, the pool was a maw of salivating death.

"Now the word 'swim' can be interpreted as meaning many things. The way I understand it, it means getting from point A, this end, to point B, the other end, any gott-damned way you can. Of course, seeing that you were so stupid to fill your packs with sand, knowing how to swim doesn't help all that much. I caution you to stay close to the side of the pool as you work your way down."

Calhoon went to a window and looked out, checking to make sure there were no officers in the area.

"Now when you step out of that landing craft, the one stuck on a reef, three hundred feet from the beach, into eight feet of ocean, you will be prepared. You will be wearing what you have on. I would suggest that before you jump in, you grab yourself the biggest, deepest breath of air you can. And that when you sink to the bottom, you bend your knees, and you push off in the direction of the other end of the pool—the beach head. And when you hit that surface, you grab yourself another one of those big breaths before you sink to the bottom again. You can travel the entire length of the pool this way—if you don't panic. If you panic and if you drown, I promise you I will make your life in hell so miserable that you'd think a piece of dog shit being cooked in a frying pan has it better. Now is there anyone here would like to go home and suck their mother's tit rather than going ashore with the 'toon?' Then step forward."

Every single boot wanted to head home.

None stepped forward.

"If you stay close to the side of the pool, perhaps your buddies kneeling there can give you a helping hand, the same way you give helping hands in combat. Helping each other is allowed."

Some strayed too far from the poolside while pogo-sticking off the bottom to the surface, off the bottom to the surface. More than one had to be pulled out by a 'toon member, Calhoon, or the lifeguards, one of whom, a buck sergeant, whispered to Calhoon, "Are you shithouse crazy, Calhoon? Someone will drown with those sand-filled packs."

Calhoon hissed, "You bet your hairy asshole I'm crazy. But better they nearly drown here than really drown on a reef before they can get to shore where they're needed."

Rhesus turned to Johnny. "And you thought those Buckman's Pond lilies and that black rat snake around your neck were heavy shit."

"By the time they get to the Ds, as in DaSilva," Rhesus said, "the As, Bs, and Cs will have drank so much pool water, it won't be up to your knees."

"I don't think Fats can make it. The little shit is so skinny, his trousers will slip down around his ankles," Righty whispered to Johnny.

"Have the guys gather around him."

"What's going on?" Fats asked, as his friends crowded him.

"We're gonna take some of the sand out of your pack and spread it among ours," Soupy said.

"Like fuck," Fats said.

"Come on, Fats," Tim said. "I don't have enough. Don't be so darn stingy."

"Cut the caca, Tim. You can't even swim."

"No, but I can breathe deep, and who jumped center for good old Rockledge High?"

"You didn't jump center with no backpack full of sand," Fats said.

"Cut the crap, Fats," Soupy said. "We don't have all day."

"Hey, back off. If I can't make it here, I can't make it there."

"Look," Johnny said, "you pint of piss, you weigh about eighty pounds. Ninety-eight-pound weaklings kick sand in your face. Besides, why drown here? I got the word 127 is gonna get shipped to the Sahara. Hand over some sand to us."

"Piss off."

Johnny reached out; Fats ducked, smiled, and mussed up Johnny's hair, if you can muss up a quarter inch of growth.

"I'm not going in the water," Pointer said. "Calhoon didn't issue no suntan lotion."

"Hey, look who's back from the dead?" Rhesus said.

"Remember the time," Johnny said to his cousin, "you put on the suntan lotion before we headed to Nahant Beach? You had on so much, you got the lotion on your scrambled egg sandwich when we got to the beach. And your stomach ached so much, you couldn't go in the ocean."

"Yah. God, my tummy hurt so much, I thought I was pregnant. But my sandwich didn't get sunburned."

"That was the day," Righty said to Johnny, "we were all holding up the blankets on the beach so Boattail could change inside them. And then we dropped the blankets and ran like hell."

"And some girl," Rhesus said, "pointed at my brother's wing wang and booed—actually booed. We laughed until our asses shattered and fell to the ground."

"I remember the one who booed. She had boobs the size of basketballs," Soupy said.

"Yah," Scoff said, "and when she ran, it looked like she was dribbling a couple of Spaldings."

Johnny remembered her . . . *They were like two soft-nosed puppies . . . swinging in a hammock . . .*

When she passed by, they took off their Red Sox, Celts, and Bruins caps and placed them over their hearts. It was like a holy moment.

"And she curtsied," Pointer said, "and smiled at Johnny. Johnny just stood there, thumb up his bum even after she looked back at him twice. No wonder my cuz is gonna die a virgin."

"Jesus," Rhesus said, "if they put any more saltpeter in our chow, none of us will have a hard-on until we're sixty."

"That's why it's important," Johnny said, "that the next time it goes up, you shellac it."

"That's not my problem, getting it up," Skinny said. "My problem is getting it down."

"Good, use it as a float. I know when my honker gets a stiffy, it's big enough to keep me afloat," Scoff said.

"How would Skinny know whether it's up or down? With the pot belly he's got, he hasn't seen it in six years," Rhesus said.

"Hey, have a heart," Skinny said.

Their talk was over; it was time to play Calhoon's game of pool.

"DaSilva! Lead the way, Pirate Long John. Walk the plank," the drill instructor said, making a sweeping bow that ended with hand extended palm open, an invitation to the walking the plank diving board.

Johnny looked at the DI, wanting to make sure he wasn't kidding, then looked around, hoping there was a second DaSilva in the outfit he didn't know about that was going to step forward.

Johnny walked out on the board. "Geroni-fucken'-mo!" And he was airborne.

His first reaction when he hit the bottom of the pool was to try to swim to the surface. He couldn't. He could feel his eyes getting big, now bulging . . . *Help . . . help . . . Oh God . . . help . . . Oh God please help . . .*

Hadn't his mother said, "God helps those who help themselves"?

Johnny looked up and could see the distorted staring faces of the platoon through the water's surface. He squatted on the bottom of the pool then shot off, his arms pumping, then the surface, the great gasp for air, then his arms flailing so he could stay on top, but the weight was too much.

He sank to the bottom and squatted. Shot up. Gasped. Several times.

But each time on the surface, he saw the same face, Righty's, eyes as large as pies, exhorting him.

Johnny was in the same spot.

Sink . . . to the bottom . . . squat . . . angle the push off . . . to the end of the pool . . .

The next face was Pointer's.

To the bottom, squat, angle the push off . . .

To the bottom, squat . . . angle the push off . . . to the end of the pool . . .

The next face was Lace's. There was no Rebel-Yankee animosity showing. Just a plea to make it . . . so we all can . . .

To the bottom, squat . . . oh shit . . . I won't make it . . . bullshit . . .

Angle, squat.

Then he felt it. The bottom of the pool shallow section. He waded toward the end, his feet on the pool bottom, head out of water . . . *I'm . . . breathing so deep . . . I must be leaving a jet stream . . . out my butt . . .*

"Let's see you"—it was Calhoon's voice—"hit the beach like a marine. Poke that bayonet in front you. Poke it again. Poke it again. Jam it in their fucken' throat. Spin 'em around. Jam it up their gook assholes. Drink their fucken' blood!"

"Isn't this a little much?" It was Calhoon's assistant DI, whispering to him.

"We'll see," he hissed back, and then, voice booming like someone beating on an empty oil drum, "DaSilva, tell the rest of the 'toon how you made it."

"I shit my pants, sir, and shit floats."

"I would say, 'Good man,' DaSilva, if you were a man," Calhoon said with sarcasm so thick, it seemed to drip from a razor's edge. "So your being a big 'shit floats' man means you don't give a pig's ass whether that BAR gunner or the company sniper or fire team makes it ashore."

"When you jump off the board . . ." Johnny started.

"Let's say 'when you jump off your landing craft.'"

"When you jump off your landing craft, don't fight it. Sink right to the bottom. But, first, grab the biggest drink of air you can. On the bottom, go into an immediate squat. Don't try to swim to the surface. Shit can your heavy gear if you can. Before you catapult yourself upward, angle your body toward the shore and push with all your might. When you break the surface, drink air so deep bubbles come out your butt plate. But don't try to stay on the surface, you'll blow your air. Sink. Then think—squat, angle, push."

Calhoon looked up and down the line of waiting boots, back to Johnny, "That's all, DaSilva. OK, the rest of you stones, one at a time, so we can babysit you the length of the pool. Stay close to the side so your buddies can grab you. You do not grab the edge of the pool."

One by one, the boots jumped in, but only after each took one last death row look for a reprieve.

When each got to the end of the pool and clung to the lip, they each had that "Is this me?" look.

Each did it, until only one remained.

"Hey, it's my turn," Righty said, crossing himself as he walked to the edge of the pool, murmuring, "and the last shall be first."

He looked back, a tiny almost man, whose pack looked the size of a Volkswagen, and his look was an "I'm not sure."

He made no move to jump into the water.

"Just pretend you're swimming bare ass at Duck Pond and Nookie Clarkson is bare butt down the other end, waving to you, 'Here it is, big boy, come and get it,'" Skinny said.

"Knock off that shit," Johnny warned.

"OK, Virgin Mary."

"Just cross yourself and go," Johnny said, turning to Righty.

Righty's first five blast offs from the bottom were progressively weaker, and he had only covered two-thirds the length of the pool.

The sixth push off didn't get him to the surface and the vital breath of air.

Everyone watched, hypnotized as he sank to the bottom. He tried to swim to the surface. Failed. Then he started crawling to the pool end, not to the side, which was only a short distance away.

The pool exploded as his buddies, some tossing off their backpacks and others forgetting to remove them, jumped in.

But Seabag was already in and shoving Righty upward.

The DI saw the faces of Rhesus, Johnny, Scoff, and Lace heading down. He handed Righty to their helping hands.

"He's dead," Joy said.

"Bullshit. If I'm dead, why do I have a hard-on?" Righty said, spitting out water and words.

Then turning to his drill instructor, "You shouldn't have done it. I was making it."

Calhoon looked into the little boot's eyes and said softly, "I know."

Then it was quiet.

It was the first time anyone had heard Calhoon speak softly.

Calhoon, hands on hips, stared into space. Then at Righty's "Baar-stan" buddies, then at a Georgian named Lace and a big guy from Michigan named Joy who had made the second entry into the pool. "Who in a good holy fuck gave the order for you people to enjoy a second dip?"

"You did, sir," Johnny said in a voice so low, he hoped that Calhoon thought he was hearing things. "We leave no one behind."

"Who said that!" the DI ordered.

"You did, sir," several answered.

"Asshole liars," Calhoon said, turning his back on the platoon as he tried to hide his smile.

"Now I want to know which of you puffy pussies is going to write and tell his mommy about today. Or write his senator. Or sneak through the night and report this poor private to some forty-day wonder officer."

"No one, sir!" Johnny said.

"Jesus, DaSilva, who in hell died and made you Col. Chesty Puller? Don't answer! Now you might think my reaction to this incident, about calling your senator, is to save my own ass. Well, you're right, because old Seabag doesn't have any more stripes to give back. And the next stripes will be on a suit issued at Portsmouth. But let me tell you that the last of the true marines will be turned out by DIs in this decade, two decades at the most. There will come the day when a DI will not be able to touch, even to kiss, a boot or swear at a recruit. God fucken' forbid. Some congressman in skirts, man or woman, will see to that. You won't be able to knee your enemy in the balls. Not under Marquis de Queensberry. No. You curtsy, bow, wave a plumed hat. Except the other guy will lop your head off when you're part way through your curtsy. Anyone who wants to make the call can do it right now. No strings attached. Just say, 'Old Calhoon nearly killed us all.' Who wants to make the call? Be a man. I didn't say a marine. For once. Step up."

Silence.

Although not one stepped out to make the congressman call, all thought they wanted to . . . kill this . . . fucken' . . . maniac . . .

Calhoon wondered how many, even with such colossal cojones as 127 appeared to be outfitted with, would fail to make it ashore from their reef-stricken "Duck," claimed by the cold water or hot lead as they step out, head down, balls up.

He remembered pushing aside the bodies of those who had almost made it to shore at Iwo. The bodies of his buddies, as well as the strangers.

They were so thick, they appeared like a giant fish kill caused by pollution, but they weren't fish, and only a few still flopped.

After Iwo, Calhoon didn't want to know names. And didn't want to remember names now and especially did not want to remember their faces.

They are eighteen- and nineteen-year-old faces . . . pissants . . . What do they know? . . . If they knew . . . they would have stayed home . . .

"Fall out. Outside!"

The platoon, dripping wet, ran from the pool and formed up.

"Dress right. *Dress.*"

The arms shot up to get the proper spacing. Water that had been cupped in folds of their dungarees poured to the deck.

"*Parade, rest!*" They stood tall and stiff.

Seeing the water fall from his 'toon's recruits made Calhoon remember the water siphoning from the bodies as the tide went out as he checked for his brother. He wanted to go home. Wanted to stay and kill.

Platoon 127 became confused as their DI stared into the distant sky. But not for long. "Ten-hut! Let's dry out, girls."

His command was greeted with a single loud thud as the 160 boondocker heels clicked together as one.

The 'toon waited for the exercise command to help their process. It didn't come.

They stood at attention.

"Perhaps he's going to let us rest," Scoff said.

"I wouldn't bet a plug nickel on it," Rhesus said.

They stood at attention.

They stood at attention.

Stood at attention. At attention.

Calhoon looked back and forth along the ranks.

Finally, "What we have here is a group of beach party nerds, swimming, yakking it up. Looking at the broads, if they were here. Don't deny it. You would have been looking at them if they existed. When you know you're supposed to be looking straight ahead. At all times. Not moving a muscle. At all times. Not blinking. Well, let me tell you, there is no replacement for obeying orders, not even getting laid. Obeying orders is what makes this man's Corps click. And the order of the day is 'ten-*shun!*' which means no winking, blinken', or nod. I'll be watching you, little ones. You will either leave Parris Island live as marines or deadwood sent home for more ninny sucking. And I'm going to determine for you which is which. No real 'move out' marine will die while you hide sniveling at the bottom of your foxhole."

The drill instructor stood back, hands on hips, unmoving, unwinking, unblinking, and not nodding. The minutes crept by, slow as molasses dripping down the hairy leg of an elephant. The sun first dried their dungarees then baked them.

The sun, bright and cheery, did its dirty deed on exhausting the dulled platoon until the pool water enjoyed a changing of the guard with their sweat.

They stood at attention until the dungarees that had once been drenched with pool water dried and were now soaked again with sweat as invisible sand fleas crept across their faces and their eyeballs biting with the brainless intensity of piranhas.

The silence was deafening.

Calhoon also stood at attention, only his eyes repeatedly sweeping the rank and file, the motion causing the sand fleas that had landed on his eyes to alight.

Johnny felt the salt drip into his eyes, burn like battery acid. At lower depths, "brother sweat" streamed into the rawness of a crotch that was an open wound from marching, running, creeping, crawling, doing sit-ups, push-ups, pull-ups . . . *What the fuck is this all about? . . . Ain't a single prisoner in any jail in the world . . . that gets treated like this . . . shit once removed . . . I'll kill this bastard if we ever get into . . . combat . . . together . . .*

He could see other recruits, their brains boiling like a live lobster tossed into a steaming caldron, starting to teeter in the heat, their balls baking, still stunned by jumping into a pool with a pack full of sand, rifle in hand. But with a small welling in their chests, a sensation many had never had before. They'd done what millions wouldn't even consider doing. Exhausted as they were not one had quit, although nearly everyone had given such an action thought.

The silence was deafening, as eighty young men stood frozen into insane pain on the orders of one man they believed was insane.

Why? . . . Johnny remembered his Uncle Tony training his new English setter . . . *What was her name . . . Churchill? . . . Nah . . . it was a female . . . Victoria . . . Queen Victoria? . . . Nah . . . she was an independent cuss of a cur . . . Oh yah . . . Ann Bolyn . . . Yes . . . I can remember Uncle Tony . . . threatening to cut her head off . . . The dog had just . . . smiled . . . God . . . what soupy nosed pushovers setters are . . . He'd made her stay . . . stay . . . and when she moved . . . she was punished . . . I hated him for it . . . but Ann Bolyn and I and Uncle Tony . . . had fantastic hunts and times together . . . She knew what she had to do . . . and did it . . . but that little pup . . . frozen in the sun . . . for what seemed hours . . . seemed so cruel at that time . . . ah . . . but later . . . wonderful times . . . and chow . . . pheasant under glass back at the farm . . . ruffed grouse . . . on a spit . . . out there in the woods . . . The smell and taste would make a rock salivate . . . the pines humming . . . the . . .*

"Da-fucken'-DaSilva! Do you mind returning to planet earth?"

"No, sir!" But Johnny daydreamed on . . . *Uncle Tony got his pup to stay using kindness . . . and now . . . this DI man treating us like dogs . . . is getting us not to retrieve a ball . . . to go instead for the throat . . . but only after we learn to stay . . .*

And staying they were, despite a heat that stopped even the cicada's constant droning as the temperature was too much for the heat bugs themselves. But of course, it couldn't get that hot, could it? But sure as God made little red-dotted lady bugs, the heat bugs had stopped twisting their bodies, snapping them, rubbing their back legs together, ceased their droning, probably to cool off in the shade.

Johnny remembered his Uncle Manny telling him you could tell the leggy heat bug females from the males because they wore long black stockings. He had looked like hell but saw no silk stockings on a single cicada. He was eight at the time and just figured he hadn't seen any females.

Anyway, on this hot day, the heat bugs decided not to drone.

Johnny wondered why . . . *Perhaps the little pricks were simply watching us . . . to see just how much shit a human could take . . . especially young shits like us . . . whose worst bad day . . . up to now . . . was staying after school . . . although Skinny got caught by his father while he was thumping his tub while looking at the* Winnie Winkle *ink drawings . . . where floppy-eared Pluto was doing her doggy-style . . . what else . . . cat-style . . .*

Then there was the explosion.

Not really an explosion.

In fact, it was in reality quite a subdued noise. One meant not even to be detected from the rear row.

But its effect on every single member of 127 was immediate. Fear installing. Fear to infinity, squared.

It was a smack.

A hand hitting a cheek.

Both cheek and hand were owned by the same person.

Someone had killed a sand flea.

Holy Jesus . . . mother of god . . .

Righty crossed himself.

The platoon's first fear was not for the flea-slapping cretin, for surely he would pay in spades. But what would the platoon pay for the flea flicker!

There was hardly a boot in 127 who believed he had enough strength to pay a penalty, no matter how small.

"Someone."

It was the drill instructor's voice.

"Killed," his second word increased in volume. "A sand *flea.*"

The crescendo stacked up from there, burning like dry wooden barrels on a bonfire whipped up by a high wind.

"We must ask ourselves, was this sand flea someone's beloved mother?

Was this little one a favorite son? Was it a secret agent sent here by President Truman, which, if it does not return to Washington, will mean punishment of the entire corps? Or God forbid, was this sand flea a tiny member of the United States of America Marine Corps, and was it carrying *a tiny fucken' M1!* Step forward, *you* fucken' order-*disobeying* pint of civilian rat piss!"

No one stepped forward.

The DI's eyes, so pale blue, it was as if they did not exist, stared through each and every one of them. The stare seared brains and hearts and then seared into the terrified soul of each.

The wet sand in their combat packs pulled down on the shoulder straps, cutting into raw flesh, making it difficult to breathe.

Time passed.

More and more of the boots teetered like tall trees caught in the wind.

Johnny stepped forward.

"You're a stupid dork, DaSilva, for many reasons, including the fact you stepped forward. Also including the fact that slap came from the rear ranks, not the front, you flaming asshole. You'll pay twice, one for disobeying the order of 'ten-hut,' and you will pay a second time for lying to a noncom."

The DI forgot for a moment that he didn't have a single chevron on his upper arm, let alone the two stripes of a corporal, the lowest rank on the noncom list.

Then he remembered, "No, Pirate Don Dirk of Dow Dee, you've done worse than lying to a noncom. Worse than lying to an officer. You have lied to a former noncom. You've got in the way of justice. I want the real killer to step forward."

He stared at the rear rank. At Pointer.

Johnny knew where his gaze was fixed.

He knew Pointer didn't kill the sand flea. He was too frightened to fuck up again. Besides, they had spent hours in the hog pen riding Bog, where mosquitoes and flies the size of blackberries walked across their faces, up the crotch of their shorts, and they had not whacked a single one of the bugs. They had been taught by Uncle Manny. Pointer, Dink, and Johnny had watched for hours as their hero Uncle allowed mosquito after mosquito to suck his blood, swell up, turn bright red with their fill, so sated, they got dizzy and tipped over.

Johnny's fear was not about the punishment of Pointer or himself. He feared his cousin would point at the person who did whack the sand flea . . . *Don't do it . . . Hang tough . . .*

He could almost feel the ground shake as his cousin's body started to come apart at the seams, by the numbers.

Don't . . .

Lace stepped forward. "You got the wrong asshole, sir."

"Lace, how could a Georgia gentleman like yourself kill our Dixie national bird? What were you thinking, boy? Just what were your thoughts when you saw it fall out of the sky in flames? I'll tell you what you were thinking. You were thinking you only killed a lowly old sand flea. Well, boy, you killed more than the national bird of the south—you killed your entire platoon. You and your 'toon were crawling through the elephant grass, real quiet. Real quiet cuz you were crawling through a bunch of little yellow men with big black guns that would tear holes in your 'toon's body and would leave their intestines hanging out, allowing flies and shit to get on those intestines and rats to eat them the next morning, while you and some of your buddies were still alive. The gooks would piss on your intestines, and for dessert, they'd cut off your cock and balls and stuff them in your mouth while you watched. They'd do the same to everyone else. Just 'cause you are a lowly tick-sucking son of a whore who would slap a bug and give away your position."

There was dead quiet.

"And why did all this happen, why is the entire 'toon crying like babies, trying to tuck their insides back inside their bodies? They are doing this because someone, guess who, slapped a bug, letting them little yellow men know a 'toon was trying to sneak through them. Rather than a slap, the next time a flea lands on you, why don't you just call out, 'Over here. We're over here. Kill us.' Let me hear you, Lace."

"Hear what, sir?"

"What are you gonna do when surrounded by people who want to blow your balls to Bali High, your special island, and back? So instead of you swatting a bug, you call out something. What is it, boy, that you call out?"

"Over here. We're over here. Kill us."

"That was good, Lace. So good, I'm letting you off easy."

Johnny rolled his eyes . . . *Oh shit . . . God help Lace . . .*

"All you have to do is dig a grave and bury this poor Devil Dog marine, yes Devil Dog, cuz this little fella was one of us. Best you thank me for being so kindly, Lace."

"Thank you, sir."

"Best it be a military burial. Regulation-size grave. Three feet wide. Six feet long. Six feet deep. Now that's not so bad, is it, Lace? Best you thank me."

"Thank you. Sir!"

"Now your entrenching tool must be pretty sharp. Wouldn't you say, Lace?"

"Yes, sir."

"Well, Lace, I'm gonna save your life. Cuz you're gonna be digging in the dark. When the mo-skeet-toes comes out to play. I fear, Lace, that you might try to kill one, with that sharp entrenching tool. Or cut your pudding head off by mistake. Then you would ride around the south, a headless horseman, scoffing little kids up, selling them to gypsies. You don't want that, do you, Lace?"

"No, sir."

"Therefore, I'm gonna let you use a spoon, Lace. Isn't that kind, Lace? Course, it is. Best you thank me."

"Thank you, sir!"

"You know I do like adjectives, Lace?"

"Fucken' thank you, sir!"

"Best you set about it now, Lace. Cuz I wouldn't want you to miss reveille. I can only be just so kind, without losing my job. You wouldn't want me to lose my job, now would you, Lace?"

"Fucken' no, sir."

"Remember, boy, I don't want to find no dead 'squitas in the morning. Fall out. But wait, it's been a long day, so why not end it with a fun game? Lace wants one more special run for everyone. Then he can return to his grave digging."

There was a groan from the ranks.

"OK," Seabag said, "I understand why you don't want to take a long run. So I'll make it a short one. A fun game."

"One two seven, ten-hut, ah-ward, HARCH!"

Calhoon marched the platoon to a nearby Quonset hunt.

"Pla-tooooon, halt!"

Seventy-nine sets of boondockers thudded "one, two" to a halt.

The eightieth set was worn by a gravedigger that hoped that after dark, he could put his spoon aside and scoop sand out with a boot.

"Now you were once kids and played capture the flag. Capture is such an important word. Capture. I love that sound. Squads one and two, on the other side of the huts. On the triple."

Within seconds, squads one and two faced the balance of the platoon, looking up the alleyway at them between two huts.

"Now the idea is, squads one and two, get all your men over here before squads three and four get all its men over there. The winning outfit gets a reward. You can run your sorry asses around the parade grounds."

"That doesn't make any sense," Skinny whispered to Scoff.

"Idiot," Scoff hissed back, wishing he could relieve the exhaustion of the day, the tension of the moment, by swiping something.

"While the winners are doing their two laps, the losers will go around twice. Let the games begin!"

The two human walls of flesh thudded against each other in the narrow alley. The smacks of muscle against muscle, bone against bone, rattled against the corrugated metal of the Quonsets. Johnny tried to go over the top, pulling Righty with him, as Pointer held on to Johnny's web belt, but a knee rushed into his crotch as a shoulder caught him in the throat, sending him smashing into the Quonset with a rattle. Johnny slid down its side stunned, with flares flashing in his brain and the metal reverberating in his brain like thunder in a gully . . . *Sun num ma bitch . . . I sound like . . . Pie . . . This racket sounds like two . . . skeletons shagging on a tin roof . . .*

He felt a boondocker step on the side of his head, crushing it against Righty's. He smiled at his friend through lips pulped to blood and spittle. "I don't think there's gonna be a lot of winners here."

"Jesus," Righty said, "if only some kind-hearted son of a bitch would kill me."

But they continued to crawl to the opposite end of the alley, over and under others, until both sides had nearly all their men on the proper side.

Retrievers went back to pull those who had fallen.

Finally, each had its men on the correct side after a swap or two.

"Guess there are no winners. You're all out of uniform.

Once around for all. And while you are running your laps, please remember the importance of the words 'capture' and 'win.' Take off like big-assed birds."

The first part of the run was on legs that felt like they had been worn down to the knees that day, was easy. Everyone, winners, losers, just wanted to put as much distance between Seabag and themselves as they could.

Near the end of the run, they were positive their legs had been torn off at the thigh, and they were running on the shattered bones and tissue.

"This makes no sense to me, Tim," Johnny said, as they staggered as fast as they could.

"Me neither. We joined to kill Communists, not each other. I'm so tired, I can't breathe," Tim said, balling his fist and pumping against his chest in an attempt to push the pain out and suck air in, as his heart thumped in his chest like a pile driver.

"My ass fell off an hour ago," Righty moaned, "and I was too tired to stop, pick it up, and stick it back on."

"Hope someone gives it a good burial," Johnny said, giving his friend the weakest noogie he had ever administered.

Johnny saw Tim look back over his shoulder.

"What?"

"Saw someone stumble back there. Think he fell," Tim said. "We'd better check."

The three turned back.

"Are you guys lost?" cried Fats, who was dragging each step as if his boondocker was stuck in sucking mud, but he turned and ran back with his friends.

"It's Stein," Righty said. "I'm not sure we owe him anythin'. He didn't even say thanks for that 'all the Jews, stand up' shit."

"Hey, he's 'toon," Johnny said.

"Yah, I know, the platoon is one," Righty said, "but holy newt shit! Come on, get up, Stein. You can do it. You can do it. Haul ass, or I'll kick your ass the final mile!"

They pulled the fallen recruit from the tarmac that still carried some of the mean heat of the day in it.

"Leave me alone. You make me puke. You assholes have done enough for me to last a lifetime. Where do you get off? Pretend heroes."

Righty hooked his forefinger and gave the fallen marine a solid chuck under the chin, "Up! Get your rear into gear! Christ, there's only a football field left."

Johnny and Tim hooked their arms under Stein's as the smallish Righty alternated between pushing with the flat of his hand on the exhausted recruit's back or running in front of him, grabbing his shirt and pulling. Fats followed, chanting, "We can do it, we can do it."

As they pulled into the finish area, all four lurched forward, fell, and lay there as the rest of the platoon trickled in.

"Seventy-six," Righty counted while flat on his back.

"We have to get the other three," Johnny said.

"Jesus, aren't we the little candy stripers?"

It was Doane, one of the Georgia reserves, built like a Rhodesian ridgeback, muscles quivering on muscles.

"I'll go," Tim said. "Come on, Johnny."

"Then I ain't going," Doane said. "I don't mind running in the dark, but not with some darkie."

"I'll go," Lace said, then looking back at Doane, said, "I don't like this either, but we can't leave no one behind."

They took off.

Righty hadn't gotten off the ground.

"Shit, I need this like a priest needs a fart while offering Communion," Righty said, finally getting up with a moan and taking off in the dark after Tim, Johnny, and Lace.

Lace was back first, a fallen recruit leaning on his shoulder.

Tim was next, his arm under the shoulder of a fallen boot.

It was more than ten minutes later that Johnny and Righty returned, the fallen recruit's shoulders cupped in Johnny's arms, his legs in Righty's. When they returned, they wondered where their DI was; would he catch them helping the weak, punish them more?

Calhoon stood in the dark, behind the Quonset huts, seeing but not seen, and told himself softly, "I'll be gott-damned go to hell. These pussies might grow dicks yet."

He only stepped out after they dressed right and snapped to attention on their own accord.

"Fire watch and guard duty are posted. I better not find any of you sneaky pieces of goat shit going back and helping Lace digging graves. Hit the road!"

The boots headed to their huts, and many went to sleep with their boondocks on, while several flopped on the floor, too tired to make it to their racks only inches away.

Seabag stood in the dark, listening to the snores that sounded like a herd of hogs sniffling for truffles in a newfound mushroom lode.

It was with some surprise that he spotted the shapes that belly crawled from their huts toward the sound of a lone marine digging a grave for a sand flea.

"I'll be a cock-knocking son of a bull's wang. They still got some life left in 'em. Looks like the Pirate Dow Dirker Dow Dee DaSilva, that little Ginzo guy, Minelli, Lisa Minelli, spumoni, or some other helicopter 'WOP, WOP, WOP' name. And the black kid. He don't need no camou face paint. And the little tattletale. The pimple they call Pointer and . . . Doane? Jesus Christ all holy mighty. My kids ain't gonna be kids much longer. Holy shit, ol' Seabag, you're talking to yourself. Well, I gotta. Who else knows what it's like to send kids to hell?" He swigged from the small bottle of Wild Turkey, gargled with the booze, and whispered, "Mine is not to question why, mine is just to eat apple pie and send them off to die." He tilted his head and finished the bottle.

Reveille came and made its usual announcement, "I can get 'em up, I can get 'em up, I can get 'em up in the morning!" They piled out of their sacks like ants out of a burning anthill. It was still as dark as when they hit the sack, yet some found the strength to sing, "I can't get it up, I can't get it up, I can't get it up in the morning."

Five weeks had passed, and while they still looked half dead, half buried, the sag in the shoulders now had a chip on it, a chip for anyone or anything that wasn't 'toon 127.

"Fall in. Dress right, dress! Ten-hut! Listen up. Regulations say you have to have thirty minutes to eat and that I have to let you have a piss call, if you believe in regulations 100 fucken' A percent. But I think if you eat fast and shit less, 127 can be the first 'toon to the firing range. Piss call, then chow down amounts to thirty-five of my regulation minutes. This can be shortened if you eat with two hands and keep both hands off your pud in the head. When I have eighty people here, we go. Stack arms. Piss call. Chow down. Break!"

The urinals in the head were stainless steel and shined like they had been married to a Blitz Cloth. The toilets were a steady stream of water heading downhill housed in a cement trough with numerous wooden seats topping it.

Calhoun came into the head as quietly as a ferret into a chicken coop and eyed those sitting on the johns and smiled.

No one liked it when ol' Seabag smiled.

And with good reason. They figured they'd best stare straight ahead.

Johnny sat on the last seat, downstream, and wondered why one by one, those sitting upstream leaped up from their potty perches with a "Yikes!" He hadn't heard anyone call "ten-hut!"

Then he bolted straight up when the flaming newspaper ball Seabag had set afire and afloat upstream seared his backside.

With a yelp, they fled the head, with a couple, Lace and Righty, arriving in the cooling air still with their trousers around their knees.

The lucky leakers, standing when the burning paper sashayed downstream, termed their hot seat buddies "hot shits."

The boots were out of the mess hall even faster than they went through the head, not knowing what their DI could do in the chow hall compared with the burning paper ship. They didn't want to find out.

Pointer was taking no chances. He was first, lined up to move out, standing at attention, as the syrup from the warm pancakes he had secreted in his dungaree pockets oozed through and stuck to his pubic hair. It was soon to dry on hair and cloth and make for an interesting march to the range some fifteen miles into the boonies.

"Ten-hut! Field transport packs and M1s. Fall out."

The boots made a dash for their field transport packs, which contained every stitch of their clothing, a pack that started at the shoulders and dragged to the knees on the taller recruits and nearly to the heels on the shorter boots.

"Jesus, Joseph, and Mary," Righty said crossing himself, "the other platoons are wearing combat packs," a small pack containing not much more than a shelter half, clean socks, and skivvies, mess kit, and entrenching tool. "Their shit is being shipped to the range."

"Shut up, you ditty bag," Doane hissed, "or we'll be loading them up with sand. If we do, the gators gonna be eating your porgy bait ass after dark."

Righty looked up at the giant. "Up your giggy with a meat hook."

"You piss me off, you pissant."

"That will be easy, you fucken' fly on the toilet seat."

Doane moved toward Righty.

"Save your energy," Tim said.

"Who died and made you Klan Grand Dragon?" Doane said as they headed out.

Calhoun broke into a fast jog. "Port arms, broken step double time, harch!"

Platoon 127 moved out with a rattle and a creak to the firing range where they would make their home for three weeks.

Platoons 126 and 128, all wearing small combat back packs, moved out with them and quickly took the lead.

"If you little girls want a bunch of pussies wearing little old ladies' knapsacks to beat you, just you lie down and cry and kick your feet," Seabag sneered, "or you can act like marines and kick their asses so hard, you get five points for a ringer around their throats. And I won't settle for no leaners. And you won't either."

With a giant step, the DI stepped it up, declaring, "You men take ten thousand giant steps, and I don't want to hear a single 'May I.'"

"You hear that?" Fats asked. "Men. We're 'men.'"

The DIs' word echoed in the ranks.

"Ah, he's getting old," Pointer said.

"Nah, it's dementia praecox," Skinny, who had gone from porky to steel in a little more than a month, said, "which anyone who smells one of Fats' skinny farts gets afflicted with."

"You're gonna wish you had that wasted breath before we get there, gooney bird," Doane said.

"Hey, don't talk so close to me so short a time after you ate dog shit."

"You ain't gonna get to heaven talking like that," Righty said, rolling his eyes.

Platoon 127 had already put some several hundred feet between them and the other platoons that called after them, "Early burnout, jerks."

"You ain't gonna get to heaven," Tim sang.

"On a pair of skates," Lace sang.

"'Cause you'll skate right by—those pearly gates," Tim answered.

Now they were really moving out, field transport packs bruising the backs of their legs.

"You can't get to heaven," Tim sang.

"On a pogo stick," Scoff sang.

"Because you'll pogo by," Johnny sang.

"Those golden gates."

The miles were piling up. The drill instructor jogged out front, never looked back.

The energy of the singing was joined by the background music of groans and quickly dimmed.

"Oh . . . you . . . can't . . . get . . . to heaven . . . on . . . a . . ." Tim groaned.

This was followed by a moan as platoon 126 stepped up its pace by increasing it cadence, "One two, one two, one two, one two."

"You . . . can't get . . . to heaven . . . come on, someone," Tim begged for an answer as 127 members sucked deep for air as they pulled the strangling backpack straps away from their chest.

Then Johnny cut in, "You can't get to heaven—doing it doggie-style, 'cause you fuck right by, those golden gates."

The entire platoon answered as one stepping up its pace for that longest mile, that mile through the sucking sand to the range, "'Cause you'll fuck right by those golden gates."

"Oh you can't get to heaven, doing it doggie-style," Johnny sang as he closed his eyes in pain as his bouncing helmet banged the sweat off his forehead into his eyes.

"'Cause you'll fuck right by those golden gates!"

"Doing it doggie-style!" It was Seabag's first words in fifteen miles as his platoon pulled into the range.

The other two platoons battled out for second place as they approached 127.

"Ten-hut! Dress right, dress. Ten-hut!"

The platoon's shoulders were so sore, they could hardly lift their arms to arrive at the proper distance between each other.

Seabag looked at the other platoons and addressed their DIs, "Staff Sergeants Moore and Geoffroy, are your ladies crapping out?"

"Fuck you, Seabag!"

"'Toon 127, do you see those, whatever they are, crapped out? Do you want to show them what you think of that sort of doings by doing a five-hundred dash out to the abutments out there? Take a look at Maggie's drawers. It will be the only time you'll see them the next three weeks cuz old Maggie only waves her red drawers on a long pole when you completely miss your target. Do you want to dash out there and back!"

"You're fucken' A John, sir!" They answered as one.

It was a raggedy ass dash, but it was their best.

Calhoon had three weeks to form them into a group that would do better than its very best.

"Look, old chicken shit is racing us," Skinny said, pointing to their DI dashing to the front of his platoon.

The dust on the range kicked up as the eighty-one bodies, throats parched to cracking, headed toward the target abutments, which appeared larger and larger as they neared them, and then they saw the ocean backdrop.

"It's fucken' Revere Beach!" Pointer said.

"He's gonna let us go in," Scott said, tears streaking his cheeks.

"Like fuck, he circled the target and is heading back," Doane said.

"You can't get to heaven," Johnny sang, taking off after the DI, "doing it doggie-style."

He was gaining on his DI.

Righty's voice reached out to him, as Seabag and Johnny distanced themselves from the platoon, which was now spread out over a hundred yards, "Go, go, *go*, Johnny oh!"

"'Cause you'll fuck right by," Johnny had said, pulling up abreast of his leader and knew he had the chicken shit, brutal bastard. Had him, and in front of those other cocksuckers Staff Sergeants More and Geoffroy. Johnny thought . . . *They're all cut . . . from the same side of rat shit cloth . . .* "those golden gates."

He was passing the DI when Seabag sent his foot out to the side, tripping Johnny and sending him flying through the air and hitting the ground, catching his own elbow in the stomach, knocking all the breath out of him like a pin put to a balloon.

The DI stopped over the prostrate boot and hissed, "All is unfair in love and war. You haven't won until everyone, every fucken' one of the enemy, is dead. You remember that," and walked to the staging area, where platoons 126 and 128 were just forming up ranks.

Seabag smiled at his fellow drill instructors. "There isn't any second place in war."

"Fuck you, Seabag," Staff Sergeant Moore said.

"Yah," Staff Sergeant Geoffroy said, adding his pissed-off two cents as well, "Fuck you, and the kangaroo you bounced in on, you . . . you buck-ass private who gets enough pay when the eagle shits to buy one draft beer."

The first of the three weeks on the firing range didn't start with a bang.

It was a snap. Little clicks repeated hundreds, thousands of times from the prone, sitting, kneeling, and off-hand positions. It was called dry firing.

Seabag's voice droned on and on as he went from recruit to recruit, assisted by range instructors, "Breathe in. Let half of it out. Squeeze. Don't pull that trigger. You can't jerk the barrel when you squeeze. Just think of a tit, a soft, warm, loving tit. You breathe deep, and as you let out part of your breath, you start to squeeze. She loves it. She'll roar with pleasure. Flames will spurt out. And you'll ejaculate, knowing your shot hit home."

The boots aimed at tiny targets set up on white sticks, breathed in, breathed partially out, squeezed, and snapped.

The action was taken time after time from a variety of positions.

Johnny wasn't hunkered low enough in the sitting position as he locked his elbows inside his knees, and was honored by his drill instructor, who chose him as a chair to lecture from.

The snapping in lasted a full week.

Later, after "Taps," while sitting around the stove in their pyramid tent city, the discussion was whether it was humanly possible to do nothing but snap in for a full week.

"Holy shit of a sultan," Fats said, "when I'm dead and buried, I know I'll be still snapping in, in my coffin. I had hopes that I could just lie there pulling my pud, hauling my ashes in keeping with the reverend's 'ashes to ashes' spiel, but no, I'll be snapping in, dry firing in my casket as I hear the dirt thudding down."

"I'll kill any son of a bitch who snaps a piece of bubblegum or an elastic band," Scoff put in.

"What gives with Lace? I saw him pulling the bulb in his tent up, saluting it, lowering it, pulling it up, saluting it, for a long time," Righty said.

"For a very long time," Tim said.

"He's still doing it," Righty said. "No one told him to stop. Wha' happened?"

"He saluted an officer with the tip of his little finger slightly higher than the other three, and Seabag spotted it," Skinny said, fingering what had once been a double and triple chin but was now little more than a reminder of a turkey wattle.

"Tomorrow we start firing for real," Fats said. "I can't wait. I've always wanted to fire a gun. Ma wouldn't let me play with guns when I was a kid. Too small."

"You're still small, you feather merchant. When that M1 kicks, it will boot your ass up into West Virginia someplace," Doane said.

"Ya hear? Doane say how the Rebs will kick our ass when the shooting starts," Pointer asked, adding, "Doane of 'head of bone' said they don't use no clickage where he comes from, only use Kentucky windage. Sticks his finger in his mouth and holds it to the wind to see which ways it's blowing. Then he said he shoots left, right, up, or down, even around corners, according to the windage. He said the wind brings messages straight from Kentucky and only to Georgians. Yup, Kentucky windage."

"He doesn't stick his finger in his mouth," Rhesus said. "He puts his thumb in his bum then sticks it in his mouth."

"What if those horse's peetoochees outshoot us?" Righty asked.

"They won't," Pointer said. "Me and Johnny and my brother Dink can shoot the wax out of field mouse's ear and not draw blood."

"And we think Doane and the Rebs are full of happy horse shit," Scoff said, swiping one of the cookies Righty had borrowed from the mess hall when he discovered a pantry window open.

"No, I shit thee not. We can shoot. Johnny spent nearly a year in the Massachusetts Eye and Ear Infirmary after he shot himself in the eye."

"Holy mother of god, what an endorsement," Skinny said, snapping his middle finger at what had been a double chin, making it flap.

"I don't give two good turds if they outshoot us. Christ, we could knock their asses off in a game of eight ball or straight," Rhesus said. "I just don't want to be the poor bastard son of a Franciscan monk who doesn't qualify."

"Yah, he'll fry the poor dork's wanger in boiling oil," Scoff said, switching a pair of his dirty socks for clean ones that were jutting out the top of Skinny's seabag.

"What was that shit Doane was giving you about you not needing face camouflage?" Johnny asked Tim.

"You know, John."

"I haven't a clue."

"Come on."

"Not a clue."

"Why do you think I was always the Indian when we played cowboys and Indians in the Big Woods?"

"Because you're the strong, silent type."

"Sure."

"Better wipe the rifles dry," Pointer said, "cause if that oil comes squirting out of the chamber, you're gonna see a lot of Maggie's drawers waving in the wind."

The bugle, as lonely as a foghorn at sea, sounded "Taps," "Day is done . . ."

And most of 127's boots were done before the final note died silently in midair.

And what seemed like substantially less than twenty winks, reviling reveille—"You can't get 'em up! You can't get 'em up! You can't get 'em up in the morning!" got 'em up.

The greetings to the bugler were varied, but all carried roughly the same message, "Blow it out your ass."

But everyone hauled ass out of bed, for the last boot in formation and not in shipshape would find his butt bouncing like a pogo stick by day's end.

The distances were one hundred yards off hand, then walked out to five hundred yards for prone, with kneeling and sitting distances in between.

Rapid fire was interesting, as the secret was to realize that you could squeeze all your shots off within the designated time and without rushing. Nearly everyone rushed to make sure there wasn't a round left in the chamber as unfired rounds counted as misses.

Each day, after the "ready on the left, ready on the right, ready on the firing line, watch your targets. *Targets!*" there were fewer and fewer Maggie's drawers drawing guffaws.

And the few that missed the target as it came close to qualification time didn't draw a guffaw because the fear was the entire platoon would suffer for anyone who failed to qualify.

Righty's shooting was pathetic. A natural righty, but because he suffered from lazy eye in his right eye, he hoped to shoot left handed using his good eye, but it wasn't allowed. Everyone shot right handed.

Righty put the rifle to his right shoulder but moved his head far to the right so he could sight with the left eye.

He had gone undetected as every time the range officer approached him, trying to figure out just what was wrong, someone had a question for the instructor about a jam, a misfire. Righty got pretty good shooting swivel head, but it was going to be close whether he qualified.

Then the day of reckoning arrived—qualification.

Johnny led all the shooters. He only needed a six out of a possible ten to be high shooter over second best, Doane.

"Your buddy needs a ten to qualify," Seabag told Johnny and walked away.

Johnny whispered directions to Righty.

Righty fired on Johnny's target, and Johnny squeezed on Righty's target.

The targets were pulled and scored.

Righty's target reappeared. A "ten." He had qualified.

Johnny needed a six to score expert. Bad. As his damned Yankees had collected a hundred bucks to bet the Johnny Rebs that DaSilva would beat Doane.

Johnny's target reappeared.

The red flag on the long white rod was waved slowly back and forth. Maggie's drawers. Righty had missed Johnny's target completely.

Seabag reappeared. "Congratulations, Minichelli, you qualified," then turning to Johnny, "I'll make sure he'll gets an office pinky job."

Doane approached Johnny as the DI walked off, whispered, "You choked."

"Yah."

Back at the tent area, Johnny collected the money from those who had bet on him and headed to Doane's tent.

As he handed the money to Doane, Lace stepped in, took Doane by the shoulder, and led him to a corner. "The asshole fired on the little ginny's target so he could qualify."

"The rotten cheating cocksucker," Doane said and pivoted away from his friend's grip and covered the distance across the tent to Johnny in nothing flat.

"Keep your goddamned money, DaSilva. You cheated. I hope your mole friend is to your right in your foxhole when the gooks come up the hill."

"Take it, asshole. The winnings go to your backers."

"Get your bandy Yankee ass out of here before I rearrange it and plant it under a bunch of roses."

"My ass hates flowers, so I'm going."

"You better haul ass."

The next day, all of 127 hauled tail from the tent area back to the main grounds.

They were nearing graduation.

First, the rifle qualification medals. Then the PFC, private first class, stripe.

Johnny smiled at Righty and Pointer. "We're no longer buck-ass privates" . . . *like Seabag . . . the bastard . . .*

"Fall *in!*" It was their DI. Johnny was certain the drill instructor could make himself appear when anyone thought his name.

"Dress right, *dress!* Parade rest. Well, you're about to become marines, and there are certain things expected of marines. You graduate tomorrow. Make sure you walk like you have a stick up your ass. Your shoes spit shined to the point where you can look down at them and up a woman's dress. You have been a fair to middling 'toon. But still the best on the island. I have gone easy on you, and I do not know why. You haven't had to wade the swamp. You haven't had to shave all the hair off your chest when I found your bayonets weren't sharp enough to make Mr. Gillette smile. No matter, you will have to do. Usually, a boot is mine for sixteen weeks. For some reason, you men only got seven weeks. But I think you still will be able to kick ass, especially when my cousin Zeke gets you at Camp Lejeune for a couple of weeks, or my nephew Zacariah gets hold of your short hairs at Pendleton. There have been some high points. Firsts."

The boots, soon-to-be marines, stiffened. They knew their DI had something up his sleeve, and it wasn't praise, and it wasn't buddy-buddy shit.

"For the first time, I had someone obey an order that others wouldn't or couldn't. Mr. Biggie Doane rapped on my hut door, and after several of my 'I can't hear yous,' I ordered, 'Knock the door down.' And you know, that son of a bitch door came down. Doane said he struck the door at its top hinge. I think he hit it with his head. That was the high point of 127. Mr. Doane gets the dumb tinkle-tinkle award.

"The 'toon's low point was a cowardly act. Someone came knocking, and I gave several 'I can't hear yous.' On the last 'I can't hear you,' the following words came through the door to me: 'Then how in hell do you know I'm out here, asshole?'

"Your ol' Seabag has the ability to move to a wise ass with the speed of lightning. But this perpetrator was gone. Pffffff. Disappeared. Now if this person will step forward, he will not be punished. I just need a recommendation of a company runner to give to the orders department. Also, the escaped one, if he steps forward, will receive the Speedy Gonzales road runner trophy. Plus a kick in the ass that will make him the first man on Mars."

No one stepped forward.

"I already have my flamethrower man, DaSilva. When the Pirate Don Dirk of Dow Dee came into my hut, and I squirted lighter fluid through the air at him and put a match to it, *woooof!* Did he jump back like anyone with a brain would have? No, he walked into it. He gets the id-git medal. Especially after he confessed he was fond of fire."

Johnny closed his eyes for a split moment. When the DI had spewed the flames through the air at him, it brought back how close he came to losing his little brother. His ma had sent Jazz to bed early as she always did. Yelled up the stairs a thousand times for him to be quiet. But not on this night, as there was not a single peep out of his little bucktoothed brother. "Go check your brother," his mother said. "And no 'Oh, Ma,' just 'Go! John.'"

Johnny found Jazz's bed roaring in flames and his little brother hiding underneath it. Johnny had picked up the burning mattress and covers and kicked out the bedroom window as the flames seared his arms and made the flesh bubble. He tossed the burning mass out the window.

Then he turned to his little brother, pulled him to his feet, and flung him against the wall, causing him to crumple to the floor. Then he picked him up, pulled him to his chest, and kissed the top of his head.

Jazz saw a single tear glisten in the corner of Johnny's eye. "That's all right, Johnny. I understand."

It seemed that since the day he was born, his mother reminded him daily that he was the man of the house and had to protect his sister and brother. But not his mother, who claimed, "I'm a tough old broad. But don't ever let me hear you using a word like 'broad.' There will be no swearing in this home."

When she learned what had happened, she pulled the little boy to her breast, kissed his head, and then bounced him off the wall, with a vigor that made Jazz appear like a bucktooth handball in action.

Johnny had successfully put his brother's brush with death and his own catching on fire aside until that day when Calhoun sprayed the fluid at him, expecting him to jump back.

As he now listened to the drill instructor's review of their tenure on Parris Island, he thought . . . *I'll get this bastard . . . not just for the flamethrower bit . . . not for the trip on the range . . . or the Long John DaSilva title . . . but because you are the shit . . . the lowest humanity . . . cruel to perfection . . .*

The DI continued, "Of course, the biggest award will be at your graduation tomorrow—when you will all be awarded a pay scale higher than me, and you will receive your PFC stripes, which you earned. Of course, that stripe is no big deal. I've been made a private first class four times. There is a rumor in the corps that I will not get a fifth chance, that my only fifth will be a bottle of Wild Turkey. But I'll go right by all those steps, PFC, corporal, buck sergeant, right to colonel, if I'm assigned to Chesty Puller's brigade. Enough bragging. Anyway, orders, stripes, leaves are all yours tomorrow. As of now, your ass no longer belongs to me. But then don't get your hopes up. It still doesn't belong to you. It belongs to Chesty and the corps. Good luck. Fall out."

The drill instructor was still standing at attention as the last of the boots headed to their huts for a final spit shining of the dress shoes, blitz polishing of the brass, and discussing what their orders might be. The Rockledge contingent had applied for guard duty in the Boston Navy Yard, except Tim and Johnny, who had opted for the infantry.

Righty and Pointer had put the infantry down as second choice to be with Johnny and Tim if they couldn't stay close to home.

As it turned out, and known to none except the four involved, only Johnny, Tim, Doane, and Lace in 'toon 127 sought the infantry grunt duty.

It didn't matter much; all were headed to Lejeune and Pendleton for infantry training. There was no "pinky" job for Righty.

Then they headed home for seven-day leaves.

Friends who remained home, relatives, and girlfriends barely recognized their old friends, sons, cousins, or companions who had left less than two short months before and returned lean and mean. Much leaner and meaner.

But then the young marines hardly recognized their friends, relatives, girlfriends as they had not been at Parris Island.

Chapter 12

WHERE HAVE YOU BEEN?

Rockledge looked the same but different as he walked through what passed for the center, which he had left two months before. He had just stepped off the Yellow Peril onto his hometown, looked skyward . . . *Wonder how Rags is* . . .

Johnny's foot warmer of a dog was an old man when he left for Parris Island. Rags still chased ground sparrows, even leaped in the air after them when they took off. And every yard within a square mile that housed star-nosed moles was dug up. His teeth were worn flat with digging away roots and rocks to get at them.

Johnny used to tell Jazz and Roma to look at their dog. "Look, he doesn't know he's old."

They all knew, even Jazz who was too young to know about death, that perhaps Rags would not make another winter of warming their feet in bed, or even under the kitchen table as they used the secret decoder to learn Captain Midnight's message. After several minutes of turning the decoder's dial, the message was still a short one—"Be very careful. Bad guys out there."

If that wouldn't put the fear of the Lord into you, what would?

After a day of chasing sparrows, digging for moles, and warming feet, the old dog's perpetual smile was more sorrowful than that of a hundred-year-old hound.

He had a lot of trouble getting up. Sometimes his feet would slip sideways.

Sometimes his kidneys would slip, and he couldn't make it to the door.

And peed on the floor. He looked sad when this happened, like he had failed the family.

Hang tough, Rags . . .

Johnny was walking past the Rockledge poolroom when he heard the familiar nasal whine, "Where have you been?"

It was Tim Lacasse, who had graduated with Johnny the past June and was a freshman at Boston College.

"Parris Island."

"Nice. My folks footed me to Martinique for a month. Lots of bare-boob and big-butt French babes there. Of course, I looked away," he said, adding, "Sure, I did," punching Johnny knowingly on the shoulder.

Johnny looked at his former classmate closely, like a desert sidewinder eyeing a fat-horned toad. He had hit Johnny on his recently sewn-on green, outlined in red, private first class stripes. Johnny didn't like that.

But Lacasse didn't notice and continued, "How were the girls on that island off Paris you went to? Voulez vous couche' avec moi, Johnny DaSilva? My folks sent me to Boston College. They want me to be a priest. I want to be a rabbi. They make more money. I'd be a rabbit rabbi 'cause they get a lot of that stuff that rabbits get. Get it? Probably because they got circumcised and are always trying to make up for what they chopped off. It's just the 'little man' bit sort of thing, like Napoleon and Hitler, overperformers. Yes, I can see those French broads on Parris Island. Did you get to see the awful Eiffel Tower?" He punched Johnny on his PFC stripe again, a dual meaning, dotting the end of his sentence with an "Aren't we buddy-buddy classmates?" smirk.

Johnny looked at him like he had never seen him before . . . *Two* . . .

"What's with this zoot suit get-up, Johnny? You rent it?"

Three . . . "Look, Tim, I have to be going."

"Why?"

"Well . . ."

"Well, what?" Lacasse demanded.

"Because as I listened to you, wondering whether you had been vaccinated by a phonograph needle, I found myself saying 'three.'"

"So? And don't say 'sew buttons on your old man's fly.'"

"Remember the joke about the old-timer who picked up his young mail-order bride at the railroad station and was giving her a buggy ride back to the farm when the horse stumbled and he said 'One'? A little while later, the horse stumbled again, and he said 'Two.' The young bride looked at him strangely. They were almost to the farm when the horse stumbled a third time. The old farmer got off the wagon and shot the horse right between the eyes. Shot it dead. The new bride started ranting and screaming, 'What did you do that for?' And the old farmer, he just looked her in the eye and said, 'One.' Well, Tim, you're at 'five.'"

"I don't get it. Come on, come on. Too good to have a beer with your old classmate? Just 'cause you got to Paris. Too good? If I remember correctly, you weren't going to no college or nothing, so that makes you not so good, doesn't it?"

"Well, maybe someday—on the college, that is. The beer with you? Nah. Never."

"You don't believe all that crap Yelena fed you about how you can go to college? From the general division! The general fuck-off division. Get real. Once a nerd always a nerd."

Johnny took a half step toward his tormentor. Stopped . . . *Don't do it, Johnny . . . Don't reach down his throat . . . and pull his asshole out . . . his mouth . . .* "Yes, I guess I am sort of nerdish," and he pivoted and walked away.

"Yes, I would guess so. I would guess those Paris mademoiselles cut off your balls. Yes. They cut off your cojones." His thoughts went further than his words . . . *You Portagee pissant . . . I ought to just walk up behind you . . . and kick your ass . . . but that monkey suit he's wearing . . . would probably bite my foot . . . or else Mr. Sissy . . . would sob . . .*

"I really have to go. I haven't seen my ma in two months," Johnny said, stepping out.

"Yah. Well, take it easy, Johnny. And good luck. By the way, is that one of those CCC uniforms your Uncles used to wear when we were kids and none of your people had a job?"

"Sort of. I mean I can't find a job either."

Johnny gave him a wave without looking back. And headed home . . . *Home again . . . home again . . . home again vagabond shoes . . .*

"John, John DaSilva. Little Johnny."

It was Mrs. Jadwinski. He hadn't seen her in several years. She was even smaller than he remembered when he used to leave off her *Boston Globe*.

"Hi, Mrs. Jadwinski."

"I knew it. I knew if I fed my little paper boy enough kielbasa, golumpki, and potato pierogi, he'd grow nearly as tall and handsome as a Polish boy."

"Thank you, Mrs. Jadwinski. You're not flirting with me, are you?"

The little old old woman's face twinkled in a smile giving it the look of a potato left in the field to shrink in sun and frost.

As she increased her smiling effort and ended up looking like a Shar-Pei, then fluffing the back of her hair with a tiny cupped hand, hair as blue and thin as Christmas angel hair, she said, "A girl could do a lot worse," then added a "tee-hee" that made Johnny smile and want to hug her close, especially when he thought of the steaming kielbasa sandwich handed him with a hot chocolate on some of those nose-throbbing icy days of January.

"You haven't aged a day, Mrs. Jadwinski. Did you steal the Fountain of Youth from Ponce?"

"Oh, Johnny, I always told my sister, told Emma, she's my sister, that Johnny DaSilva could have been Irish that sweet way he slings the blarney. Could have been Irish, and she said to me, yes, that you could have been Irish, and so cute, and she started getting the paper from you. The *Post.* Remember?"

"I think it was the *Boston Record.*"

"Now don't you go sassing none. What are you doing for a job? You're too old to be delivering papers."

"I joined the marines."

"Why? What for? The pay good? They treat you right? How's your mother? I hafta go," and she turned and walked swiftly away, talking to herself, "Oh what a cutie, sweet talker like he was Irish, built strong like a good Polish boy, pretty like a Portagee. Didn't Emma buy a paper? The *Globe.* And she couldn't read English."

"Good-bye, Mrs. Jadwinski." . . . *Why did she ask why I joined up? . . . I remember the first gold star in her window . . . Thaddeus . . . and then the second one . . . Stanislaus . . . so why . . . the why . . . but thank you . . . for the boiling kielbasa . . . on those freezing . . . hungry . . . days . . .*

As he headed homeward, he spotted the first trees turning color . . . *Swamp maples . . . always the first to turn . . . Uncle Manny always said . . . but he never said why . . .*

Johnny often wondered why the swamp maple leaves were first to turn yet last to fall. Some even held on till spring and then were finally buried behind the profuse thrust of the new bursting greenery.

The white birch were starting to color cream and rouge. He wondered why they were best for Tarzan swinging.

They had been great trees to climb until their weight made the trees bend to earth. The competition was to see who could get the treetop to touch the earth first.

Then one day, gentle Tim noticed that many of the young trees that they had made bend to their desires never straightened up again. They had spent days trying to straighten them. Made them splints. Did rain dances around them. Wa-hooping and chanting and such.

Their rain dances were similar to the ones the Big Tree Gang did with ballicky bare-ass swimming in Duck Pond and in the showers after a football victory, all the time snapping towels off each other's ass . . . yi . . .

ti-yi . . . ti-yi . . . yi-yi . . . They always finished their victory dances in a way unknown to Indians; setting up a forward rocking motion, flipping their boy-toys against their stomachs, and ended up with a "Yipped I a ki yeah!" So much for Indian talk.

Johnny, realizing he was doing the old birch saving (modest) rain dance while traveling through the town center, looked around embarrassed, but no one was looking.

Then they graduated from swinging in the birches to the young maple trees, those six- to eight-inch-thick, thirty-foot-high youngsters, which would swing . . . swing and sway . . . with Sammy Kaye . . .

They would swing and bend like the pole of an Olympic vaulter but always snap up straight after their big bend. They played tag in these sapsuckers, getting a tree to swing so they could transfer to the next as they gave chase or were chased.

Later, the maple trees were great for pirate sword fights. Armed with long hollow reeds, they would get their tree swinging like the top mast of a sailing ship in a storm and then board the ships they were taking over.

All the time, they swung their pirate swords, cutting the air with such vigor, they expected sections of the sky to fall at their feet. If you could break the other guy's sword, give him a good switch to the cheek of the face or cheek of the ass and make him yelp, you'd won the day and the imagined spoils of war.

And you climbed down the main mast to the deck to claim the spoils you had dreamed of. Johnny had dreamed of freeing Yelena from the pirates. She was so out of reach to all, so far above. He had untied her from the main mast. Gently replaced her one exposed breast in her blouse, somehow without actually touching it. The other pirates mostly dreamed of Nookie. They kept her as a slave. Johnny couldn't free her because Yelena said he must always look straight ahead as someday he would be an admiral with his own fleet and return to the seas to wipe out the pirates who had caused her indignities. He could at the same time free their classmate, and she could become Yelena's handmaiden.

Of course, of all the trees, it was the Big Tree that served as the center of their young world.

Johnny started to change direction, from his home to the Big Woods and the Big Tree . . . *Our young world* . . .

But then he returned homeward bound . . . *No more* . . . *quote the raven . . . never more* . . .

The raven was wrong. He jogged through the Big Woods and found himself climbing, climbing, until he swayed from the very top of the Big Tree.

But it didn't seem quite as big as before as in his young world.

As he climbed down, he spotted a single chestnut hanging far out on a limb.

He hugged the branch and crawled toward the end as the branch bent, threatened to break if he continued. The large boulder at the base of the tree looked very uninviting, but he continued out.

The chestnut was still in its quilled shell, looking much like the mines set afloat at sea during the big war, World War II.

He reached as far as he could. The branch groaned beneath him. The nut was only inches from his hand. He started sweating . . . It's not the fall that will . . . kill me . . . It's . . . the sudden . . . stop . . . cornball stuff . . .

The branch was now caught in a new breeze, surprisingly stiff. Johnny realized that it would be difficult to get back to the safety of the trunk. The boulder appeared to thrust upward as the branch swayed in circles. If the boulder hit him or he hit it . . . the sudden stop . . . *Would my gray matter . . . or my white matter . . . ooze out my cracked skull? . . . Doesn't matter . . . Ma could sweep it up with my cerebrum . . . Will my blood be sanguine . . . tangerine? . . . You're the one I love . . . I'm sure it would be . . . sanguine . . . rather than red . . . 'cause I heard Uncle Manny say . . . say . . . all us Portagees . . . have . . . lots of lead . . . in our pencils . . . and lead is like iron . . . Gotta get back . . . without this limb . . . breaking . . . Rockabye baby on the treetop . . . down will come . . . Johnny . . . cradle . . .*

The wind picked up even more, and the limb had a wicked will of its own, like a buggy whip . . . *Come on . . . Lord . . . Get my ass back safe . . . I'll be good . . . perhaps . . . Don't be an asshole . . . and kid with the Lord . . . when you want him to save your worthless hide . . .*

Then he ended his thoughts of backing up toward the tree trunk and instead shot forward and grabbed the chestnut.

That's all he remembered, his grabbing . . . *that . . . fuckin' nut . . .*

He was running home, home, before he had an opportunity to crush his coconut skull again.

Then he saw it, his home. Nothing had changed. It was still the most rundown home in the town. With wood shingles . . . *older than God . . . There's no place . . . like home . . . There's no place . . . like home . . .*

Home, with windowpanes so loose, they rattled in the wind . . . *like dead man's bones yardarms from a hanging tree . . . like the tracks under old engine nine . . . as she steamed home here . . . home . . . home again vagabond shoes . . . Why did you let me stray . . . stray so far away . . . Take me home again . . . home again . . . Please let steps four and nine stairs . . . still be missing . . .*

He was on the front porch. The slats creaked beneath his feet like an old vessel dry rotting in dock.

The door handle was still as loose as always . . . *loose as a goose* . . .

"Ma!"

"I'm upstairs!"

One, two, three . . . skip . . . five, six, seven, eight . . . skip . . .

"Ma! They're still missing!"

"I'll get them fixed now that I'm getting some overtime at the box factory, and have the government's sending me part of your pay. I'll give it to the Salvation Army if they keep it up."

"Don't do it. I want nothing to change until I come home for good."

Then they were hugging, like "two bugs in a rug," as she said before Johnny was no longer a little boy and was embarrassed to be hugged.

Embarrassed, they pushed away. They hadn't hugged for years. Theirs was an unspoken thing. Their thoughts comingled . . . *John . . . you're the oldest . . . You watch out for your brother and sister . . . Ma, I'll watch out for you . . . You're the only ma . . . I got . . .*

That outward thing, hugging, kissing, some other stuff had been put aside.

His outward thing became very different. Hadn't he for years, when walking with his friends, gone a block out of the way when he spotted his mother?

And she, on spotting him with his friends, went a block out of the way so he wouldn't have to recognize his mother in front of his friends.

She held him at arms' length now. "My good little boy."

"Ma, I'm a big bad man now."

"I see, but that's only to the rest of the world. You'll always be my little boy."

"Come on, Ma. Knock it off. Where's Jazz?"

"In the closet, being punished. He hoisted his leg and let a gas noise. The he looked at me and smiled."

"He learned that from you, Ma."

"Yes, but I don't think it's hilarious and go bragging about it, like he's built the Empire State Building or bought the Brooklyn Bridge or did something real great. Besides, I always said 'excuse me.' Or blamed Rags. And later, I always apologized to Rags for blaming him. Your brother is so stubborn that I don't know where he came from unless the devil delivered him here instead of in hell."

"Can he come out? I'm only home for a little while."

"He can come out.

A muffled little "yeah" came seeping from the closet.

"After he says 'excuse me.'"

Their mother thought she heard the word "excuse" come from the closet and said, "OK, come on out, but never another windy without saying 'excuse me.' Everyone who does one of those in nice company says, 'please excuse me.' It's only polite."

Jazz hadn't said "excuse me." With the combination of being wrapped in swaddling closet clothes and operating with buckteeth that could eat potatoes through a potato masher, little brother had challenged, "The cops will get you for child abuse, Ma."

Abuse? Excuse? Close enough for a mother who wanted her child out, and the child who wanted out, because big brother was home from the Marine Corps. Home from Parris Island where everyone must have been so nice, as for the first time in his life, he hung up his clothes.

Jazz ran to his brother, crushed his head into his stomach, and wrapped his arms around him.

"Didya kill anybody yet, Johnny! Didya?"

"Not yet. Pretty soon. Maybe sooner than you'd like if you don't start saying 'excuse me' when you fa— ah, when you let fly with flatulence."

"You mean fart? You never said 'excuse me.' You always blamed the dog."

"Where is Rags?"

"He's with Roma. Ma said that without you around and me spending all my time farting, someone had to protect her from the boys. She's starting to grow those water wing things up front. You know." Jazz gave his big brother a knowing smile. "So Rags has to protect her."

"Who is going to protect the boys from Sis?"

The two brothers walked down the stairs, arms around each other, counting the stairs, stepping safely over nine and four, in the expert cadence of marines in close order drill.

"Ma?"

"Yes?"

"Don't fix the steps. At least until I get home from Korea."

"Do you have to go? I think I read something about it in the paper. Or on the Pathay News at the movies. The war takes time away from the sing-alongs and that."

"Yes."

"Yes, what?"

"I have to go."

"Why you?"

"One, someone has to stop them there so we won't have to fight them here."

"Who?"

"The Reds."

"Cincinnati? Does Ernie Lombardi still play for them?"

"Nah. He ended up with the Boston Braves. In fact, in 1942, Lombardi won the battling title with a .331 average with the Braves, and Ted Williams won it with the Boston Red Sox with .356. You know that Ted is flying a fighter plane for the marines right now."

"No, son, he fought in World War II. The war to end all wars."

"No, Ma. He's headed into the Korean War right now."

"Then why did we fight World War II? Why did your father and all your Uncles get shot up? And why did Mrs. Jadwinski have two gold stars up in her window? I always knew when a new gold star went up. You'd come home from delivering your papers and wouldn't say nuffin'. I'd try to hug you, and you'd push me away. That nice little old woman always smells of those foreign foods. Someone ought to tell her."

"Hey, Ma."

"What?"

"Just trying to get you to return to planet earth."

"So you didn't answer my question. Why you?"

"I want to."

"Not good enough."

"Besides, we're poor," he added.

"Don't you ever say that again as long as you're under this roof I put over your head. Ever. Again. I mean it! Don't smile. And don't turn away so you can try to sneak a smile. Don't *ever!*"

"I didn't mean it that way, Ma. What I meant is I can send money for you and Jazz and Romola. She can have a real rocking chair and a doll all her own and won't have to sit in the store rocking a doll, while Jazz and I keep the store manager away. Jazz can have his teeth fixed."

"Your brother can join the Marine Corps and get them fixed. They fixed yours for nothin' . . .'"

"Yes, but they forgot to give me novocaine."

"Don't be funny."

"God's honest truth."

"Don't you go using the Lord's name to cover up your fibs."

"Then honest injun."

"The only injun I know is Tonto. And how do I know if he's honest or not? Although he hangs out with that clean-looking Mr. Lone Ranger. And don't you go turning away so you can laugh at your old mother. Remember, I brought you into this world."

"Yes, *Ma.*"

"And don't go being sassy."

"No, Ma."

"Didn't I tell you . . ."

"Yes, Ma."

She grabbed her son and pulled him to her. "You're my oldest. You always took care of everyone, but not your mother. I don't need no one taking care of me. Save your money. Give it to the church where it will do some good. Give it to the Salvation Army."

Jazz started singing and dancing, "Salvation Army. Put a nickel on the drum, save another drunken bum. Salvation Army . . ."

"See what you taught your younger brother? Now are you happy. You'll both end up in the electric chair or even reform school."

Johnny opened his eyes wide, stood up straight and stiff, and shuddered—"The lights dim, the smell of burning flesh."

Jazz duplicated his brother's look of sheer ludicrous terror, shuddering as he pretended the electrical current surged through his body.

"Go ahead, you two, make faces, but someday the good Lord will freeze them that way."

"Just to show crime doesn't pay," Jazz said.

"He's your brother. Do something about it."

"Here's a dollar. Go buy yourself an ice cream," Johnny said, reaching in his pocket.

Jazz's eyes, still locked in the open terror of a man on death row, got even bigger. "A buck! I can buy ice cream for a month, double scoops."

And he was out the door.

"You won't help anyone rewarding bad works that way."

"I know, Ma. I'll talk to him, when we're alone, man to man."

"Neither one of you is a man just yet, Mr. Smarty Pants, and don't go forgetting that. Now go change out of that tight uniform. It shows muscles bulging all over. What did they do to you?"

He went to his room, took off his uniform, folded it neatly and hung it up, placed his socks in his shoes and put them under his bed, and lay down, hands behind his neck.

It took a little while of staring at the water-stained ceiling, but finally, it was there, the head of a lion. And sure, that's the alligator. And, oh, oh, that breast, still so pert, a bluebird could perch on it.

He hummed softly, keeping in tune with the slight whisper of the wind moving the windowpanes, whose rattles provided a sensual moaning that made him harden.

He closed his eyes ever so slightly, peering through his long lashes, as the water-stained breast became more real. *Yelena's . . . yes . . . but, no . . . too large . . . Bernadette's then . . . no . . . think of Yelena . . . I love her, Yelena . . .*

He got up slowly, still watching the breast, which, through his nearly closed eyelashes, appeared to be coming to life and moved undulating toward him; his lips parted. His eyes closed.

He moaned softly as he unscrewed the big brass ball on the bedpost. It was still there. The picture of Betty Grable. In a bathing suit. In high heels that flexed the calves of her legs.

Johnny was sure, well, almost sure, that you could almost see, almost see . . . a nipple . . . showing . . .

He was back on the bed, looking down. He knew he was very big . . . *too big . . . a Leaning Tower . . . of Pisa . . . How do you . . . apologize . . . for being too big? . . . Can I go on a diet? . . .*

I'll just straighten . . . the tower of . . . tower of . . .

"Ohhhhh. Bernade . . . I mean . . . Yelena . . . I mean Betty . . .

His actions left him with a feeling that Vesuvius was exploding, killing everyone in Pompeii. And God, seeing what he had caused, struck him dead by firing a bolt of lightning down the highest point of his body,

He slept.

"Johnny!"

It was his mother. She was in his room.

My god . . . do I still have my hand . . . on my . . . donk . . .

He looked down. He was completely covered. "What?"

"Do you feel OK?"

"Of course. Why?"

"Your clothes."

"Yes?"

"They're all hung up."

"So?"

"So do you feel OK? You've never done nothing like that before."

"Ma, I ain't sick."

"Don't say 'ain't.'"

"I know. Ain't 'ain't' in the dictionary? But it should be."

"Look, I'm warning you, don't make me get the broom, Mr. Too Big for His Britches, little boy. I'm not a cripple yet. And I'm not going to stand by and watch you fall into ungodly ways. Ways that would make your grandfather Shiverick be ashamed of you.

"And make your grandmother cry all because that girl Bernadette walks by our house real, real slow a thousand times a day. What does she want? Never mind. I wasn't born yesterday. Her trying to look innocent and all that trickery."

"Ma?"

"And you, peeking out from behind the curtain at her. And all that stuff. You are not only calling the house of the Lord down around your ears but the ears of everyone. Your grandfather Shiverick would have had the good Lord bring down his terrible swift sword on the head of his own grandson. That no-good Burnitdown, whatever her name is, girl has walked by this house several times today."

"Bernadette, Ma. Bernadette."

"Bernadette was some sort of Catholic saint or something, and this girl—a saint, she ain't."

"Ma—"

"While those black Catholics worship all those gold things and ring bells and make smoke in a pot while ringing the bell, when people die, they still believe in God. No matter the priests face the wrong way and speak in a language called Latin that no one understands. They still believe in God. And when I say that girl isn't no Bernadette, the saint, I mean it. Why, her and her father . . ."

"Ma! Thumper time."

"OK. OK. Like I always told you, like the mother of Thumper the rabbit said in *Bambi*—'If you can't say somethin' nice, don't say nuffin' at all.' I'll be quiet. But—"

"Ma."

"All I was going to say is that nice girl Yelena came by while you slept, wouldn't let me wake you, and said she had two tickets to the movies, and if you are interested, well, stop by her house about seven."

"Did you put in a telephone like I asked when I sent you the money?"

"We don't need a telephone long as the good Lord gave us lungs for walking and talking and kids to run messages. I saved it for you."

"Yah. Sure. Thanks for nothing. You keep it."

"I don't need nothing. Long as the good Lord gave me these two hands." She turned away. "I'll just go, I'll just go and—mind my own business."

"Ma."

"You'll miss me when I'm dead and gone."

"Ma."

"Then you won't have no one to put down."

"Ma."

"But you'll be better off without me."

"Ma."

"'Cause the good Lord takes care of little children and id-gits."

"Which am I?"

"Both."

And then she was gone.

My good happy Jesus . . . did she catch me . . . jerking off . . . Oh . . . what unhappy shit . . . There wouldn't be a fan big enough for it to hit . . . I could hide under an ant . . .

He smiled as he put his uniform on. Of course, she would ask him about the PFC stripe. And he would tell her that it put him a full rank above the very man who trained him when he was a lowly boot . . . *The medal . . . you ask about my medal . . . It was not only for shooting . . . expert . . . but for also . . . throwing myself on a grenade . . . well, practically . . . to help a comrade . . . qualify . . . samee, samee . . .*

He neatly knotted his field scarf . . . *When I tell Yelena that a necktie is now called . . . a field scarf, she'll laugh . . . I'm a poet . . . my feet are Longfellow's . . . poet, poet, she'll say . . . We'll both laugh, laugh . . . and then . . . kiss, kiss . . . We'll laugh finding ourselves so close . . .*

Suddenly, his trousers, M1 green, were entirely too tight around the crotch, and a tiny wetness spread, forming its own tiny Rorschach in white, a message that would not require the efforts of one of the world's top tea leaf readers to interpret.

He would kill his mother if he ever again caught her checking the insides of his trousers, like she did when he was a kid in high school.

"What's this!" she would demand, pointing to the inside of the fly of his tattered trousers.

"Ma."

"Don't 'Ma' me, young man. What is this white stuff inside your pants? You're only in the tenth grade"

"It's just paste. We were pasting up Christmas decorations in art class."

"And how, young man, did it get on the inside of your pants? I suppose you want me to believe your art teacher makes everyone wear their pants inside out?"

"Ma."

"Don't stall for time. Out with it. What's what here?"

He felt like laughing out loud when she said "Out with it," but for safety's sake, he didn't.

"Simple, Ma. I had toothpaste on my hands when I went number one in the bathroom."

"Oh, aren't we the cute one?"

"Ma." He felt a little sheepish, a killer marine "oh ma-ing" his mother.

"If I ever hear about you and a girl doing . . . doing . . . doing it, I'll . . ."

"I didn't do, I didn't do that word, 'it.'" . . . except in my mind . . . *Why can't I just keep the wet in my mind . . . so I won't get my butt . . . in trouble . . .*

The field scarf in place, after one last blitzing of his belt buckle—the eagle, anchor, and the ball—it was Semper Fi time. Stand sharp for Yelena, walk tall.

The cap was next, just a tilt off center like they were worn by those Flying Tiger pilots that blew the Japanese Zeros out of the sky.

His cap was the marine version of the Generalissimo Chiang Kai-shek Czech cap, with the shiny black visor and strap that went around it or could be lowered under the chin when on parade, and he thought . . . *Or when strutting . . . your stuff . . . in little old Rockledge, Massachusetts, USA . . . home of PFC John DaSilva . . . US Marine . . . lean and mean . . . and made to be seen . . . and gook asses to clean . . . a killing machine . . .*

A short while later, the willowy Yelena was walking beside him, her hair, rippling like the honey-colored wheat in a soft summer wind. They had met at the Rockledge Library just like old times.

He would have loved to look at her but was certain she was looking at him . . . Walk tall . . . walk straight . . . and the only way to do it . . . is to walk like you had a corncob up your butt plate . . . one with a long stem . . . like the one Gen. Doug MacArthur puffed . . .

"Does your back hurt, Johnny?"

"No. Ah. Our backpacks were so loaded that if we leaned forward, we'd fall on our face."

"It had to be rough. When do you start officers' candidate school?" Yelena asked.

"Oh, yes, I remember my letter to you now. The Marine Corps wants me to fight first. Yes. Fight first, and become a general second."

"Will you win a medal for me, the highest one?"

"That's the Congressional Medal of Honor. I think that, most of the time, you have to die to get it."

"I don't want that, maybe the second highest then. Or you could wear the Medal of Honor. Who would know the difference?"

"Me."

"Oh? Yes? No one would know. You could just wear it when you were wearing your parade dress blues and when we're in New York City watching South Pacific. I'd love you for it. Who would know?"

"Me, myself, and I would know."

"But you would never tell on yourself. No one would ever tell on himself. I wouldn't. If anything happened tonight, I wouldn't tell a soul."

"What's at the movie tonight?"

"Would you believe I don't know and I don't care?" she said, taking his hand, bringing it softly to her lips. I hope it has Van Johnson and Betty Hutton, John DaSilva and Yelena Smoltz."

Johnny hoped the Pathay News would show some of the fighting in Korea. So Yelena would know what he faced . . . *God . . . please don't let it be over . . . before I get there . . .*

But there was no news about the war. There was a story about a chicken that adopted a duckling. Just as well, everyone enjoys something like that more than people, especially Americans, getting killed.

They held hands all through the movies, except when she had to go to "the little girls' room."

He tried to put her out of his mind while she was there . . . *No . . . she doesn't sit there . . . like a stupid puffin on a muffin . . . She sits like a . . . like a queen . . . I wonder if she gets . . . dew on her little rose . . .* Johnny visualized himself as a bee seeking honey from such a flower . . . *Knock that off, Private . . .* He laughed . . . *I don't mean my private to knock it off . . .*

He thought of her sitting there. He hoped she would only do water, a lovely stream like a beautiful waterfall tumbling down from a lush bush head wall above. He couldn't bear to think that she might be doing the other thing . . . *No . . . she wouldn't do that . . . number two . . . not while on a date with me . . .*

The movie wasn't Van and Betty. It was Errol Flynn and a group of females—women, girls, dogs, horses, men that he gave every appearance of wanting . . . *to corn hole . . .* Johnny thought, as they left the theater.

"A penny for your thoughts."

"I was just wondering whether I could grow one of those little pencil mustaches, like Errol Flynn."

"If I was the Bernadette girl, I would say, 'So you could get in, like Flynn.' But I wasn't brought up that way. Forgive me, Johnny, for being cruel."

"You could never be cruel."

"You could grow the greatest grandest mustache in the world if you put your mind to it."

He took her hand tightly in his and picked up the pace.

Yelena knew what this heated pace meant. More than one boy had tried to take her hand, pick up the pace, but she would have nothing to do with it. She was saving. Saving for the right person.

She looked at Johnny . . . *Saving for the right . . . savior . . .*

She felt her upper lip break out in a warm sweat. The bottom of her bra started to dampen, soak. She half closed her eyes as he led her on more and more urgently.

"Here we are."

She opened her eyes.

They were at her front door. Yelena stared into Johnny's eyes. "Would you like to come in for a moment and have a Coke or something?"

"I . . . I . . . I will call you as soon as I get back from the farm. I'm heading there tomorrow."

And then he was gone. Running in the dark . . . *Jesus . . . Jesus . . . why . . . stupido . . . stupido . . .*

Jazz and Romola spotted Johnny's soaked-cat and hang-dog look as he bounded up the stairs. They heard his crash, a first. He wasn't counting the stairs, and his leg fell through the stair tread void and sank to his crotch, slamming into the missing stair's riser, making a noise similar to that of a walnut being broken in a nutcracker, causing a cry more sorrowful than pained.

"We want you to have Rags tonight," Jazz said to his big brother as Romola nodded her agreement. A first. This agreeing on who got the foot-warming dog.

"Nah, you guys have him." Another first.

Jazz took the Heinz 57 different varieties old dog in his arms and handed him to his brother.

"Yes," Roma said. "We want you to have him every night while you're home."

Jazz added, "'Cause someone said you might not be alive when you come back from over there."

"Stupid," his sister said, shoving him against the wall, "no one said no such thing."

"A friend of mine whose brother is an Eagle Scout and has all kinds of medals said so," Jazz said but stopped when he saw Romola hold her forefinger over her lips in a "shhhhh" indication, and said, "Remember what Granddad Shiverick said when he was a six-star general in the Civil Defense? He got to tell people to close their black shades as the air raid sirens went off to tell us there was an air raid. And you could never tell whether it was a test of Nazi loof-waffle bombers overhead. He said, 'Loose lips sink ships.'"

"Oh, yah. I get it," Jazz said." Rags is always farting. Can't help it. Johnny, will you and me fart all the time when we get old? All real old people over thirty fart all the time. Anyway, Rags farts, and I take the blame so Ma won't put him out in the cold. I don't mind taking the blame."

"Jazz, you're the man of the family while I'm gone, and it's a good thing to take the blame for Rags's farts. It's good for Rags not to get sent out into the cold. And it's a good thing to apologize to Ma after you fart. She needs it."

"She'd die if I ever apologized."

"Well, ah, good. Ma's lived long enough."

They all laughed, knowing full well their mother would live forever.

Rags was housed in both Romola's and Jazz's extended arms.

Johnny took the old liquid-eyed dog, that dog that he had taken hunting a hundred times, the dog that had only sniffed field mice from under leaves and chased cats hunting meadow larks out of the fields, but was a great and spirited companion when hunting. "If he farts on me, I'll beat the tar out of you two."

"Better start now," Jazz said, taking an old-fashioned boxer's stance.

Johnny came at him, circling with his arms like a push lawnmower blade.

"Hit him in the balls!"

"Whoa up! Just whoa, up little lady," Johnny said. "Where did you learn that type of talk?"

"I taught myself the talk. With you gone, I'll have to take care of myself."

"Knock off the dirty talk," Johnny ordered.

"All marines swear, it's the number-one thing," Romola said.

"In this man's Marine Corps," Johnny said. "The Corps and my M1 are first. Praying to God is next. Col. Chesty Puller is God. But don't tell Ma that, or I'll zip your lip closed with your belly button. I still love our civilian God too, but you tell Ma, and you get a fat lip."

"You and whose army!" Jazz said, hugging his big brother.

"You don't need that street talk, little brother. You can whip anyone twice your size."

"Three times," Jazz said, playfully sinking his teeth into Johnny's knee.

"Anyway, I'd give you two punks a kiss good night if you don't tell anyone."

The two puckered up like they had swallowed bad cider.

"Except you two make me puke."

He banged their heads together and grabbed the old dog from their arms, looking it in the eyes and lovingly crooning, "You fart, you're dead."

"Johnny?"

"Yah, Roma?"

"Don't get hurt, but if you do, can I have your slingshot that you made?"

"Don't worry, I'm coming back for my own David the Giant Killer. But I'll make you one. I'll even peel all the bark off to make it fancylike, like Tom Mix's pearl-handled six-shooter. But I'll be back with bells on. You know me, I do the hurting."

"Johnny?"

"Yah Jazz?"

"Will you kill someone for me?"

"Sure. I'll get a dozen of those slant-eyed Commies for you."

"Nah. I want you to kill my art teacher. She told Ma that we weren't working with paste in class the other day when I told her we were, 'cause of some white stuff in my pants."

"Yah—I mean, yes. I'll feed her a dozen chalkboard erasers."

"Loaded with chalk?"

"Yah. Yah. Hit the rack."

The next morning, Johnny was up and running.

The farm was twenty miles away. He was sure he could do it easily in less than two hours or so in his marine dungarees and boondockers. Hadn't he done it in less than three hours in a heavy snowstorm when he was young?

He was positive as he ran that both Pointer and Dink would be at the farm. They had the nose when he was on the run.

As he jogged, he thought of his bucking bronco Bog the Hog and his first bullfight with Betty Boop, the cow with the attack teats. Then there was the underground tunnel Dink, Pointer, and he had taken weeks to dig from that little knoll to the outhouse, where once and for all they planned to discover whether "it," the girl's honey hole, was underneath or in the front below the belly.

In boot camp, the word was that an oriental women's "it" was sideways rather than up and down. His thoughts jumbled and tumbled as he jogged . . . *If it is sideways . . . does the man or the woman . . . lie on the table . . . while the other stands? . . . Hey . . . no one ever said life was . . . without problems . . . No one ever said life would be easy . . .*

He wondered what Uncle Manny meant when he overheard him talking with the boys and said, "My wife makes me doggy style. I have to sit up and beg."

The run time went easy, and time flew as both his brain and imagination had turns clicking on stage.

Suddenly, his mind said . . . *Here . . . now . . .* and he left the road and cut through the back fields of the farm. He slowed as he neared the faded, whitewashed house. He looked skyward like he wasn't paying attention, so when Dink and Pointer jumped out of the bushes and tried to tackle him and give him a noogie and Indian burn, he'd surprise them with a little of that fancy boot camp footwork. They rushed him with a war whoop. He ducked, making Dink trip over his back and fall to the ground. Pointer was even easier. Johnny placed one foot behind his heel and pushed on his shoulder, and leverage did the rest; he went down backward.

The three gave a circle hug as they walked slowly toward the weathered door of the farm. All the dog and cat scratches that gouged out the soft wood, leaving the harder grains like veins stand out, was a beloved sight as it led to a small room, "Mine's Little Room," where she had hundreds of fat and beeswax candles burning for the souls of sinners and loved ones.

Johnny spotted the candle she had lit for him when she learned he was going off to fight a war in a country named Korea, wherever that was, instead of staying on the farm where there were no wars.

Johnny wished his Uncle had not made them return the statue of the Virgin Mary they had borrowed . . . *Now I have my own . . . candle . . . I wish Uncle hadn't made us return . . . Mary . . . She was so beautiful . . . No wonder everyone wants to be . . . a Catholic . . . and you get to cross yourself . . . when you come to bat in a baseball game . . . and you're so frightened, you fear that you will pee your pants if you strike out . . . Catholics can cross themselves . . . and concentrate on getting a hit . . . because they don t have to worry about . . . peeing themselves . . . and if you strike out . . . you can blame God . . .*

Dink, Pointer, and Johnny swiped . . . borrowed . . . sweet corn, raspberries, dug up three big potatoes, and then they squeezed Betty Boop's teats to get enough milk into Johnny's well-dented Boy Scout canteen, the one he discovered in the town dump while shooting rats with his slingshot, his very dependable David the Giant Killer.

They munched raspberries high in the big hill beside the farm, cooking the corn and potatoes over the fire they fed with dead branches they had gathered.

After burning lips and tongue on the hot food, they soothed the stinging with Betty's sleepy cow-tit donation to their cause.

As the sun set, they lay on their backs, watching the embers of the fire join the fireflies that flittered overhead and then spiraled skyward to disappear among the stars. The droning baritone cicadas joined the alto tree frogs to sing them to sleep.

It was the caws of cruising crows that nudged them out of their sleep. They meandered through the filtered morning light toward the river, borrowing their breakfast of frost sweetened apples from an abandoned orchard, which were covered with honey from a honey tree they had shooed the bees away from away, with a smoky piece of burning newspaper they had secreted in each of their pockets for a good ass wipe in the woods.

To find the honey tree, they had captured a honeybee from a Devil's Paintbrush bloom and squeezed raspberry juice on its rear end. Thus, butt painted, they could follow its flight, reading when they released it and it made a beeline to the tree that hummed, giving the honey hive away.

They picked bunches of dry wild grass and greenery to add to their smoking torch that they stuck into the tree hollow. There is little more helpless, at least for a short while, than a dizzy bee. They acted quickly, plunged their arms into the opening after wrapping giant elephant ear leaves around the thrust arm, and came out with scoops of dripping honey with which they covered the apples with. Then they had a feast that would make a bear cub smile.

The rope that they had left on the river edge was still there, so they bucked up to see who would go first. Johnny was the winner of the finger-tossing gamble. After rubbing Dink's and Pointer's noses in invisible imaginary cow shit, he swung, skyrocketing out with a Tarzan "Ahahahaaa," sounding much like a kid with his foreskin caught in his zipper.

Dink was next. He swung out and over the water and then back to the bank. Then as he headed out again, he placed his feet in Pointer's back, sending him ass over tea kettle into the river. He released his grip on the rope just in time to cannonball Johnny, who was floating by on his back, holding his pecker in the air, and declaring, "I'm a sub. Periscope up."

Later, they lay bare ass on the bank, drying in the noonday sun.

After chewing on long stems of wild grass that shivered in their mouth like timbered trees, the cousins loped through the woods like young antelopes until they could see the farm far below.

Johnny said, "Gotta go see Yelena," took one last look at the farm, turned, and said, "Keep your finger on it," and started the twenty-mile return run.

Yelena was in her yard, banking rose bushes, putting the first seeds of fall in the bird feeder as he jogged through the Knob Hill section of town where Tudor houses stood, large and majestic. The mansard roofs had fish and bird designs cut into the slate, with white wainscoting trim as elegant as swans gliding in the snow.

She looked up as he passed near, smiled softly, and whispered in the wind, "Tonight. Seven. Under the Big Tree."

Johnny thought . . . *How does she know about the big tree? . . . Did I take her there? . . . And now . . . she wants me to . . . really . . . take . . . really take her there . . . do her . . . she wants . . .*

"Yes," he called, weakened by the gentleness of her smile, unsure whether he could cover the last half mile to home.

Her elegant voice that would fit naturally into a New England snow version of *Gone with the Wind*.

Her voice followed him, "Someday you'll win the Boston Marathon," and then it drifted off, "For me. Run for me. Now. Like the wind. The wind."

His injured football knee throbbed as he headed homeward bound with a gait that was that of a horse that had thrown a shoe.

He was running now among the four-story battleship blocks of the area known as Chinatown, a name given when a number of Orientals were imported to sew shoes in the long-gone shoe factories that now stood like mothballed battleships.

The salt from his sweat trickled down his legs into his boots, acid in the broken blisters.

"Johnny."

Was it the wind?

"Johnny."

He slowed. It was Bernadette.

She was sitting on the curb, elbows on her knees, hands under her chin. "You're limping. Let me take you to the little brook. And wash your feet."

Take . . . wash my feet . . . "Do you think you're Jesus, or what?" he asked offhandedly, immediately sorry for being flippant, and not expecting an answer back, or what he got. She looked up, her eyes huge and sorrowful as a wombat's.

"Don't cry, for Christ's sake, don't cry," he said.

Johnny slowed to a near walk. "Look, Bernadette, I'm sorry—Meet me tonight at seven, under the Big Tree. Wait. You don't know where it is."

"Yes, I do."

"How could you?"

"Seven. Tonight. The Big Tree." She thought . . . *How many times . . . did I follow you . . . through the dark . . . watch you climb high . . . higher . . . I watched you so many times . . . alone up there . . . terrified you'd know I was there . . .*

He ran to Righty's house. He would ask him to take a dip in Spot Pond for old time's sake. After the Big Tree meeting with . . . Bernadette . . . "Oh, good happy horseshit" . . . with Yelena . . . *Where am I? . . . What will I do? . . . Righty and I will take a dip at midnight in Spot Pond . . . after dark . . . maybe take a last leak in the town water supply . . . have it bottled . . . send it to Seabag . . . That wouldn't work . . . I'll put it in another bottle . . . toss it in the ocean . . . and some poor kid in Africa would find it . . . think it was a pirate note telling where the gold was hidden . . . but instead . . . all he would get would be . . . piss on his hands . . . old pee to boot . . .*

"Jon-a-nee!" It was Righty's mother. "Are you-ah OK? OK? You look confugeled. Cunfoozed. Kung fu-ed. You knowa whatta I meana. Come-ah in and havea some homemadeah breada and a spa-get. While'll we wait for my boy. He's such a gooda boy, likea you, Johnny."

"Thank you, maybe later," and he headed home.

"Where have you been? What are you doing, Johnny?" his mother asked, watching him jump the front porch steps and head up the inside stairs, counting aloud so as to leap over the missing ones and . . . not fall like a dumb shit . . . a turd . . . in a drop toilet . . .

He was just finishing packing his seabag when his mother came into his room.

"Your leave hasn't even hardly started. I want to show you off to my friends."

"I know, Ma, someday I'll explain. If I can." . . . *maybe be able . . . to tell you . . . I love you . . . then someday . . . say it aloud . . .* Then he admonished himself . . . *You no good fucken' asshole John . . . asshole to the tenth power . . . squared . . . Am I meeting Yelena or Bernadette at seven? . . .*

"Good-bye, Ma."

Once outside, he yelled, "Brats!" Little sister with little brother in tow came from the back of the house, each with a fist full of four-leafed clovers held out for him.

"You have to do me a favor," he said. "I want you, Romola, to run to Yelena's house and tell her I was called back to base and had to move out early. Little brother, you know Bernadette that lives in Chinatown—well, you go there and tell her the same thing, that I have already left got called."

They both swore solemn oaths.

Romola said, "On my Girl Scout honor, I'll do it."

Johnny kissed the top of her head, looking around first to be certain there were no witnesses . . . *There's none of . . . this stuff goes on here . . . like Bernadette's dad does . . .*

Jazz swore, "I'll get the word to your Chinatown girl, I swear on my Captain Midnight Secret Decoder Badge."

Johnny roughed up his little brother's hair and told him, "You're the big guy of the house now. And Bernadette is not my girl."

"What about when you get back from killing bad guys, after you kill my art teacher?" Jazz said, giving Johnny that eating-corn-through-a-picket-fence bucktoothed smile that would charm a coyote out of its fresh kill.

"I'm out of here," Johnny said, pivoting, so they wouldn't see his eyes, nor he see that theirs glistened as well.

He had a plane ticket from Logan Airport good seven days hence, but at a little before seven that evening, he was on a Greyhound cross-country bus to Oceanside, California, home of Camp Pendleton and a mixed batch of hardtack, trail mix, and moxie band of regulars, recent boots, reserves, long-timers and short-timers, that was to bulk out the First Marine Division, FMF, Fleet Marine Force in Korea.

When he arrived at the California base, he was greeted by others who, for some reason or no reason at all, had not taken their full leave time.

He sat silent and alone in the transient barracks among strangers. He was frightened and not knowing why, for the first time in his young life.

And he felt sick to his stomach; he had forgotten to say good-bye to Rags.

Chapter 13

PARRIS—A LOVELY ISLAND; THEN THE OCEANSIDE

His friends finally started trickling in to the Camp Pendleton transient barracks with most barely making it under the wire, sucking every little last drop of milk from the teat of their boot leave.

"Everyone asked what happened to Johnny, your leaving before your leave was up." Righty said. "I tried to be evasive and polite and told them all to mind their own fucking business," punctuating his words with a noogie that would have made heavyweight boxing champ Rocky Marciano wince, right on Johnny's PFC stripe, a painted black stripe on his green dungarees.

Johnny gave him a noogie back, "Hey, don't bend the stripe. I want Seabag to salute me when he sees me."

"He'll salute you with a good kick in the tail," Johnny said, giving Righty a boondocker to the butt with the side of his foot. "Three points! All bologna aside, I guess we form up starting tomorrow. We'll probably go over as a company rather than replacements 'cause the word I got is we're really kicking ass over there."

"Yah, if you believe the papers."

"I'm not that stupid," Johnny said, "but I hope we get there before it's over."

"Word is MacArthur wants the boys home by Christmas, according to the paper," Righty said, running a patch down the barrel of his M1 for the fiftieth time.

"I'm going to sack."

"Still hate the newspapers? Hey, what happened that night at home? I was at Spot Pond at seven, and you never showed." Righty said.

"I'm going to be evasive and polite," Johnny said, "like a friend of mine. Mind your own fucken' business."

"Whoa, look who's got the rag on. Why didn't you at least call your congressman and have him give me the leave time that you didn't want? Everyone figures you're trying for a Section Eight, not using up your leave."

"All I did was pull my pud an extra week," Johnny smiled, making a penis-size fist and working it back and forth in the air.

"Yaz-sur, that's fun, but Rasmus here, he like asbestos. Ass-best-us," Righty sang. "I'm comin' to the Promised Land, oh, Lordie Lord."

"Do you cross yourself when you talk like that, you sacrilegious sack of scat? Just don't stand near me during a lightning storm."

"Hey, Pointer!" Righty called out, spotting Johnny's cousin who just made it under the wire. "Another minute, and you would have been over the hill. That's an empty rack top of me."

"I almost went AWOL," said Pointer. "Dink kept telling me time after time that I could get killed for nothing, for a bunch of gooks. A bunch of little guys fighting each other is none of our business. These little guys don't have a horse's petouchee touch of anger against you and me. Dink told me it was a bunch of fat-assed politicians that moved pins on a map, and the more of us they could get killed, the more money they could make. I nearly had a nervous breakdown while at home! 'Get a Section Eight as a Loony tune,' he said. Dink said he was the only one in the world who could love me 'cause I'm so ugly. He said I could get a Section Eight for being ugly, that the government would even send me money, money for being ugly. He says ours is a great country at home. There's a piece of pie for everyone at home. He's gonna become a fireman, a firefighter, as he says. He'll get paid to sleep all night and then get up and go home. Maybe he'll start up a small daytime business like drywalling and hire some other firemen to do the work. He said he'll try and do us all a favor and give our girlfriends plenty of loving but that he can only do so much for his friends and country."

"What a guy. If he's so smart, how come he ain't rich?" Righty asked.

"He's too smart," Pointer said proudly, "but I was smarter on this one 'cause when we went out hitting the dance joints, I wore dress blues."

"We didn't get issued no dress blues," Righty said.

"My momma didn't give birth to no id-jits. First thing, I went out and bought a set at this army navy store. Anyway, I got laid, and he didn't. That made him think about joining up, but only for a second. He said our momma didn't give birth to no idiots. Anyway, he figured he could wear his firefighter's uniform and along with a fist full of money made by having other guys do drywalling for him, he'd do OK. And without getting shot at."

"What about our motorcycle? Is he taking good care of it?" Johnny asked.

"Is he! He's had so much poo tang riding back of him that on Sundays, he lets guys sniff the seat at a buck per."

"It's getting a little deep here, hold off a second while I put on my hip boots," Skinny said.

Other transients gathered around the bullshit session, and one, a tall thin farm boy from Sturgis, South Dakota, had a tiny head and ears that should have had warnings, "Stay out of high winds," on the flaps. He had "Matuzawitzski" stenciled on his dungaree front pocket followed by 1139936. He stepped forward with a cardboard box full of penny candy.

"Make your choice, boys. Mint Juleps, Bull's Eyes, nonpareils, nigger babies, jelly beans, licorice sticks," a cross section of nearly every penny sweet offered, "Tootsie Rolls, pick your favorite and, you don't even have to thank old Ma Toots. It's just the joy of giving."

As each searched the box for his favorite candy, Ma Toots smiled and laughed. Surely the nicest guy in the US Marine Corps of America, they thought.

Johnny searched for a Bull's Eye, that piece of rolled caramel that housed white frosting in the middle. It was a long search, as the box was filled to the brim. He almost settled on a Mint Julep . . . *Nah . . . they make the roof of my mouth itch* . . . Then there it was, a Bull's Eye.

Each sucked, chewed, rolled cheek to cheek, savored their favorite candy, not quite understanding that the joy of a home town treat was tempered by the fact it reminded each of his hometown.

Johnny's approach was slightly different. He unrolled the caramel in his mouth, freeing the sweeter white middle, which he allowed to melt on top of his tongue. Then he took little nips from the caramel to see how many actual bites he could get from one piece of candy. Once, when skiing down the sandbank on the farm, Pointer, Dink, and Johnny had had a contest. Dink claimed he was winner, reporting thirty-seven nips from his Bull's Eyes.

Pointer pointed at his brother and chanted, "Liar, liar, pants on fire."

Johnny had set a personal record of twenty-nine and made sure his tongue could feel each individual nip between his teeth. He didn't believe it was possible to take any more than that . . . Why do I feel . . . if someone beats me at something . . . that perhaps . . . they had to cheat . . . to do it . . .

He couldn't match the twenty-nine-nip record, partly because thinking of Rafferty's Little Store back home made him hold the candy in his mouth a little too long, softening it, making clean nips nearly impossible.

"Well, I'm gonna put the sweets away for now, boys, but old Ma Toots will have it out again. Have it out again," and he roared with laughter.

And they all smiled.

"What kind of name is Matuzawits-ski?" Pointer asked, "and how did your head get so small?"

"My name is Japanese. Although my parents tell people they are Polish. And wear a kielbasa around their necks instead of rosary beads or garlic, like you eye-talians do to prove it. The 'ski' on the end is an honorary title. My parents were both winter Olympic Games gold medal winners," he said, locking his hands behind his head, sitting back proudly.

"Where'd you get that tiny head?" It was Lace. "Find it in a haystack?"

"I wear this tiny head with pride," Ma Toots said. "Sturgis, South Dakota, where I come from, is the motorcycle capital of the world, at least the Harley world. It is where bikers come from all over the world. Where man is as leaping free as the prong horn antelope. Where the deer and the antelope play. Where seldom is heard, a discouraging word, and the skies are not cloudy all day."

Righty scratched his head in wonderment, listening to this harmless bullshitter.

"Doesn't explain how you can fit that head through the eye of a needle," Lace said.

"Sure, it does. While the bikers are wonderfully behaved for such free spirits, after all, they are doctors, lawyers, Indian Chiefs, and there are many, many wonderful ladies with dancing boots enhanced by rides over rough roads, there are a few spirited and traditional practices that take place."

"Shit or get off the pot," Lace said. "What about the tiny knob you call a squash?"

"Ah, yes, my hat size. Anyway, one of these wonderful traditional boons is that if a gentleman seeks in proper tones, a boon, from a well-endowed person of the opposite sex by utilizing the magic word to her, 'tits,' as often as not, a sweater will be pulled up or a tank top down."

"So bike broads show their knockers. How about your head?"

"Well, to my amazement, I discovered, through research, that if you followed up on the request for 'tits' with a 'please,' that as often as not, a kindly lass will take your head in hand and place said head between her fair bosom and—*voila!* The thus graced human head is compressed, and if you look closely at mine, you will see it is reshaped to that of the female boo-zummm. Boo-zummm yum!"

"My good happy bullticky, he's got more bullshit than seen at a Madrid bullring," Johnny said. "He's going to be my foxhole mate."

"Sure," Righty said, "if you don't mind getting smothered in your sleep by those wing flap ears."

"A man who loves sugar tits can't be all bad," Johnny said.

"My goodness, doesn't end there. Further research has proven after the fact that 'tits', with a 'please' after it, gives you a pass to heaven's gate. And a 'thank-you' for your fleshy smothering will at times give you a visa directly to heaven, an introduction to bifurcation."

"Bifurcation?"

"Yes. Bifurcation, that wonderful, wonderful body part that branches out, the nether land that all roads lead to."

"Jesus," Lace said, "now he's a tree surgeon."

"I only speak of the limbs of love," Ma Toots said, reaching down and buttoning the fly of his dungarees.

"I'm impressed," Johnny said. "Somehow the US God Almighty Marine Corps has signed up one of these multimillionaire evangelists we hear on the radio all the time," Johnny said, reaching in his wallet, taking out a dollar bill, and dropping it on Ma Toots's stomach.

The former sanitation worker from Sturgis placed the bill in his pocket. "Bless you, son. I will buy candy for the poor and double my purchase of Bull's Eyes. Alms for the poor, alms for those who want more Mint Juleps, Tootsies. Your dollar will name the candy."

"Jesus God Almighty," Lace said, "this son of a bitch must be a Southern Baptist."

"He fires more words per minute than a Thompson submachine gun firing does," Righty said.

The ghostly "Taps" being sounded in the distance, as lonely, lovely as the cry of the loon, signaled lights out.

Ma Toots's voice sang softly in the new dark, "Good night, sweet dreams, tomorrow is another day."

"Jesus, I'd even take Seabag's tucking us in to this guy," Pointer said, accenting his statement with a leg lifted high and a braggadocio type fart—"To the winds."

"Ho!" Ma Toots said.

"I one it," Righty said.

"I two it," Lace added.

"I three it," Ma Toots said, all the way up to Righty's "I seven it" and Johnny's "Pointer ate it.

All was still, except for a gruff giggle or two, after Pointer's denouement, "Nice."

Reveille started the three-part day. It was followed by hurry up and wait. Then "Taps" again—"Day is done."

The training and conditioning were such that they were often too tired to eat or sleep, but never too tired to bitch.

"Geeezus, you scratch your head, bring your hand down, and you're missing all your fingers" were Fat Burn's words after a day of crawling the infiltration course with live fire over their heads.

"You're lucky you've got a bony ass. Look at poor fat-assed Skinny Potts. They had to issue him a pair of pants with a bulletproof butt," Johnny said, "and when that California high noon sun set in, it got that metal seat of his so hot, we could have boiled tea. God knows it's hot enough on the piss pots we have to wear on our head."

"We're getting some kind of cover for our helmets," Tim said. "It's camou and also won't make noise when you're crawling through the bush."

"I heard that some guy was crawling the course today when he saw a rattlesnake right in front of him, stood up scared shitless, and had seven brand-new belly buttons stitched in within a split second," Rhesus said, "but later learned it was scuttlebutt."

"I thought I stuck my head into a hornet's nest when it started flying just over our heads. I plowed a furrow with my nose, I kept so low," Tim said, picking up his copy of *Walden*.

"Were you reading as you crawled under that the burst of the thirties?" Scoff Burns asked.

"What makes you ask that?" Tim asked.

"I figured you was reading the Bible. I never heard you swear in my life, yet clear as hell's bells, you said 'good Jesus.'"

"All I know," Lace said, "if there was a pack of shit-eating dogs around when that shooting started, they could have just followed me and had their fill. That's what I thought of those thirties whining over my head."

"Y'all," Ma Toots started, but was interrupted by Lace.

"Enough, since when did you all earn that Southern accent?" Lace asked, pointing a finger at Ma Toots.

"Since I was born in South Dakota, and since the day I looked south and saw the most interesting part of my body—Little 'Fella.' I named him after Pres. Franklin D. Roosevelt's little dog."

"Here goes," Righty said.

"Anyway," Ma Toots said, "I was crawling on my back trying to determine whether the bullets flying overhead were .30 caliber or bigger, when that noonday sun sort of baked the crotch of my trousers, and Little Fella started panting like a hound dog after a good rabbit chase. I started thinking 'bout some of those biker ladies and my 'please' and 'thank you' boons. I really started to get A-roused, and that's Aroused with a capital *A*. Then it hit me. And I immediately switched my imagination to my crawling bare ass in the snow with a winter wind howling up my butt-tocks. I didn't want Little Fella growing from a 'little close to the ground dachshund' to a tall in the saddle Afghan hound. At that moment of truth, I realized I could get my donk shot off. I started sobbing like a little baby with such a thought. Thank the good Lord he held his powerful quick sword from this worthless body protrusion."

"Hallelujah, brother," Lace sang.

"And you think Marie Antoinette had it hard," Johnny said.

"What do you know about her love life? Had it hard," Rhesus said.

"Not much, but I know Ma Toots was greatly enhanced by the salvation of Fella. And the arse he was attached to."

"What do you call yours?" Righty asked Johnny.

"Loafer. The girls always called it 'shooo, getaway.' How about you, Scoff?"

"Romeo."

"Get some imagination," Rhesus said.

"What do you call yours, wise ass?"

"Julie-eat, like in Romeo and Julie-eat."

"Holy mackerel, anyone or anything normal around here except the doorknobs?" Tim laughed.

"I am," Skinny said, taking his lower lip and pulling it upward over his entire nose as he roughed his hair downward to his eyebrows until only his eyes were showing. And he had crossed them.

Looking at Skinny, Johnny said, "Marry me."

"Can't, you're knock-kneed."

"So?"

"If you're heavy hung as all other Portagees, your knees are battering your ram."

"Can we elevate this conversation a couple of clicks?" Rhesus said. "Let's talk about pussy rather than peckers."

"Mary had a little pussy, its fleece was cold as snow," Lace said.

"Dum-dum," Rhesus said, "Mary had a little lamb, she also had a bear, you always saw her little lamb, but you never saw her bare."

"Boo. Third grade," Fats said.

"Hey, toothpick," Rhesus said, "you're the one they call needle dick the bug fucker."

"First grade."

"I can't believe we're going to be heading across an entire ocean to fight people we don't know," Tim said.

"We'll know 'em soon enough," Johnny said.

"Too soon."

"I wonder how long we'll be here. Combat training is usually about three to six months," Pointer said.

"Boot camp was supposed to be sixteen weeks. We got seven," Johnny said.

"They need warm bodies," Lace said.

"Not funny," Scoff said, pointing at the doorway, and when everyone looked in that direction, he swiped a pair of dress socks from Righty's rack.

"I saw that," Lace said, grabbing Scoff's wrist and twisting slightly.

"Hey, don't get excited, big guy," Johnny said. "Anyone missing anything can just check Scoff's locker box anytime."

"Yah. Fine and dandy," Scoff said. "But I'm not gonna go easy on any guy that swipes something from my locker box while checking for his own gear."

"Let's take a look right now," Lace said, increasing the torque on Scoff's wrist.

Ma Toots grabbed Lace's wrist. "Should be no problem here. Mr. Scoff obviously has a dishonest face and thus can be trusted."

"What are you talking about, Man Who Wears Elephant Ears?" Lace said.

"It's mostly people with honest faces you've gotta watch," Ma Toots said. "So why don't you just release the wrist of Mr. Robin Hood, who could be taking from the rich to give to the poor?"

"Oh, sure," Lace said, releasing Scoff's wrist followed by Ma Toots releasing Lace's as if it was a hot coal.

"The two of you are lucky I'm in a good mood," Lace said, glaring first at Scoff and then at Ma Toots.

"You're the lucky one," Righty said. "Look at Scoff's new hero. If he doesn't look like an ax murderer, I don't know who does."

Johnny took Ma Toots hand and raised it over his head. "Introducing the new Lizzie Borden, whose parents can't be here to congratulate him because of mitigating circumstances."

Tim smiled. The rest wondered what Johnny was talking about.

"Anyone for T-town this weekend?" Fats asked.

"Heard you can get anything you want there. Anything, even getting your shoes shined by a live pussy," Pointer said.

"You can also get a dick with more leaks than a lawn sprinkler," Johnny said.

"Hey, we get issued rubbers, soap, a pro kit," Lace said, "plus all the girls are virgins. Ask 'em."

"Tomorrow we get to fire the BAR, the backbone of the corps, the Browning automatic rifle, the backbone of the fire team," Righty said, turning and spraying make-believe bullets around the barracks.

"I won't be able to sleep. Five hundred shots a minute! They say if you have a good assistant BAR man feeding the magazines into it, you can fire enough shots quick enough to melt the barrel," Pointer said. "I could have used it when Dink, Johnny, and I rabbit hunted with our .22s. Wonder if they kick?"

The next day, they discovered that indeed not only didn't they kick but they also tugged your arms slightly forward, upward, and to the right. To fire straight, you fired bursts of three or four.

They weren't as impressed by the fact that a BAR could tear a man-shaped target to pieces as they were with the fact their three instructors manning BARs fed by three other instructors could play the Marine Corps Hymn on the guns.

"Could they play 'Bar, Bar Black Sheep'?" Rhesus asked.

The shooting of the weapons came easily to Johnny, Pointer, Righty, and Lace, who had hunted as kids, but not quite so easy to the others who, other than boot camp, had little experience firing.

What came with difficulty to Johnny was grenade tossing. Since the day he could walk, he had tossed tennis balls to Rags, baseballs to little brother Jazz, and footballs in pickup games when the linemen got to be the backs and the backs played the line.

The grenade tossing was done with the arm straight and stiff, and the grenade was lobbed, rather than thrown, with a snap of the wrist and follow through like a pitched baseball.

The highlight was when they sat crouched in their pits with an instructor waiting for their number to be called. When Skinny's number eleven was called, his voice cried, "Shit! Oh my god! I dropped it!"

Everyone ducked deeper in their pits and were finally relieved when they heard the grenade explode some sixty feet away. While Skinny was bemoaning, his instructor was picking up and tossing. Luckily, the instructor was ambidextrous and had a free hand to grab Skinny's belt, keeping him from bolting the protection of the pit as he tossed the explosive.

The only thing swifter than the instructor's action was his ability to not only line up hours of tossing dummy grenades for Skinny but also to line up scrub details at what appeared to be the decks of every marine barracks on the West Coast. He also arranged for Skinny to peel potatoes stacked Matterhorn high and to perform assholes and elbows field-stripping of cigarette butts on what appeared to be more turf than the African continent.

He did not make their first weekend liberty, T-Town.

The bus to the border sounded more like some sort of giant boom box of a radio, at times causing the windows to rattle.

Lace sang, "We are three *caballeros*, birds of a feather. *Aha! Si*, I'm not a gay caballeros!"

"I'm going to have two at a time, both with big cabooses," Rhesus said. "Bahama mama, for me."

"Oh Lord, help me," Righty said, rolling his Mama Mia eyes skyward. "I've saved up a caboodle of hard-ons."

"No concubinage for you, my friend," Johnny said. "I promised I'd keep you out of trouble."

"Don't do me any favors. It's my sworn duty to get a little something. I haven't touched my loved one I plan to marry. We Italians want virgins, virgins, even in our olive oil."

"You little greaser Ginzo," Lace said, trying to be funny, failing. "If you don't need no olive oil, if you fall out of one of the amphibes, you'll leave an oil slick to find you."

"Hey, Big Stoop," Righty said, pushing his jaw forward and upward, the top of his head almost reaching Lace's chin, "No one calls me a ginzo."

"Except friends," Johnny added.

"Yah, except friends," Righty said.

Lace grabbed the little marine by the wrist and started twisting.

Ma Toots grabbed Lace's wrist. "I'll check your pulse, patient, while you check my little friend Righty's."

"Ma Toots, you can call me Ginzo. But I don't need any help with Big Stoop here."

"You guys are wasting a lot of energy that could better be used with hard-ons," Rhesus said.

"I don't need no help from no one," Righty said. "It's the other guy that needs help when he crosses swords with me."

"Yah, I'm shivering," Lace said, releasing his grip and turning to Ma Toots, glaring from beneath his heavy blond eyebrows. "Yet I've got the hots at the same time 'cause this pinhead is holding my hand again."

Ma Toots released his grip on Lace's wrist. "Sorry."

"Hey, there's the border! Tijuana!" Rhesus cheered.

Ma Toots struck up song, "Mama zita, Rosalita, no ca peeta, you're the one for me. Please don't think, I'm a fool, serenading a mule—"

The next thing they knew, they were in T-Town, and there was a real-live mule. For a dollar, you could put a serape around your shoulder, put on a giant sombrero that said "MEXICO" in giant letters, sit on the mule, and have your picture taken.

"I'm going to have my picture taken and send it home," Johnny said.

"I'm gonna spend my money on real ass," Lace said.

"Here, here!" was the group cheer.

"I'm here sightseeing. I'm sending a picture to Yelena," Johnny said.

"Goody two shoes," Rhesus added.

"Maybe you could get two prints made," Righty suggested.

"Yah, my ma would like one."

"Better get three made then."

"For who?"

"Better give it some thought."

"You guys gonna sling the bologna all night, or are you gonna play a little T-ball and plan to swing the old war club at a dark-eyed lady? Stick to golf?" Rhesus asked.

"Fore," Johnny said.

"Four? And I was only gonna have two at a time," Rhesus said. "Bookend broads."

"I'm going for a six-pack," Skinny said.

"I wish I had six to pack," Fats said longingly, scratching his crotch.

"Careful you don't tear off a tie-tie," Johnny said.

"They only count the tie-ties on your skivvies in boot camp."

"Don't bet on it."

"Forget the tie-ties, they tear the skivvies right off your body here," Scoff said.

"And they eat 'em," Rhesus exclaimed.

"You guys are acting like barbarians," Johnny said, his grin appearing to swallow his ears.

"You know what Ralph Waldo Emerson said?" Tim asked.

"Of course, I do," Johnny said. "Ralphy boy said, 'Pass the kielbasa and horseradish.'"

"True," Tim said, smiling at his friend, "but he also said, 'The end of the human race will be that it will eventually die of civilization.'"

"I don't think we have to worry about that," Johnny said, climbing aboard the donkey as its keeper wrapped the serape around Johnny and placed the sombrero on his head.

Lace saluted Johnny.

"What's that for?" Johnny asked.

"Because you look like Seabag sitting on top of our boot platoon."

By the time the pictures had been taken, Johnny had lost sight of his friends.

Pushing through the crowd made up of sailors, marines, tourists, whores, and passing pimps, Johnny heard their voices, "Roll me over, Yankee soldier, roll me over, lay me down and do it again."

"Hey, you guys didn't wait for me."

"Let's hit this club here. It looks interesting," Rhesus said. "It's underground."

They walked down the ramp that led to the club cellar, which was dark.

Those that remembered their night training had little trouble getting their eyes to adjust to the dark. They merely closed their eyes tight and thought . . . black . . . and when they opened them, they could see shapes.

Most of the tables were full, and the bar was three deep.

"Tequila!" Rhesus ordered. "And skip the worms. I've already got 'em. I need this kerosene to kill 'em."

The others drank beer.

Johnny just went through the pretense of sipping his suds. He didn't believe what his mother said when she stepped on her temperance soap box: "Beer has worms in it, and they'll eat your insides."

He mostly skipped beer and the hard stuff because he didn't like the taste.

"I thought this town was wide open," Pointer said. "Other than some guy having a broad by the bubba, I see nothing special."

"It's just because you're as blind as you're stupid," Rhesus said.

"I'm not completely blind, but I am completely stupid, Dink told me when I walked in the house in uniform."

"Take a look at that table over there," Rhesus said, nodding to a nearby table at which three sailors and two women sat.

"So?"

"So look underneath. Either that lady on her knees underneath the table has lost her way to the water bubbler or is giving that swab jockey head."

"My good Jesus."

Johnny didn't know how to act or what to think on seeing the scenario under the table. He did what was necessary and pushed the woodie that's climbing upward toward his navel back down his leg and whispered to himself, "Lord, help me. I joined the marines to see the world, not someone going around it." And thought . . . *I'm actually blushing . . . Haven't done that . . . since I was in the fourth grade . . . and had to wear . . . knickers that whistled . . .* "I'm going to up anchor."

"Stick around," Pointer said. "You always said you wanted to write a book someday. Take notes."

———

231

"How in unholy Hanna do you take notes when your hands and knees are shaking?"

The darkness was cut by red lights that girls shone on their faces, sort of a catwalk show. More than one girl turned out her light and did the drinking at the bubbler deed. The voice of a young marine who looked so young that he'd have to forge his birth certificate to get into the Boy Scouts was under a table, drunk as a skunk, his head cupped by a girl sitting back in her chair, telling her cohorts he was working off his department for service rendered. "Let go my ears, I know my business," he said, as his mates cheered him on, "Hut, two, three—four and a half."

Overhead, the shaded red spot light moved smoothly, slowly to a corner, where a tall woman with hair so dark, it was a blue black, sat back, almost elegant.

Johnny felt weak when her black eyes sparked like flint on steel as she surveyed the room and stopped at him.

He looked at his shoes . . . *She's . . . too . . . beaut-i-ful . . . to . . . be . . . real . . .*

Then there they were. Her red high-heeled shoes were between his marine-issue dress shoes.

"Come, dance with me."

Her voice was surprisingly soft, throaty.

Without looking up, he shook his head no.

But when you pull liberty with your buddies, the individual doesn't always get to make the decision; it is a group vote that involves pushing and urging. He felt himself being lifted upward, unsure how hard he should fight, as he wasn't much into making himself the center of attention in public. He especially got his feet slip-sliding, the result of part of his youth when he shuffled his feet because the loose soles of your shoes flapped, and the socks were pulled downward to cover up heel openings in them.

The woman with the blue black hair that undulated like the wings of a gliding raven's pulled him to his feet and led him to the dance floor. Holding him at arm's length, she led him expertly across the dance floor to the rhythm of the waltz played by seven blaring trumpets and three soft and low violins.

The only one he had ever danced with was Yelena, but she had counted for him . . . one, two, three . . . slide . . . together step . . .

On the slow dances with Yelena, he simply held on for dear life. Although it was . . . wonderful . . . just holding on . . .

Several times, he had thought about dancing with Bernadette, feeling bad that she sat alone, not being asked to dance. Johnny did not ask her, as he was afraid what Yelena would think. She was the one who was training him to dance, to study, to talk the King's English . . . rather than American . . .

In the final run, he hadn't asked Bernadette to dance, not because he was afraid of disappointing Yelena; she had danced with other boys. Nor was he afraid of his friends, moaning "Nookie" as he danced by; he could always fix their asses later. He just didn't want Bernadette to think he was after her . . . big . . . jugs . . . *and what if I suffered . . . a . . . woodie? . . . What in hell do you do if you have a boner . . . on the dance floor? . . . Call a cop . . .*

But this tall beautiful Mexican woman was every bit the lady, even when the cat calls from his buddies urged her to "put it to him."

She just danced, looking into his eyes.

Johnny wasn't sure she even said it. It was so low. "I have never felt like this."

She pulled him closer but not so close that he would bolt.

Yet he could feel the heat. Were they dancing on some sort of rug? He could feel the static giving his body little shocks.

Then she had him close her leg between his legs. She leaned back.

The marines and sailors groaned and catcalled.

He could feel himself start to grow, expand, down there, and thought . . . Oh, good, happy . . . horse . . . shit . . . they'll destroy me back at Pendleton . . .

Then all the lights were thrown on.

He was blinded at first, but when his eyes adjusted, he could see the long dark hair had been pulled off, exposing a man's partially bald head with the blue black of a beard that the powder couldn't cover completely.

The crack of Johnny's fist sounded like a rifle shot. Johnny's dance partner did not fall at first, did not fall over backward pole axed. Instead, his eyes glazed and his legs buckled, and he seemed to unfold into himself, like air shuffled cards coming back into the pack.

Where all the Mexican bouncers appeared from was complex, but they came down on Johnny like lava.

But they didn't quite make it to him.

Righty's "Semper Fi!" led a wave of marine green that met the bouncers head on, laid a few low. Then they turned and headed out the door, hit and run after one yelled, "Merrill's raiders!"

The marines took up the rear behind the sailors who had yelled "Anchors away" and fled the scene.

It might be one thing for a navy corpsman to risk his life dragging a badly wounded marine off the field under fire, but to lose a good liberty in Sugarland by spending it in the Tijuana lockup, well, hell's bells, that was another thing.

233

They spewed out of the ramp onto the street, took a quick head count, and took off like big-assed birds.

They didn't land until they blended with the sea of green-and-white uniforms that strolled the boardwalk shopping for goodies some believed they might not see for a long time, or perhaps never again.

They quickly wiped the blood from the corners of each other's mouths and noses, straightened field scarves, and arranged their shirts so missing buttons could not be easily discerned, as nothing in the world rains on the parade of marines on leave like the shore patrol.

"I didn't join the marines to fight," Rhesus said. "I joined to make love, not war. Quickly, lead me to your whorehouse." He started chanting, "My little engine puts puta, puta, puta."

And within moments, a very dark little man in a white suit was by their side. "We take taxi. Good girls. Do much stuff. All virgin stuff."

He flagged down two cabs, and they poured in.

In the lead cab, a little man with the Fu Manchu mustache and in a dark suit rattled off promises, "Clean, all clean. Like Ivory Soap, 99 44/100 percent pure."

"It's that other half percent I worry about," Fats said. "I'm not sure I'd buy a used car from this guy."

"All first-time girls. You cop cherry."

"Sure," Rhesus said, "their cherries are pushed so far back, they can use them as taillights."

"That's right. Some girl she light. Some girl, she dark, change your luck kind. Very cheap."

"Please at least say 'inexpensive,'" Skinny said.

Pointer turned to Johnny, a shit-eating grin on his face. "We don't have to marry them, do we?"

"If you're any type of decent person, you do."

"Hey, *que sera, sera*, whatever will be, will be."

The cabby slammed on his brakes, sending those in the backseat piling into the front and those in the front into the windshield.

But because God takes cares of fools, no one was hurt.

It reminded Johnny of the time down at the Cape this old guy came into Barnstable Harbor with a giant tuna.

The Japanese would pay big bucks for it, but he had to get it to Plymouth where they did their buying, and fly the fresh tuna to Japan.

There was a truck there for just such a transportation. It already had four giants in it, loaded there by a hoist on the truck.

The old guy had a young woman with him and was pretty much puffed up with his double catch of a delicious tuna and woman and believed himself to actually be Puff the Magic Dragon.

"I ain't about to pay no big bucks to move my giant down to Plymouth. I'll move it in my station wagon."

Puff had enlisted all the able-bodied hangers-on, including Johnny and his father, to load the tuna in the back of the wagon.

They could only get a little over half the tuna in the wagon.

"No sweat," Puff the magic dragon said. He ordered his girlfriend into the wagon and hopped into the driver's seat.

He had everyone's curiosity up. No way could he drive all the way to Plymouth with only half the tuna loaded as a good steep hill could leave the huge fish slip, sliding away and skimming along the highway.

Puff floor-boarded the wagon and went screeching down the large parking lot.

What in hell was happening? was the overall question.

Then he slammed on the brakes of his tuna taxi, and the giant fish slid forward.

It worked. Well, a little bit too much.

The tuna not only slid forward but also slammed into the front seat and sent the couple forward, jamming their heads along the top of the dashboard into the windshield with the head of the tuna jammed, big eyed, in between them. The couple was uninjured. The tuna? Didn't matter much, as it would be on a flight to Japan shortly.

Now their Tijuana taxi driver slammed his brakes to miss a drunken doggie whose army uniform was half torn off his body, jamming the marines forward. Righty's eyes were wide in surprise, not unlike those of a smaller tuna, a bluefin schoolie, hooked in a gill net.

Johnny laughed like an idiot remembering the Cape Cod adventure with Puff the Magic Dragon and his tuna.

"What in hell are you laughing at?" Soupy asked.

"Nothing, just brain damage," Johnny said.

The cab unloaded, and the friends gathered behind the little man in the white suit who whispered through a partially opened door to a woman whose lipstick appeared to be smeared from ear to ear, or else she had had her throat slit.

Then Johnny, Righty, Pointer, Rhesus, and Soupy moved up behind Ma Toots, Tim, Scoff, Fats, Lace, and Skinny, attempting to peek through the partially open door into the room.

But before they were allowed in, the woman with the ear-to-ear lipstick looked them over from head to foot.

"She's checking to see if we're wearing ties," Johnny said.

"Tie-ties," Rhesus said.

"In! Come!" lipstick lady said.

"Yah, your income all right. I hope she's only in charge of swabbing the head," Rhesus said.

"Hey, ugly or not, she makes plenty," Fats said.

"She doesn't make near what Rhesus and Boattail made on the pond lilies I picked at Buckman's," Johnny said.

"We put a little something in a bank account for you. So make sure I get back safely," Rhesus said.

"Hey, man, it's every man for himself in Korea," Scoff said.

"Who said anything about Korea? I'm talking about this whorehouse."

"You going in, Johnny?" Righty asked.

"Nah. It's too, well, shabby."

Tim smiled at Johnny. "Idealism increases in direct proportion to one's distance from the problem."

"Emerson?"

"No. Galsworthy, John," Tim said.

"Galsworthy, balls worthy, I want to dip my wick in some of that salsa," Rhesus said.

Skinny said, "I want to dip the entire candle."

Tim, Righty, and Johnny stayed outside as their friends went in.

"We better go in," Johnny said. "You know these guys could get in trouble in a confessional."

"They're big boys," Righty said.

"I don't know," Tim said. "You know Rhesus picked himself up a German Luger."

"Didn't know. What for?" Johnny said.

"Seems he read James Jones's *The Pistol* and wants to make sure he has that one extra card in his hand to play in combat."

"Yah," Righty said. "The Rhesus always had an extra card up his sleeve. Don't you monkey with the monk is his byword."

"We better go inside. I'm sure they have some sort of a waiting room," Johnny said.

"Waiting room? This ain't no maternity ward," Righty said.

The three laughed like the silly little kids they had been a few months before.

"Yah, it's more like a dentist's waiting room," Righty said, "except the patients there are waiting to have one filled and two pulled."

"Corn," Johnny said, giving Righty a noogie, as Tim opened the door to the house but was immediately stopped by the madam.

"No come-ah in-a without-a knocking."

"We wait inside-a," Johnny said.

"I didn't know you spoke Spanish," Righty said.

"It's-a the same-ah as Italiana."

The three stepped around the woman who was built as close to the floor as a duck, weighed well over two hundred pounds, and despite being well into her fifties, had a small lovely face free of double chins and wrinkles.

Righty whispered to Johnny, "She must have had a head transplant."

The women not doing business sat around the room chatting like a flock of feeding flickers, but while the meadow woodpeckers looked alike, the women did not. All had eyes as dark as inkwells, their variety of hair colors was jet black to scarecrow orange. They were dressed in everything from G-strings and bras that appeared to be made out of soaked nose tissue to a floor-length, high-necked gown. And everything in between. One wore a short-short skirt like the one that got Bob Hope kicked off the radio for saying, as Righty remembered it, "If it got any shorter, she'd have two extra cheeks to powder and one more head of hair to trim."

The three friends were looked over from toe to head. Tim's height, well over six feet, and broad shoulders, were in contrast to Righty's narrow shoulders and diminutive height, but his swarthiness was more than a match for Tim's coffee-bean coloring. However, the ladies' eyes immediately turned to Johnny.

Righty said, "Here in this house, I stand taller than Tim, as here, a man's height is measured as he stands on his dollar-filled wallet, and his erection is on the top of his head!"

He commenced to wave what appeared to be a thick wad of bills, made thicker by the multiple blank papers he had cut into bill size and inserted between the real green stuff.

The women flocked to Righty as he danced around like a bantam rooster, singing, "I'm cock of the loft!" Then he pushed them off with "I'm queer. My money is for the church and little boys," and he wet his eyebrows with his little finger to emphasize his pretended preference.

Meanwhile, Tim's words were not truly understood, "No thank you. No thank you."

A young girl about fourteen approached Johnny and asked him, "You like to go bang-bang, sir?"

"I think she means 'you like to do the dirty deed, buddy?'" Righty said.

"No speakee English," Johnny said, giving her a smile that left her warm, even though in her two years of working there, she had seen every look from that of Chief devil Mephistopheles to the Archangel Gabriel.

She put aside her coy whore come-on and gave him a young girl's smile and looked him in the eyes and said, "Then you don't understand this, Mr.

Speak-Only Greek, but I think I would break all the rules here for you. Give you a kiss. What language do you speak if you don't speak English?"

"Well," Johnny said, "I speak everything but Greek."

"Then you speak Spanish," she said, lifting her long skirt just above her ankles, turning in a circle as she did a flamenco stomp.

"That's Greek to me," he said, sitting down.

"And you accused me of corn," Righty said.

"May I sit down?" Tim asked the madam.

"Don't give me-ah that snotty 'may I,' big man,'" she said, turning her back and walking through a wool navy blanket that served as a door.

"Rosa." It was the young girl.

"Johnny."

She smiled.

He returned her smile, his thoughts were questions . . . *Why . . . here . . . probably caught . . . a tiny field mouse . . . like Bernadette . . . Rosa and Bernadette . . . tiny field mice . . . caught in the giant rat trap . . . we call life . . . Wow . . . when did I get a transfusion? . . . From Plato . . .*

"Everyone get their fuckin' hands up!" It was Rhesus's voice.

He had a gun in his hand and was waving it around like a bird feeder suspended by a wire blowing in the wind.

He was bare ass, except for the handgun.

Johnny was speechless, never having seen a bare-ass man with a hard-on in one hand and a handgun in the other.

Finally, finding his voice, Johnny demanded, "What the unholy fuck are you doing!" Johnny demanded.

Rhesus paid no attention to him as he pushed aside each of the blanket doors to the little rooms, ordering the occupants out and into the main room.

Everyone stood against the wall, including all his friends, except Johnny, who said, "You pie-ass drunk, put that down, or I'll shove it up where the sun doesn't shine!"

"You might know it's some asshole jarhead," said a sailor who had nothing on but the black scarf all sailors wore.

A second sailor, naked, except for his white cap, which he wore low over his eyes like Popeye the Sailor Man, said, "Jesus, Joseph, and Mary, it takes me ten minutes to get the thirteen buttons undone on my pants, no easy task with a hard-on like a battleship's big guns, and this asshole comes along and spoils it."

"Shut the fuck up," Rhesus said. "I've had it. I was getting laid, and I happen to look back between my legs, no easy job, as it's like looking through a maze of stalagmites hanging between my legs, and I see someone lifting my wallet out of my pants that are hanging on the other end of the bed."

"Stalactites," Tim said. "Stalagmites are the ones coming up from the floor of the cave. Stalactites hang down."

"She's right, she's right," Rhesus said, appearing to get more intoxicated as he waved the gun around.

"Who's what?"

"The whore mistress, Tim, when she called you uppity," Rhesus said.

"I wouldn't run with that one too far," Johnny said.

"Hey, John. It's me. Rhesus. I've got the gun. I give the orders. I just want my wallet. It has everything the eagle shit last pay day in it."

"We'll all throw in a couple of bucks," Fats said, his skinny body shaking as Rhesus turned to him, causing the gun to make circles around the top of Skinny's head like some sort of halo.

"Jesus, Rhesus, I just came here to get a little."

"Yah. I know. I'm sorry. I shouldn't drink," he said, lowering the Luger.

His friends relaxed just a bit, but were snapped to attention again when it was brought up again, "But I need my wallet. It was a graduation present. Luckily, I had my revolver . . ."

"Automatic, actually, a semiautomatic," Tim said.

"Oh, shit, I get no respect," Rhesus said. "Luckily I had my pistol in one hand, while I had my pecker in the other, otherwise, the son of a bitch who copped my wallet wouldn't have gotten away. I'm fishing everybody."

"I've got nothing to hide," the bare-ass Ma Toots said.

The sailor wearing his hat like Popeye said, "Hey, let all of us doing the dirty deed go back to the sack."

"Hey, I make the decisions around here. Take off the fucken' beanie."

"Make me."

"The beanie or the balls," Rhesus said, lowering the gun.

"The beanie," the sailor said as the cap came off.

"Wise decision. You nearly had your brains shot off."

"You wouldn't be so brave if you didn't have that gun."

"Yah, you're right, but I got the gun, mop-ass. And it's a beauty."

"Mr. General Marine Man, we will take your beauty." It was a police officer.

Rhesus was surprised that so many of the Tijuana police could have slipped into the house behind him, and the gun was taken easily from him. He was grabbed by both arms and ushered toward the door after his head was slammed into the wall like a battering ram.

"I'll give you ten bucks if you let me kick him in the balls," the sailor in the cap offered.

Ma Toots spoke for the first time since hearing Rhesus's "Everyone get their fucken' hands up." Crossing his eyes, while wiggling his ears, he looked at the sailor with the hat on and said, "Hey, sailor boy, give me the ten bucks, and I will personally kick his ass back at Pendleton."

Once outside, Rhesus's buddies formed a circle around him and the police bringing him in.

"Ola, gringos, you're all under arrest," the officer in charge said as they all drew their weapons.

The Big Tree Gang was ushered into a large van that was empty, except for a lone paratrooper who was prone on the floor, trying to do the dog paddle in his own barf.

Johnny looked first at the swimmer, then at Rhesus, who looked even more naked without the handgun drawing attention away from his nudity and declared, "War is hell."

"How can you be funny at a time like this?" Soupy asked. "We're chin deep in whale shit and being put into a jug where a giant egg beater will kicko-a-poo."

They were all tossed into a large cell at the Tijuana jail, except the smell-bad paratrooper, who was dragged into a second cell after one officer accepted a two-dollar bribe from a naked Rhesus.

"Where in hell were you hiding that bill?" Johnny asked his naked friend, laughing so hard, he could feel the warm water trickle down his thighs.

The cell door was slammed behind them. They watched as the officer opened the top drawer in the one desk, a rickety thing that didn't look unlike a rabbit hutch, Johnny thought, and placed the Luger in it.

"Not bad here, sort of like the Ritz," Righty said, looking around. There were no seats and only a single hole in the floor for relieving themselves.

"I should have brought my entrenching tool to dig a slit trench," Johnny said.

"How in fuck can you be funny when we're in jail?" Soupy said, his head in his hands.

"Hey, the good news is," Fats said, his thin body still trembling, "the corps doesn't like troublemakers, and we'll be sent home. Drummed out. Section Eights."

"Yah, we'll be sent home all right," Skinny said, his once-chubby now-muscular body tightening, "by way of Portsmouth."

"I like New Hampshire."

Ma Toots said, "It's not a Winni-pee-saukee vacation, dipstick. It's a place where every sadistic swab jockey and grunt in the navy and corps is sent as a guard, and every morning for breakfast, they flatten your balls in a hot waffle maker."

"Without any syrup added," Scoff said, swiping what passed for the toilet paper and tucking it under his shirt.

"We'll be in double deep doo if we don't get back in time for roll call," Fats said.

"Sure as shit the Mex will hold us for court," Soupy said.

"They didn't even book us yet," Righty said, shaking the cell door. "Book us, you gook bastards."

"I think they're called spics," Ma Toots said, as the giant grabbed the cell door and gave a real shake.

It opened.

"They never locked it," Ma Toots said. "Let's hightail it!"

He led the charge toward the door.

"Wait!" It was Tim's voice. "We'll never get Rhesus back across the border bare assed."

They all looked at their drunken friend.

"Not while he's naked as a jay bird. Whatta we do?" Soupy asked, hunching his shoulders and putting his hands out to the side, face up.

"Let's kill the stupid son of a bitch," Skinny said.

"Yah, he caused all this shit," Soupy said.

"Wait. There's the paratrooper. Strip the doggie and get the clothing on Rhesus."

"I ain't wearing no doggie shit," Rhesus said. He kept repeating this as they held him down and dressed him in the trooper's clothing.

They remembered little about how they got back to the base, except their trying to keep Rhesus in his soldier's clothes from returning to the Tijuana jail to get his Luger.

The next morning, when the gunny in charge of the transient barracks saw them, he just shook his head. "Even Chesty Puller wouldn't want you sorry sacks of shit. Even for range targets."

Chapter 14

BILLY WEIGEL'S TWIN SCREWS

"What an ark," Johnny said, climbing upward into the ship that had the coloring and wear history of an old car muffler.

"Noah really fucked up on this one," Righty said, looking around at the green-clad marines that streamed double file up the gang planks boarding the troop ship. "We're all the same animal."

"No," Tim said, "each one of us is an individual, fighting for the freedom that will keep us that way."

All within earshot laughed.

"What's with the laughter, Johnny?" Tim asked.

"Tim, take a look down at the dock. What do you see? Never mind that, what don't you see? You don't see a band or any people. Remember the flicks of them boarding to go fight in Europe during World War II with thousands of people cheering, bands playing?"

"Yes."

"Well, patriotism appears to be a little bit out of fashion. No one understands anything as old fashioned as patriotism. It's flat out of fashion. Everyone thought you were making a ha-ha, a joke."

"You're old fashioned too. You said if we don't fight them there, we'll fight them in our country, or our town."

"Tim, understand I'm sneaky enough to hide it, my patriotism, me lad. The next thing you know, they'll be taking the Frenchie face off the Statue of Liberty and putting yours in its place."

Johnny studied Tim's dark-chocolate face . . . *They won t let him piss in my toilet . . . in the capitol of the country of world freedom . . . Well, no one in this world will keep me from pissing where I want . . . even that one that said blacks only . . . Cheez . . . his natural coffee color . . . is the same hue . . . as the tan we were always trying to get . . . at Revere Beach . . . and on our ballicky boulder . . . at Duck Pond . . .*

"John, you're the one wrapped in the American flag that is responsible for me heading up into the bowels of this boat."

"Better say ship, not boat, or you'll be climbing down the line over the rat guard with a rat trap on your private, Private."

"How come they named this tub after some guy in the army?" Scoff asked no one in particular as he joined some two thousand other marines and a Puerto Rican army reserve unit. It was hoped the *Gen. William Weigel*, a twin screw troop ship, could cut several days off the trip from San Diego to Japan.

"Probably because it won't float," Soupy said, his face becoming even more hang dog as he chewed on his own words. "Jesus, I was stupid enough to get talked into this by Johnny who said if we join the marines, we wouldn't be cooped up in some submarine or airplane. We could have our feet on good old terra firma when we win our medals. This tin lizzy is a terror firma all right and an in-firma."

"I think it's a banana boat," Rhesus said. "Look at those monkeys looking us over." He gave the crew members a middle-finger salute.

One of them yelled down, "Did you mangle your fingers when you tried to pull your head out of your ass, jungle bunny?" His buddies scratched under their arms like itchy apes. One even jumped up and down, giving a "Hmm-hmm hymm-hymm, hurrrrr."

Soupy held his arms out like helicopter blades and spun around in order to have the helicopter blade action to accompany the "wop-wop."

"OK, let's knock off the crap," Johnny said.

Soupy brushed off Johnny's corporal stripes. The rest of his buddies wore the single stripe of a private first class, except Pointer, whose sleeve was bare, indicating he was a buck private, the lowest of the lowly whale shit.

"What kind of geese don't fly?" Righty asked.

"Port-o-geese," Soupy sang out.

The shorter marines coming up the gangplank, being piped aboard by whistles from fellow marines acting like boatswains, paid a double boarding initiation fee. Their field transport packs, which contained every piece of issued gear other than dress uniforms, started above the head and carried below the calves, rapped away at the Achilles heels. Some carried the combat pack, which could be detached from the top of their field transports in their hand.

"I'd rather have a Pekinese biting at my heels than this thing," Righty said.

"Hey, you don't have to lug all those records," Pointer said.

"Talk to Johnny about that," Righty said. "He carries the Victrola."

"You've got a mind of your own."

"Hey, he's bigger than me, and I'm a coward. Besides, I might need him to save my life," Righty said. "Who else but Johnny would save a wop like me?"

Rhesus made the "wop-wop" sound of helicopter blades, smiling at Johnny, who had a Victrola perched on the very top of his pack. Its double bend crank handle, when wound, provided record player power. Rhesus said it looked like a miniature tank with a crooked cannon.

"You're so dumb, you reinvented the word 'stupid.' You're actually afraid of nothing," Fats said, providing a light noogie to Righty's helmet. "Knock-knock, who's there? Nobody home."

"Come on, let's get on this rub a dub-dub, two thousand men in a tub," Johnny said, "so we can play a little Glenn Miller."

Johnny looked down. There was no Glenn Miller music coming from the dock below. There were no proud waving families, little brothers or girlfriends . . . *Maybe the navy gave them the wrong anchors aweigh time . . . Where have all our . . . flag wavers gone? . . .* Johnny closed his eyes. Imagined Yelena, a single tear . . . red . . . white . . . and . . . blue . . . rolling down her cheek as she waved tiny American flag after flag. Someone was handing them to her, but the flags hid that person's face. Both the flags that Yelena waved and the ones handed her by—someone . . . *It's . . . Bernadette . . . but why would she be here? . . . She already told me . . . thank you . . . just for my knocking . . . that asshole . . . on his asshole . . .*

He turned to Righty. "Cheezzz, it's bad enough I'm swearing all the time now, but Christ, I'm even fuckin' swearing in my thoughts. That's bullshit. I need some succor." He reached behind him and patted the Victrola on his back and then patted the records on Righty's.

"Got anything besides Miller? I'd rather have some bebop," Fats said, "something you can jitterbug to. Bebop, I love you baby. Bebop, I don't mean maybe."

"Great, you can dance with Rhesus," Johnny said, giving Fats a noogie on the butt of his M1. "You know Glenn Miller was a patriot?"

"You mean he hid behind the stone walls at Lexington and Concord?" Rhesus kidded.

"He took great risks during World War II playing all over the front for the guys. And he was in a plane flying low over the English Channel. It exploded and disappeared. They think some crippled Flying Fortress or

Liberator had to unload its bombs and didn't know the Glenn Miller band was flying below them."

"Did you make that up?" Righty asked.

"God's honest truth."

"Maybe sitting back and listening to Miller isn't so bad after all," Fats said, rolling his eyes in Rhesus's direction.

"Sure," Rhesus said, "just in case you don't have any sleeping pills to give us when the gook artillery is being laid in."

"Will you sewing circle ladies stow the chatter and get up that ladder?" It was Gunny Murphy, a twenty-year man. He had waded ashore on Tinian and Tawawa as a frightened kid buck-ass private. Now an old warhorse at thirty-two; a wolf-of-war urging what could have passed for lambs heading to the little old veal maker.

Murphy looked down to make sure he had his most important appendage, his Thompson machine gun . . . *It sure isn't . . . a shepherd's crook . . . They'll do OK . . . I was one of them at one time . . .*

"Whatdagut, money in the bank, talkin' to yourself, Gunny?" Righty asked.

"Nah. Well, sort of, a little, very little, none, but I'm gonna buy a boat and charter fish when I finish my twenty," Murphy answered, looking them over again, then said to himself, "A bunch of virgins waiting for that one great first fuck-over called combat."

"You got us worried, Gunny," Rhesus said, "talking to yourself."

"Waddam I gonna do, talk to you idiots?"

Then the long climb up the gang plank ended and the even more difficult one, climbing the ladders downward to their racks while outfitted in field transport packs into the bowels, of the *Billy Weigel.*

The ship's crew had had the ladders clean, white glove clean, but the oils, sweat, and filth of many hands built up a slippery veneer. It meant those who didn't employ the old mountain climbers' method, always three appendages grasping, either two legs and an arm, or two arms and a leg, could take a leg-breaking spill. They could get in more trouble by slipping a foot into the face of someone descending just below them and, in return, getting a rap in the testicles with the business end of a rifle.

The transport packs seemed to be continuously attacked by evil spirits that did chin-ups on them, pulling down on shoulders already sore from hours of wearing the strangling straps.

"Jesus, can you imagine having a big set of boo-zooms and a bra strap pulling down on your shoulders all day long?" Soupy said, his hangdog eyes taking on a little glint of merriment.

The chatter continued as they headed down compartment after compartment.

"I wished you hadn't talked tits," Rhesus said.

"Yes, we know," Johnny said. "You were breast-fed until you were eighteen."

"Sure, but I didn't start until I was sixteen."

"Can we talk about something besides jugs, boobs, knockers, tits, and suckees?" Rhesus said pontifically.

"Like what?" Scoff asked, working a hanky out of the back pocket of the guy in front of him, wiping his brow, and tucking it in his own back pocket. Then remembering how easy it is to swipe one from a back pocket, he put it in his front one. "Like what, Rhesus?"

"Well, we could talk about pussy."

"One-track minds, tsk, tsk," Johnny said. "Is there anything else in the world?"

"There's booze," Lace said.

"That's a start," Johnny said.

"I've got a chopped and souped-up Model T Ford back on the farm," Pointer said.

"I collect stamps and am going to be on the lookout for them in every country we visit," Tim said.

"Tim, how in hell did you get to be a high-scoring, 'outrun 'em or run over 'em' football scat back, talking like some fruitcake that snuck out from under the Christmas tree?" Righty asked, laughing and giving his friend a loving noogie to the nose.

"How do you nigras get those wide nostrils," Lace said, "by putting a claw hammer up there and pulling the handle down?"

"How would you like a couple of extra assholes reamed, you rebel touch hole?" Johnny said, glaring up at the tall Southerner.

"I didn't know you loved me, boy. Someone surely should have warned me about you. Maybe one of you other boys from Bars-ton could have warned old Lace: beware of Bars-ton Greeks bearing grease."

They all laughed. Even Johnny had to laugh at that one. The hammer and claw bit was forgotten with a "consider the source" wave of the wits.

"You guys seem in a pretty good mood, but the old *Gen. Billy Weigel* will take care of that," Gunny Murphy said.

"What's this two-thousand-ton banana split holder gonna do, give us a tum-tum ache?" Rhesus asked.

On the bottom deck, they were greeted by bunk after bunk set on top of each other, only inches between each. Giant, dark-green slabs of bread were waiting for the meat to be stuffed in, a la Dagwood Bumstead sandwich.

"You're lucky you lost weight, Skinny, otherwise you'd be wedged in there tighter than a fart trying to escape from between chubby cheeks," Rhesus said.

"Who cut one?" Pointer asked, now climbing downward as one hand was over his nose. "I bet it was you, Soupy, you pig. Farting while we're in flight like helpless bluebirds."

"I'll only give the initials of who cut it—it was Tim Yanders," Rhesus said, knowing Tim would not lower himself to defend the honor of his tail section.

"Well, young George Washington," Johnny said, "blaming others for his buttocks butt-talk and egg crackle."

"Corn, John, pure corn," Fats said, the smile on his thin face was that of a little simian's.

"Pheeew. PU! Pee-fuckin-yoo. Probably the same person that cut one on the way down here, and I had to make it down the ladder with both hands squeezing my nose," Pointer said.

"The stinking son of a turd should have a plug put in his ass," Soupy moaned, his real gag noises mixed in with the fake ones of his buddies.

Even the real fartee, Pointer, entered a fake gag and nose holding.

"Pointer, you farted. You want to get some innocent bystander killed?" Rhesus said.

"Can't we give Pointer a rack near a port hole and wedge his ass out it?" Ma Toots asked.

"Why don't we all just cut his ass into grits and set up a chum line for the sharks?" Lace said.

"It was Johnny who let fly," Pointer said.

"Now you turn on your own flesh and blood," Johnny said, pounding his cousin's arm and demanding, "Come on, farm cuz, let's hear your 'the mail must get through, the mail must get through, the mail must get through.'"

"What's the mail bit?" Lace asked.

"When someone cuts a purple poots-en-popper, he has to say 'The mail must get through' three times, whistle three times, and rap on wood three times. Until you do, you get pounded."

They all started pounding on Pointer, his arms, his butt, his pack, and his helmet.

"The mail must get through, the mail must get through, the mail must get through," Pointer said, rapping on his head three times in lieu of real wood, but found it impossible to give the required three whistles; he was laughing so hard.

Everyone stopped pounding and started laughing at Pointer's inability to get out the required whistles, attempts that ended up as just wind blowing through his lips.

"All I know is when we get to Korea—doesn't it sound like 'gonorrhea'?—I'm sleeping in a rack and then a foxhole, located megamiles from el stinko Pointer," Soupy said.

"Listen to the Campbell Soup kid, who soaked in a bathtub full of it to get rid of the skunk smell and still reeked of woods pussy even after that," Scoff said.

"Not me," Johnny said. "I want to be in the same foxhole. No enemy in his right mind would come near you. Check out this scenario—the gooks are coming up the hill, we're all out of ammo, the entire company. What do we do? We feed Pointer a can of Friends Baked Beans. He digests same, aims his ass at the enemy, and lets fly with bandoleer after bandoleer of rapid-fire farts, which the gooks mistake for heavy machine gun fire that stank. They back down the mountain, pleading, "Merican GI Joe, no more fartee-fartee, pleeze.'"

"This is gonna be some trip," the gunny said. "Did the Crops check you guys out of some funny farm? Let's get with the action, stow the gear and stow the clap trap."

There was no storage room, and the packs, M1s, helmets, and web belts, were hung from the racks like so many bodies from a gallows.

The bunks were six high, and it meant continuous climbing over each other.

"If I buy the big one, make sure I get my own grave, a huge hole with plenty of room," Soupy said, nearly bringing himself to the edge of tears imagining his own death.

"If you buy the farm, can I have your Daniel Boone skunk cap, Soup?" Rhesus said.

"Fuck you and your kangaroo too."

"Bestiality will get you a free walk home, even right out of combat, out of the corps," Rhesus said.

"Where can I steal a sheep and get out?" Scoff asked no one in particular.

"You don't need one of the innocent beasts. Just let some gold bar–wearing ninety-day wonder, catch you giving our little monk Rhesus a kiss—that's worth a Section Eight," Soupy said, making gagging sounds in accompaniment.

"Anyone want to hear a little Glenn Miller? Give me one of those platters, Righty," Johnny said, winding up the old RCA Victrola he'd unhitched from the top of his pack. Righty undid the small pack that was heaped on top of his field transport pack and pulled out a record and handed it to his old Eastward Ho school buddy.

"I can't take this torture. I'm gonna set up a poker game," Rhesus said.

"You got that tailor-made dungaree jacket, the one with the bell-bottom cuffs?" Johnny asked.

"You know me better than that," Rhesus said, smiling, as he pulled an ace of spades from his sleeve.

"You better remember, your playmates are going to be carrying KA-BARs and .45s. Those guys who ruminate about your wrongdoings in cards will find your rack and stuff a hand grenade up your sleeping ass and pull the pin," Soupy said.

"Better play it a little careful," Johnny said.

"Yah, thanks for saving my life."

"I wonder when in hell chow down takes place?" Pointer asked.

"Who gives a good rat's ass?" Scoff said. "The food is probably the pits."

"Shipboard food is supposed to be sensational," Pointer said.

"Yah, but that's what they feed the swab jockeys, not us," Scoff said.

"Then why do you have three of those chow punch cards they issued us?" Soupy asked.

"Just so those three dog faces I relieved the chow cards from won't get ptomaine."

"Hey, what's that noise?" Pointer asked, looking around wide-eyed.

"They just started up the diesels to let them warm up," Tim said, looking up from his copy of Tom Sawyer.

Johnny looked up from his book despite the fact author-adventurer Richard Halliburton had just swum the Hellespont and for his next act would be to secret himself in a Harem, with the undisputed fact he could end up as one of their eunuch guards if detected. Johnny said, "I'm seasick."

Everyone laughed.

"This tub just started its engines," Fats said.

"No, not from the *General Weigel*, from swimming the choppy waters of the Hellespont."

"We're headed to the point of hell," Soupy said.

"This Hellespont is in the Dardanelles."

"Oh, la de da, it's now library hour. So you read a map once," Lace said, then turning to Pointer, "I'm looking at grits and chitterlings, my little fart flowing, shark porgy bait chum."

"And who thought that all poets came from Amherst?" Johnny smiled.

Then the engines that powered the giant twin screws were under way, as was the poker game, the letter writing, the reading, the never-ending rifle cleaning until the weapons shone like the sun on the sea, the bayonets sharpened until the blades could, as the boys said, split a cunt hair so it could be divided up between two hungry jarheads for nourishment.

And they steamed out of San Diego Harbor and into two beautiful days of calm seas, sunshine, and acres of dolphins. They sighted in heavy and light machine guns, Thompsons, M1 rifles and carbines and BARs at targets towed behind the friendly *General*. At times, a herring gull bit the water after flying into a bullet from a company sniper. They dragged lines with their dungaree clothing tied to them off the fantail. This was not so much to get their recent issue clean as to give that salty look that all marines strive for, even when there were boots getting hair shaved off at Parris Island or the San Diego Recruit Depot.

Scoff was happy he had three chow down punch cards, two of which were kindly donated without the previous owners knowing about the transfer. He was eating for escape, solace, and succor. Besides, the chow down was good. So good, he stashed his porgy bait until the tiny corners of his pack could not hold another morsel.

On the third day, the dolphin disappeared, as did the sun and, finally, the flat sea. The waters later were replaced by whitecaps that at first were merely the foamy suds on the top of a good beer, then became the mouths of lathered-up pit bulls, and finally, the giant waves were toothy sperm whales, having no mercy on this shipload of kindly young Geppettos.

Now every time Scoff looked at his three chow cards, he became violently ill. And he was joined one by one, two by two, and then platoon by platoon of barfing marines and soldiers.

Then the weather got rough, junkyard dog-foaming fierce.

The USS *General William Weigel* itself became seasick as its bow plowed into the ocean and its fan tail shot into the sky, allowing the twin screws to shake the ship like a dog shaking a rag.

The two thousand warriors became helpless subhumans who bounced around in the leftover World War II Liberty Ship's stomach, and intestines were strangled by a peristalsis that squeezed the very life out of them, first in the form of vomit. Once empty, the dry heaves followed, and last came the fine sprays of stomach blood and thin silver strings of stomach lining dredged up when the sump pumps of the human body could pull up contents.

The toilets in the heads of each deck also got sick, plugged up, then retched out the water and its human flotsam and jetsam. The spew streamed down the ladders from deck to deck, collecting more heavings, finally settling on the very bottom deck, forming a nearly knee-deep pond that would make a goat heave. The top hatches were battened down, not so much to keep the sea out or from sick soldiers being washed overboard, but rather to keep those so very sick from jumping overboard and drowning, for relief.

With this in mind, the brass ordered that all ammunition be collected and secured. No one was going to escape duty by emptying his brains against the bulkhead. But rather than becoming suicidal, they were becoming murderous. A few thought about suicide, but that was quickly dismissed because those entertaining it believed the chicken shit corps would follow them to hell where they would be made to scrub the cerebellum gray matter off the bulkheads. They knew from swapping sea stories with combat marines that the stubborn brain crap could stick to anything like a fly to flypaper.

The partially and mostly sick tried to offer comfort to the very sick, but the reaction moan was always the same, "Leave me alone, please, or I'll kill you."

On the fifth day, only a skeleton crew left with some stomach lining made it to the galley.

Johnny was one of those few that stood at the waist-high, long, steel tables.

And he wasn't feeling much better than a kitten in a burlap bag tossed over a railing into a river, but he maintained his strength by remembering what his father told him when they used to row a couple of miles out of Salem Willows. They mostly fished hand lines on the bottom for those cellar-feeding, white flaky flounder.

They had also cast lead jigs into the schools of porgy that swam by, snagging them, schools that were miles long and ten feet deep. They cut the porgy bellies into shiny strips and cast for the sleek mackerel.

The oily mackerel that both sets of grandparents loved would strike the porgy strips like Joe DiMaggio lacing a fast ball down the middle of the plate.

But when the rolling swells got big, they were even tougher to take than the fiercer appearing choppy waves, his father would break out the Saltines and Mine's homemade bread, and they both would munch. "It helps to hold the stomach in place," his father said.

The old Liberty Ship took to more than just heel and toe, bow under, fantail out; bow up, fantail under, teeter board dizzying action, it became a binnacle and yawed left and right as well as up and down, a rampaging bull.

He was the last of his group making it to the galley. Pointer had given in two days before, pointing blame at Rhesus who, when feeling well, had a piece of raw bacon he slid in and out of his mouth, while smiling at Pointer.

Pointer's only consolation was that on one lurch of the ship, Rhesus had swallowed the raw bacon and became immediately sick, beating Pointer to the only shit can not overflowing.

Righty had hung tough. "I'm sicker than a bull with its balls caught in a barbwire fence," not wanting to desert his friend.

Lace as well had held on until the day before, the ninth day of debauching weather; held on the grounds, "There ain't no Yankee can outlast even the poorest white trash of a Rebel."

"This isn't no civil war bit," Johnny had told Lace. "Eat some bread. Stuff it in. Eat crackers."

Lace declined, an act punctuated by two silver strips of stomach lining that suddenly appeared in the corners of his mouth.

The others had exited by a variety of methods from grand to gross.

"I joined the marines so I could be on God's good ground" were Tim's words as he wandered from the chow hall, head high, hoping to make it out of everyone's sight before putting his hands over his mouth and filling them.

Scoff left with the lament, "Someone swiped my stomach," and then he caught his Vesuvius eruptions in a Colgate college T-shirt swiped from the second lieutenant that headed up the heavy weapons platoon.

Skinny left off all eating with the reasoning, "I already lost forty pounds in boot and Pendleton."

While Fats said, "I got to go practice my part. They want me to replace William Powell in the next *Thin Man* movie."

Rhesus stayed in character, "I bet you two to one I'll be back at the next meal."

Soupy was most elegant when he barfed himself from galley to rack. "It is a sad day for humanity, not fit for man nor beast."

Johnny stood with his feet set wide apart, relaxing one knee, then the other as the ship yawed and played its giant stacked deck game of teeter board.

The SOS, "shit on a shingle," on his tray looked nearly as gray as the faces of those both sick and not quite sick, a bit like Pointer's face when he looked up from his rack as Johnny left for chow-down and wished him "Bon appétit."

It was a big wave that buffeted the ship and sent Johnny's metal tray sliding away from him. His stomach was flipped like a flapjack.

"Righty, do you feel as fantastic as I do? I wish I were a stinking camel.

I hear they have two or three stomachs. Then I could switch to a good one when one went sour."

"Look at the dark side. If you were a camel and all your stomachs couldn't hack it . . ."

"And I only had one throat to toss three stomachs out of."

It wasn't his runaway tray that got to Johnny. It was when the ship lurched in the opposite direction between a giant wave trough and his tray slid back to him; it was complete with the stomach contents of several other marines the tray had traveled past.

He wanted to cry out the same kind of "oh shit" that General Custer's troops muttered, but his mouth was full of the first eruption of warm bile.

Oh . . . shit . . .

Everyone—the sea took no prisoners—was feeling more than a touch mean. Thankfully, they were too ill to voice this feeling in any type of violence.

Thus, it should have been no surprise when they pulled into Yokohama Harbor after nearly two weeks at sea and the lines were being tossed to the dockworkers below, that a mean cheer and angry growl accompanied the fall down a ladder by a young officer, who obviously broke at least one leg and an arm.

The cheer grew in crescendo as others out of sight of the accident learned of it.

The colonel in charge of the marine replacement-battalion, on viewing the reaction, turned to the light colonel beside him and said, "If I could get these boys into action today, they would mop ass from Pusan to Peking, and maybe all the way to Moscow for good measure."

The steps down the gangplank put their feet on Japanese soil.

Most had never been outside their own state. When they finally got to travel, it was from one base to another, then to a country fifteen thousand miles from home.

They were getting to see the world, but mostly entombed inside a couple of inches of steel.

Their introduction to Japan was a man dressed in a World War II Japanese army uniform, sitting on a little wooden platform with wheels, similar to a mechanic's dolly used to slide under cars with. But this man wouldn't be sliding under cars, or into second base for that matter, as the cart was made necessary by the fact he had no legs. A former soldier, a rare one that had survived Okinawa and had metal artificial legs somewhat rusting.

Traveling down the street was a truck that looked like something put together from a Tinker Toy kit. It was full of dying, flopping sharks whose tiny blobs of slime were sent airborne by the man-sized fish thrashing out their lives gasping for air. Several blobs landed on and stuck to several marines whose comments ranged from "cocksucker!" to "cocksucker!"

A young girl, dressed in a colorful flowered kimono and as delicate as a spider web, glided past them.

"Fucky sucky Jo-san," Rhesus said, holding his fingers to the corners of his eyes to make them slant and jutting his front teeth out beyond his lower lip.

"Enough." It was Johnny . . . *I hope Jazz is taking good care of . . . Roma . . . and doesn't end up in . . . reform school . . . doing it . . .*

Rhesus was going to say something but decided better.

As they moved past the Japanese soldier on the dolly, he smiled at them, neither friendly nor angry, just knowing.

Lace pointed his thumb at him. "Sharks get cha?"

"Yah, probably Second Marine Division sharks. My brother was with them when they waded in," the Kentuckian Quince Carrey said. "He left an arm there."

"That ended his two-hand set shot career," Rhesus said.

Carrey started toward the little redhead.

"Nah," Johnny said, laying his hand on Carrey's shoulder, "Rhesus means no harm. He's just practicing to become king of the doodle doofuses."

Carrey brushed Johnny's hand off with "Look, Barse-tonnn, keep your pet monkey off my back, or the only nuts he'll eat will be his own."

Rhesus stepped toward the larger marine, but Righty stepped in. "No dancing without music, boys."

"Hey, the Japs, even the ones without no legs, are still starting wars," Lace said. "Right, DaSilva?"

Johnny was having difficulty thinking about the past war, that old, old one, the one where large crowds saw our boys off and welcomed them home. He was having difficulty thinking . . . *Jap rat . . .* "Poor bastard." . . . *He probably didn't ask . . . for it . . . the war . . .*

They boarded trucks for Itami, where they boarded antiquated R4Cs, which only recently had been taken out of mothballs where they had been stored in the Arizona desert.

"Don't we get no liberty or to go to a gee-sa whorehouse or nothin'?" Soupy asked sadly.

"Geisha girls aren't whores," Tim said.

"Hey, another world heard from," Lace said.

"They're trained performers, artists. They sing, recite poetry, dance, and play instruments."

"I've got an instrument for them to play."

"Come on, move out." It was Gunny Murphy. "The war's waiting, guys. Get aboard."

"I wanted to at least eat some rice with chopsticks," Soupy said.

"They'll be plenty of rice in Korea, Emmett Kelly," the gunny said.

"What's with the Emmett Kelly?" Soupy asked sadly.

"Emmett Kelly is the best known of the sad-faced clowns," Tim said.

Then they were aboard, and the ladder was wheeled away, the door shut and locked.

The R4Cs engines started after a cranky coaxing.

"This thing sounds like a dentist's drill," Pointer said.

"It sure as hell doesn't have enough power to take off," Soupy moaned.

"Nice talk," Fats said.

"I can still smell the mothballs in this thing," Righty said, smiling.

"I christen this tub the Mothball, son of the *General Weigel*, Rhesus said. "You know how to smell mothballs?"

No one answered. They had all heard it a hundred times.

"Spread its legs."

"Jesus, you'd have to scotch tape a million moths to get this rock to fly," Ma Toots said, swallowing his upper lip and nose with his bottom lip. "Do I look like a moth?"

"Moths are too small, too weak to help this thing to fly," Scoff said, moving his head as if he was following the flight of a moth, and while everyone tried to pick up the flight of the moth that wasn't there, he borrowed a half-eaten candy bar from the lap of the marine sitting beside him. "Yup, moths are too small to help."

"Maybe we should have brought dragonflies," Soupy moaned.

"No sweat," Johnny said. "While we're taxiing down the runway, everyone sticks their arms out the windows and flaps like fury."

Not only did the Mothball make it to Korea, but it also circled the dirt emergency landing strip several times as a dozen marines tried to get an ox off it.

The beast moved when an old Korean farmer said something to it.

"He probably whispered to the fucken' ox that he'd clang its balls between two bricks if it didn't move," Ma Toots said.

"You see the nuts on that thing?" Fats exclaimed.

"If I had those thunder balls, "Ma Toots said, releasing his nose from the grasp of his lower lip, "I'd be the King of Siam."

In his best female voice impersonation, Skinny said, "Balls, cried the queen!"

"If I had two, I'd be king," Ma Toots said, taking on a regal look, wiggling his ears.

"Can you wiggle your ears to march music?" Lace asked, drumming up a Sousa march, complete with drumrolls and trumpets.

Ma Toots's ears kept perfect step to the march.

"Holy shit!" Soupy said. "They forgot to put any hot top on the landing strip."

The plane hit the deck, bounced in the air like a golf ball dropped from a balcony, joining the wrenching noises of the plane's metal with that of the troop's weapons, mess kits, and helmets into a series of metallic clangs that sounded like a tin band.

"It sounded like this sucker was coming apart," Righty said.

"Sounded like a thousand skeletons getting laid on a tin roof," Ma Toots said.

They unloaded quickly and started up a road that kicked up so much dust that it quickly coated their tongues and throats.

"What the hell's the hurry?" Soupy complained. "My legs haven't made up their mind whether they are on the *Weigel* or Mothball. I've got one sea leg, one air leg, and we're supposed to be ground grunts."

They all laughed.

Ma Toots imitated the bowlegged walk of a Popeye the Sailor Man then jumped in the air several times, flapping his arms. "I'm confused too."

"You were born confused," Rhesus said.

"The men sound in pretty good spirits, Gunny," Lieutenant Smith said to his platoon sergeant.

"More important than that," the gunny said, "they're complaining."

Within minutes, the two long thin trails of marines were stretched on each side of the road chewed up and spit out by tanks, jeeps, and four-by-fours, never more than a roll away from a ditch.

"Korea. We're in Korea," Rhesus said. "Boy, that was fast. I didn't even get a chance to make a Nip mamasan Mona in a kimona."

"Promise me one thing," Righty said, turning to his friend with the orange hair and face of one million freckles, "when we get back and are civilians again, you won't make any attempts to become a poet. Promise."

"Up yours."

"You should do so good."

"Rhesus?"

"Yah," he said, turning to face Johnny, who was on the opposite side of the road.

"Are we good friends?"

"I ain't lending no money."

"Nah. I just wanted to know if when sometime we're crapped out and bored between firefights, if I can join all your freckles with a pen."

Rhesus squeezed his cock in his hand. "Join this."

"Oh, such a naughty, naughty boy."

"I don't hear no shooting," Soupy said, his sad eyes, as always, looking close to tears. "They're probably waiting until they have us surrounded. They'll probably wait until we're taking a shit. I can see my gravestone, 'He died with his pants down.'"

"I ain't dropping into no slit trench full of shit if I'm spread eagled over one when the shooting starts," Scoff said, checking his pocket for the roll of toilet paper he had borrowed while shipboard.

"When the shooting starts," Ma Toots said, "it's any port in a storm. Course, being an old Boy Scout, I'm prepared. Right before I jump in that shit pit, I reach under my jacket, haul out those two shit-eating birds I kidnapped in Congress, Washington DC, USA, and toss them in that slit trench before me, and after they're done eating it clean, I toss in a grenade."

"What gives with all these people walking around those rice paddies with those giant jugs on their heads?"

"Those giant jugs are honey buckets," Gunny Murphy said, "the honey being human crap."

"You mean they grow their food in human . . . stuff?" Soupy asked, close to tears of disbelief.

"Remind me to stay clear of their supermarkets," Ma Toots said, licking his chops as if he had finished a fine filet mignon.

"When we get up there, where the fighting is, do we all get to stay together?" Tim asked the gunny.

"Depends. We might form up a new company and stay together, or we might get put into a pool and sent to the four winds."

"Do we have any say?"

"Sure, you have a say," the gunny said, smiling. "You get to say 'yes, sir!' or 'yes, sir!' to everything. You never volunteer, and you never fail to get out of your hole and move out when the word comes."

"We joined together, we stay together," Johnny said.

"I'll take a hundred bucks on that and give you ten-to-one odds," the gunny said. "Decisions aren't made at the kindergarten level."

"I don't hear no shooting," Soupy repeated.

"Don't rush it, don't rush it," Scoff said.

"What's this?" Soupy said, pointing to the small mud huts with thatched roofs that made up what appeared to be a tiny, two-oxen town.

"It's New York City—west," Ma Toots said.

Old men, dressed in white smocks, topped off with tall black hats, smoked long, thin-stemmed pipes. Not one looked up at the long columns of marines.

"I've never seen anything like this. Those are octopus hanging there. I thought they were in the ocean," Fats said, "and they're covered with dust."

"This is the market. How would you like to chow down on that?" the gunny said, pointing at a chow dog that was shaved down, gutted, and was hanging on a spit beside the octopus and a rack of dried fish.

"He'd woof it down," Rhesus said.

"Oy." It was Stein, the Jewish kid from New York, the one they all stood up for in boot camp.

"Gar-felta fish, it ain't," Ma toots said. "What kind of religion feels up fish."

"I'm with the ditty-dum-dum-ditty boys, communications," Stein said, "and we got caught up in a wire jeep. They just mounted a .30-caliber job on it. So along with the wire, one guy walks. Just as well, who wants to drive up the middle of a road here?"

The jeep had a giant wooden spool of wire mounted in the rear, the machine gun on the passenger side in the front, meaning that the gunner pretty much had to rest his butt between the large wooded sides of the spool.

"No ride-ee," Rhesus said to Stein. "Looks like you're going to have to keep up all on your own this time. Even a retard like Ma Toots keeps up."

Ma Toots farted, "A kiss."

Rhesus smiled, squeezing his face together, bringing all his freckles in tight together into one brown surface. He took off his helmet and brushed his carrot-top hair back.

"You could be Tim's brother when you make that brown-faced smile," Lace said.

Johnny stepped toward Lace, but Ma Toots's words stopped everything, except the laughter, "Nah, Tim doesn't have orange hair."

"Can't get that octopus back in the village out of my mind, eight arms, octo, eight. Octopus," Ma Toots said, "Like October. The eighth month of the year."

"Whew," Johnny said, counting on his fingers.

"Can you imagine how great it would be to have eight arms?" Ma Toots said. "My right arm gets so tired from thumping my tub. Ghee, I could beat my haddock in the attic four times as much."

"Sure, sounds great," Johnny said. "But how in hell do you figure out which are the four right arms and which are the four left?"

"You have to ask it. Which is your left, Mr. Octopus?"

"Nah, stupid, just follow it down the street. When it makes a left turn, see which four arms make the left-hand signal," Johnny said.

"Johnny," Righty said, "I'm going to ask you for the same favor I asked Rhesus, our little monkey, for when you get out: don't make being a comedian your profession."

"Johnny is gonna be a great surgeon someday. I heard Yelena telling the girls that," Scoff said.

"I heard Bernadette say he was going to be a red hot lover," Skinny said.

"Why not? She's a red hot mama," Rhesus said, forming a circle with the thumb and forefinger of his left hand and pushing the middle finger of his right hand through it repeatedly.

"Enough," Johnny said, "unless you'd like your teeth pushed so far back, they'll be providing smiles for your asshole."

"Hey, DaSilva, monkey nuts, save it for the gooks," the gunny said.

"I didn't know he could read sign language, Gunny," Rhesus said.

"Anyone got any pizza? I got the anchovies," Scoff asked as he opened his dungaree jacket to display the wares he had scoffed up as they passed through the town—a sheath of dried fish, a bottle of P'ohang-dong wine, and a live chicken.

"How in bad balls did you get that chicken without it making a noise?" Ma Toots asked with admiration.

"Genius," Tim said, "Scoff is a plain genius, but then again, don't ask him to explain genius. Did they ask young Yehudi Menuhin how he got to play the violin like that, or Ted Williams how he pulled the pitched ball out of the catcher's glove with his bat? Did they ask Margaret Truman what she did with the money daddy Harry gave her for her piano lessons?"

"My god, Tim, you're actually funny," Soupy said, the sad look on his face approaching pathetic at the thought that the one person who always made sense was being funny.

The long line had slowed slightly. Ten miles in a field pack after a long boat ride and a short airplane ride will do that.

Their transport packs with the total gear were left back at the motor pool and were allegedly slated to keep up with battalion headquarters, but no one planned on it.

"I think it's raining up there behind the mountains. That thunder is rolling," Fats said.

"That, my boys, sounds like the artillery of the Eleventh Marines, and the North Koreans' answer," Gunny said.

"It's a sad sound," Soupy said.

"Y'all is a sad sound, you creepy shit," the towering Lace said menacingly, pushing down on Soupy's helmet until it pushed the smaller man's ears down. "What in hell did you join this man's Marine Corps for?"

"So I could meet nice people like you. You know, Mr. Lace, that Northerners like me blow Southerners like you."

"Yes, you do."

"Yes, we blow you on the back of the neck when we stick it up your butt."

"You're dead, pissant!" Lace said, moving toward Soupy.

"You stupid rebel piece of putz, I'm holding the BAR," Soupy said, turning his back on the giant.

"Look, tough guys, save it for the gooks," Gunny Murphy said.

The new troops didn't understand the distant noises of war. They sounded like pops and rumbles, rumbles and pops, not ear- and body-shattering explosions.

Pop, pop, pop. Like a bunch of kids blowing bubbles until they burst.

As they got closer, the explosion of the artillery shells sounded like the moans of an arthritic old dog in front of the fireplace.

The only thing that seemed real were the Corsairs that winged in the air over where it appeared the bubblegum pops and old dog moans were coming from.

Even then, the young marines' view of the planes was that they were only real in the sense that they reminded them of when they were kids, and they held small planes in their hands, moving them overhead in circles. But they were in miniature.

Johnny studied the gull-winged, close air support fighters . . . *They look like the gulls . . . off Revere Beach . . .*

Turning to Righty, he said, "Don't they look like the gulls at Revere Beach? I heard some guy say the Corsairs were from a carrier, and another said they were from MAG 33, the Marine Air Group on a P'ohang emergency strip. I go with the aircraft carrier."

"Its-sa not a big boat-ah," Righty said, "as how would a ground grunt know about a ship at sea? They must be from P'ohang Big Dong."

Ma Toots said, "The gunny landed at someplace called Incheon back a bit. He said they kicked ass and the gooks ran so fast, it was tough trying to find a bullet that could catch up to them. I want to chase some rabbits too."

"What the hell is Incheon?" Pointer asked.

Ma Toots, in his best imitation of a girl, moaned, "It's all the way in-John."

"Hey," Johnny said, "all I said was that the Corsairs looked like the gulls at Nahant."

"Revere," Righty corrected. "The birds from Revere Beach were real hot stuff. Nahant girls were snobs."

"You bet," Rhesus said. "You'd take those Revere girls on the Cyclone, and when that old roller coaster dove nose first down that first steep one and they started screaming, you could feel the tits right off their body, and they wouldn't know it."

"The ones from Somerville were best. I don't know what they fed them, but they were all built like brick shithouses," Fats said.

"And every brick had been laid," Rhesus said.

"Jesus, I joined this man's corps and traveled fifteen thousand miles to escape that sour old stuff, 'every brick had been laid,'" Soupy said.

"I remember the girls at Revere Beach," Righty said.

"You should. You're practically engaged to one. Ah, Maria," Johnny said, "and I remember being in such pain with a Malden girl, her boo-zoom was like absolutely over ripe peaches, full of warm, sweet juices." . . . *Oh . . .*

"Yah, boobs and buttocks," Rhesus said.

"The pain was your fault, John. You could have had the pick of the litter. What gave?" Righty asked.

"I don't know. I guess I was always saving myself for the next football or hockey game."

"I don't think so, John," Righty said.

"Do you realize you always call me John when you're serious, Mr. Minichelli?"

"I guess so, but you practically had anyone you wanted. You had them for the picking. But something always stopped you."

"I always had this hang-up. Ma had me protecting Romy around the clock. No one wants to think he'd be doing it to someone's little sister."

"I want to think it—do it to someone's little sister, big sister, same-size sister, and even Sister of St. Cecilia of Rome," Ma Toots said, punctuating his feelings with a heartfelt fart.

The dark was falling quickly now, and the good-natured kidding was replaced by whistling-past- the-cemetery kidding.

"I hope those gooks are good shots," Rhesus said. "I don't want one of them hitting me by mistake."

"Take off your piss pot and let them see that orange hair so they'll know you're one of those monkey faces," Ma Toots said.

"I don't think I'm going to like someone trying to kill me," Pointer said.

"I wonder what it's like to have someone trying to kill you," Righty said. "What do they think when they aim and shoot? I'm not sure I can kill someone."

"Bullshit," Lace said. "We all can kill."

Righty turned to Johnny. "I don't know. In the back of my mind is the thought, I could maybe be killing someone else's Big Lefty."

"Big Lefty?" Lace said. "Is that the hand you use when the right one gets tired?"

"I think constantly about getting killed," Soupy said.

"Then you're the kind of guy who won't buy it," Fats said. "I read that someplace."

"Well, I'm sure as shit not afraid of the devil himself," Lace said.

"You're a better man than I Gunger Dinn, Gunger Dinn, you're a better man than I, Gunger Dinn," Tim recited.

"What are you saying?" Lace asked, looking at Tim from beneath eyebrow-darkened eyes.

"I worry too," Pointer said, "a lot of the time, and when we get into the shooting, I'll worry all the time."

Johnny belted his cousin on the shoulder. "You've got to be like the wild animals. They don't worry about dying. They don't think of dying. Ever. But they are always cautious. I saw this time after time when deer hunting with my dad and Uncles."

"Well, I'm not a wild animal, and I think it can happen to me."

"Then don't think of getting killed. Think of killing."

"Easier said than done," Righty said.

"Can we change the subject?" Pointer said. "I don't want to kill, and I don't want to be killed."

"You're not going to have a lot of choices, cuz," Johnny said, clapping him on his back.

"Why do you keep hitting me, Johnny?"

"So you won't get nervous."

"This way, men." It was the gunny. "Battalion is up there someplace. When we get there, stand close to the guys you want to be with. So when they say 'you, you, and you,' it can be the you, you, and you, you want. Then again, maybe they'll form up a company. But it will be tomorrow or the day after that you guys break your cherries. Or months from now. Hurry up and wait is the order of the day from generals to you porgy baits."

The bandy legged sergeant led them up a valley that picked up the pop-pop and dog moans from a different angle. The sounds, rather than being outside their ears, were now inside, inside their heads, and getting more personal.

By the time they reached battalion, it was nearly dark when the captain or major—they couldn't tell which, as the insignia of rank on the helmet cover was black rather than shiny gold or silver, shiny metal known as "Hey, here I am, bullet!"—said, "Relax."

Pointer started to salute the officer, but the karate chop the gunny gave him stopped it in midair and nearly broke his wrist. If the chop hadn't stopped Pointer's arm in midair, the officer's look would have.

The hiss that followed seared into the would-be saluter, "You ever salute again in this here country, and I'll cut both your wrists off at your asshole."

"Jesus," Pointer whispered to Ma Toots, "where the hell is there a toad stool to crawl under when you need one?"

"What did you expect? A salute in the daylight could cost an officer his life. Here, have a piece of penny candy."

"Thanks. Where in hell did you get that?"

"Shut up. Just accept the fact that your Ma Toots loves ya. And if you piss me off, I'll salute you in front of the gooks."

Johnny kissed Pointer on the ear and said, "Don't you go taking no candy from strangers."

Ma Toots said, "You stop getting in the way of my love life, you boy that speaks with the broad A. Just paark the kaar in Haar-vaard yaard and drink your tonic."

"Any more candy?" Johnny asked Ma Toots.

"Only for those that officers and gunny sergeants hate," Ma Toots said, handing Johnny a Bull's Eye.

The gunny and the officers were huddled a short distance away, a black amoeba changing shape as the dark cloaked in. Their whispers were the hisses of garden snakes escaping before the sharp prongs of a gardener's rake.

A single figure broke off and approached the men. "OK," the gunny said, "we gonna head up there. Dog Company's dike has a few holes in it. We're the little Dutch boys. DaSilva, you can see in the dark. Take point. Come get a compass reading but stay on the lip of the dingle. The dingle itself could have a set of boobies in it. Set the lead one off, and the downhill string will make beef jerky of all us following."

"OK," Johnny said, hunching low and starting up the mountainside that was as black as the inside of a mole's belly . . . *Why oh why . . . did I ever leave . . . Loch Lomond . . . or was it . . . Wyoming . . . ?*

"Crazy Polack, Minichelli, go. Up there," the gunny ordered.

Ma Toots and Righty formed the wings of Johnny's point as they headed "up there," a mountain peak that was a black dagger that cut through the dark heart of sky.

They heard Pointer's voice behind them, "Can't we crap? We've been moving since five this morning."

"I'm gonna pretend I didn't hear anything this time," the gunny said, "if you get the idea. You follow me, single file. Keep below the ridgeline. No silhouettes. Ever!"

Fifty yards in front of the main body of replacements, the three-point men stumbled and cursed, legs raked by crippling rocks that sledgehammered shins, already black and blue, raw.

Eye-whipping stunted pine branches took their minds off the hot sweat that poured down their faces and the bitter winter cold that ate them alive, a paradox love-hate beyond their comprehension. The sweat and tears joined in.

The gunny had overheard Johnny in an earlier bull session when he told his buddies that if he kept his eyes closed tight in the dark for five minutes and concentrated his mind on seeing in the dark, that he could see in the dark. After that, he got nearly every night detail going . . . *Why in diddilly shit . . . don't I keep my big mouth . . . shut . . . ?*

But the mouths of all three, as well as the trailing replacements, were wide open, trying to suck enough air in to keep moving upward, before their hearts burst.

"Password."

It was a single word, hissed, that came out of the dark and stopped them in their tracks.

"Password!"

"Give him the password, someone," Righty said.

"I have no idea," Rhesus whispered.

"Last time. *Password!*"

"What's the word, Johnny?" Ma Toots asked.

"Shit, I don't know."

The demand "password" hissed into their ears and hearts.

They all heard the safety click off the gun held by someone who would kill them over a single word.

"Look, you porgy bait asshole . . ." Johnny said in frustration.

"Did you say porgy bait?" the voice from the dark said. "Then pass. Those porgy bait, Southern Cal educated gooks never learned that word in English 1."

They advanced toward the voice and came face-to-face, actually, foot to face, as the voice was down in a deep hole with only its head above ground. The voice's shoulders and hands were sticking up just high enough so he could cut the legs out of anyone who didn't know the password or had sense enough to call the challenger a porgy bait asshole.

"Would you have shot us?" Righty asked the head in the hole.

The head answered, "Do bears shit in the woods? Does the pope, when he's making the sign of the cross to all those below the balcony, whisper to the crowd, 'Will all you ginnies get off the goddamned grass'? Of course, I'd shoot, touch hole."

"Hey, Minichelli, he's insulting your leader," Ma Toots said, shoving Righty's shoulder affectionately.

"No one gave us the word. I was just gonna yell out 'Babe Ruth.'"

"That sure as shit would have got you killed. The Japs were yelling Babe Ruth in WW II," the listening post sentry said.

"Well, then," Johnny said, "I'm glad I didn't say it."

"Jesus, I hope you goofballs aren't Dog replacements."

"Us goofballs is," Johnny said.

"Look, head up the spine, keep below the ridge, about a hundred yards, you see Dog headquarters, a palace among bunkers. The password is 'Semper Fi.' So even you gooney birds with your heads up your poop-chutes can remember it."

"That's original," Rhesus said. "That's all we've heard since joining this man's corps, but how did you ever remember it once removed from a turd yanker?"

Turning his head toward Rhesus, the listening post lookout, whose piss pot was so big on his small head that he had to keep pushing it upward and away from his eyes, said, "You won't feel like being a wise ass after tomorrow. Every gook that tries to infiltrate our lines guesses the password is 'Semper Fi,' but the slant-eye goombas pronounce it 'Slemper Pie.' Now get the fuck out of here before you draw some night fire in on my innocent ass."

The gunny appeared next, and the watch asked, "Gunny, you better make sure none of these goofballs give the password with an oriental twang, or we'll need replacements for the replacements."

"What's your name?" Fats asked the sentry.

"We don't ask each other that question until you've stayed alive for a full week, and then you don't ask it," the head in the hole said.

"God, you're as funny as a rubber crotch," Fats said.

The head in the hole said, "This guy's good. Why don't you mosey on? You draw incoming, you are outgoing. In pieces."

"Up your giggy with a meat hook," Rhesus said.

The head in the hole said, "I lied about the password. Guess it, when you get close to Dog," and disappeared into the dank and the dark of his stand-up foxhole. The listening post marine said, "There's another listener above. I hope you guys are checking your ass, as the gooks like to sneak up on our tail-end Charlie and quietly do the deed."

"He was kidding, right?" Righty asked, "about lying about the password?"

"Nah," Ma Toots said, "he was giving the straight poop. I can always tell when someone is lying."

"How?"

"Simple. I'd stand in front of a mirror and tell the truth then lie, tell the truth then lie, watching my face all the time."

"But it's pitch black out. How could you tell the look on his face?"

"No problem. After sunset, I look with my asshole—it sees in the dark."

"These gooks won't have a chance against our brain power, with jarheads like me, Mr. Ma Toots," Ma Toots said between attempts at catching his breath.

"Never mind that," Righty said. "What about the password? Did he give us the right password?"

"Doesn't really matter," Ma Toots said.

"What if some trigger-happy son of a bitch shoots!"

"Hey, walk backward on your hands," Ma Toots said, "and then if someone shoots, they hit you in the ass, and you get a free ride home. And get to wear a ruptured goose on your chest, and everyone says, 'There goes the skinny ginny, wounded in action. Wounded in ass-tion."

"Jesus, is everyone a clown?" It was Gunny Murphy. "I had to break my ass to catch up to you. We could hear you like you were calling for the gook mortars. Their gunners aren't bashful about putting a round up your butt. Move out. Get up ahead. Speed it up so we can get inside of the Dog perimeter before spring."

"You're just kidding, right, Sarge? About the big ones?" Righty asked.

The gunny headed back down the mountain to lead the followers, while Johnny moved the point forward without a whisper exchanged, covering the ground much faster.

"Password!"

It was another hiss in the dark but not as authoritative as the first.

"What the fuck is the password?" Ma Toots, who was walking point, whispered back to Johnny.

There was no answer.

"Password." The voice was low, a tremor in it.

Ma Toots, imitating what he figured a gook's voice would sound like, answered, "Babe Root and Slemper Pie, assho . . ."

But never got to finish the sentence as an eighteen-year-old, four months in the corps, eight months out of high school, marine on his first listening post did as the sergeant of the guard had instructed him to. He fired his M1 into the voice, and the bullet exploded in Ma Toots's face.

The curses, "Shit, shit, shit, shit, shit!" convinced the shooter that indeed they were Americans.

No gook could utter the words "Shit!" "Cocksucker!" "Asshole bastard!" so clean, so swiftly.

"Oh, my good holy shit," the shooter uttered.

"Is everyone all right?" Johnny called out.

"Yes" was the answer from Righty.

"Ma Toots?"

But Ma Toots would never give out his penny candy again.

Never laugh his fool head off at his special candy-carrying box that only he and Johnny knew about.

"Anyone know who's down?" the gunny asked, coming up behind the point.

Johnny crawled forward in the dark until he bumped into the body. "Sorry, Sarge."

"Sorry for what?" Gunny asked, crawling forward toward Johnny.

"For bumping into you."

"You never touched me," the gunny said, cupping a small penlight in his hand, shining it on the fallen marine's face.

"Ma Toots," Johnny said, taking his comrade in his lap, "you goofy bastard. You goofy bastard" . . . *you poor goofy bastard . . .*

"Go ahead and cry, kid," the gunny said, lighting a cigarette. "Fuck the gooks. Let 'em see us. Give it a cry. The first cry is the toughest."

"No," Johnny said.

"The listening post sentry cried for every marine in the world."

"We can't take him back to battalion. We're needed up ahead," the gunny said. "I need you guys to bury him."

"Right here? Don't we at least send him home?" Pointer said.

"Right here."

"The ground's frozen," Rhesus said.

"Pile some pine boughs on him and hold 'em down with stones."

"I'll do it," Johnny said, adding, "What the hell are you staring at, Righty?" His friend's face was in the sergeant's flashlight beam.

"I hope Big Lefty didn't stare like that when . . ."

"Get your asses up and follow me," the gunny said.

"I'll help," Tim said.

The gunny said, "Put one tag in his mouth and his teeth on it. Give the other to the company commander, whoever he is. Don't forget his piece and the ammo. The rest of you follow me and shut the unholy fuck up!"

The sentry who shot Ma Toots kept up a constant moaning, "The gooks use 'Babe Ruth' as a password more than they use Semper Fi. Oh shit. Oh good shit. Will I get in trouble? Babe Ruth. Babe Ruth? Anyone would have shot."

It was only a short distance between the crying marine shooter and the sergeant of the guard, who was hissing, "Jesus, you shit bird fuck, I didn't mean it literally when I said 'shoot and ask questions later.' They'll hang both our asses from the same tree, you tit-sucking baby girl."

"No, they won't. Get your asses in your holes and shoot any son of a bitching sound you hear." It was 1st Lt. John Smith, who headed up one of Dog's rifle platoons.

Johnny and Tim didn't hear Smith's order. "You men get your asses uphill. Wait just below the peak. Stuff your asses in your sleeping bags. Tomorrow you go over the top and get a luxury suite in a Hilton Bunker."

Johnny and Tim stayed behind breaking off pine boughs and prying frozen rocks free with their bayonets.

"Should we wrap him in a shelter half before we lay him down?" Johnny asked, not expecting an answer.

He felt Tim gently remove Ma Toots's head from where it was cradled in Johnny's arms.

"We'd better wrap him. I saw the worms eating a dead fox one day," Johnny said. "Oh shit. Oh shit. Oh shit. Oh shit. Oh shit." . . . *Oh good unholy shit . . . Ma Toots . . . why . . . in good unholy shit . . .* "Oh shit. Oh shit. Oh shit."

Tim cradled Johnny's head in his arm, unknowingly bringing the dead boy's head close to Johnny's.

"I'm not crying, Tim. I never will."

"Yes, I know. I never will either."

Tim released Johnny's head and used both arms to pull the shelter half over Ma Toots.

"Did you get his dog tags?"

"I got 'em, Johnny. One stays with him."

They lowered boughs over the tall marine.

"Aren't we supposed to say something, Johnny? I'll say it if you don't want to. He was your friend."

"No, I'll say it. I probably would have been a preacher if my grandfather Shiverick had lived a little longer."

"OK."

"Dear God in heaven, I hope the good fuck you know what you're doing. I only knew him a short while. But he thought enough about me to tell me why he laughed so hard when he gave out his candy. He only told me, and I loved him for it."

Tim, trying to untie the knot in Johnny's chest with small talk, said "What was the poop? Why did he laugh so? When he had us pick out our favorite candy from that box? Always that same old box. I wanted to give him a new one. I was afraid scum would build up in that old candy box."

"Well, it seems . . ."

Tim had finished covering their comrade and put the entrenching tool he had whacked off the pine limbs with back into the case on top of his combat pack. The two young marines sat on their haunches like the old Koreans they saw squatting in their mud huts near their terraced rice fields far below.

"I don't know how they do it," Tim said, "sit this way."

"Guess his father, whatever his name was, probably Big Ma Toots or something, owned a candy store back wherever he came from."

"I mean I've been sitting on my haunches for only a couple of minutes, and I—"

"And he sent Ma Toots this great variety of penny candy, no matter where he went—"

"I have these fantastic aches in my thighs, calves, butt, and—"

"Ma Toots bored easy, and one day, he got this great antiboredom idea—"

"Both my back and butt ache. So you tell me how these Orientals sit so long with their knees folded up beneath their fanny," Tim said.

"He told me why he laughed while giving out the candy. Told me when we were crawling the transition course at Pendleton and the bullets were snapping branches just over our heads. Carefully measured, of course, but the measurements didn't allow for no standing up—"

"Those old Korean papasans could sit that way forever."

"Someone said their knees grow right out of their asses," Johnny said. "Anyway, sure as shooting, just like those guys who lied to scare the crap out of you by saying rattlesnakes littered the course. We all knew it was crap."

"Hours, and not ever change positions," Tim said.

"Except there was a rattler that one day. It wasn't crap, it had a body thick as a pythons."

"If they changed positions, I never spotted anyone doing it."

"Ma Toots was frozen with fright while crawling through that Camp Pendleton transition course, under the barbed wire, the live ammo whizzing over our heads. He knew he'd bought the farm when that rattlesnake popped up. Ma Toots could stay on the ground and get bit by a rattler or stand up and get bit by a .30 caliber."

"Johnny, I don't think those old Korean papasans ever did change posit—"

"I grabbed that snake by the tail and snapped it like a whip. Its entire guts came shooting out. Ma Toots said to me, 'Whatever I've got is yours.'"

I said, "Why do you always laugh so hard when you give out the candy?"

"I'll tell you why. I laugh so hard when I give out the candy; the guys search through the candy box looking for their favorite," answered Ma Toots.

Tim said, "Hey, my knees!"

"'I owe you forever,' Ma Toots said. I said 'No way.' That would leave me uneasy, having a coo coo nut like you owing me. So I said, 'Do me one thing.' 'What?' Ma Toots asks, and I said—"

"I think those Koreans died and were freeze dried in these positions."

"I said to Ma Toots, 'Tell me why you laugh your goofy ass off when you're giving out the penny candy.'"

"Ma Toots said, 'I'll tell you, but you can't tell anyone.' I promised, but now I think he would want me to tell so he can get that one last laugh. Well, he says, 'You know how when I hold that box of candy and everyone concentrates so hard, looking only for the kind of candy they like? Mint Julep. Bull's Eyes, Squirrel Nuts, and nigge— and Tiger Babies?' 'Yah,' I answer because I was always looking for my favorite. Mint Juleps. They stuck to the roof of your mouth. Made it itch. I liked that. Ma Toots says the next time he came around with his box of candy, instead of looking for my favorite, check out every piece of candy in the box, forget your favorite. Look 'em all over. The next time, I did."

"Yah? Yah?"

"And when I found out what was what, we both roared, and we roared each time he offered the pick of the box to each of the others. Rhesus. Righty. Pointer. You . . ."

"So? What was what?"

"He had torn a small piece out of the side of the box."

"So?"

"And there among the penny candies."

"John, come on!"

"Was his pecker. He had his fly undone, and his wanger was cascading through the tear in the cardboard, unbeknownst to all, hidden among the other variety of sweets."

They weren't sure how long they sat around the rough grave on their haunches. Certainly, it wouldn't have been much for the old Korean farmers, but it was a long time for legs not used to haunch hunkering.

"What are we doing, just sitting here, like we're on a Boy Scout campout? There are people out there that want to kill us," Tim said.

"I guess we're afraid to start moving. It will put this unreal thing in motion."

"We better find Dog before they send out a search party," Tim said.

"I hate to leave him alone, Tim."

"I know, but I'm afraid he might not be alone all that long."

"No! No way! I'm not letting no one else get killed. I can watch over everyone. I'm not afraid. God, better be a better fucken' person to my friends, or else."

"Sure, buddy. Sure. I understand."

"I know, Tim."

They moved slowly toward where they thought the company perimeter was, listening for the slightest sound.

Then it came. A hiss whisper, demand—"Password."

"You'd better not be the same trigger-happy cocksucker that shot Ma Toots," Johnny said.

"It's Johnny," the challenging voice announced to no one in particular, "and Tim."

The two marines closed the distance quickly in the dark before realizing the challenge came from Skinny, who post haste had sped up the dangerous gully.

"Any chow left, Skinny?" Tim asked their once-chubby friend as he came out of the dark, carbine at a high port.

"K-rations. Except Scoff's got some smoked fish."

"Good."

"Not so good. I don't know what came over him. He keeps talking survival shit and doesn't want to share."

"He'll share," Johnny said, "or I'll break his ass into more pieces than Humpty Dumpty's."

"There is a hole for you, Johnny, left over from two guys who bought the farm. One sleeps and one peeps. Then we get our own holes and bunker. Another fifty yards, and you'll be inside the company perimeter. Tim, Rhesus is alone in his hole," Skinny said.

"Thanks," Johnny said, "but if the company perimeter is up there, why are you out here alone?"

"It's called a listening post. You'll get your turn."

Righty was already wrapped in his sleeping bag and poncho; his arms and legs outside their warmth.

"Put your arms and legs in the bag, dummy," Johnny said, climbing into the two-man foxhole.

"No one sleeps with arms and legs inside their bag. Orders of the CO. Seems a couple of throats have been slit or something like that. Actually,

I guess the NKPA got past the listening post before they started their charge, and some of the guys in their bags couldn't get out in time."

"Great. But thanks for our new home."

"It was apparently started with a grenade. It ain't much, Johnny. We got worried, you and Tim were out there a long time."

"Home, sweet home."

"I'm afraid so."

"Long as no one shovels dirt over our heads, it's our home," Johnny said, "any port in a storm."

"And scuttlebutt has it that there will be a storm tomorrow. There's another hill over there somewhere in the dark that has failed to fall for weeks. We just sit and shit while they throw stuff at us, and we throw stuff at them. Took a couple of hits, and that's why all us replacements ended up with Dog."

"That's comforting."

"I know what you mean, Johnny. I'm scared shitless too."

"I'm not scared. You just keep your skinny ginny ass down and stay close to me. Things will be fine."

"Sure, Johnny. Johnny?"

"Yah."

"If you're not scared."

"Yah?

"Then you sure are stupid."

"So, good buddy, what's new?"

"You want me to take first watch, John?"

"Nah. We'll both take it. Seven eyes are better than one."

"Seven?"

"Yah. My eyes. Yours. And you wear glasses, little four eyes."

"So what gives with the seventh?"

"My fly's open, and my one-eyed Big Ben is on snorkel watch."

"I've been biting for your bait since the first grade, Johnny."

"Yah, I know. That's what I love about you."

"Do you think Ma Toots will be all right out there?"

"I can't answer. I'm sound asleep."

"Really."

"Really. And Righty?"

"Yah?"

"It's all right to be a little afraid."

"I just didn't like the look on Ma Toots's face. He looked so surprised," Righty said, taking his helmet off and wiping the sweat off his forehead despite the early morning cold.

"I know, like someone else knew why he laughed when he handed out the candy to all of us."

"You know why he laughed, Johnny, don't you?"

"Yah, yah. Now conk out. I'll keep watch."

"OK, an hour on and an hour off. Till dawn."

"Of course. What do you think, I'm going to let you get more Zs than me?"

Johnny peered into the pitch dark. A noise? A snapping branch? Set the hair on his neck on end.

But it was the quieter than the quiet "tic tic," like a tiny watch, that sent a chill down his spine, into his buttocks . . . *My asshole is shimming . . . like a hula-hula dancer . . . with ants in her pants . . . I hear a tic-tic . . . Do they have some sort of Chink wristwatches on . . . a time bomb . . . ?*

He cupped his ears forward to pick up more sound, remembered that this meant he didn't have a hand on his M1, and released his ears.

Then he heard the thumping, like distant Indian drums.

He talked to himself, "I know the fuckers blow bugles and all that shit when they charge, but Indian drums? Shut up, you crazy fucker. Looking for a Section Eight?" . . . *I hear the drums . . . I feel them . . .*

His hands tightened on his rifle. He could feel his finger tighten on the trigger. "Is the safety off? Should it be? No, Jesus, I could shoot myself. Stop talking to yourself before the guys in the white coats get you."

The drumming was getting louder. He peered into the dark, forcing his chest against the edge of the foxhole." . . . *Shit . . . shit . . . shit . . .* He realized the drumming was his heart pounding, trying to get out of the locked room whose walls were closing in on him.

He pulled back from the edge of the foxhole. Took deep breaths, short ones, three in, three out. The beating drums went away.

There was deadly silence, which was worse for Johnny than the spasmodic small-arms fire from the Chinese line . . . *Probably shooting . . . at one of the few surviving night animals . . . near their company perimeter . . . dumb dicks . . .*

Shit . . . Was that a stick . . . that cracked? . . . He peered into the dark until his eyes burned, his temples throbbed, and his stomach tied in knots that proved a harsher, slower strangulation than a hangman's noose.

He kept seeing Ma Toots's face in the dark. Staring. Surprised. No longer that look . . . that shit-eating grin . . . *How in hell . . . do I . . . keep . . . my friends . . . alive? . . . How do I keep me . . . alive . . . I never saw a dead person before . . . only old ones . . .*

He talked slowly, less than a whisper, "Jesus, Jesus, I'm tired. And, Jesus, I didn't mean that crap about you'd better be a better person, or else

I'll, I'll kick the crap out of you. I never used your name in vain before." . . . *It would break Grandpa Shiverick's heart . . . Grandmother Mine's . . . too . . . if they knew . . . I threatened you . . .*

"Jesus, don't let me fall asleep. Everyone could get killed. I could get shot as a traitor. Jesus." . . . *Am I swearing . . . or am I calling out for help . . . ?*

"So, look, I need an answer."

The potluck shot fired from a Russian-made T-34 tank that had been buried in the ground with only its camouflage cannon showing hit nearby, showering him with torn earth tossed into the sky. The tank had survived the napalm dropping marine Corsairs during the day and only came out at night to play. A second round from the T-34 rocked the company perimeter, jarring Johnny's teeth together in the middle of his talking to himself.

"Jesus! The name, that is, not the curse using your name in vain, that's not the answer I wanted." . . . *Christ . . . no one would believe me if I told them . . . the incoming hit, just as I demanded an answer from . . . Jesus . . .*

"Don't get excited, men." It was the gunny's voiced coming through the dark. "They're just firing a few fun ones to piss you off, ruin your sleep. We'll find the fuck of a tank tomorrow."

"Hey, John," it was Righty's voice coming from the bottom of their hole, "can't you keep it a little more quiet up there?"

"Anyone hurt? Killed?" It was Lieutenant Smith's voice this time.

"Hey, Lieutenant, you're a minute late and a pound short. If we're dead, how do we tell you, sir?"

"Who said that?"

"If you don't know, you sure as hell aren't going to find out, sir."

The replacements recognized Rhesus's voice. Lieutenant Smith didn't, and that was lucky for the little monkey's ass.

The gunny, smoking in the bottom of his hole, muttered, "The poor eighty-day wonder. Eighty days to make him an officer. Eighty seconds in action, and a walking, talking body bag."

A third round, this time from a North Korean mortar, hit on the back slope where the marines thought they were safe.

"What's that, Johnny?"

"Just some gook can't sleep, probably got some bad rice."

But Righty didn't hear the answer; he was already snoring, a much louder noise than an over-the-hill explosion of a roaming round.

Then the line was quiet.

Johnny continued his staring into the dark, long past when he was supposed to wake up Righty. He could vision Ma Toots staring wide eyed despite being dead. Johnny could swear he heard his friend laughing wildly, chanting stupid nothings: "You can't kill me, I'm already dead! Here, pick your favorite piece of candy, the piece I'm pissing on." "Righty, wake up. I'm going out."

"What? What you talking about? Going out, why?"

"Never mind. I'll give a password to you, 'pound sand,' when I come back here to home sweet home."

"John, what you talking about? Where in hell are you goin'? What if you hit a section of our perimeter and you call out 'pound sand' for the password?"

"It will be light in an hour. I'll be able to see."

"You bastard, you'll let me sleep while some gook is crawling around."

"There's no gooks in our lines."

"Promise? Cross your heart and hope to die?"

"Kissadeech, buddy, I'm just going down to check on Ma Toots," and then Johnny was out of the foxhole and crawling through the dark.

He had crawled some three hundred yards downhill when his head hit something soft. A body. He tried to get close enough to see who, what.

It was where the tank shell had landed earlier, just short of the Dog perimeter.

He felt the body in the dark. Ran his hand down the leg, past the leggings made of rags, to "Sneakers. Split toe. A fuckin' gook. What the fuck was he doing here?"

He ran his hands up the body, down the arms, to the right hand. There was a small homemade mine in it. His other hand held an ice pick for plunging into the temple of sleeping marines.

Johnny thought . . . *If there is one gook planting mines . . . there are more . . . General Custer . . . Private DaSilva here . . . sir . . . What am I doin' out here? . . . Son, you are fighting for your country . . . OK, sir . . . long as it's not for your personal glory . . . and get a haircut, General . . . What did you say, boy . . . Shouldn't call me boy anymore . . . it's either . . . man . . . or . . . baby . . .*

He wanted to move on but was afraid the body would come to life and plunge the ice pick into his temple.

He felt for his KA-BAR and unsheathed it. To slit the body's throat. But there was no throat to grab. Slit. There was only that feeling when as a kid fishing for catfish at midnight with his dad and uncles, and reaching into a can of worms. Except this time, the worms were what were left of a heart and lungs. Only crushed thorax contents pushed up from the gut to the only opening it could find, the missing throat.

Johnny wanted to crawl back to his foxhole . . . *Have to find . . . my home sweet . . . home . . .*

He started back to Dog. Stopped. Turned the top of his body in the opposite direction. But his feet wanted to push him back to his foxhole. To be safe . . . for at least one night . . . *but only if we stayed awake . . . and didn't let any one . . . with an ice pick . . . find us . . . with our entire bodies . . . inside our sleeping bag . . .*

Then the upper part of his body won the tug-of-war, and the lower part followed, away from his company, toward where Ma Toots laid.

His search seemed like forever. He wanted to quit, go back. He started back several times, but every damned time, the upper part of his body, head, heart, arms, won over the lower part, a stomach that wanted to shit his pants and an asshole that agreed to go along with it. Then there was his cock that pissed when it wasn't supposed to, not to mention legs that wanted to run or crawl to safety.

Then he found his friend. Luck was with him. He felt the pine boughs, the rocks holding them in place, the few entrenching tool shovels of dirt tossed over the stones. It was Ma Toots.

"Guess you're all set, old buddy. I just worried the pricks wouldn't let you sleep. We're moving out tomorrow, but we'll be back to get you." He moved slowly away . . . "I'll take you back to the States," . . . *and all that great candy . . . and that great hidden pecker in the box . . . What kind of shit is this . . . talking to myself . . . and a dead man . . . a worthless big guy . . . with a little head . . . and big . . . big ears . . . and a hidden pecker . . .* Without knowing it, he had crawled back into the company area shantytown of foxholes and bunkers.

"I'm talking to myself."

"You sure are," the voice from out of the dark said.

Johnny jumped up so fast, he left his M1 on the ground.

It was Righty. "You must have money in the bank, talking to yourself. I heard you twenty feet away."

"What the hell you doing out here? You could get your skinny ginny with the meatball eyes shot. You could get killed, asshole."

"Ahh, I got worried."

"Jesus, Righty. How you gonna stay awake tiring yourself out creeping around like a shit-eating night crawler?"

"Believe me, after those shells, we'll all stay awake."

They crawled back toward the company area when Johnny bumped into the North Korean's body.

"The traffic director here," Johnny said, taking the dead North Korean soldier's hand and placing it in Righty's.

"You prick! Why did you have to do that? What are you doin' now?"

"Just borrowing his tool of the trade."

"You're not cutting his pecker off?"

"Nah. Just taking this off him."

He let Righty feel the ice pick he took from the body before he slipped it into the top of his right boondocker. "Just a little extra insurance."

They continued whispering as they made it to the company perimeter and their hole.

"I know the insurance policy I wish I took out."

"What's that?"

"The 'keep your mouth shut, stay home' policy. Then 'go to college and let the dummies fight' policy."

"College. Sure. That's why we prepped in the general course. Arithmetic and basket weaving," Righty said.

"You're right; we're here because the Marine Corps said, 'Give me your poor, your dumb bells.' Yelena said I could go to college, but I can't see me graduating in some smock."

"Frock. Frock. A smock is for a pregnant woman. A frock is a college graduation gown. I read it somewhere. A frock, frock. Gee."

"Ah, sure, frock you. Into your whole junior gee man. Your turn to sleep."

"Ah, I can't. I can't. And fuck you too, you cocksucking groom of a whore, roaring asshole. The next time I go out at night, you stay home. How can I take care of you and the others as—"

"Good gracious, John, what language. Do you know any English?"

"Good gracious, little lady, what makes you talk that way?" Johnny said, pinching his friend's cheek.

"Ah, I don't know which end is up. I just got tired of swearing all the time. Pass the fucken' beans, let's get the fuck out of here, those fucken' fucks. My mother would really be weeping if she knew. She'd wear her rosary fingers to the bone."

"Yah, I know. Before I joined up, my ma only caught me swearing once. I had nearly taken my finger off while carving a whiz stick to start a fire on one of our Cub Scout pack cookouts in the Big Woods. She had snuck up, just to make sure we were OK, and heard me. She let out a roar. We didn't know what was what, thought it was a banshee. We ran pell-mell home. Didn't stop to clean the shit out of our pants."

"Yah?"

"She was fast and waiting for me when I came through the door. She used so much soap washing out my mouth, I farted soap bubbles for a month."

"Yah?"

"And they hurt 'cause she used that homemade laundry soap that Grandma Shiverick made out of lye."

"So, Johnny, why the fuck do we have to swear so much?"

"If we didn't, we wouldn't fucken' understand each other. Besides, swearing keeps you from getting super shit scared. Fats, who wants to be a head shrinker when he gets out, feels the swearing is to relieve pressure, build up courage, And promote camaraderie. Let's face it. With guys from the south and west and north speaking different ways, the fucken' swearing is the only language we all understand. Why are we talking like Aristotle and Socrates in a set-up for us to kill rather than being philosophical?"

"Hey, Fats needs his head shrunk. Can you imagine Fats actually gained a little weight in boot and at Pendleton? Course, it's muscle, not fat. Yah, and Skinny lost all his fat—it changed to muscle. Remember when we used to set pins . . ."

"At the old Sundown Poolroom and Bowling Alley."

"And it got so hot under those lights in the pits, we'd take off our shirts."

"And Fats was so skinny, you could see his ribs through his back."

They laughed out loud.

"Shhhh," Righty said, "might be a gook around."

"Nothing is louder than a whisper. We know one gook that was around doesn't have an ice pick anymore," Johnny said.

"A fart can be heard farther away than a match lit at sea. But you can't tell if it's one of our farts or ones of theirs. Course, theirs smell like garlic, while ours smell like a cross between beans and shit on a shingle. Ah, what would life be without SOS? But back up a bit, we had a lot of fun at the poolroom. That's where you started making up nicknames for all the guys."

"And for revenge," Johnny said, "everyone called me John. Period. Rhesus pointed out it was fitting. A John being a shithouse."

"We're lucky, Johnny, all of us ending up in the same outfit. Most of the time, you're in a company where everyone is a stranger. I heard one of the long-timers telling Soupy, everyone is a stranger 'cause the faces change all the time. My Big Lefty said after a while, he didn't want to know any of the names of the new guys. I just hope someone knew Big Lefty at the end."

"They did, Righty, honest. They did. We do. We know each other."

"Yah. John," Righty said, lowering his voice to the weakest of whispers, "no one challenged us when we came in."

"Yah, something's wrong, very wrong."

They stood up, looked around, no one was in sight.

"Where have you assholes been?"

They jumped in the air on hearing the fierce voice.

It was Lace.

"We went to check Ma Toots."

"Sure. He was going to get up and go to the high-school prom. I told Lieutenant Smith you pussies deserted."

"The company's at a staging area. Baker is joining Able heading up first. Dog's in reserve. We're taking 209."

"Is that when the bus leaves?" Righty asked.

"Funny. It's a hill number."

"Cheez, we just got in this God-forsaken country," Righty said. "I would have liked a chance to see some scenery, have a hot meal."

"That's Dog up ahead, I can see Smith's fat ass," Righty said.

"That's Lieutenant Smith's fat ass," Johnny said.

"Do you guys from Mass-of-two-shits with your paaark da kaaars ever get serious?" Lace asked.

"Serious is a good way to die of fright," Johnny said.

"Where did this snow come from?" Righty asked, "and it's still coming down."

They caught up with the "tail-end Charlies" of Dog.

Pointer told them, "That's Tim's fire team going up the hill to join Baker. Baker is under strength. Baker sent four guys out on night patrol. They didn't come back. Hopefully, they're in a Seoul whorehouse or something. Jesus, the four of them looked small. Even tall Tim looked tiny. They were pooped to start up with and now were loaded down with all the gear they got stuck with. Extra ammo boxes. Wire. Tim took the most gear. He looked slow. Almost weak."

"Tim wasn't exactly a club foot when he carried that football around end. He was fast even with a couple of guys on his back," Righty said.

"That was a million years ago," Fats put in.

"And Fats, without those rubber heels we glued to his feet so he'd be tall enough to get into this man's corps, looked even smaller, like Bridget the midget, carrying that horse of a BAR," Pointer said.

"Yah, Scoff and Soupy should have each picked him up by an arm and carried him up," Skinny said, "except Scoff was carrying that two-ton mortar base, and Soupy had six BAR ammo belts; he looked like a Christmas tree decorated with bullets."

The visitation to Hill 209 started simply, slowly enough with a single pop, like the first kernel from a popcorn popper. A gook had fired at a rattle of a can attached to their barbed wire, not caring whether it was the wind, a marine, or a mythical snow tiger that caused the rattle. But the gooks had no cans; they carried their rice in laced bags.

Then six quick, louder "pops" slightly silenced in the deep snow to their left flank, where Tim and his fire team sweated bullets despite belly bumping, face first, through the snow.

Then the first automatic fire had entered stage left, Phantoms of the Opera outfitted with burp guns.

The curtain call, an early one, was when the cellar of hell, where all the human shit and flesh was stored, exploded as the first gook mortar rounds rained down on them, shaking the earth, bouncing bodies about.

The Eleventh Marines answered, their artillery voices louder than the North Korean People's Army mortar "woofs." The air was so thick with shells and shrapnel that those moving into the action wondered whether the Earth Mother had fucked up and couldn't make up her mind whether it was day or night, as bursting shells lit up the snow, and the lull brought on the dark again.

There was more airborne shrapnel than usual as occasional rounds kissed overhead, shattering, scattering their smashed metallic bodies of steel and lead downbursting them, leaving men on both sides dead, some with a single sliver the size of a toothpick catching them in the throat; others catching the entire bag, ending up looking like discarded fish guts bloody, silver, and slimy.

As light replaced dark, the F4U Corsairs of MAGs 33 and 45 winged in, their dark-blue fuselages with "Marines" or "Navy" boldly printed in white, tumbling their napalm end over end like poorly thrown footballs, meeting the earth, exploding into blood flames like angry clouds out to rape the heavens.

Single napalm blobs, some golf ball size, others the size of the gull-winged Corsairs that released them, bounced out of the holocaust, out of control, sticking themselves to whatever or whomever they hit, cooking victims alive, no swift death like the lobster dropped into boiling water.

It was a wonderful sight to the marine ground grunts, those Corsairs winging close to the ground, their pilots, eyes straight ahead, giving thumbs-up to the men below, bombs dropping, wing guns chattering death. Then they were away.

The marines jumped to their feet, most jogging, some running, screaming, crying with adrenaline pushing caution out of the driver's seat, climbing, shooting, tossing their grenades, picking up the enemy grenades rolled down at them, and throwing them back. In some cases, the complete return of an enemy grenade did not come about and an arm and half a face disappeared.

Johnny couldn't find a target as he worked his way through the heavy black smoke that combined with his efforts of running up a mountainside overloaded with gear, to choke what seemed to be the very life air out of him.

A tail-end Charlie, an F4U finally finding its target, winged overhead, releasing its napalm into the smoke, lit up the earth as it bounced like the sing-along bouncing ball at the drive-in theaters.

Johnny couldn't understand how he could think about the days of the drive-in while running into hell to kill or be killed . . . *We hid so many friends . . . in the trunk of Soupy's father's old Lasalle . . . that the front end kept lifting off the ground . . . as the Soup drove it into the outdoor theater . . .*

Johnny remembered Scoff's words in the black of the trunk, "The first one who cuts one is dead!" And then he set about looking for any change that might have fallen from the pockets of his friends who formed the ball of kids wrapped together like a ball of worms.

"Shit!" Johnny's foot struck a fallen marine, and he went down when his boondocker lodged in the large hole that once had been a rib cage. To add to the punishment, a blob of napalm burned around the wound hole. The flame sang its silent song as the screaming soldier begged for death before a final indignity visited him, crying for his mother while his bowels filled his pants.

Johnny was close now, so close, the firefight seemed to be taking place inside his head.

Then he saw his first enemy running directly at him, but not interested in Johnny, as he attempted to brush the napalm off his body but only managed to fan the flames, which climbed upward and clung on his face as a gold tooth melted within a grimace. His face melted and dripped like a slab of bacon in a sizzling hot, fat-popping frying pan . . . *Oh my good Christ . . .* "Fall, you stupid son of a bitch!"

Johnny fired his BAR at the burning soldier, trying to bring him down. But the automatic fire, the closeness of the two, only managed to keep the inferno with the now-melting eyes upright.

Then he fell. Johnny slid a second magazine into his BAR, stood over the blackened body, staring at once had been a face but now was only a set of smiling teeth.

Why didn't the teeth melt? . . . The lead melted . . . Jesus . . . the lead fillings . . . dripped down . . . like black lava . . . down a blackened hillside . . . Oh shit, I'm sick . . .

What had been a mountainside was now a smoking earth, shattered trees, shattered gook hoochie huts similar to the marine bunkers, shattered people.

Then as quickly as it started, everything was quiet, except for the silent screaming of the dead, whose voices were louder than the agonized cries of the wounded. A few marines ran down the few surviving NKPA soldiers, shooting them in the back, bayoneting the wounded, these strange young men who had killed marines, not really knowing why.

Wounded men crawled around in anger and fright, ants on their damaged anthill.

Johnny watched as one of the wounded jumped to his feet and ran downhill close to the ground . . . *Christ . . . he looks like some sort of a small fullback . . . trying to make it unseen through giant defensive linemen . . . He looks like that rubber tire in the farm sandpit . . . bouncing down the hillside . . .*

Johnny brought up his BAR, snapped off a single shot; watched as the runner kicked forward, his head between his legs, a perfect 10 in any gymnastic meet. But the gook wasn't dead, or was dead and didn't know it, and moved along in a mime's duck walk . . . *Coachie made us do that duck walk . . . for hours . . . He knew we hated it . . . but then again . . . we never had any ankle injuries . . . What the fuck am I doing? . . . Concentrate . . . Think staying alive . . .*

The living enemy wasn't answering. Surely, the artillery and napalm had blown all to smithereens or dissolved them to ashes. It was the chatter of the Able company BARs and M1s, with the sharp "sprinnnn" noises of M1 empty clips flying out of the gun breach announcing, "I'm empty" to all that showed that some surviving gooks were wrong way Corrigans and had retreated right into dead pointblank fire.

But then these rabbits, exhausted from the exertion, also got tired of being chased and turned to greet the hound dogs that had been disemboweling them on the run and returned fire. The whining in the air was both that of American and gook guns, bees from different hives gone insane.

The retreating North Koreans were replaced by hordes of charging Chinese troops that had crossed the border without being detected by American intelligence. Intelligence had informed those fighting on the front lines that there were no Chinese in North Korea, despite the capture of Chinese troops by marines.

The first hordes were stacked up like cordwood at the barbed wire, yet many made it through the point-blank fire to die a barrel length away from the young marines of the high-school graduating classes of 1949 and 50, high-school drop-outs, old salt regulars from classes of 1941 and '42, and reserves from Augusta and elsewhere. In close, the Chinese soldiers were hit so often that at first, their riddled bodies were held in the air, dancing like puppets on their hot lead strings, before the decency of falling in death was awarded them.

The firing slowed, stopped. The thin green line of marines stood staring at their new antagonist, who also stood without firing; both were mostly out of ammunition.

Then a voice cut through the air, "Dog, let's move those bastards." It was the Dog Company commander. "Fix bayonets."

Almost in slow motion, the bayonets clattered out of the scabbards and onto rifle ends.

The clattering transfixed Johnny for a moment . . . *It sounds like my aunts . . . washing the dishes . . .*

The Chinese troops, fearless in the face of gunfire, turned and ran, walked and crawled away before the fixed bayonets.

"Let's get the bastards," someone yelled, and Dog gave chase again, reloading with ammunition taken from their own dead and wounded, shooting from the hip as they advanced.

But they ran into the Chinese reserves and were caught in a crossfire of enfilade and defilade from the enemy, fire that chopped up men like branches being fed into a tree limb chipper. The Chinese left their hiding spots and closed in on the trapped Americans.

The Dog Company commander radioed and called in all the artillery and mortar fire on the marine position as they spread the word to hit the holes. Some made it into a hole, and some did not, as the incoming screamed in their ears and exploded.

Johnny, looked for any hole dug by human hands or the fiery spit of the cascading mortar and artillery rounds. He thought he was hit in the legs by gunfire, but it was the shards of shattered rocks sent ricocheting by the incoming artillery rounds of the Eleventh Marines. He hit the deck, where he lay facedown in the snow that looked like a Salvador Dali painting done in blood and soot. The snow he munched was good; tasted better when the artillery fire stopped. One by one, the marines dug their faces out of the ground and brought their weapons up in front of them from their hugging positions.

When he looked up, there was nothing, no one standing. The Chinese who had overrun the company were skewered, along with several marines that didn't make it to a hole.

That's when Johnny heard the familiar voice, "Johnny, you sure look silly."

Johnny slowly turned his head, trying to determine whether it was still on his shoulders.

It was Soupy. He was sitting against a shattered tree, holding himself steady with his arms to the side, a grin on his face.

"What's that shit-eating grin for?" Johnny asked.

"Skunk pissed on me again. I'm just glad you're here to get me home, like you did that day. Remember? The polecat piss burned my eyes so

I couldn't see. Darn pole cat followed me all my life." His eyes looked downward.

Johnny followed them.

Soupy's legs were mangled; pieces of bone showed through the flesh like the wooden ribs of a long-lost three-mast schooner rotting in the sun and sands of Cape Cod. "It's going to be tough trying to climb the Big Tree now," he said.

Shots snapped overhead. Then one of the bodies that was mangled so badly, you couldn't tell whether it was a marine or an enemy, sat bolt upright, energized by gas and shattered nerves ends, and sprayed automatic fire and blood through the air. Then slowly returned backward to the earth like someone completing sit-up exercises.

Johnny had hit the deck when the dead man fired then crawled back to Soupy, who was still smiling. As Johnny burrowed through the snow, he hoped his ass or head wasn't showing above its surface. He thought of the moles that burrowed through the bluegrass lawn of his Aunt Hope, how lucky they were to be moving underground. She would challenge the lawn wreckers with her "Come on out and fight like a man, you darn moles." . . . *Darn . . . she was so ashamed . . . thinking darn was a curse . . . but she sure hated their furry little asses . . .*

"Fuck it," he said, standing up and walking toward his friend, "if they want to kill me and the fucking camel I rode in on. Well, fuck it and the old oaken bucket to boot."

He felt like he was standing upright, at high noon, on the midway shooting gallery, and he was the little metal bear who, when you hit one, would fall over, or turn and walk in the other direction, as if it wanted to get shot in its bare ass. It did all this when the shot hit the shoulder, and a bright light lit up.

Johnny looked at Soupy's legs. What was left was twisted like strands of spaghetti, steaming spaghetti as pieces of hot metal smoked out of his flesh.

Johnny rested the BAR against the tree, went to his knees, and hugged Soupy's twisted legs. His eyes were wide, as if they would inflate like a balloon.

"I'll make a tourniquet."

"Don't bother."

"I can stop the bleeding in both legs."

"Sure, in the legs, but not here." Soupy took his hands off his stomach. The smoke and the blood fought for the one body exit.

"You're fine. You're gonna make it."

"Remember the day I dropped the flat rock on that sleeping skunk? Jesus, you looked surprised when I did that."

"Yah, that's an understatement."

"After that, the guys wouldn't even let me into the Big Woods, let alone the Big Tree."

"Yah."

"But you started chasing them around in the Big Tree like a chimp chasing baby monkeys to make them behave. Then all was OK. I climbed up there. Those were the days."

Johnny didn't want to look into Soupy's eyes. They looked like those of a Bassett, saddened beyond explanation.

"John."

Johnny looked up and into his eyes. They were too bright. He stared into Johnny's. The corners of his mouth were turned up as if he was smiling, except blood was leaking out of the smile.

They both knew he would never climb the Big Tree again.

But there was no time for mourning as the angry runaway lawnmower sounds came down from above. The Chinese were standing and fighting again.

The sound of the weapons on both sides indicated it was turning into a one-way conversation as the American guns stuttered and stopped.

"Let's move out!" It was the gunny, off and running at a slow trot, Tommy gun at a high port. "Sounds like Able needs help."

Johnny looked at Soupy, his smile lost in death. Johnny wanted to close his eyes, wipe the blood from the corner of his mouth, take his fingers, and put the smile back on that sad face.

Instead, he jumped to his feet, screaming, "The cocksuckers! Cocksuckers! Kill the slant-eyed cocksuckers!"

He was charging, running up hill at top speed, wondering why the thin line that was once Able, Baker, and Dog was so slow . . . so very slow . . . keeping up with him.

"Kill!" He heard the shrill voice scream. Looked to the side as he ran to find out who was with him, doing the screaming . . . *Fuck me . . . it's fucken' me . . . It's me . . . screaming . . .*

Now he could see the muzzle blasts from behind trees, stumps, and rocks.

The fuckers . . . want me . . .

Every fourth and nine steps, he feinted one way, dodged the other . . . *fourth and . . . ninth . . . steps missing, hit the deck . . . roll . . . fourth and nine . . . Jazz . . . remember . . . four and nine . . . be careful . . . like Roma . . .*

It was the explosion of the Dog Company bazooka being fired from behind him that got his attention.

He asked himself . . . *Why behind me . . . ?*

He glanced back down the mountain. The angry bees' spit by the Russian-made burp guns were below him.

Why . . . below . . . me . . . ?

He glanced back below. The killer bees now were being spit out of the mouths of weapons from both sides as they battled for control of the very air they, the American and Chinese troops, sucked in.

Johnny had caught up to his mates and ran through their lines and through the enemy line. He was now looking back on both fighting groups, his thoughts unable to focus, and he drifted in the middle of a firestorm, backward . . . *The enemy is spitting bees . . . at little brother and me . . . at Jazz . . . We were knocking down dead trees . . . near Mahoney's piggery . . . We were Indians . . . with our war clubs . . . Jazz and me . . . then the bees . . . nested in that one rotten tree . . . spitting . . . stinging . . . me pushing Jazz ahead . . . killing the bees on him . . . My pants were falling . . . They stung the crack of my ass . . . I wanted them out . . . but the bees were after Jazz . . . Kill them . . . A bee got in the crack of my ass . . .*

In my ear . . . but Jazz was home-free . . . Now the bees want me . . . Who will kill them? . . . They want to eat me . . . alive . . . eat me dead . . .

But the killing ridge was below him . . . The shitten gooks . . . look like black ants down there . . . easy pickings . . . like tires hardly moving down the farm sandpit . . . They hauled too much gravel out . . . The farm's sandpit was flattening out . . . I'll fix their asses . . . They won't even know . . . where their death came from . . .

He dove behind a large rock. His body bounced. Like a fornicator without his girl beneath him.

Below, the remnant rags of the three marine companies were nearing the enemy.

He could turn the tide. Easy pickings. They weren't looking behind them. Johnny felt great joy. Now they would pay.

Johnny didn't shoot.

The marines were in the same anthill below with the enemy shooting, stabbing, and ripping apart by hand.

He hadn't shot. Couldn't, as in his insanity at Soupy's wounds, he had charged upward, leaving his BAR . . . *It's leaning on Soupy's tree . . . Soupy has two rifles . . . He doesn't need even . . . one . . . now . . . I need one . . . can use a thousand of them . . .*

Johnny watched as the enemy line below broke and headed uphill toward him, now in full retreat.

He hugged the ground and tried to dig a hole with his torn fingers, with his teeth. They were coming.

Toward me . . . Soupy's last look . . . bright . . . glazed . . . no light . . . ever again . . .

Johnny started sobbing . . . *Please God . . . help me . . . help me . . . because . . . because . . . because I'm crying . . . crying for . . . not for Soupy . . . for me . . .*

He saw the burp gun leveled at him. The frantic eyes.

Such a little man . . . such a big gun . . . Big Tree . . . Big Tree . . . ma . . . ma . . . maaaa . . . baaaaa . . . Those aren't the . . . goat's . . . testicles . . . hanging from its neck . . . maaaa . . .

He saw the dirty hand on the trigger of the burp gun . . . *Such a small hand . . . with its tiny fingers . . . tightened on the trigger . . . Little boy . . . please put away your toy . . . You already ruined a Soupy doll . . . Besides . . . you smell of garlic . . . brusha, brusha . . . brusha . . . with the new . . . ipana . . .*

Less than a second passed from the time he saw the dirty finger on the burp gun, the tiny fingers aiming death at him . . . *Bibles . . . I need bibles all over my . . . body . . .*

Johnny felt the blast of the burp gun, could feel the cold heat of bullets whiz through his clothing. The burst slapped his jacket against his body with such force he was sure he had been flayed.

He went down. Everything was black.

"DaSilva. DaSilva!"

Johnny could feel himself being shaken. He opened his eyes. It was the gunny looking down at him. "Where you hit?"

Johnny couldn't check for injuries. The dead enemy soldier with the tiny fingers was on top of him, his blood splattered now like a sloppy Salvador Dali art all over him. He was the canvas of death.

The gunny rolled the dead soldier off him.

"Thanks, Sarge. The gook's breath smelled." He looked at the blood all over himself. "I guess I bought it."

The gunny checked Johnny for wounds.

"Nothin'."

"I felt the blast. I felt the fucken; blast. The gook's bullets clipping me!"

"They were mine clipping through this sucker with the burp. You're only gonna need a new field jacket. You lucky cock knocker."

"My good Jesus. You mean I'm alive?"

"Nice job."

"What, being alive?"

"No, porgy bait brain. Your heading up into the Chinks, cryin', 'Get the cocksuckers' got us all off the deck and heading up after those cocksuckers that did it to Soupy, Able, and Baker, and tried to do it to Dog. 'Cause of you, little big man, we did it to them. Did it doggy-style. You're some sort of half-arse hero."

"The guys—"

"Don't know. We gotta count heads. But the bastards are on the run. These were the last of the stubborn ones, but now they've joined all the other sprinters heading to Manchuria. It's like a shooting gallery. They're running in the open, in full daylight."

"They're not all running, Sarge." It was Lace, carrying a flamethrower. "Some is Southern fried chicken."

"Yah. Yah. Good work, Lace."

The tall Southerner smiled, "Gonna go cook some more goose. See y'all."

"Yah. Yah. Be good."

Lace disappeared in the bush with a Rebel cry.

"I mean be 'careful,' Reb. Not good." Then turning to Johnny, "Where's your BAR? Did you jam it up some gook's ass and have one of those .30-calibers greet a garlic fart head on? I'd bet on the fart."

"Yah. Yah. I have to go get it. Had to put it down a bit, to pick up rocks to toss at the gooks."

"I bet. I bet you burned out the barrel. Melted it. Bet you shattered it over some gook's head. Better get what's left of it, so we can get it bronzed. Get it, or the Marine Corps will make you pay for it."

"Seriously?"

"You bite for every piece of shit put on the hook?"

Johnny walked downhill to the ridge that took most of the punishment. Corpsmen were treating the wounded. A chaplain was praying over one.

Johnny looked at the priest in disbelief . . . *Where in hell did . . . he come from . . . ?*

"Hey, padre, where in heaven did you come from?" Johnny asked. "Can you come down to my friend?"

"Where's Soupy?" It was Righty. "Last time I saw him, the burps were all around us, and he was complaining about no hot chow in four days, while we got shot at. He's one hot shit, a sad sack hot shit. Then we got up and ran at the bastards. The Soup was complaining with that sorrowful, sad, hangdog look of his that we ain't had no hot chow in a month of Sundays. Complaining he was already tired of sleeping on the ground, that even the troop ship racks would look good right now. All this during the shooting."

"He had a small smile, almost happy when I left him, Righty."

"Good."

"No. Not even a little bit good. It's as ungood as it can get."

Righty stared, wordless. "I can't buy that. I can't buy it."

Johnny put his arms around his little friend as they rested their heads on the other's shoulders.

Tim appeared from out of the smoke, saw his friends, and wrapped his arms around both. "No Big Tree here to escape to. I'm guessing the Big Woods is lost forever."

"No," Johnny said, "we're going to sit in the Big Tree again someday."

They separated, each walking off in silence, and kept busy helping the corpsmen with the nonambulatory, while the walking wounded headed down mountain toward the battalion and what passed for the field hospital.

Johnny put off working his way to Soupy, building up his courage, lying to himself that the wounded had to be taken care of first, but all the walking wounded were already out of sight. Others were carefully rolled onto stretchers, and then were gone, lugged by exhausted marines, carried as gently as a small girl carrying a butterfly in her palms, down the steep icy slope. Yet despite their gentleness, litter bearers fell, and wounded crashed to the frozen ground, their own shattered bones stabbing into them. The dropped wounded were often buried in the snow and had to be found and dug out by hand, screaming out in pain or whispering in supplication. Nearly all were blind as the swirling snow froze in the eye sockets, the nostrils, even inside the lips.

One wounded marine, his frozen blood gluing him to a makeshift poncho stretcher, pointed to a burning body and asked to be carried there so he could get warmed.

It wasn't his wounds stuck in his mind. It was the thoughts of others frozen and with frostbite, hands and feet that first turned a bright red, then white, blue, then black. It was black that allowed toes, nose, or fingers to be snapped off, like breaking off a turkey leg at Thanksgiving.

Others did not let out a sound as the fall was the final indignity as they died, spew in their mouth, excrement from their bowels soaking their trousers, a baptism into death with shit and puke serving as substitutes for the oils and holy waters. There would be no oohs and ahs of proud parents and friends as there were at their baptism into life.

The last face the dying saw on this earth was a stranger, a caring one, a very sad one, a young face old beyond years, but a face that was thankful it wasn't him looking up one last time.

When Johnny came across Soupy, he had slid down the tree that had supported him in such a way that his and Johnny's rifles had formed a cross on his chest.

The dead man's hands, soaked in his own blood, rested on Johnny's BAR.

God . . . you're just not a happy god . . . just killing him . . . You want to crucify him . . . You're not going . . . to get away with . . . killing . . . my friends . . . I'll never talk to you . . . again . . . ever . . . you bad god . . .

Johnny propped his dead friend against the tree. Freed the two rifles. Slung his over his shoulder . . . *They're gonna bronze it . . . because I'm a hero . . . Heroes don't cry . . . forget their rifle . . . have to throw rocks . . . I can't tell them . . . I charged without my rifle . . . I can't tell . . .*

He walked slowly away, turned, looked at Soupy, and returned to the tree and sat beside him.

"Just like the Big Tree, huh, little buddy? Huh, little buddy? Cat's got your tongue? Come on. Come *on!* Don't get me mad. *Come on!*" . . . *please . . .*

"You bastard God." . . . *Grandfather Shiverick . . . never would have pulled this . . . shit . . . if he was god . . . especially on people that love . . . you . . . loved you . . . oh god . . . like I love Soupy . . . You know, God . . . I was with him the day he dropped that giant rock on that sleeping skunk . . . I was there . . . It was one of the great days in . . . history . . . All he really wanted to do was . . . wake that little skunk up . . . It was as if he woke up Old Faithful . . . It pissed all over him . . . but what do you care, God? . . .* "Don't give me that shit about a caring God. Don't give me that crap that we're all your children." . . . *You don't kill your children . . . do you, God? . . . Tell me if you do . . .*

"Soupy, you smell worse today than that day you rocked that skunk to sleep."

Johnny watched as that one big waft of the dead marine's body heat escaped, leaving a misty aura.

"Jesus, Soupy, you scared the living shit out of me."

Johnny had seen body heat escaping before, when he had shot the giant whitetail buck that had hid out for years on that too-faraway mountaintop swamp. He was sitting on a rock beside the animal when the last mist of its heat left, heavenward, in the exact shape of its body. Then the body mist disappeared as if it never was. Much of the exhilaration of the hunt became a new mystery.

Johnny took his friend's face in his hands, kissed his forehead, and sang softly, "Swing low, sweet chariot, coming to a carry you ho—"

But the word "home" would not come out. *Not come out . . . come out . . . you fucken' bastard word . . . come out . . .*

"Comin' to a carry you ho— ho. Yah, ho-ho, home. A real good laugh on us, God, you unholy ghost."

He felt the arm around his shoulder. "Come with me, John." It was Tim, squatting beside him. Righty was on the other side, helping him up.

"It's not your fault, Johnny." It was Pointer. "I don't know who. It's someone's, and we'll find out who. We'll get him."

Johnny sang softly as he was led away, "For I cherish the old rugged cross—"

"Are you OK, brother?" Tim asked, looking at Johnny's soot-covered face . . . *Now we're brothers forever . . . Johnny . . .*

"For I cherish the old rugged cross."

The others tried to sing with him, hummed along with him, unable to get the words out.

"Form up, you killer assholes! We're chasing those bastards out of the country."

The voice was familiar, but there wasn't an officer's bars in black stencil on the collar. Not even the single stripe of a PFC on his sleeve. Not all officers had the black stencils of rank on their collars. If captured, it meant a torture far beyond that of the enlisted man. These noninsignia officers showed rank with voice presence.

The figure trotted off in the direction of the fleeing North Koreans. "Let's get 'em."

The figure outdistanced them.

Then Johnny remembered the voice, "Seabag!"

"You're shittin'," Righty said.

"No, he's right," Tim said.

"Let's go, Marines!" It was Gunny Murphy now, first waving his arm in a "come forward" motion, and then giving it the "double time" pump overhead.

There was a roar as Dog formed up behind him, running at high port. To where? They did not know. Into what? They did not know. They did not care as the endorphins kicked in like spurs into a racing horse's ribs.

"Saddle up," Lieutenant Smith shouted to those wounded and exhausted that could follow. They trudged, snowmen colored with blood.

The only enemy to shoot was the wounded. Some of whom still tried to reach their weapons.

What surprised the young marines was the lack of fright on many of the faces.

Johnny tried to figure. What was there? Anger? Acceptance?

The "Whoa up" went along the line.

Then "Form up, we could be running into another trap."

The 'form up' wasn't that stiff at attention on the parade ground.

Troops stood slumped, sitting propped up on a rock or stump or a pile of frozen snow as the head count was taken.

Dog had received twenty-two replacements the day before.

And would need twenty-four from the next draft landing in Japan.

"The first day, and we lose twenty-two out of 180 men. In a week that nearly everyone is gone," Scoff said.

"This was their last stand. This hill," the gunny said. "This was their rear guard. A holding action so their Ching Chong Chinamen buddies can hightail their rice-eating asses back up north."

"What are you saying?" Fats asked.

"I'm saying that most of our losses will be to the clap and syph from here on in, or heart attacks chasing these guys. That's what MacArthur says, home by Christmas! We shall return."

"He shall return, MacArthur thinks he's on Bataan," Scoff said.

"We're gonna chase these diddly-doos right into Manchuria." It was Quince Carrey, who claimed he was an Indian and called himself Walking Jay, a tall thin Kentuckyian who had landed on both Iwo and Tawawa. In both cases, he had only made it less than one hundred feet up the beach from his landing craft before getting whacked.

He had gotten out after World War II ended, but when Korea came along, he'd realized that the quiet of the catfishing and squirrel hunting that he had dreamed about as he island-hopped was not enough.

He had dreamed of plinking gray squirrels in the high treetops, arm wrestling catfish from beneath the banks, and cooking them up in the same frying pan, even as he hunkered low in the landing craft, and when he hunkered low in the mosquito-infested jungle.

Walking Jay dreamed of squirrel hunting and catfishing all the time, even the two times he was hit on the beach and stared into the boiling sun. "Yes, sir, I'd rather be catfishin'."

He was wrong. He talked slow and walked slow. But he needed the fast lane of combat, despite the fact that the first time the Japanese artillery had pounded down on them. He had scratched in the earth with his hands, his feet, shaking like a mouse before a cat's maw. But then he realized that this fear gave him the most fantastic erection of his life. A real-live hardwood woodie! One if used as a bat by the Splendid Splinter Ted Williams would crack home runs with the power of a constipated cow finally farting.

He never understood this "erection under fright" syndrome. He rarely was given the boon of even a modest stiffy during the workaday week.

It was a double scoop when he re-signed up for Korea, not only would he get possible future hardwood woodies but he would also be presented with the stripes of a corporal as well.

The triple scoop of reward for re-upping came later when he got to tell sea stories to the new replacements.

His and their favorite of course was his discovery of the "terror hard-on."

"There I wuz, diggin' with my feet and hands, diggin' like crazy. My head and feet would be hidden beneath the surface, but my ass sure and shooting could get torn off by one of those 'no ticky, no laundry, sake-suckin' little yellow guys. I realized my entire body was now beneath snow, diggin' at the frozen top soil with my entrenching tool, digging right along with my hard-on. I asked God to shoot out my heart first, a heart over hard-on choice."

"You telling us," Righty said, "that you got a hard-on because you was scared, that your private did some digging? That you shipped over for a hard-on!"

"Yup, but first of all, young sir, anything as fine as my dingus is not a private. I think general, or at least full-bird colonel, would be more fitting rank for such a fine piece of manhood equipment."

"Here's a bird for you," Rhesus said, throwing his right hand in the air, the middle finger extended high.

"Why, young Mr. Rhesus, I didn't realize your hand was mangled in that last battle."

His buddies gave Rhesus the razz.

"I haven't eaten since Methuselah was a pup," Johnny said, "except for that hardtack and beans. What a combo, I could nail a buffalo hide to the wall with my fart dart."

"I bet the navy is eating steak right about now, taking a hot shower, going to a soft bed," Fats said.

"Hah!" It was the corpsman, only known as Chief, an American Sioux.

"You're not navy, you're corps," Fats said.

"Yes, but the navy eagle shits for the Chief."

"What was that 'Hoka Hey' you were chanting when you went into help Able and Baker's boys when they got all shot up?" Tim asked.

"That was some good happy horse shit you pulled, Chief," Skinny said. "You didn't have a rat's ass chance in hell to survive that crossfire. It was hotter than a whore's ass in Augusta in August."

"Yah, when I heard that Hoka Hey chant," Johnny said, "I figured it was some kind of Injun fire water cry that you had run out and needed more. No one sober would have gone in there."

"Able and Baker went in," the Chief said, "and then Dog. All chanted, 'Hoka Hey.'"

"Well, tell us what we were chanting then," Johnny said.

"Hoka Hey, it's a good day for dying."

"Isn't that what Crazy Horse said?" Tim asked.

"No. Custer said it. But only when he had no other choice."

"And you didn't even get a scratch, when everyone around you was put down," Pointer said.

"Too busy to get shot."

"You're gonna get a fucken' medal, along with Johnny," Righty said.

"No medal. I didn't even have a gun. Only morphine and compresses."

Johnny wanted to confess that he had left his rifle behind. He couldn't get the words out. And instead said, "I just threw rocks at them as I headed up after them."

"Jesus, John Wayne revisited," Rhesus said, adding, "How long we gonna keep moving along?"

"We're clocking some miles all right," Johnny said.

"Aren't we supposed to dig in or something before dark? Someone's screwing up, probably Lieutenant Smith," Pointer said.

"Keep moving, Gouveira," the gunny said.

"I'm sick. I'm reporting to sick bay," Pointer said. He had been holding his breath off and on to build up that look of having a fever, a trick that worked in school on warm days when the largemouth bass fishing was good.

"Listen, Gouveira, and listen closely. You've used up all your sick leave. Don't call in again back at battalion unless it's to call in dead."

"Funny, really funny," Pointer said.

"In fact, you look so good, take that mortar base plate from your buddy Fats. And how in hell does a skinny bastard like Fats get that name? Never mind, grab the plate."

"I'm not hungry."

"In Bobby Doerr's last twenty trips to the plate—he has eaten. Get it? Trips to the plate—instead of getting a hit on his trip to the plate, he ate instead," Rhesus said, imitating a baseball announcer.

"Shit, that mortar plate weighs a ton, it's Two Ton Tony Galente. Fats is even stronger than he looks. Give it to Lace. It can keep his flamethrower company. He can cook hotdogs on it. He won't even realize he is carrying it."

"I don't want this little goofy taking this man's plate," Fats said.

"Shut up. Give it to him."

"I've got a pack on my back. If I put it back there, I'll fall over backward," Pointer said.

"It's got straps. Put it on your chest."

"I'll fall forward."

"You little piss cutter, Gouveira, it will take exactly two and one half steps to get to you and kick your ass forty yards for a three-pointer," the gunny said.

"All right."

Johnny helped his cousin get his pack off and put the straps of the mortar base plate around his shoulders in such a way that the heavy plate was on his chest. Then he helped slip the combat pack back on him.

"This is lousy. I'm gonna write to my congressman," Pointer said.

The gunny took a step toward him.

"I'm gonna recommend you for a medal," Pointer said.

"Don't worry, Gun, my cousin's going to learn to fire that M1 rather than shooting off his mouth," Johnny said, winking at the platoon sergeant.

"How do you figure this shit?" the gunny said, moving out to the front of his men again. "Both got the same blood in them. One guy runs right into the gooks, right though them, in fact. Who knows how many he killed, and this other thing was shitting his pants."

"Where do you figure we heading, Gunny?" Tim asked.

"Somewhere."

"That's what I guessed."

"My first guess is up the Seoul-Kaesong Highway, that's the way all those chopsticks are thumbing rides to, to keep ahead of us."

"I can't figure it, Gunny," Quince said, working his hand under his helmet and scratching his head without taking the piss pot off. The skinny Kentuckian, who had had a full mop of curly blue-black hair when he had joined the corps, had started losing his hair during his World War II island-hopping and could not get used to the fact it was gone. It would be a hot day in the Arctic before he would be seen with his hat off. "From Incheon, all through Seoul, they fought to the last man. Some of the silly shits seemed to still be pumping lead even after they were dead. They gotta be half Jap."

"They took some tonnage. The navy, artillery, our planes poured it on with us. It was like the earth opened and hell said hello to them," the gunny said.

"Thing that surprised me most was the size of these guys. I always thought Orientals were small," Fats said, "and that I'd be a giant among them."

"You wouldn't be a giant even if you hung out with the Seven Dwarfs," Lace said, waving the nozzle of his flamethrower like a maestro's baton. "Put a butt in your mouth, Fats. I'll light it for you, Dwarf Dopey."

"And Snow White would puke just looking at you," Fats said.

Lace stepped toward the little marine.

"Will you guys save a little bit for the real cockfight?" Carrey said.

"You give a guy a couple of stripes, and he becomes Napoleon," Scoff said.

"Another country heard from," Rhesus said. "You come out of hibernation. Eat all your fish?"

"Up yours."

"It would be the best you ever had."

"Last time! Save it for the NKPA and Chinks," Carrey said.

"What the hell's that? I heard of the WPA, 'we poke along,' the NRA, the FBI, the IRS, but no NKPA," Skinny said, blowing across the end of his carbine barrel, trying to get it to whistle.

"North Korean People's Army, dipstick," Carrey said.

"Take his head and stick it up my ass," Lace said. "I think I'm a quart low."

"You know something?" the gunny said. "I don't think you guys understand we're gonna be walking. Then walking some more and maybe even some more. Right to China, so save your breath for up the next hill, and the hill after. You just might want to save a little of that gas too".

The road was narrow, and they walked single file on each side, ready to do a barrel roll into the ditch if it hit the fan.

The troop movement was relatively quiet. The new men learned from the survivors how to quiet their equipment.

Then the single shot rang out. Like a bell.

"I'm hit!"

It was Pointer. He was flat on his back in the road. The rest were in the ditch.

Johnny was the first to look over the edge of his protection. He could just reach Pointer's hand. He started to pull, trying to keep hunkered low. While Pointer was a feather merchant, the combat pack and mortar base made him a handful. A second arm reached out, took Pointer's other hand, and helped pull him to safety. It was Lace.

"Hey," Pointer said, "take it easy."

The two had pulled Pointer in with such fury that he flew into the ditch, landing on top of Rhesus, who was in the very bottom, and said, "No one farts."

"Let me take a look." It was the Chief.

The big Indian checked Pointer over from head to foot. "Can't find nothing."

"Where'd you look, in his head?" Lace said.

"I had a guy die in my arms, not a mark on him," Carrey said. "Later we found a tiny sliver of shrapnel in his throat."

"Oh, Jesus Christ, thanks," Pointer said, clutching his throat. "Check my throat, Chief."

The giant corpsman checked his throat. "Goiter."

"Goiter! Am I gonna die?"

"You asshole, eat more iodine," Lace said.

"I'm not eating no medicine they put on cuts," Pointer said.

"Fish, eat fish to gain iodine to shrink that throat that looks like it swallowed a yo-yo in action. It looks like your Adam's apple is having sex on a string, you touch hole," Lace said.

"Where'd you get hit?" the Chief asked.

"Right in the chest, Chief."

"The chest? You're right. Here's a ping right in the middle of the plate."

"It hit the mortar plate!" Pointer exclaimed. "Tell the gunny the corps doesn't have enough men to get this plate back from me! You tell him I'll kill anyone who comes after it. The son of a bitch never mentioned it made you bullet proof."

"Keep your fuckin' heads down," Quince Carrey said, "unless you need a free haircut. That sucker sniper is still out there, lockin' and loadin'."

"OK, knock it off." It was the gunny. "DaSilva, Yanders, you saw the position Pointer was in when he got knocked down out there. What position was he in on the deck when he was whacked?"

"His head was near the ditch, Sarge," Tim said. "His legs out straight. He fell backward. Like a tree."

The gunny sketched Pointer's position in the snow and studied the sniper's bullet nick in the mortar base.

He took off his helmet, held it just above the edge of the ditch with his right hand, while placing a clod of mud and snow on his head, and slowly raised his gaze, scanning a section of the mountainside opposite them.

Nothing.

"I think one of us has to stick his head out for a split second to draw a shot so we can spot the prick," the gunny said.

"I volunteer," Rhesus said, "for Pointer to stick his head up. The Chinks can't hit a pin."

"Fuck you, numb nut."

"Shut the fuck up," the gunny said. "There's a big splintered tree at ten o'clock, about ten clicks up from the road. And a patch of heavy brush just to the left of it. The fucks gotta be there. Take a quick peek. OK. When I give the word, I'll count to three, we pop up and piss all over it."

The marines in the ditch near him nodded in agreement.

"Three!" The gunny skipped one and two so he could get off the first spray from his carbine. His men followed suit, and leaves flew through the air as bullets shredded the bush like branches fed into a forester's chipper.

The sniper shot upright when he caught the first round in the groin but didn't have a chance to fall to the ground as the heavy fire poured into him, holding him upright and pushing backward up the hill several steps.

The gunny was not heard in the firing at first. "Whoa! Are you pussy fuckin' deaf or somethin'? Cease fucken' fire. What the fuck you think you're doing wasting fuckin' ammo like fuckin' that?"

"I just wanted to see if I could walk him to the top of the hill," Pointer said. "After all, the dick breath tried to kill me."

"Oh, you like to waste ammo, is that it? You carry the ammo boxes for heavy weapons tomorrow, Mr. Jesse Fucken' James," the gunny said.

"Only if I can carry my motor plate too," Pointer whispered to his cousin.

Johnny smiled and kissed him on the cheek.

"I get him first," Rhesus said. "You get sloppy seconds."

"Sure," Lace said. "How come there's no smoke coming out of your barrel?" pointing at the muzzle of the unfired M1.

"Shit, I musta left my safety on. If I hadn't, I would have gotten him first."

"Left your safety on, left your safety on, you mutton head. I bet you're still wearing the rubber from when you got your ashes hauled in Tijuana town."

"How'd you like a bayonet up your keeister?" Rhesus said.

"I didn't know you could speak Italian," Righty said, touching his fingers to his lips then flicking a kiss to Rhesus.

"A bayonet up my ass, you say?" Lace said, leering at Rhesus, bending over, and spreading the cheeks of his buttocks. "Try your finger. You might fall in love."

"Better not go with the finger, Rhesus," Johnny said, smiling. "I saw him put a set of false teeth up his coo-lo this morning. They'll bite the hand that feeds you."

Lace laughed.

"Lace isn't feeling good," Righty said. "He's smiling, and no one got their head caved in."

"Talking about butts," Rhesus said, changing the subject, "remember that corpsman in Boston—that 'skin it back, turn around, bend over, spread 'em, shove off' one? When he got to the spread em' part with me, he doesn't say 'shove off,' instead he says 'you got red hair on your ass as well as your balls.' I knew the three dollar bill was falling in love. He was falling in love with my butt-tocks. I tried to fart. Just as well, I couldn't. He would 'ave come."

"Go on," Johnny said, "this sounds like that Stella Dallas radio show my mother used to listen to."

"Anyway, to break up this budding romance, I accused him of practicing proctology without a license."

"My old man was a plumber," the Kentuckian Quince Carrey said, "and always bragged that one man's shit is another man's gold."

"Well, I wasn't letting him do any mining in my butt," Rhesus said.

"OK, listen up." It was Lieutenant Smith walking up the middle of the road as if was walking through Boston Commons. "Captain Hundley wants us up on that ridge for the night."

"OK, you three, take the point," the gunny said, pointing to his choice.

Tim, Johnny, and Righty found themselves as point, out ahead, as dark took them in like the black shroud put over the condemned man's head.

While the second lieutenants tried to get point men to believe it was their job to "see what you can see," the point realized being the point meant "draw fire so the platoon and company commanders can see what they can see."

The climb at certain points meant grabbing a small tree and pulling yourself upward. Other times, it was so steep that only crawling on all fours meant progress. Then there were the steepest sections that called for crawling on your stomach. This also meant having to hold your weapon, ammo box, mortar plate, light machine gun tripod, whatever, off to the side and dragging them along like a bird with broken wings trying to crawl. Then there was the sheer ice near the peak, which called for pulling yourself along on your stomach by digging a KA-BAR knife into the ice.

Despite the bitter cold, the sweat and swears fought for the right to be the meanest. The swearing sounded like good stuff, but the sweat, although silent, won out, as it burned eyes, made cargo slick, and boiled the snow-soaked balls, leaving the men steaming in the mean high wind and cold.

Dog stopped its upward climb at 0100, on the defendable ridge.

"Corporal Carrey, get the listening posts out. Set the trips. Put two BARs on that ravine." It was the gunny.

"Aye-aye."

"Keep that aye-aye off me. You want me to get shot by some sniper who thinks I'm a naval officer?"

"Aye-aye. That's the last thing I want, you catching it. Then they'd probably make me gunny. We don't have any staff or buck sergeants hanging around after yesterday."

"Skinny, get that Anglar Nine souped up for the captain." It was Lieutenant Smith giving the order to the radioman to start pumping away to build up the power for a radio message back to battalion.

Captain Huntley was a career man who, even in exhaustion, stood as straight as a flagstaff.

"Great target," Righty said.

They could hear the company commander speaking in a hushed voice, the whirring pings of the radio's double handles whipping up the needed power as Skinny pumped his arms like the legs of a bicycle racer. The bitter cold had him double-timing on the handles.

The radio and pumping gear squeaked and whined and groaned until it sounded like a droning wind song.

"The radio sounds like an old *Inner Sanctum* radio show. God, that show could frighten the skin off me," Tim said.

"It was *I Love a Mystery* with Jack, Doc, and Reggie that made me fight for old Rags to keep guard on me," Johnny said. "You couldn't sleep after listening to it. I'd go to sleep with the slingshot in my hand. I used to change Rags's name to Fang after watching the scary show. I'd keep call him Fang, so if any madmen were hiding in the dark, they would hear his name and beware."

"But Rags was such a little dog, John. He wouldn't frighten a flea off," Tim said.

"Sure, but I had an answer for that too. I'd talk to Rags, ah, Fang, and tell him, 'Fang, old ball biter, I'm glad I trained you to jump waist high and snap!'"

"If I were a madman," Righty said, "I'd be gone, I shit thee not."

"The Anglar Nine squeaking reminded me of Jack Benny," Johnny said. "Remember when he'd go down to his vault to count his money, that squeak when the safe opened?"

"Yah," Righty said. "Remember the old guy in that vault, I forget his name—was it Digger O'Dell? He'd ask questions like 'Mr. Benny, is Mr. Coolidge still president?' and that sort of stuff."

"Digger O'Dell was the friendly undertaker," Pointer said.

"Is this Mickey Mouse time! Keep digging those holes," the gunny said.

"Gunny, send out three men to check the entire perimeter to make sure we aren't setting up camp in the middle of a gook ping-pong tournament," Captain Hundley said.

"DaSilva, you love the dark. Minichelli, Gouveira, out! The word to get back is 'piss ant.'"

The three looked at each other as the gunny set the company guards and sent out listening posts, "Yanders, Lacy, out about fifty yards. 'Piss ant' is the word. Carrey, take a crew and set some trips to the flanks and rear, put out another set of wire."

"Why are we catching this night shit all the time, Johnny, just because they overheard you saying it's safer? That's bullshit," Pointer whispered.

"Hey, they can't see us."

"Are you shittin' me? Our dark bodies on this fucken' snow!" Rhesus said.

"OK. Let's shush," the lieutenant said.

"'Shush'—is that the same as shut the fuck up?" Lace guffawed as the three perimeter men hunkered off. They walked slowly through the pitch black, staying in contact by listening for each other's breathing. Everything that could rattle had been taped down or had rags stuffed between metal and metal.

Each step called for setting the back edge of the heel first, then not meeting something that could cause a snapping sound or set a loose rock clattering. The rest of the foot was lowered slowly, still feeling for noisemakers.

Johnny had taught Righty and Pointer the ways of the still hunting deer hunter well. They were noiseless.

Then Johnny felt his heel set in something soft.

Something's not right . . . Nothing could be worse . . . than this . . . feel . . . on hard ground . . . oh shit . . .

The softness was a body.

Its owner hadn't been dead that long, as rigor mortis, which *Merriam Webster* defines as the stiffness of death, had yet to set in. The Brigadoon dance of death would not be high kicked again.

Johnny felt with his foot in an attempt to determine whether it was an American or gook. No canteen, no bayonet, no quilted clothing, no rice bag . . . *Something's wrong . . .*

"What?" Righty whispered in his ear.

Johnny didn't answer. Instead, he squatted and ran his hand along the body. It appeared to be wrapped in some sort of wire. He untied the shelter half from his cartridge belt. Pointer undid his, and they were joined together, making a small pup tent, which they placed over the body. The open end was covered with Righty's poncho so they could light a tiny flashlight inside without giving their position away.

Pointer took lookout, as his friends crawled into the pup. Johnny took out his penlight, cupped the beam in his hand, and shone it on the body.

"Holy good Christ in heaven, I'm gonna be sick," Righty said, holding his hand over his mouth.

———

The body was naked, an American, and was completely wrapped in chicken wire. Sticks were worked through the wire at various spots, and when twisted, the wire dug into the body, causing the flesh to pop out between the wire. Every other piece of flesh was cut out and was on the ground, appearing like the giant scales of a filleted fish.

"Whoever it is didn't talk," Johnny whispered. "Otherwise, they wouldn't have worked so long on one man."

"Maybe they weren't interrogating. Maybe they were just having fun playing chess or body checkers."

"Shut up. I have to get the tags." Johnny turned the body over, snapped off the tags, put one in his pocket, placed the other in the mouth, a mouth that was missing its lower lip as a result of the game of tic-tac-toe.

The nose was missing.

"Jesus," Johnny said, clamping the teeth on the dog tag of the dead marine, who, despite his mutilation, was still recognizable by the men he had trained in boot camp.

Johnny read the tag . . . *Seabag . . . my Christ . . . Seabag . . .* "My god, it's Seabag!"

"What's happening in there?" Pointer whispered. "I hear gooks moving in the dark. Come on out. We'll get our throats slit."

Johnny snapped off his penlight and crept out of the tent, stuck the snap sections of their shelter halves in their mouth, and undid them so as not to make any noise.

"Jesus," Righty said, "I could hear you guys in there like listening to a bass drum. The only thing noisier than a whisper or a fart in church."

"Let's get back to Dog," Pointer said, pulling on Johnny's arm.

"Get some stones. We have to cover him."

"He ain't going nowhere," Pointer said. "You couldn't find a stone if you wanted to. We'll just put some snow over him. He'll keep. Let's get back to Dog."

"We know Seabag never talked. Probably spit in their face after they cut his lip off," Johnny said. "Come on, let's git."

They crawled back toward their company perimeter, stopping every time they heard a noise, or thought they did. There were no noises in the snow.

The voice cut through the dark, "Who the fuck goes there?"

"Piss cutter," Pointer stuttered.

The voice came back with a hiss, "Piss ant, you porgy bait touch hole. Get in here."

The three ran close to the ground toward the voice.

"Oh Lord, don't let it be one of those gooks that went to UCLA," Pointer said. "I saw that in a John Wayne movie, I think."

"Good Jesus, Mother of Mary. Oh shit Mary, mother of Jesus, please shut up," Righty said. "I have to get into my fart sack before I fall asleep standing."

"Might know it was you three," Lace said.

"Why you guys back so fast?" the gunny asked.

"The gooks deposited a welcome note for us," Johnny said, "a body close to our lines. We never heard them."

"Any chow?" Pointer asked. "I'm so hungry, my asshole is eating my underwear."

"My underwear are frozen stiff. I had to piss in them. I wasn't about to take Mr. Bo Bo out in this cold," Rhesus said.

"Just dig your hole and shut up," the gunny said.

"I'm eating first," Pointer said.

"You're digging and digging deep."

"You can't even chip out a tiny piece of this frozen crud. I'll die on top the snow. I'm crapping out," Righty said.

"You're digging."

"A three-man hole OK?" Johnny asked.

"Yah. Dig it deep. One on watch all the time. Only the bottom half of your body goes in the sleeping bag, weapons on top your ditch. No one in Dog gets their throat cut in their bag."

"Gunny?"

"Yah, DaSilva?"

"That ain't the way my mother tucked me in."

A voice cut though the dark, "'Mel-lic-can, you die."

"What the hell was that?"

"One of the gooks who doesn't know he's dead yet," the gunny said. "I spotted him while checking out a spot for company headquarters. He's got roughly a half mile of his intestines dragging behind him. We left him that way so if any of his buddies try to sneak in, they'll step on his guts and fall on their ass."

"I'm going to go finish him off," Johnny said. "I wouldn't want to be out there like that."

"Johnny," Righty said, holding his friend's arm, "forget it. It's probably the bastard that sliced and diced Seabag."

Johnny took Seabag's dog tag out of his pocket and handed it to the gunny. He felt in his other pocket. "Forgot to give you these two," and handed the platoon leader Ma Toots and Soupy's tags.

"Thanks. I guess."

"'Mel-lic-cans, you die."

Lace yelled out, "Shut up, you stupid bastard, or I'll strangle you with your own guts."

"Die! I saids. An fluck yoo, 'Mel-lic-can plicks."

"Guess he didn't go to UCLA. Just a working Joe. I could get to like that guy, although he's a little corny," Johnny said, as he dug the pick end of his entrenching tool into the hard ground. "Gunny, what's the chance of a single spurt from the flamethrower?"

"About the same as your chance of getting a filet mignon delivered."

Righty chipped away at the opposite end of the foxhole to be, talking and digging, both at the rapidity of a machine gun—"Skinny had one of 'em jamming his radio all last night. Over and over again, 'Amer-lic-cans you die, mer-ic-cans you die,' for hours. Just like the Japs did in WW II."

"Great," Johnny said. "How did we send out for pizza and beer if the radio was jammed?"

"Please don't mention food," Righty said, stopping his chipping and grabbing his stomach, hugging it in an attempt to end the ping-pong game using molten ingots taking place in his guts.

Skinny broke radio silence and told the jammer, "Shut the fluck up, you fluckin' Chink flucker!"

"Betcha, if his mother heard him talking that way, she would wash his mouth out with soap," Johnny said.

"'Mel-lic-cans, you die."

"Shut up," Lace yelled at the radio.

This time, the voice did not come over the radio but rather from no man's land directly in front of the Dog Company line—"Ma-leens eat shit."

"Hey, it's live entertainment," Skinny said.

"Let me go get that bastard, Gunny," Lace said.

"That's just what they want, some idiot crawling around out there alone.

It took an hour for the three friends to finish digging their hole. And then it took some doing for all three to squeeze into it.

"No hard-ons," Johnny said.

"No farts," Righty said.

Pointer sang softly, "Show me the way to go home, I'm tired and I want to go to bed. I had a—" but he fell asleep before finishing the words.

The three were like butterflies-in-waiting, laced together in a single cocoon.

"Johnny?"

"Yah?"

"Do you love me?"

"I don't think so."

"Then get your mouth off my neck."

"I was just pretending it was a ham on rye."

"Back off, Dracula. Johnny?"

"Yah?"

"The bastards could come back in big numbers and overrun us. Cut our cocks off and put them in our mouths."

"At least you'd have a tiny snack and could stop complaining about how hungry you are."

"But I'm so tired, I can't be scared anymore."

"Lullaby, and sweet dreams," Johnny crooned.

And the three fell asleep.

"You fucken' assholes!" It was the gunny, and somehow he managed to kick all three with a single swing of his boondocker. "I said one man stays on watch."

"I'm the one on watch."

It was Lace's voice from the single hole beside them. "We agreed on it."

"Bullshit," the gunny grunted and was off checking holes.

"Thanks," Righty said to Lace.

"Fuck you, ginny. Stay awake. You get me killed. I get pissed."

"Conk, Lace, I'll take over," Johnny said.

"Suck a bull, deenni, I'll stand watch for myself."

"I won't be able to sleep now," Pointer said. "The son of a bitch of a gunny kicked me right in the ear. I'm colder than a witch's tit. The only consolation is misery loves company, and everyone is frozen. Jesus, you could cut me up and fill a hundred ice cream cones with me."

"You think you're cold? My balls are hiding under my armpits trying to get warm," Righty said. "And besides, I think Gunny broke my tooth when he three-pointed me from the fifty-yard line."

"Nah, he didn't break your tooth," Johnny said. "Otherwise, you would have said, 'I think he broke my tookus . . .'" but before Johnny had finished trying to be funny, his two foxhole companions were asleep.

"I'll take the first watch," he said to his sleeping friends . . . *I better stay awake . . . Winken . . . and blinken . . . are nodding . . .*

He tried to conjure them up with the gang in the Big Tree. Failing, he tried to conjure the three of them at Duck Pond, skinny dipping in the bright sun. Nothing would conjure, except Seabag's butchered body and an enemy soldier crawling around out there, dragging his intestines like a dog sneaking off with a string of stolen sausages.

All he got was an old silent movie flickering of his mother, her lips telling him to be a good boy while he was far from home, and his cousin Dink mouthing, "Keep your finger on it and don't take no wooden nickels."

He wanted to dream of sleeping for forty years or gorging at a Roman food orgy. And wanted to be lullabied . . . *swing low . . . sweet chariot . . . coming to carry you . . . home . . .*

But Righty and Pointer's snoring and farting sounded more like a firefight, and their groans were those of the wounded.

Don't worry, guys . . . We made it through the day . . . the long-timers say . . . That's the toughest thing to do . . . making it through . . . the day . . .

Johnny took off his piss pot, found the stub of a pencil in his dungaree pocket, and felt along the helmet's camouflage cover until his fingertips could find the small lines etched there, marking his first three days in this country . . . *Only 362 days to go . . . oh . . .*

He wondered if he made another 362 day marks of the camouflaged helmet cover whether they would send him home the next day.

They didn't.

"Up and at 'em!"

"Well, well, it's Corporal Quince of Kentucky," Lace said. "Y'all could have been a Southerner, if they accepted ya."

"I wish I could turn him into Kentucky fried chicken," Righty said.

"You gonna hike alone today, Righty, if you insist on talking about food," Skinny said, rubbing what had once been a soft and sizable paunch.

Johnny had noticed when he had his dungaree jacket in the warming tent checking for lesions the day before that his backbone showed through like the keys on a xylophone.

"I got a can of beans that I found that you can have," Righty said, "I scoffed them from Scoff."

"Hey, you saved 'em when everyone else ate theirs. You eat 'em yourself. Don't be an ass."

"Nah. You have them. My ass is so sore that if I am forced to fart, all the sad and sorry seams on my body will come apart, and the sawdust will fall out."

"You sweet talker, Righty," Fats said. "Hand them over."

He took out the tiny M1 can opener that came with the rations and opened the beans and offered it around.

They all dipped in with their KA-BAR knife tips and ate the beans off its razor tip.

Johnny watched as the can of beans emptied. Righty licked the inside of the can with his tongue like an anteater dining on an anthill. Then let out a yelp like a red ant had tied into him, as he caught his tongue on the jagged edge.

Johnny watched as they saved and savored the last few beans in their mouths, trying to make them last forever, like a child trying to keep milk chocolate from melting in his mouth, a hopeless chore.

He felt like grabbing his friends, squeezing with all his might, catching the beans as they spewed out of his friends' mouths. He felt like the days in the school cafeteria when a thick sandwich was offered around, and when no one accepted the offer, it was tossed in the trashcan. He felt like . . . diving in . . . after it . . . *Why didn't . . . I? . . . Ma would have known . . .*

"Pick it up, pack it, let's move." It was Gunny. He motioned them to follow.

Skinny put his combat pack on his chest so he could pack the radio on his back.

Pointer grabbed the mortar base, feeling the nick of the enemy bullet in it. He frowned as Johnny helped him on with his combat pack and handed him his M1.

"Wish I could get another one of those plates for your back," Johnny said. "I promised Dink I'd get you back home safe and sound."

They walked slowly down the mountain spine toward the thin road below. It was barely visible in the morning mist as the sun warmed the frost that had set in.

"Keep below that ridge line, Gouveira," Lieutenant Smith said.

"Aye-aye."

"Don't 'aye-aye' him. You'll get your butt kicked so hard, it will horseshoe around your neck. And worse, you'll get him peeved," Tim cautioned.

"I know. When you gonna learn to curse, Tim?"

They gathered on the road, reforming their fire teams, squads, platoons, and checking out the replacement companies new to in-country.

"Look at those sorry shits," Rhesus said. "Clean dungarees, scrubbed faces."

"Dog Company?" a short stocky marine leading a small group asked. "Punderson here."

"La dee fucken' da," Rhesus said, "You bring any chow?"

"We're replacements for Dog," the little man said.

Johnny looked at him, wondering how anyone in this man's Marine Corps could look pudgy.

"How about cutting off a piece of that suet you're wearing around your waist?" Skinny said, lamenting the fact that not only had his pot disappeared but also that his stomach was actually concave now.

"Hey, Skinny, you're down to a six-pack gut. This Pun has a twelve-pack," Rhesus said.

"Watch that crap," Punderson said. "I'm up for corporal. It just hasn't caught up to me yet. I'll have your ass up before Captain's Mast."

"Do you ladies mind moving along while reading the minutes of your sewing circle?" Quince said.

"Hey, Napoleon is up for corporal," Rhesus said.

"I'm up for seven-star general," Pointer said.

"I'm up for the highest rank in the corps. I'm up for Chesty Puller," Fats said.

"Watch it," Punderson said, "that's holy ground. You wouldn't amount to Chesty's dick tip. Chesty, that's holy ground."

"Your ass is hole-E, E being for ever ready," Fats said.

"Yah, beware of Greeks bearing grease," Lace cautioned, with a fiendish wink for the new replacement.

"By the way, replacement," Righty said, "look over there," and when Punderson looked, he relieved him of a red bandana from his back pocket.

But Punderson wasn't an easy mark. "What the hell you doing!"

"Sorry, little buddy, nonregulation, otherwise, we would all have been issued one. Besides, that red among our camouflage would give a fighting bull a hard-on."

"Give it back, and I'll owe you a cookie."

"What?"

"I get sent a lot of good stuff, all the time, by my family. I need that to wipe my forehead."

"Wipe your forehead with my ass."

"Talking about ass," Rhesus said, "I dated your girl when I was home on leave. We played 'dromedary or camel.'"

"What the hell is that?"

"She wanted to know if I wanted one hump or two."

"How would you like a . . . what's that noise?"

"Sounds like one of those Russian tanks," Rhesus said.

"Sounds like a North Korean airplane," Quince said. "Some goopy bastard would fly a biplane, honest to goodness, one of those old two-winged biplanes, over our area in the pitch black and toss hand grenades out at us. Never hit shit."

Pointer dove into the ditch, calling out, "I'm not waiting around to see which or what."

Before the rest could follow suit, an American Jeep that covered terrain—followed by a four-by, came in on a cloud of dust without a "Hi-ho, Silver."

A skinny, bucktoothed marine covered with more dust than home plate at Fenway Park during a game between the Yankees and Red Sox, with a face as tiny as that of a spider monkey, but the most beautiful person anyone in Dog had ever seen, yelled, "Hot chow and mail! And long coats, and Mickey Mouse baby booties."

"Which first, warm clothing, mail, food?" Righty asked.

"That's a no-brainer," Pointer said, digging into the first food other than rations they'd had since hitting Korea.

The steaks and boiled potatoes were carried in fifty-gallon steel containers. Many of the men learned they could chew both a steak and a spud at the same time, that they didn't need a mess kit to hold their food, and that it was possible to stuff your face with two hands at once. They learned that an entire slice of bread could be swallowed by merely using the tongue to fold it over like a taco, and five fingers to give it a boost.

And there were the other joys of the supplies catching up to the infantry, including real-live toilet paper, which doesn't sound like all that much of a luxury unless you've been wiping your ass with straw, leaves, and pieces of shelter halves no longer needed by the dead.

"Oh, the joy," Rhesus said, kissing an issue of potty paper, "prettier than any girl I've ever seen. If you don't believe me, ask my ass. Besides, it does such a good job, I won't have to wash my tail with frozen mud after a dump."

"Why don't you just marry it, you dumb crap," Lace said, hoisting his leg and letting a fart fly at Rhesus. "Here's a kiss for ya."

"Where'd you get that fart? We haven't had enough food to fuel a fart," Pointer said. "You've been holding out."

"Another world heard from," Lace said. "I thought that fart blew you away."

"Kiss my ass."

"I wouldn't know where to start, you're all ass."

Then it was the long coats and Mickey Mouse thermal boots.

"Hey," Johnny said to Pointer, "that one's too long for you. It drags to the ground. You look like Dopey of the Seven Dwarfs."

"I chose this one on purpose. I'll be as warm as if using Snow White's tits as pillows."

"Hey, cuz, now you're thinking," Johnny said, looking at the shelter half that broke just below his knees. The long ones were grabbed first.

"Hey, mail call," the marine with the tiny monkey face yelled, enjoying his moment in the sun. "Got it all packaged for ya."

Each greedily grabbed their mail, except those who knew they had no one to write to them. Some read their mail, while others were too frightened to open it; it could be a greeting, "Dear John, I sent your saddle home."

Johnny sorted through his. "Ma. Jazz and Roma, Yelena—what the hell, Bernadette?"

His mother's message was pretty much like those of other frightened mothers whose sons fought to kill and to stay alive ten thousand miles from home: "Johnny, you make sure you button up, stay warm. Keep your feet dry. Get plenty of sleep. How's the food? I heard the navy feeds best and have all that thick metal around you for safety. And those giant guns to keep those bad ones away. Can you get transferred into the navy?"

"Hey, Walking Jay," Johnny yelled over to the navy corpsman, "you think I can get a transfer? My ma told me you swab jockeys eat better and are as safe as a baby in a crib."

The Sioux, gave Johnny a friendly grunt and said, "Good medicine. You listen to your mother. She give good totem. Mine tell Walking Jay keep feet dry, get plenty of sleep, sleep in tall teepee so no hit head. Good dear woman, very wise. She also say, don't talk to marines, they pull their dicks."

"Kiss my dick, Tonto," Rhesus said, groping his groin.

"Doctor say you die, Lone Ranger."

"None of us pull our pud in this cold weather—the damned thing would break off," Pointer said, pulling his collar up high enough to meet his helmet as the bitter wind whistled under the edge of his helmet and circled several times before dying out, only to be replaced by the next freezing gusts that at times seemed to pierce the eyeballs. "It's just too cold. Baby, it's cold outside."

"Yah, you're used to beating your haddock in a nice warm attic," Fats said.

"Hey, listen to the old skin and bones, the guy who has to wear glasses and has hair growing in his palm because of so much love play with his constant love companion, Merry Palm," Pointer said.

"Hey, you'd thump your tub if you could find the string attached to it," Fats said.

"Hey, all Portagees are hung like the jolly green giant," Pointer said. "Ask Johnny."

"Sure, we are," Johnny said, holding up his forearm to emphasize size."

"It's not size that matters, it's how you use it," Rhesus said.

"What if you got size and know how to use it too? That gets the girls," Pointer said.

"Johnny doesn't need either with his movie star good looks," Skinny said, smiling like the Cheshire cat as he wet his eyebrows in the standard clowning imitation of a homosexual.

"Would you jolly good ladies talk about something besides beating your meat, such as tearing the heart out of a gook and eating it?" the gunny said.

"Like what?"

"Like, pussy," Lace said.

"What's that?" Rhesus said.

"That's what makes the world go round, puts the starch in a woodie."

"I haven't had a hard-on in a month. They force-feed us so much saltpeter. If it ever goes up again, I'm gonna shellac it," Fats said.

"Read your mail," Scoff said.

Johnny's mother's second letter was a short one: "I was so glad to hear that you're staying in Japan rather going to Korea. Why would they put you in charge of growing rice there? Oh, well, I'm sure the government knows what it's doing. I put in two dollars in case you have to buy anything. Love, Your Mother. PS Please come home quick. Your brother is going to spend another year in the sixth grade; he won't study and needs a spanking for being fresh. He told me not to worry, he'd get promoted because his teacher hates him and wants him to move on. I found a white spot in his trousers. Different than I used to find in yours. Your spots were from the paste you used in art class. You always told the truth. You were always a good boy. Never no trouble."

Ma . . . your PS is longer . . . than your letter . . . "Hey, Punderson, you want to sell one of those thousands of cookies you said you had? Two bucks."

"I don't have any more cookies."

His sister Roma's letter was short: "I hope you're happy, Johnny. You embarrassed me in front of the entire school. I can never go to school again. I did what you said to fill out at top. I got two hamburger buns from the bakery and wore them up top at the school dance. I even snuck into the home ec room at intermission and warmed them in the oven. And then one fell to the floor while I was doing the jitterbug with Danny Obara. I had been working up my courage for weeks to ask him to dance. Everyone could have seen the buns fall out. No one did, though, because Danny picked them up and ate them. Sort of like destroying the evidence. Still, I hate you. Everyone could have seen. Then Danny said, 'Roma, you're great. The next thing I expect is a hamburger to fall out.' I told him to buzz off. Ma is mad at Jazz. He beat up some ninth-grader who said I was skinny. The kid probably told Jazz he had buckteeth. Regardless, I hate both of you. But Ma said that more than anything in the world, I had to tell you I love you. I didn't really mean I hate you. Just sort of.

"I miss your drawing paper dolls for me, and the clothing you drew for them was the most fantastic, most awesome ever. Even though I don't miss you, Rags misses you. Please be very, very careful. For Rags. The newspapers say you're chasing the bad guys all the way to China, and Mr. MacArthur says you're gonna be home by Christmas.

"I love you. But you know I don't mean it. Your sister, Romola. PS Jazz wants to write something."

"Johnny, I beat up a ninth-grader. Ma got the money you sent home to get my teeth fixed, but she said I'd probably get them knocked out before I get to the dentist, so she's saving it for you."

"Ma sent me to a Catholic school. They call it a parochial school. She said the nuns would straighten me out with a good left. They can belt you in Catholic school and get away with it. They only let me go there one day. I chanted with the rest of the class, but the nun must have rabbit ears and heard me say, 'Holy mother, full of grace, I hope your father spits in your face.' The nun said I blas-flemed God and suspected I was a black Protestant.

"Ma didn't get real mad at me for some reason. She just said, 'Your grandfather Shiverick would have been proud of you. I didn't rat on Danny Shea who taught me to say that 'Holy Mother' thing. You told me never to fink. PS Wish cousin Pointer was here. He would have finked and fingered that rat Danny Shea. Gotta close. Uncle Manny told me to tell you to keep your ass down. I don't know what he means. Keep your ass down where? PPS Kill a bad goop for me."

"Gook," Johnny said aloud, wiping the tears of laughter from his eyes. "Should have told Roma sticky buns as a bra filler, sticky buns, they won't slip out."

"Everything OK, John?" Tim asked, "Your ma OK?"

"Yah, everything's great."

"Why you crying?"

"My bra's too tight."

"What with the 'sticky buns' bit, John?"

"I was just thinking, the steak and spuds were good, but could have been great with sticky buns."

"What are sticky buns?"

"They're just buns with a lot of honey and sugar, and you stick all the buns together and then pull them apart and eat 'em."

"Hmmmm."

"It was the only thing my mother made, the rest came out of a can. She worked long hours."

"I know, John."

"Anyway, Roma wanted to make them one day, and were they sticky. I made fun of them, and she threw one at me. Then Jazz threw one at her.

They stuck to everything. Ma told us to knock it off. And Jazz threw one at her, and it stuck to her. She got mad as heck and tossed one at Jazz, and when it stuck to his face, she laughed, and we all tossed them. Jazz tossed one at Rags, and it stuck to his butt. He looked real sad, but ate it anyhow."

"What's new with you, Tim?"

"Ma said I've been accepted to Princeton."

"You shouldn't be here, Tim," Johnny said, returning to his mail.

Yelena's letter smelled of lilac, and Johnny thought . . . *Please don't say . . . "Dear John . . . I've sent your saddle . . . home . . ."*

Yelena wrote, "I read the good news today in the *Christian Science Monitor*. Dad says it's the only paper that tells the truth. Everyone that is in the service at present will get something called the GI Bill. They will pay your way to college! Although I'm positive my father would help. He might have to when you go on to medical school. By then, we'll be married and have three children, two boys and a girl. The girl will be in the middle. The boys will be Moses and John, after my father and you. The girl will be Gladys, after my mother. I've been elected Carnival Queen here at Smith, and a boy named James VanHolt from Amherst College was elected king. It's a pretty big thing, gowns, floats, and figure skating. A hockey game and a big dance. While I'm dancing my heart out, I will be with you and you only. You would like my dance partner, although he isn't you.

"I remembered what I said to you before you left and how horrible I was. I asked you to win me a medal. I didn't mean for you to take chances or anything like that. Just a small one will be fine. I talk to all the girls about you. They ask what Korea is. I showed them your picture in your dress blues, and they all said 'Woo-woo!' and asked why you are fighting. And I tell them to save our country. Like you said. They just shrug their shoulders, especially the girls from Long Island. They hate the other photo of you in camouflage and with that rifle thing. But do they pant when they see the one of you in your dress blues. One asked if her boyfriend could borrow them.

"I ran into Bernadette Carlson. You remember her? Maybe you don't. Remember I told you the first time I fell for you was when you struck that horrible Ted Nitzke during the football game. He had said something foul about her.

"Now she doesn't even go out with boys anymore. She looked sort of pretty until I showed her the picture of you. Then her face got all contorted, and tears streamed down her cheeks. She knows how you adore me and felt sorry for me.

"Did I tell you, you were beautiful! Or what! We're perfect for each other. As I am beautiful. Oh what a bigheaded girl I am. You will swoon, what a childish word coming from me, but you will when you see the photo of me at the winter ball, a queen. Yes, it's almost frightening how beautiful you are, my male Pygmalion."

Johnny looked at the picture she had sent him in her queen gown. The king had a smug look on his face, his arm around her, and he wondered . . . *What would the son of a bitch . . . look like . . . with a bayonet . . . between the cheeks of his ass . . . shoving a grenade with the pin pulled deeper . . . where the sun doesn't shine . . .*

She had included a reworked picture of Johnny in dress blues where she had dubbed on red stripes down the trouser leg and wearing captain's insignias. Johnny was a lowly private first class, and only corporals and above got to wear the blue trousers with the red stripes down the side . . . *Geez . . . a PFC . . . with red-striped trousers . . . me . . . a PFC . . . soon to become a buck-ass private . . . wearing officers insignias . . . Holy toad shit . . . I'll get court-martialed . . . if they see me . . . in red trouser stripes . . . I'll be in stripes all right . . .*

Yelena continued, "I hope you're not angry, Johnny. You do look more handsome in that dress blue uniform with the red stripe. I always disliked that dark-green one. Please understand I would love you in sackcloth, but if you can wear dress blues instead, well enough said. Until we meet again, sweet prince.

Your adoring Yelena."

Johnny rubbed his eyes, thinking . . . *So tired . . . I wish you had sent me a picture of . . . just you . . . not one of you with Van Holt . . . Jesus . . . please kill me . . . but after I butt end my M1 . . . into that smug face . . . She said . . . "you would like him" . . .*

Despite the bitter cold that ate into his core, he felt flushed with anger, a double anger, as he was helpless . . . helpless . . . here . . .

"John, you sure you're OK?"

"Tim, if feeling helpless is OK, then I am OK to the tenth power, squared, to infinity."

"Why do I feel you're not all that great, Johnny?"

"Hey, Tim, you lucky dog." It was Rhesus.

"Lucky? How by?"

"Punderson told me that you brown guys get it for nothing in Japan. All you have to do is get her to believe you're a giant Hershey bar."

"Thanks. I'll remember that."

"What's this chocolate bit, Tim?" John asked, setting his opened mail on his lap. "Far as I know, you're the same as us. Maybe a touch smarter or a touch dumber. You could be in college, king at some winter ball."

"The same? John, I'm sure you knew why I was always the Indian when we were kids playing cowboys and Indians."

"Sure. You were the silent type, like an Indian. Unafraid."

"Thanks. You forgot a letter," Tim said, pointing to Bernadette's unopened one on the ground beside Johnny. "And thank you, Rhesus, you monkey's pogo stick, for telling me I'm a Hershey bar."

The little redhead pretended he didn't hear the tall dark marine and didn't see the "what the fuck" look Johnny shot at him.

Johnny looked down. There was still an unopened letter. He stared at until his eyes blurred in the cold. The wind whipped his frozen eyelashes and brows into his eyes, leaving them medium rare. Was it five seconds or an hour resting in his hand? But still he made no motion to open it. His eyes closed.

"Afraid it's from your draft board, John?"

He looked up, but between being half asleep and cold numb so that his teeth ached, all he could think of was the warm wax his mother used to put in his teeth so they wouldn't ache in the cold New England early mornings.

He was unsure who the letter was from. Everyone put a return address on the envelope, but all this letter had in the upper left hand corner was a *B*.

"It's me again, your buddy Tim. You used to lead the blocking around end for me. I was the runner that kept pushing you from behind."

"Tim. Yah. I must have conked out, sacked out standing up."

"Everyone else is zonked. It's the food, or lack of it. Perhaps we're not used to handling a full stomach. And the cold."

"We could have had our throats slit if we all slept."

"Nah. Quince and Gunny got the listening posts and guards out. No one kills this company in its sleep. Anyway, you've got a letter in your hand unopened."

"Probably my acceptance at Harvard."

"Come to Princeton. I'll need a blocking guard there."

"Sure, all I have to do is gain a hundred pounds."

"Then go to Harvard. They're lightweights there," Tim said, smiling and drifting off.

Johnny looked down; the letter was still in his hand. There was no return address on it. Just his FMF, Fleet Marine Force, address and the *B*. The writing looked frightened to him . . . *Nah . . . that's weird thinking . . . so what's new . . . pussycat . . .*

He stared at the writing for several minutes. The words looked frightened, moved on the paper.

The pen hand had been frightened—"I have no right to be writing to you."

Who the hell is . . . it . . . ?

He opened the letter slowly, and it read, "I have no right to write to you, but I became so frightened thinking of you so far from home. You don't know who I am, but I had to say I love you, although I have no right to. So I am not signing this letter. You already have a beautiful woman who loves you. I saw Yelena at the movie. She even remembered me. She is so nice.

"Please be careful. I could not live if something happened to you. And you didn't get to live out your life with that wonderful girl.

"With all my love. Someone who thinks you are very dear. PS I have no right to say this. I love you."

Johnny stared at the letter . . . There was that shadow . . . in the woods . . . that time . . . when I carved in that tree . . . I was a little frightened . . . too much listening to inner sanctum . . . That's stupid . . . but I did get the hell out of there . . . and it seemed to follow me . . . always in the shadows . . .

"OK, saddle up!"

Johnny jumped at the voice that snapped him from his reverie. The hair stood up on the back of his neck. Tingled. His sphincter puckered like a fish struggling for oxygen.

It was the gunny. "We're moving out. In case you guys forgot, the front's that a way, and the Chinks and gooks are planning a little party for us. But we'll make sure they do all the dancing. So take off your dancing shoes and put on the ass-kicking boondockers!"

Most had on the new thermal boots. But weren't ready to give up the tried and true traveling man boondockers. But not one set of the Mickey Mouse thermal boots were left behind.

"Move 'em out, Sergeant." It was Captain Huntley.

"Jesus, I wish he wasn't so tall in the saddle," Righty said. "If he gets it, Smith takes over the company."

"He ain't so bad," Quince Carrey said. "I saw shavetails in the World War II that were like him. All they needed was to get the bejesus scared out of them, get laid, killed, or all of the previous mentioned, and they were all right. Christ, a second loony usually only buys about five minutes in combat before catching it. And that buys you and me time. Because if they live through that first five, they understand they can die and take better care of themselves and us. Seems that Quantico doesn't tell their future officers they can die no more than they tell you pipsqueaks that no one lives forever."

"Could we change the subject?" Pointer said.

"Hey, Johnny," Pointer said, "Brother Dink wrote that you'd better take good care of me, or your ass is grass when you get back to the farm."

"Don't worry, cuz. We're all gonna make it, I'll see to that."

"Mind if I ask how you're gonna do that?" Quince asked. "It's hard to keep your own ass alive and breathing."

"Sticky buns," Johnny said. "Yes, that's it. The secret of life is sticky buns, ones that can even stick to a dog, stick to your ma, and stick to Roma's flat chest. They can stop bleeding. They're bulletproof."

Lace elbowed Pointer. "What the hell is he talking about?"

Pointer just hunched his shoulders as they moved out, files on both sides of the road, always eyeing the ditch for a quick Geronimo into it when the heat of enemy fire was added to the bitter cold that appeared to be eating them alive with its rusty razor freezer teeth.

"Stow the chatter," the gunny said.

There was no need for the "stow the chatter," as the bitter cold invaded them to the core as they reached new altitudes. They moved steadily under full battle gear, always upward, through the narrow winding road that gradually changed complexion as the rice paddies disappeared, replaced by a steep, seemingly perpendicular mountain on one side, a deep pitched valley on the other. Many failed to see either side as they were sleeping, walking zombies, as exhaustion claimed them one by one.

Despite covering miles too long, endless advancing, the fighting seemed to remain the same distance ahead of them, leaving them wondering, *Where's the line? Did we cross the line?*

Johnny took off his helmet and checked his writing on it. He faithfully kept marking the days off on his helmet cover.

He looked around at the newer replacements; he was slowly becoming a long timer in this country . . . *Great* . . .

He counted the day marks . . . *Ten . . . only, only 354 more days . . . eleven hours . . . let's see . . . about thirty-seven minutes . . .* "Fuck the seconds."

"Talking to yourself, money in the bank, DaSilva?" Lace said. "Hey, see what I got."

Johnny looked at the tall Southerner. He was carrying the flamethrower, the weapon with a tongue of fire that could reach out ninety feet and toast someone like a marshmallow on a stick.

"Jesus, stay on my right," Johnny said, thinking that invariably when hit, the human body turned to the right. You wouldn't want to be there, if the thrower's finger was on the trigger when he got hit.

They had all heard the horror story of Easy. When the guy carrying the flamethrower got hit and went down, he took his entire squad with him. Thirteen burning bodies.

Johnny winced . . . *Only for Jazz . . . only for Jazz . . .*

"Quince, what do you think?" Righty asked, squinting his weak right eye, trying to improve the sight that had been lacking since birth . . . *Jesus . . . I was lucky to get in . . . with this bad eye . . . They sure were rushing us . . . Now they check your eyes . . . with these optical machines . . .* "I was lucky."

"Jesus, everyone got money in the bank from up North," Lace said, "even the ginnies."

"Eye-talian," Righty said, "you ferkin' Klu Klux Klanner."

"Fuck you, and fuck God while you're at it."

"Hey, don't stand near me, Lace," Johnny said. "I don't want to get hit by the same bolt of lightning that's gonna get you."

"I've got my lightning here in hand," he said, aiming the flamethrower at Johnny.

"Do that again, and I'll have to give some serious thought to your death."

"What do you care about my death, DaSilva?"

"I care about that snot-throwing dragon you aimed at me," Johnny said, leveling his BAR at his waist toward the tall marine.

"Would you low-grade idiots save it for the gooks?" the gunny said. "Don't piss me off, or I'll piss you off."

"What are we, Sarge," Rhesus said, with that lopsided, ear-eating grin, "the flies on the toilet seat?"

They all laughed, even Gunny.

"Where the unhappy fuck did you get that redheaded monkey?" Lace asked. "Bet his ass is as red as a baboon's."

"You're a monkey's ass, you fucken' Rebel sheep fucker," Rhesus said, spitting through his front teeth with most of the spray settling on his chin and chest.

The day and night of forced march slipped faster when the men ragged each other. Silence meant a long, never-ending day.

"Are we ever gonna get to catch up with those running slant eyes or not? If we moved any slower, we'd be going backward. We've flat assed the tail-end Charlies," the gunny said. "Even the dog faces are ahead of us."

"And they'll probably get shot in their dog asses," Righty said, taking time to gnaw on an octopus tentacle he had appropriated off the rack it hung from in the four-hut town they passed through.

"You eat that shit, your eyes will slant," Skinny said.

"Shut up, Potts, you ain't getting none."

"I'd rather eat yak shit."

"Then eat shit. Just stop the yakking."

"Oy, you corny bastard."

"Please don't talk about food," Righty pleaded. "I'd eat bat shit if you put a little relish on it. Whatever happened to that guy with the little monkey face that brought all the goodies? Punderson."

"You notice how Punderson's breath always smells of cakes and other sweets?" Rhesus asked.

"Nah, I never tried to kiss him, but you're different, dear Rhesus," Johnny said, blowing him a kiss while wetting his eyebrow.

"What about Yelena's kisses, you two-timing piece of newt shit?"

"Rhesus, your brother used to pocket money when we sold the water lilies in Melrose Highlands." Johnny quickly changed the subject.

"I knew it. I knew it! That thieving piece of grunt. It runs in the family."

"Hey, Gunny, why are we always tail end?" Righty asked.

"We're rear guard. Don't want no gooks nagging at our rear, like Beetle Bomb."

"Nice. Why didn't someone tell us so we could check back over our shoulders?"

"Don't have to. Lieutenant Smith is covering our ass with his 'toon. You hear shooting. You hear me say, 'about-face, please,' the gunny said.

"Shit, how can we ever win this war? Even the gunny's a clown now," Lace said.

"Hey, Gunny and Quince won World War II, and this is just a police action, according to Truman," Tim said.

"Bring back Roosevelt," Johnny said.

"No fifth term," Tim said, smiling.

"A cow's tail is soft and silky, lift it up and you'll find Wilkie," Johnny said.

Tim smiled even wider. "Remember the pins we collected during elections? Those were the days. We were sure we won the presidency for them."

"Look at the little grunt coming up. How in hell does anyone have that kind of energy?" Righty said, pointing at the tiny figure as it closed the distance.

"It's Mattress Back," Punderson said.

"Mattress Back?"

"Yah. She sewed a small mattress on the back of her jacket, the seat of her trousers, and the back of her hat so she can get laid in comfort, and not on the cold ground."

"What is she, an orphan or somethin'?" Fats asked, getting a little puffed up, spotting what he believed was another marine shorter than he was. He had saved the soles he had glued on the bottom of his feet to pass the corps height requirements. It was his grandest accomplishment, a coup.

Except for the high-school baseball state finals. He had sat on the bench through high school without getting into a single baseball game. Until the state finals played in Fenway Park. Can you believe that shit, Fenway. The coach had used everyone on the bench except him. It was the last of the ninth, bases loaded, two outs. The batter was Skinny the fat-ass slugger. He got so unnerved, he shit his pants, a big-time load, one that even one of those Barnum and Bailey elephants would have been proud of.

He had to leave the game.

That left only Fats.

He remembered Soupy's words when he took his bat out of the rack: "The bat is bigger than our resident shrimp. He can't even hit the air with his swing."

For some strange reason, the tiny Fats had turned to Soupy and said, "In my last twenty trips to the plate, I have . . . eaten."

Coachie threw his hands in the air. "All is lost. Forget getting a hit. Just get hit. Get hit by the darn ball. Please."

The Lynn English pitcher figured a brush back pitch was needed so he could work the rest of the plate. It was a zinger, but not near the batter, just a little inside. But Fats, who had pulled the front of his shirt out on his pants in such a way that it appeared he had a big pot belly on that tiny frame, went through the acrobatics of pretending to have to dodge the ball.

The ball thumped into his shirt.

He was hit.

Tim jogged home.

Fats collected the ball. It hung in his room.

"She's no orphan," Punderson interrupted. "The mattress is so she can give curb service. I heard she usually follows Fox Company, but it got all shot up and taken off the line."

Mattress Back now entered Dog Company lines.

"How in the hell did she get past Smith's platoon without getting shot?" Johnny asked.

The girl turned her attention to Johnny. She was very young. About Roma's age. Perhaps fourteen at the most and looked like a miniature angel dressed in camouflage.

She smiled at Johnny. "Fuckie-suckie?"

Lace reached, took her small face in his ham of a hand, and squeezed and said, "Get the fuck out of here."

"Leave her alone."

Lace stared at Johnny.

"Oh."

"Yes."

"She's only a whore. Maybe she's a princess to you, but you're not even a poor man's Sir Galahad. You're willing to get your ass kicked all over this crummy country for a whore with a chest full of Purple Hearts for getting shot while getting laid during a firefight?"

"Only if I have no choice," Johnny replied.

"Man, you're a bigger shit head than I thought."

"I'm a shit head? If I remember correctly, that back in boot camp, it wasn't only me that lay on the deck so the M1s that hung from Pointer's thumbs wouldn't pull them out by the joint."

Lace remembered his lying beside Pointer's rack to relieve the pressure of the rifles pulling down on Pointer's thumbs.

"I'm not that fucken' smart either," Lace said, releasing the girl.

"Where'd she get those Purple Hearts?" Pointer asked.

"I heard that every time she got wounded, someone picked one up for her," Punderson said.

"Why in hell doesn't she just service the rear echelon?" Fats asked.

"Combat pay. Combat pay," Punderson said.

"Are you chewing something? Something good?" Righty asked Punderson, staring him down with his good eye.

"Nah. Just a piece of grass."

"Better be. If I eat one more frozen bean, well, I won't look kindly on you, Pilgrim, if you are an unsharing cookie carrier," Righty said.

"Jesus, John Wayne moved into the outfit," Punderson said, separating himself from the group.

"I don't like the guy," Righty said. "His breath smells of cookies or something."

"I wish mine did," Johnny said, giving his friend a noogie.

"Hey, you eating cookies too?" Righty asked Johnny. "Where'd you get the strength to give a noogie? How many miles you figure we've covered today? Thirty? Forty? Feels like ten thousand. Why are we moving sideways across this country? How many miles we gone?"

"About a quarter of a mile, but who counts?"

"All I know is I could do without another single foot of this mountain climbing. When I get home, I'm moving to the Florida Keys. I heard the highest point there is three feet above sea level."

"And all the girls there have an extra set of tits on their shoulder blades for dancing," Pointer said.

They all laughed just moments before the machine gun fire rattled into them, like bees gone insane, and sent the column scurrying, like ants scattered when their nest was spread asunder.

The machine gunner only got off one burst, as unbeknownst to him, the flanker group on the mountainside was just above him when he opened up.

The brush he was hidden in disappeared in a rain of grenades and automatic rifle fire. The body parts mingled with the shrubs, hung there like grotesque Christmas ornaments on a raggedy ass Christmas tree.

Slowly, the marines on the road peered over the edge of the ditch.

Fats was still standing in the middle of the road. He had never hit the deck and rolled into the ditch with the others.

They couldn't figure out how he had avoided getting hit. It was a miracle.

Johnny stared at his friend standing there. He looked so small . . . *Grandpa Shiverick . . . don't paint his shoes red . . . His mother will be so angry . . . at him . . .*

His heavy long coat was shredded at the stomach but kept the blood from the bullets from splattering. When Johnny opened the long coat, sticky red rivulets of blood interwove with the glistening white stomach parts mixed with shit and slithered down his pant legs, into and over his Mickey Mouse boots, which overflowed with blood.

Fats held out his arms, his hands, pleading, "Johnny, am I killt?"

Johnny reached out to catch his friend but tripped on Fats's shelter half and sleeping bag, which had been blown off him.

And Fats fell face first onto the road.

Johnny got flat on his stomach to look into his eyes. They had a distant look as if he was searching for a last look at the Big Tree and all his buddies.

"I'm kilt."

Johnny put his arm around his little friend. Remembered his room, a little room with his two proudest possessions, the inner soles that got him into the Marine Corps, and the baseball, the one with which he got his biggest hit ever, when the pitched ball thudded into his jersey and Tim trotted home and Fats yelled, "I drove in the winning run!"

Johnny's voice rang through the valley—"Fats!"

Tim lay beside Johnny and put his arm around him. Righty and Pointer knelt next to them and dared anyone to come close. No one would touch their little friend, only those who had climbed the Big Tree with little Fats could touch him.

Johnny looked up at his friends. "I want to go home."

"We all do, John, we all do," the gunny said, "but we gotta move out."

They didn't look back as Fats's body, which even appeared frail in the heavy long coat, and was piled on the Jeep that was returning to the rear along with the frozen bodies of the hard-hit Fox Company. Their arms and legs had to be broken so they could be stacked like cord wood and more could fit aboard.

Tim had forced the long purple intestine that had pulsated its way out of Fats's stomach back into his body, but now it hung out over the Jeep and dragged several feet behind the vehicle like a string of sausages at market.

Scoff had collected one of Fats's dog tags and had handed it to Johnny, who had become the unofficial carrier.

"We should say something to God about Fats," Righty said.

"What?" Pointer asked as they trudged like twisted robots whose batteries were wearing down.

"How about," Johnny started, "we all should have stayed in the Big Tree. Fuck God!"

"I'm not ready to say that just yet, Johnny," Righty said, putting his arm around his friend.

Johnny brushed Righty's arm off him. "Put it there when you're ready to join me in my kind of eulogy."

"John?"

Righty looked up at Tim, wanting him to say something.

"Cuz," Pointer said.

"I'm all right. Sorry about my cheap shit talk."

"Hey," Righty said.

"Hey," Johnny putting his arm around him.

"Johnny?" Pointer was looking at his feet.

"Yah?"

"I don't know if it's in the front or underneath, or either."

"I know."

"What is 'it'?" Righty asked.

"Something Cuz and I have never seen. We almost got to see one, but our grandfather set the shithouse on fire. We almost gave our lives just to try and see a pussy."

"At least your near final sacrifice was for a real cause," Righty said.

They smiled weakly at each other as they walked up the road in the approaching dark, never looking back at Fats's helmet on the bayonet, now gently moving, like a child's Hula-Hoop, in what was swiftly turning into a chilling wind.

"We've got to be careful. It's getting dark, and we don't have a password," Tim said. "They'll shoot. Maybe even without anyone asking for a password."

"We'll shoot back," Pointer said.

Johnny said, "By the way, guys, I didn't mean that fuck-God bit."

"Yah, we know," Righty said. "I told the pope. We pie-zons talk."

They walked in silence, and Johnny thought . . . *Heel and toe . . . away we . . . go . . .*

"Put 'em down, pick 'em up," Pointer said, almost as if reading Johnny's mind. They had an old math teacher who, it was rumored, graded his classes' tests by tossing them up the stairway in his house. Those that landed on the top steps got A's; bottom steps, flunks. He sorted them out.

"I'll kill some gooks for your friend," Lace said to Johnny.

"Forget it. The stupid bastards don't want to be here any more than we do."

"Listen up." It was the gunny. "We're digging in up there. We can hold it. Wire and trip flares, full watch."

"Jesus, Gunny, couldn't you pick something steeper for us as a favor?" Rhesus asked. "This hill would even make a demented mountain goat think about getting sick on the thin air up there."

The steep climb up the icy slope in the dark left steam streaming from their bodies, giving them the appearance of poltergeists on parade.

The defensive line they set up in the snow was loosely knit, and the word "fuck!" was the order of the day as they slipped on ice underneath as they set out the defensive wire, often slipping and landing on it.

"It's darker than a Walpurgis night nightmare," Johnny said.

"And we're a bunch of wallydraigle," Tim said.

"What's that?" Skinny asked.

"If you're a wallydraigle, you are a feeble, imperfectly developed, slovenly creature," Tim answered.

"Here, here," Rhesus said, adding, "Where in a cat's ass did you get those big W words?"

"Don't you remember in Mrs. Paquette's English class, we had to come in with three new words each week? And she would give us a letter to chose our words from," Tim said.

"I'm too tired to talk," Righty said, as they finished up the wire laying and searched the area for old Chinese foxholes. "Let's conk. John, I'll take first watch."

"I'll keep you company."

They hit the deck, pulled their great coats around them, and rolled themselves into tortillas inside their shelter halves. they pressed against each other in an attempt to squeak out even the slightest ounce of warmth and block against the brain-bursting wind that sliced and diced their bodies.

As the body heat built in, their tough climb before disappeared; the warming sweat froze and turned into a mask. Grimaces made the ice masks crack, leaving them looking like Phantoms of the Opera.

"I wish Rags was here," Johnny said to no one in particular.

"I'd fight you for him," Righty said.

"Once I had a hard-on in church," Johnny said.

"What is this, confession?" Tim asked.

"What did you do with it," Righty asked, "put it in the collection plate?"

"Nah, I sort of hid it, and dreamed I was naked in the snow and wind that made my asshole whistle 'Dixie' so it would go down. My ma would have beaten me to death if she spotted it."

"Hide it! Hide it? How do you hide a boner in church?" Righty asked. "It would be easier to bury an elephant in a sandbox and keep its trunk hidden."

"Don't make me laugh, I don't have the strength," Tim said.

The wind picked up, carrying up the mountainside, found tiny spaces in their great coats, and penetrated through their bodies like icicles.

"You know I wasn't even going to come to work today, but I couldn't call in sick. I've used up all my sick leave," Johnny said.

"Should have called in dead," Pointer said.

"You're about as funny as a rubber crotch, cuz."

"Remember Goda?"

"Good idea, now we'll warm up," Johnny said. "When we worked the fields, I used to dream of using her as a plow, so to speak. She would be on her stomach. I would pick up her legs and push her forward like a hand harrow, and I would look between the two handles and see her forest fire of pubics. Her breasts, great heaving beasts of burden, would part the earth. I would be that earth."

"Jesus, Johnny, you're a poet," Righty said.

"All I know is, she just got my teapot boiling just before I froze to death," Johnny said.

"It just isn't possible to be this cold," Tim said.

"Can I tell you guys something?" Pointer asked, not waiting for an answer. "I don't know whether I'm frozen more from the fucken' cold or the fucken' fear. Those Chink burp guns sound awful close. Right now, I'd welcome a firefight. I like the word 'fire.'"

"Hey, why complain, Johnny? A hard-on is a hard-on," Rhesus said.

"You're not alone with a shaftie caused by fear, Pointer," Johnny said, putting his arm around his cousin. "You're not alone."

"Johnny," Rhesus said, "you know when you mentioned Goda's pubic hair, well, I have a confession to make. When I get home, I'm going to make my own pillow and fill it with a thatch of pubic hairs from each woman I bop."

"A noble cause," Tim said.

They slept.

"Get your asses up, it's already 0500, in the a.m." the gunny bellowed.

"Hot coffee?" Pointer asked.

"God, you're a saint," Righty said, blessing himself, wondering where the coffee and the fire could have come from. It wasn't in sight, mostly because neither existed.

Pointer said, "And while I'm cooking, how about some sizzling bacon, eggs popping in fat, steaming pan fries, hot waffles drenched in warm maple syrup taken from sun-drenched Vermont trees, at high noon. Sausage, more bacon?"

"You sadistic prick," Righty lamented, "you'll burn in hell."

"I'll take it! I beg that Lace turns his flamethrower on me."

"Forget it, you'll freeze in hell."

The gunny said, "We're moving out. Dog is heading to that flat valley below."

"Jesus, we just hiked up here last night from down there," Rhesus said.

"One fire team will hike the mountain side and make sure no Chinks take pop shots at us from up here. DaSilva, Yanders, Minichelli, take point. And DaSilva, take your cousin—he's too funny for me with his sizzling bacon talk."

"Yo," Johnny said.

The company started its slip sliding away trek down mountain, while Johnny's fire team moved along the mountainside, with Johnny as point. "Tim, you, and Pointer watch the flanks. Righty, keep an eye up your ass. Protect our rear."

The first of Dog was just hitting the road far below as the four marines moved high above, easily breaking though the drifting snow, hoping they would not slip on the icy crust beneath it.

"Are we supposed to stay up here?" Righty asked.

Johnny shrugged.

Some forty minutes later, they saw a single figure climbing toward them. It was Rhesus, the new company runner who replaced the Georgia reserve who had bought the farm. And not the one he had always talked about, but the one he now laid stiff on, on the makeshift platform of the body-carrying Jeep.

Rhesus said, "Just back from Hawaii, I brought you some hula-hula girls in leis to warm you up."

"No thanks. I'll just take a dip in an active volcano, if you're giving gifts. It's so fuckin cold up here, we have to put our words in a frying pan to thaw before you can hear them. Got any food?"

"Sure. A sizzling hamburg and french fries OK?"

"You know, some things just aren't funny."

"Including stupid questions."

"Where are we headed?"

"Why don't you ask God? He's the only one with the poop, and he ain't talking. Anyway, the skipper wants you down below. And faster than immediately. This is a no-shitter."

They followed Rhesus as he turned and bolted downward, finally catching up to the company in a mood much more than very foul.

Captain Hundley, Lieutenant Smith, and Gunny trotted up and down the company line, repeating, "Move it!"

"Hurry up and wait, what a fucken' way to run this man's army. Bet it ain't that way in the navy and air force," Punderson griped.

"I don't know," Righty said. "Some swab told me he was serving aboard a ship when the words came over the loud speaker, 'All men fore, report aft. All men aft, report fore. All men amidships—stand by to direct traffic.' Those swabs probably obeyed the order."

Pointer said, "I heard this one about some air force base. There was an order posted on the bulletin board: 'All men who have two mess kits, turn in one. Men with one mess kit, draw a second.' That sure sounds crazy."

"Real crazy," Johnny said. "Fly boys don't even know what a mess kit is. They eat off china plates."

"I told you the Chinks were everywhere. Now they're in the air force dining rooms," Rhesus said.

"All I know is if we cover another thirty miles today, I'll be walking on my knees—my legs will be worn off that high," Righty said.

"Your fucken' feet sweat in the Mickey Mouse boots when you're walking, and when you stop, the sweat freezes," Rhesus said. "I'm shit canning them and wearing my boondocks."

"Better not," Johnny cautioned. "It's colder than an Iceland rat's ass now and expected to get colder than a nun's tit."

"A nun's tit—why'd you have to go and mention a warming device like a tit when my face is freezing? Add to this the fact that I love 'em, those bubbers. When I get home, I'm taking my combat pay and putting in a rug of tits in my bedroom. The room will have a two-foot-high ceiling so I have to crawl in them," Pointer said.

"Hey, you know what they say, cuz, once you've seen one pair of boobs, you—want to see 'em all," Johnny said.

"How do you know, Cousin John?" Pointer grinned. "The only set you've ever seen is that old cow at the farm, you know, Betty Boop, the one we used to bull fight."

Rhesus said, "Ya hear the one about the farm girl who fell asleep in the field and woke up and a cow was standing over her? She just looked up at those old cow udders hanging down and says, 'One at a time, boys.'"

Johnny looked skyward, "Oh Lord, what did I do to be a captive audience to this?"

"He makes me want to let a crap," Skinny said, taking the radio off his back. "Anyone got any paper?" Not getting an answer, he said, "Guess I'll just use my skivvies."

"So what's new?" Lace said. "Just make sure you shit downwind. You shit upwind, I burn your ass."

Skinny went into the ditch, started to pull down his trousers, and squat.

"Not there, Potts. Just in case we have to hit that ditch in a hurry on the way back. Hit that dingle down there," the gunny said, pointing to heavy brush below, "and don't go waving your whitetail like a flag in case some lost deer hunter passes by."

Skinny, continuing past the ditch to the brush, not bothering to pull his dungarees up, muttered, "Jesus! Jesus!" Then went silent.

The company stared down into the brush but couldn't see the yelling marine, and Lieutenant Smith ordered, "Gouveira, Eurasian, hightail it down there and find out if he stepped in his own crap."

Pointer and Rhesus moved their weapons off their shoulders and to a high port and headed down.

"Hey, leave the mortar plate here," Quince yelled to Pointer.

"No, fucken' way."

"That's an order."

"Send me to the fucken' brig. I don't care where, San Diego, Portsmouth. Rockledge. This fucken' plate saved my life. It's part of my body and more valuable than my dingy-whacker."

Quince shook his head, smiling, "If we win this God-forsaken war, it will be a miracle."

The company watched in lazy curiosity as the two marines approached Skinny, who was standing stiff as a railroad tie. They could see that despite the wind, cold, and sun that had turned his face a bronze, that he was white as the snow that had started to fall again.

Rhesus arrived first. "Jesus!"

Pointer, a moment later, "Jesus. Good Christ."

Within moments, most of Dog were down the ravine, looking at the remains of what had been the nineteen members of an army recon patrol.

They apparently had been close to starvation. Most had small rice bowls in their hands and, while waiting for food, were shot in the back of the head. They had been prisoners, starving as they tried to keep up with their captors.

"Those fucken' gooks will pay. I'll cut off their cocks and cook them with my torch right in front of their eyes," Lace said, waving his flamethrower wildly in front of him.

"Get these men up on the road," the captain said, taking one of the dead under each arm.

"They don't weigh anything," Tim said.

"The cocksuckers didn't even let them have their last meal," Johnny said. "I'd almost forgot why we're here. It's the innate cruelty of Communism they want to force on the world."

"That's awful heavy stuff," said a muscular black marine named Mulligan, who had come up with Punderson and the other reserves. "Me? I just couldn't find a job. And then I talked with this recruiting sergeant that came to Public School 128 in Chicago, and I knew that being transported all over the world, being outfitted in dude uniform clothes, and getting laid in fifty different languages was *theee* job for *meeee*. But fight Communism? These rice fuckers didn't do nuthen' to me."

The heard a clack as they climbed out of the ditch with the bodies. It was a false teeth plate that fell out of the mouth of the trooper being carried by Johnny . . . *Must have played hockey* . . . He bent to pick them up.

"He doesn't need them, keep moving," Lieutenant Smith said.

Johnny stooped, picked up the plate, and put them back in the trooper's mouth.

"A wise guy, huh?" the platoon leader said.

"No, sir." Johnny hoped he had addressed the little officer with the "sir" loud enough so if there were any snipers in the area, they knew where to look for extra points.

On the road, Captain Huntley gave the order to straighten the legs and put the arms down beside the body.

"What the hell's that for?" Pointer asked.

"If we leave them in that frozen pretzel position, you can't stack as many in a four-by," Quince said. "I had a brother that served on the Russian front during WW II. He told me they had to break so many legs and arms to stack them, it sounded like a walnut-cracking competition."

"Great."

"Hey, Mulligan, was that the name of the plantation owner your folks came from," Lace said."

"Knock off the Klu Klux Klan stupidity," Tim ordered.

"Yah? Do you think you can do it?"

"You'd better believe."

"I don't need no defending, brother," Mulligan said to Tim. "Nor does my name. It has nothin' to do with plantation bosses. My dad, Mr. Piper, said a Mulligan is a 'gimme' in golf after you foul up a shot and you take a free shot. My dad was sort of a golfer. He hid in the rough and sort of borrowed balls that got in the woods out of the sight of the golfer that hit them. He looked at me when I was a baby with big eyes that he thought looked like golf balls, figured I looked like a baby that would grow up into someone that would be out of bounds, and he named me Mulligan, Mulligan Piper."

Tim and Johnny looked at each other and burst out laughing, joined by Mulligan, and suddenly, Lace did not exist. The friends suddenly felt sheepish as they remembered the dead army troopers that had been executed.

The troopers were loaded gently onto the Jeeps, piled carefully so more could be carried on the jury-rigged two-decker racks.

There was a frozen body in the Jeep passenger seat, a marine that the Jeep driver had found on a knoll beside the road when answering a call to pick up the dead troopers.

Johnny looked at the dead marine, "Tim. It's Scoff."

"I know. He went back hoping to borrow anything we could use from anyone's supply department. He didn't make it."

Johnny kissed the dead friend on the cheek, but in doing so, his lips froze to the barrel of Scoff's rifle that was used to prop him up. Johnny attempted to breathe warm breath on his lips but failed to free them.

Tim tried to free Johnny's lips with his breath, and his froze to the M1 barrel.

"You talk about two monkeys fucking a football," the gunny said, tugging the backs of their helmets away from the rifle, ripping their lips so their torn skin stuck on the metal and flapped like small flags.

All the troopers would not fit on the racks, so Johnny and Tim climbed onto the stack and tried to arrange them sardine-style so more would fit. Their crawling snapped icicles off the troopers that contained frozen blood and brains and excrement and some body parts that stuck to them, leaving them looking like horror movie Christmas trees.

"Hubba-hubba, with the loading," the Jeep driver said. "I don't like freelancing back to battalion without a body guard. There is something about being the only target. Better to share the wealth. Betters my odds."

Once loaded, the Jeep drivers came as close to burning rubber as you can on ice heading back behind the lines.

"Jesus, he's gonna get a ticket," Rhesus said.

"The taxi drivers are afraid of the dark," Lace said.

The Jeep was barely out of sight when Dog Company heard the Chinese and NKPA burp gunners cut loose on the driver and his cargo.

"Let's go get 'em," Quince yelled.

The company commander said, "Hold! We're heading up. Get on the radio and give battalion the gook position."

"If it's any consolation, the poor bastards can't get killed twice," Quince said.

Dog took nearly an hour to catch up to the troops and convoy forward of them despite their near double-time foot travel. Someone had told them they were needed at the front, as the forward marine units were getting exhausted just chasing the retreating North Korean army and the few Chinese volunteers captured with them.

"What do you figure? All this double time?" Tim asked.

"I would guess we've got them on the run," Johnny said.

"Someone said Able Company and First Cavalry have been capturing more and more Chinks despite the brass in Japan still declaring there are no Chinese volunteers here."

"As long as they don't slow us down so we can get to Manchuria, then rush back to Seoul and catch a plane home for Christmas. Everyone is talking home for Christmas."

"But the poop is we're going too fast. Some of the guys we're bumping into say there are big gaps between us and the army and the ROKs. And some guys are wondering whether the Chinese will let us go right up to their border."

"The reason we're here, Tim, remember, is so the Commies won't pull their tanks up to our border. I can't imagine them letting us pull ours to theirs."

"Then why are we putting our head down and going full speed ahead?"

"I don't know. Let's call MacArthur in Tokyo."

"Let's call Hairy Ass Truman in Washington. He appears to have all the answers. He called this a police action, the flaming asshole."

"I heard a Chinese ambush wiped out a ROK battalion," Righty said.

"Where'd you hear that scuttlebutt?" Pointer asked.

"Some runner from battalion. I gave him a glass of wine some farmer had lying around his barn, probably hiding it from his mamasan."

"Ours is not to question why, ours is just to do or—" Tim said.

"Can we change the subject?"

Pointer interrupted, "Anyone here like tits?"

"I'd like them if they were covered with steaming mashed potatoes, and they would breast-feed me hot chocolate," Johnny said.

"John, what do you plan to do when you get out?" Tim asked.

"You trying to take our minds off food? I'm not sure what I'll do when I get out. Yelena would like me to become a doctor like her father, except instead of just making lots of money, she would have me make lots and lots of money. Then we would help the poor, but keep tons of ras-buck-niks for ourselves."

"What would you like to do, Tim?"

"I don't know. Perhaps go to college for a couple of years to find out what I want to do. But, first, I want to do nothing for a very long time, just to thaw out."

"What kind of nothing?"

"Maybe write stuff."

"What kind of stuff?"

"Just stuff that tells the truth. The truth is tough to get published sometimes, but maybe it's possible to sneak the truth in once in a while."

"You'd be happier just being a lawyer and lying all the time," Rhesus said.

"Maybe. What do you really want to do, John?"

"I think I would like to be a teacher but a different kind of teacher. I would start with kindergarten kids. It's not too late for them. Then I would follow them from grade to grade. Elementary to their middle years, then junior high. Senior high. Then college. Then they would go out and do the same thing, take kids from kindergarten to college. And then those kids would do the same thing."

"And what would they teach?" Tim asked.

"Simple stuff. The Constitution. The Ten Commandments. Teach what Thumper's mother told him in *Bambi*, that 'if you can't say somethin' nice, don't say nuffin' at all.'"

"That's heavy stuff. But great. Anything else?"

In a Bugs Bunny stutter, made easier by the biting cold, Johnny said, "Da, da, dat's all, folks."

"You make a great Loony Tunes bunny, John."

"Thanks. It sounds loony, as loony as Tim trying to write the truth. We humans aren't ready for it. The truth has to be sneaky, palatable."

"Hey, Socrates, where does all that heavy crap come from?" Righty asked. "It's weird listening to. How about some reality? Wanna share a couple of pork chops?"

"Remember that off-limits shit kidding about food isn't funny," Johnny said.

"I found them on the front seat of one of the officers' Jeeps. He probably left them for us, as by now, he is probably back at the Waldorf at Division headquarters, Righty."

Rhesus handed chops to Tim, Johnny, Righty and Pointer.

Rhesus grabbed his benefactor's hand and kissed it. "I kiss your ring, oh holy man."

"Give me back the pork chop, you goddamned sex fiend."

"Fat chance."

They slowly chewed the pork to the bone and then sucked the bones, finally snapping them between their teeth and sucking out the marrow.

Johnny looked at his cousin. He could barely see his face, hidden deep in the hood of his long coat, a scarf pulled up over his nose. He looked a very, very old seventeen who had lied that he was an adult eighteen . . . *Maybe I should turn him in . . . get his ass home . . . Seventeen is too young . . . It's the rules . . . but what makes eighteen old enough . . . to die . . . ?* "You warm enough, Pointer?"

"Jesus, Johnny, don't be funny."

"Yah, I know."

"Anyone want a smoke?" Rhesus asked.

"Where'd you get the deck of butts?" Righty asked.

"They fell out of the pocket of that second looey who was in charge of the convoy gooney bird."

"You're living dangerously, swiping fags from an officer," Tim said.

"So let him sue me."

He handed the package around. No one refused anything.

Everyone smoked. Drew the warm smoke into their mouths, lungs. Coughed painfully and drew again. The snot from their runny noses dripped onto the cigarette, then the hot coals, finally putting them out.

"Captain Huntley's coming," Lieutenant Smith said. "Get ready, we'll be moving up."

Lieutenant Smith drew up as if to salute. "Don't you dare, Lieutenant, unless you want to become company commander. Men, we're staying put. It seems the Chinese have entered the war, which we knew. Just the generals didn't know. We're heading up that ravine to the top and digging in. Lieutenant Smith, send a fire team up as point—two teams on the flanks. Corporal Carrey, take a couple of men and protect our tails. Move out."

Johnny's fire team took point with Johnny, front; Tim, right flank; Righty, with his Browning automatic, to the left; and Pointer, his assistant BAR man, in the rear, completing the diamond-shaped advance.

Pointer had the most difficulty. He hadn't given up carrying the mortar base on his chest despite the fact the light mortar, along with its carrier and the ammunition carrier, had been vaporized during an artillery attack while assigned to the heavy machine gun platoon for the day.

Everyone wondered how the North Koreans, while running hell bent for election, could muster time to set up a mortar. Now they had the answer. They didn't, but the Chinese coming up to join them did.

The climb meant shrub grabbing, crawling on hands and knees, chilled to the bone, knees hit by lightning strike messages to the brains delivered by hidden rocks and shards from shattered trees, while peering upward expecting hidden slant eyes from above rolling grenades down on them. But there were no strangers in wait above that would kill them.

The enemy had been there. Several well-hidden bunkers were dug into the mountainside. They were complete with log roofs packed with dirt. Metal barrels had been used as stoves. Some wood was left behind by the NKPA troops that had lived there. The North Koreans had fortified lookouts zeroed in on the narrow ribbon of road far below. The marines were quick to set up home in them, as the bunkers were already arranged in a defensive position that would allow their holders a superior hand.

"OK, Corporal, pick two men and check the hoochies for booby traps. Everybody else, away from them," the gunny said.

The troops that had already entered the bunkers wanted to stay in out of the biting wind.

"Out!"

Each waited for the first person to exit a bunker. Nothing. No exit takers.

That is, until the gunny said, "Gentlemen, don't argue. Those who enjoy the comfort and heat of the bunkers perhaps will have to enjoy the fact that the NKPA or their friends, the Chinese, took the quadrants on each and every bunker and plan to drop a welcome gift down the smoke stack. Fuck it, we use them.

"After they're clean, Captain Huntley wants the first engagement bunker to have both a BAR and a light machine gun. So DaSilva's fire team, plus Punderson and Mulligan, get. The rest of you guys, follow me. Gouveira, where's your mortar plate? Mr. Potts, you and the monkey find the captain and the radio and stay close to him like you're wearing one pair of skivvies between you. Get the idea? Keep the gooks away from that radio at all costs."

"Yup," Skinny said, heading out with Rhesus.

The remaining Dog members set up housekeeping.

The bunker was dug into the mountain, probably with gook grenades. Its sides were dirt, its roof was logs packed with dirt, stones, and hunks of metal off abandoned vehicles.

As they reentered the bunker, a raft of rats slithered off. Except for one, a fellow so long and skinny, he looked like a rolling pin. His ears were extra large and had several bites out of them.

"Look at that silly bastard," Punderson said. "It looks like his buddies thought he was a piece of cheese—he's got so many holes in him. I'll fit his rat's ass out with one big hole."

Punderson drew the .45 from its shoulder holster and took aim.

"Leave 'em."

The stocky marine turned to Johnny. "What are you talking about? Who made you keeper of the rats? I'm the corporal-to-be here."

"And I'm the buck-ass private in charge of rats. So best listen."

Punderson turned back toward the rat as it attempted to scratch its ear but was missing it by about a half inch. The look on its face indicated a question as to why he was scratching and the ear was still itching.

"Leave 'em."

"I'll get it later. Hope he shits in your canteen, DaSilva."

"Just as long as you don't drink from it."

"Jesus, a real-live roof over our heads," Righty said. "It's like home."

"Yah, if you're Bog the Hog," Pointer, back in the bunker, said, staking out a corner of the cave as his.

"Who the hell is Bog the Hog?" Mulligan asked.

"He's a, a Harley biker."

"I wish we had some chow," Mulligan said. "I'm so hungry, my asshole's eating my underwear. Tie-ties and all."

"Wish in one hand, shit in the other," Righty said.

"You talk like that, Righty, and you're not leading the prayer session tonight," Mulligan said.

"Look, let's knock off the crap," Johnny said. "Let's figure out our fields of fire. Righty, dig that gun port out a little more so we can sidearm a grenade. Tim, take Punderson and Pointer and set out the trips. Mulligan, you go with them. While they're setting the flares, dig a listening post. Make it deep. A two-grenade hole."

"I hate to use up my grenades to dig a hole," Mulligan said.

"Just do it."

They headed out.

Johnny peered out the holes in the sod and logs that would serve as gun ports, lined up fields of fire, took a reading on rocks and stumps to mark them, and then set out with a machete to cut a new field of fire.

They all returned to the bunker in silence. One thing about exhausting, dangerous work performed in the cold and black, it leaves you too tired to talk.

Tim and Johnny peered out the ports as the others sat on the frozen ground.

"What do you think, John?"

"We'd better get some rations up here fast, or the harpists will be showing up to play a tune or two on our ribs."

"All I can think of is food, filet mignons, lobsters, pork chops, fries so hot they burn from your lips to your buttocks. That's it. Filet mignons smothered in pork chops, with a sizzling prime rib chaser, hunks of lobsters in hot melted butter."

"And hot apple pie and steaming homemade bread on top of it."

"John, we have to stop this."

"I know. I can't spare the energy needed for a drop of salivation."

"The carriers got the ammo up here. Why in a good goose fuck didn't they bring the food up first?" Righty asked.

Johnny said, "The food has to follow. You can't kill a gook with a can of beans. We all look as goofy thin as Laurel and Hardy. Which one was fat, and which one was skinny? I'm too pooped to remember. You guys look like customers in a Nazi concentration camp. Except Punderson. Look at him asleep, fat as a porker."

"I heard these noises coming from his foxhole when his foxhole buddy was out on listening post the other night. I think our fat fellow is filling his face after dark."

"Nah, John. We all share, even Punderson the prick."

"How about a little bet? We pretend we're all asleep, you, me, Righty, Pointer. Then when we hear him break out his goodies and start munching, we turn our lights on the little turd, take his goodies, eat them, spank his bare ass, and then piss on him."

"Sounds like a plan," Righty said, "but what if we turn our lights on him and what we heard was him breaking out his beads and saying the rosary?"

"Then we elect him fucken' pope."

"OK. Pope Punderson."

Righty and Pointer joined them at the gun holes. They watched, as the two men manning the listening post walked downward like ghosts.

"The poor pricks. Getting really dark fast," Righty said.

"Getting colder, faster," Pointer said. "My hands and feet are so cold, I wish we had an elephant in here so I could stick them up its ass to get them warm. This cold could make me cry."

"Cry? Give me a break, cuz. Marines don't cry, especially us Portagee jarheads. Especially my cousin."

"I ain't no Portagee. I'm a fucken' American, and you know full well us Americans have rights, and I have the right to head home right now."

"And now that I think about it, looking around this country with its five-star asshole rating, and knowing that you got me here, I ain't got no cousin."

"Tim, isn't 'ain't got' a double negative or something?" Johnny asked, taking off Pointer's helmet, mussing his hair, then holding the helmet waist high and pretending he was taking a leak in it. "Pointer, toss a tea bag in it."

Righty whispered the plans for Punderson's midnight snack exposure.

"What are you guys whispering about?" Punderson asked from the back of the bunker.

"The stars are bright," Tim said, ignoring Punderson.

"They seem as close as when our gang sat high in the Big Tree late at night," Johnny said.

"It was like being in a diamond mine," Righty said, "like you could just reach out and pluck one outta the sky."

"And make a wish on it," Johnny said.

Tim squeezed Johnny's arm and whispered, "John?"

"Yah?"

"Someone's moving toward us."

"Where?"

The four of them tightened their eyes, hoping the squeezing would let them see in the dark.

"I don't see anything," Righty said, his voice so filled with the unknown that the words kept breaking in half.

"There could be a million of them," Pointer said.

"He disappeared," Tim said.

"No," Johnny spotted the figure. He had closed his eyes as usual, as keeping them in the blackness allowed him to see slightly better than his comrades. "To the right. Small."

"Must be a gook," Pointer said, lifting the BAR into the gun hole.

Johnny held his hand on Pointer's arm. "Hold, steady, wait."

Johnny headed out the opening of the bunker.

"What the fuck," Pointer whispered.

They could now see the outline of the figure as Johnny approached it. They became one, returned to the bunker.

"My good happy horseshit!" Punderson said as he and Mulligan came to the front of their cave, "Mattress Back! How did she make it through the trips and tin cans?"

The little Korean girl was shivering, nearly out of control.

"Whatee you do here, Jo-san?" Johnny asked.

"Didn't know you spoke Korean, John," Tim said with a smile.

"Get rid of her," Punderson said.

"We can't send her out into that cold," Johnny said.

"What the hell are we, a haven for rats and whores?"

"Look, Punderson, you jerk off, you take the first watch. Then Righty, me, Tim, Mulligan, and Pointer. Hit the rack, guys."

"Whattee me?" the Korean girl asked.

"Take this," Johnny said, tossing her what was left of his sleeping bag.

"Whattee you?"

"Me fine," Johnny said.

"You need fartee sack self. You want freebee?"

"Thanks, but no thanks. Let's hit the rack."

"What rack is that?" Mulligan asked, immediately spreading his sleeping bag on the deck, climbing in, and zipping it around his head.

"Bags only zipped to half mast, partway up, weapon inside, but make sure the safety's on so you won't blow off a ball or toe and get a free ticket home," Johnny said.

The others spread their bags on the deck and crawled in.

Johnny set up his bag for the tiny Korean as Punderson looked at him like he was crazy.

"Just don't touch my bag while I'm on watch," the stocky marine growled.

Johnny ignored him as he lay down, drawing his great coat around him.

Within minutes, they were snoring like an elephant farting into a wind tunnel lined with tweeters and woofers. But they weren't sleeping. After an hour, Punderson left his lookout port and moved slowly toward his stowed gear.

He returned to his port and asked, "Any of you guys awake?"

He was only answered by a snore that sounded like a muffler-less hotrod starting up.

Johnny and his fire team had heard Punderson rummaging in his pack, then papers being unwrapped, and then munching.

The fiercely hungry men snapped on their flashlights and surprised Punderson, his eyes the size of ostrich eggs, the crotch of a pair of women's panties that had been hidden in his pack now in his mouth.

"I'll be darned, the son of a bitch is one of us!" Righty said.

There was no spanking. Just a few congratulations before Righty took the cookies from Punderson's pack and told him, "You can keep the panties."

Johnny, munching a frozen cookie, summed his mates' feelings up with a singular opinion of Punderson's cookies and panties, "Punderson, you are my hero."

"You flucklin' lats!" Punderson growled, the underwear still firmly grasped in his mouth, much like a pet doll in the salivating mouth of a Lhasa apso.

"Take the undies out of your yap and speak clearly," Righty said.

That he did. Punderson spoke clearly, "You fucking rats!"

The exhausted marines roared with laughter.

"Righty, take the watch. Punderson has got to be exhausted with all that munching."

The tears streamed down the laughing men's eyes. Except Punderson's.

"I always fall asleep after breakfast at the Y," Pointer said.

"No, please, no more," Johnny said; the laughter on a hunger-pinched stomach was painful.

Tim was sobbing.

"You all right, Tim?" Johnny asked.

"Yes, John. But my stomach is in double hurts from hunger and laughter."

"What time is it?" Mulligan asked.

"Waddaya got a date?" Righty asked.

"Yah."

"Not Mattress Back, she's just a kid," Johnny said.

"No way, man, I've got a sister her age. Anyway, you gotta respect a woman wearing four Purple Hearts."

Then it hit the fan! Big time!

The enemy artillery and mortar fire poured in, round after round, on Dog Company.

"How in hell did those running NKPAs come up with artillery?" Righty asked.

"Beats the living piss out of me," Johnny said, "unless they were keeping it in their watch pocket 'cause you don't carry artillery shells in your arms while running away. Gotta be Chink. At least they built these bunkers strong."

"Yah, it's gotta be the Chinks," Righty said as the nearby rounds shook the earth, showering dirt by the shovelful down on them as log splinters slashed the air, sending them to the ground terrified.

Only Mattress Back remained calm and munched on one of Punderson's cookies that Johnny had left in her sleeping hand.

Then as suddenly as it started, it stopped.

The silence was eerie, disturbed only by moans and an occasional scream, "Corpsman! Walking Jay!"

There was no need to call for Walking Jay; he was crawling from man to man, the calf on his own right leg blown away, leaving muscle and sinew showing like the leg of a wildebeest being gnawed by a crocodile.

Then as suddenly as the screaming had started, the wounded quieted. Silence again, worse than the screaming.

A bugle sounded.

"What the hell!" Johnny said. "They bringing in the cavalry or something?"

A whistle blew.

A lone voice called out, "Ma-leens, you die. You fluckers!"

"Jesus!" Righty said.

"Ma-leen, you die!"

"He must fucken' think we're all Marleen Dietrichs."

The incoming rounds had shredded the air, filling it with smoke and settling debris. Burp guns filled in the notes between the trumpet frets.

The trip flares went off, exposing a solid wall of charging humanity, except it wasn't charging exactly, as withering return fire from the marines stopped the human wall, changed its shape into a bloody pulp.

A single figure shot through the slaughtered mass of quilted Chinese soldiers and headed directly at their bunker and through the bunker opening, where he was met, throat high, by Tim's KA-BAR.

Johnny shone his light on the fallen figure. He looked like the young boy that waited on them at the China Sky back home in Rockledge.

"Oh god," Tim said, "what did I do? I killed a kid."

"It's OK. It's OK, Tim," Johnny said.

"Oh god, John. Chinese. He's wearing Chinese insignias. We saved China. Did they forget?"

The wall of wounded and dead Chinese soldiers was being built closer and closer to the company's last line of defense.

"They're gonna overrun us!" Pointer said.

"Like fuck. Just fire!" Righty said, the barrel of his Browning automatic rifle starting to glow.

"Fire! Lay it down!" Johnny said, "while I get some ammo."

He was out of the bunker, running hunkered close to the ground and dodging the foxholes that were lined with wounded, dying. He fired as he ran, ducking, as if you can duck a bullet.

He spotted Lace. No ducking there. The Southerner was up and at 'em, pouring it on.

Jesus . . . old Lace . . . looks like a real . . . fucken' . . . marine . . . "Lace, where's the ammo?"

"There. They took a hit."

He found the body of Captain Huntley behind the logs, a huge wooden sword-size splinter sticking from his chest and out his back.

"Oh my good holy Jesus!"

Walking Jay was sitting beside the company commander, staring into the stars, chanting, his leg blown off by the same round that had claimed their captain. He cradled the leg in his arms, rocking it like a baby, crooning, "Hoker bey, yea, yea, hoker hey, yea, yea."

Johnny spotted the ammo supply and was about to load up when he saw the radio and its operator. Skinny was on his stomach with not a mark showing until Johnny rolled him over. Most of his face was missing, except his eyes that stared almost knowingly at the stars, one was full of fear and surprise, the other at half-mast, rest.

Johnny could see the figures running among the company, firing into foxholes like broken field runners in a football game . . . *Who started the Fourth of July bonfire . . . at a football game . . . won't be able to see the first down markers . . . dumb . . .* "Skinny, don't fuck with me. That playing dead shit isn't funny."

He shook his friend and saw the eyeball that had been severed from its nerves slide down his face. It was so clear, so white, among the pulp.

The eye appeared to be looking at something. The radio.

It was undamaged.

The Chinese were everywhere. Some were being shot off their feet, but it would only be minutes before there was no one left to kill them.

Johnny got the radio up and working. "Bring it in on us!"

The Eleventh Marines artillery officer on the other end asked, "Are you sure? Very sure? On top of you?"

"Fucken' Fire!"

"Roger. OK."

"Hit your holes! Hit your fucken' holes! Incoming!" Johnny yelled to the survivors now standing to meet the charging enemy eye to eye with fear replaced by fierceness.

The high explosives of their own artillery pulverized the piece of earth they groveled in.

Johnny felt hot slivers injected into his body as he ran with a box of ammo to the bunker. "Better tuck your head between your legs and kiss your ass good-bye," Johnny yelled.

"I can't," Righty said. "I shit my pants."

Johnny and other Dog Company survivors were stunned or knocked unconscious in their holes and hootches as the artillery wiped out the standing, either grinding them into hamburger or vaporizing them.

The bombardment ended as abruptly as the drop of a guillotine blade.

It was the quiet of a corpse in its casket.

There were no moans. Those above ground did not exist to moan.

Those hidden in holes were either unconscious from concussions or exhaustion, or a delicious combination of both.

"Johnny?"

The voice sounded like it was coming from the horn of an old hand-wound Victrola, scratchy, faraway, surreal.

The smoke and smell of cordite filled the air, joining the dark of night in a mixture that was especially concocted for Walpurgis Night and Walpurgis Night only. Only the devil danced.

Despite the smells of cordite from the explosives and the copper from the blood, it was the smell of a dirty sneaker and the foot inside it that won out as it rested in Johnny's lap, looking like a mock-up a kid might carry around while playing trick or treat on Halloween night.

What's with the sneaker . . . with a Chinese foot in it? . . . How do you know it is Chinese, John? . . . It stinks . . . like garlic . . . phew . . . pee-fucken'-yoo . . .

"Johnny?" The voice appeared to be going back into the bowels of the Victrola.

Don't . . . I know this guy . . . called me . . . Johnny . . .

"Here." The voice was low, weak, further filtered by the blood that trickled out of his nose, his ears, into his mouth . . . *Who said that? . . . Here . . . someone is throwing his voice . . . into my mouth . . .*

"Here. Please. Here." The voice was Johnny's own, heard by him through his own blood.

He was being lifted by the arms by Righty and someone even smaller than his friend. It was Mattress Back. Blood trickled from the corner of her mouth.

Johnny looked at her . . . *A fifth . . . Purple Heart . . .*

They laid Johnny on a long coat placed on the snow. He watched as she took off her jacket, the jacket with the mattress sewed to the back, and wrapped it around his shoulders . . . *She will have five Purple Hearts . . . I'll have only one . . .*

She wore a Daffy Duck T-shirt. The yellow of Daffy was a mite dirty, and looking him in the eyes, she said, "Me Mai Ling care you."

She folded the tattered sleeping bag he had given her and placed it under his head.

By forcing the blood out of the one corner of his mouth, he could moan, "Name? May Ling Daffy Duck?"

She said, her voice amazingly clear, like a Tinkerbell in a slight breeze, "You rest now, Mr. Johnny."

"Johnny, save your strength." Righty was checking his chest, stomach, for any wounds that might signal a quick end. He saw the bloody bone sticking out of Johnny's stomach and moaned. Then realized it was not

Johnny's but was a sneakered foot his friend was holding. Johnny had dodged the bullet; a concussion grenade had sent him into tweety-bird, but his head cleared quickly.

"Oh shit," Righty said, taking the enemy foot and throwing it behind him.

Mai Ling took the foot and placed it in a hole dug by a burp gun still firing as its dead carrier fell to the ground. Its owner was not to be found.

She covered it with the loose sod erupted by the barrage and bowed her head.

"Pointer? Tim?"

"Both OK, Johnny. The Chinks charged into our bunker like Chinamen in a bull shop. Tim was as calm as a flat sea, methodical, working his KA-BAR in close. And Punderson, the little prick that I expected to run, cleaned their clocks, swinging his rifle, and spitting into the air like your Red Sox hero, Teddy Boy Williams, telling the Fenway sports reporters to go to hell. I think Punderson thought they were trying to steal his pink panties. You OK?"

"I think so."

"Anyway, Punderson got a million-dollar wound, the lucky little prick, half his ear and the tip of his nose came off during the slice-and-dice time. I didn't do scratch. I can't remember. Except Tim almost diced me, and Punderson nearly took my head off with those wild man swings of his M1."

"What about Mulligan?"

"That son of a five-leaf clover was in the listening post, Chinese crawling all around. Not one spotted him. You sure you're all right?"

"Yah. I think all my bells were rung, and I feel like I was taped inside a clanging Big Ben, but no holes. But Chinese? It changes the picture. There's billions of them. Every time two pieces of rice get together, they have a little pigtail baby."

"Mulligan said he didn't see or hear them at first, just smelled a shit pot full of garlic. Johnny, you sure you're all right?"

"Come on, Righty, Mulligan's in a hole, enough Chinamen to do all the fucking laundry in America around him, *and he survives?*"

"One of the little shits looked right down into the hole, right at him."

"Then?"

"Then nothing. The guy smiles down, pretends like he doesn't exist, and crawls away to join his buddies. Jesus, they're gonna change the name of the Blarney Stone to the Mulligan Stone."

"Jesus, God must be a golfer and gave him a Mulligan. Pointer?"

Righty was quiet. Looked at the ground.

"Pointer? Did Pointer make it?"

Silence.

Johnny grabbed Righty by the neck and started to shake him. "Pointer!"

"He's OK. He's OK."

"Then what the fuck is what?"

"Tim and I went looking for him."

"Yah?"

"We found him."

"Cut the shit. What did he lose? An arm? An eye?"

"He had not only dug his foxhole outside our bunker but also dug a second room down the bottom of it. A two-room hole. And hung a piece of burlap over it. Crawled inside it and forced the mortar plate into the opening. We could hardly get him out. He was shaking like a leaf."

"You mean shivering? It's colder than the heart of an icicle."

"No, he was shaking, terrified."

"A round landed beside his hole."

"No."

"Where is he?"

"Tim's with him."

"Oh, Dink."

"What's the Dink bit?"

"I told him I'd watch out for Pointer."

"Johnny, get with it. We're a company, 180 fucken' men, or what is left of us, all depending on each other. We can't look out for one. That's, well, it isn't right, it isn't the way the corps does it, the way we do it."

"Hey, Plato." Righty turned.

It was Quince. "When you and Socrates are done, we need help. We have to get these bodies down to the road before they freeze. If they freeze in tough positions, carrying them down will be impossible."

"Get your asses into gear!" It was the gunny. "Marine body parts go into a shelter half. Check for identification. Dog tags. Wallets. Anything you recognize that belongs to someone. Move it. Move it! On the double."

But the "move it" and "on the double" didn't have its usual immediate effect.

They went about their job like zombies, saying nonsensical things, doing a duty that left them more bloody than their fallen brothers.

"Carrey, put together a work party, get the bodies down there."

The tall Kentuckian nodded. "Lace, DaSilva, Mulligan, you, you, and you," he pointed to Tim and Righty, "saddle up. Straighten their arms and legs by their side. Drag them down headfirst. Every single body comes down. The corps doesn't promise your mamas much, except to do the best to get your bodies back to the States." His voice drifted off. "That's all anybody can ask."

The trips down were nightmares. The stretchers were all being used by the corpsmen to get the wounded down the hill.

Exhaustion set in with some of the body movers and several of the dead marines being dragged downward by the legs, their heads bumping.

"By the arms, men," the gunny said.

Johnny saw an exhausted marine, his eyes as hollow as that of a cadaver, pulling a marine down by the ankles.

Johnny recognized the dead marine. It was Skinny. His intestines that Johnny had tucked back into his body had worked their way out and slithered behind him like a blue, green, brown, slimy snake. Skinny's bouncing head appeared to be trying to bite into his own guts like a dog chasing its tail.

"Stop, you son of a bitch!"

"Look, fuck head," the hollowed-eyed one hissed at Johnny, "if God wanted this guy carried, he would have whispered in my ear and not had some asshole screaming 'stop.'"

"Fuck God. He lost my fucking vote. Leave him."

"Hey, good luck." The leg puller headed back up like a hundred-year-old man to bring down another body.

Johnny carefully set down the body of the young marine that was on his shoulders. "Sorry, buddy. I'll be back." He went over to Skinny and whispered, "It's OK. It's OK. Johnny's with you." . . . *We're heading back . . . to the Big Woods . . .* "To the Big Woods."

He heaved his friend across his shoulders and started down the trail that was slippery with ice and blood.

Quince was ahead of him.

Tim had the company commander's body on his shoulders. He had removed the wooden spear.

Johnny spotted something moving beside him. Was a body attempting to crawl off this hill of hell?

It was Righty, on all fours. Johnny's small friend couldn't handle the body of the giant Walking Jay, but rather than pull it down hill by the ankles, he had gotten down on all fours over the Indian's body, tied Walking Jay's hands behind his own neck, and was doing a firefighter's carry.

The problem was that sometimes the body slid on the blood, and instead of being carried by Righty, it pulled him along behind it as it tobogganed downhill on a field of ice and intestines.

"Hold off, I'll be back to help Righty," Johnny said, adjusting Skinny's body on his shoulders. Johnny's own bleeding from his nose and ears stopped, as the blood froze solid. He felt like he had the weight of the world up there . . . *Where are you, Atlas . . . when I need you? . . . You know, Skinny . . . you'd be impossible . . . if you weighed as much now . . . as you weighed in high school . . . Smartest thing you ever did to lose weight . . . joining the crops . . . We're crops all right . . . to be harvested . . . then planted . . . We are grunts . . . the lowest of the low fighters . . .*

"DaSilva, you OK?" It was Quince.

When Johnny didn't answer, just nodded, the corporal turned back downhill.

The sweat was pouring from beneath Johnny's helmet. The wool hood and scarf he wore underneath his helmet were meant for slow travel and not tonnage of exertion. Yet while his head boiled, his body froze.

The heat of lugging the body kept him warm, but his snots froze in his nose. He tried to suck air through his mouth, but he couldn't open it wide enough to meet his needs. At first, he didn't understand why his face wouldn't move, thinking he was paralyzed. When he put his hand to his face in an attempt to determine why he couldn't move his cheeks or jaw, he realized that the sweat was now freezing on his face as quickly as it dripped down from beneath his helmet.

The exertion, the steep, rough terrain, and the bouncing body pushed his helmet over his eyes . . . *Fucken' piss pot . . .*

He didn't see the long green snake slither through the snow from behind him, pull alongside, and pass him. It was Righty's intestines.

Johnny stepped on them. He felt his feet go from under him and shoot into the air. The teeter board effect slammed his head and shoulders into the ground. Despite the cushioning of Skinny's body, the wind was knocked out of him.

He didn't move as the remainder of the intestines caught up with him. Those fresh out of the body were warm against his cheeks.

Johnny didn't bother to push them away; he just lay there staring at the sky, a sky the color of a shark, a snow-spitting shark.

"I quit. Quit." He could barely hear the words, wondered where they were coming from. But similar ones whispered like the wind in his brain . . . *I quit . . . I'm sorry . . . I quit . . .* "I fucken' a-John quit."

"John, we don't have that option. Honest."

Johnny looked up at Tim.

"What are you staring at, John?"

Johnny laughed.

"What are you looking at, John?"

"You. Your face is covered with ice. You look like a Swede, not a . . ."

"Go ahead and say it, John," the tall cocoa-colored marine said, "why I was always the Indian. But if we were playing cowboys and Indians today, with my white face, I could at last get to be one of the cowboys."

The two of them laughed and then hugged what was left of Righty.

Johnny got up slowly, taking out his KA-BAR as he did. He reached over and cut free Skinny's intestines . . . *Just like freeing . . . your fishing lure of weeds . . .* "Did you want to be a cowboy all that time, Tim?"

"It would have been nice once in a while."

They were walking downhill now, their burdens lightened by the out-of-place laugh.

"Funny, I always wanted to be an Indian."

"But they'd never let you."

"Because I could drink the hard stuff, the whiskey, when we played."

"Never understood how you could drink all that water with a ton of pepper floating on the top, not to mention turning over your white stones. Sorry. Gold. You could put down the fire water."

"That's why the older kids never made me an Indian. White men couldn't serve liquor to the redskins. I heard Jimmy Stewart accuse some bad guy cowboy of 'liquoring up the redskins so you can get their pelts for broken pieces of mirror.'"

On the road, several different companies were gently placing their dead in neat rows, evenly like they had been ordered "Dress right, dress!" And their arms had shot up to get the proper distances between each other.

Johnny set Skinny off to the side, holding his hands over his chest, then changed his mind and put his hands inside his jacket. Pulled the collar high around the dead friend's neck, wrapped the scarf that was tied in a knot under the helmet tighter around Skinny's ears, and looked his friend in the remainder of his face one last time. His eyes somehow had swung into the section of his head where they belonged. A snowflake landed in the middle of his right eye. He didn't blink.

"You bastard. You bastard!" . . . *You had no right to do this to me . . . to die . . . What were you thinking . . . ?*

"DaSilva." The voice was familiar, but softer than usual. It was the gunny. "You OK? Soon as I can, I'm gonna get you some R & R. They fly you to Itami. You head to one of those electric trains. And head to Koyoto. There is a synagogue or something there. It was Hirohito's father's, and it has these giant carp."

The gunny put his hand on Johnny's shoulder. "And these carp will come up and eat right out of your hand. Sacred. Or something. And they got these giant gold statues of Buddha. He's a god or something to them. They're big. Bigger than a defensive lineman for the Chicago Bears. And maybe . . ." He tried to wipe away a tear that started down Johnny's cheek, but it had turned to ice. The old sergeant looked at it in his hand then sheepishly said, "I thought it was a sliver of shrapnel. Was afraid you'd get it in your aiming eye. Good happy Jesus, it's cold. It was so warm on Tinian that worms grew between your toes. That's the biggest difference between WW II and this one, where your toes freeze, turn black, and fall off."

The gunny tried to help Johnny to his feet, but the young marine was like a sack of water where if you lifted one end, the other filled. The gunny was exhausted. What made him different from his troops was that he had to pretend that he wasn't exhausted.

Johnny could feel the exhaustion in his sergeant's attempts. "You'll like Koyoto, DaSilva. No coochie coed on every corner, but rather some high-class stuff to study. Be careful when you take that train to Koyoto cuz the conductor keeps calling out something that sounds like Kyoto. But isn't—Koyoto."

The gunny sat Johnny down and sat beside him. "But maybe you want some of that sideways stuff, five bucks and you get the works."

"Mustard and relish?"

"So you are alive. No, the five bucks includes the jo-san, and she washes and starches your uniform before you wake up. Sings softly. And if you say 'dozo' and 'alligato,' please and thank you, you might get a little for nothin' from her later on. They're very courteous. You OK?"

"Yah."

"Then get your bandy ass up and movin'. You think your shit don't stink? You think your asshole shits filet mignons? Move it!"

"Sergeant?" It was the new company commander, Lieutenant Smith.

"Aye-aye."

"What's happening here?"

"Waddaya mean, Lieutenant?"

"The Chinese overran a number of positions and then disappeared."

"What month is it?"

"November. I don't know. What's that got to do with it?"

"If it was December, I would say the Chinks want us to be comfortable for Christmas and prepare to be sent home."

"A couple of the young officers said you'd been around, might know something about how these Chinamen fight."

"The Japs never disappeared. They were always in your face, even when they were dead. With their last breath, they'd booby trap themselves. Rule was never look for no flags and swords from a dead Jap that has a smile on his face."

"So you know nothing."

"One thing for sure, you check their knapsack, and you'll find rice or dough rolled in millet that you add water to for about three days' ration."

"Yah. Thanks. Why didn't you say that in the first place?"

"Lieutenant?" It was Tim.

"Yes, Yanders?"

"I've read some Mao. His plan, and it sounds much like Chang's during World War II when the Japanese were in China, is to retreat when the enemy advances, harass when the enemy digs in, attack when the enemy gets exhausted and confused from chasing, and when the enemy retreats, chase them."

"Where'd you learn this, Private? At West Point? Well, we don't retreat," Lieutenant Smith said., "They're the ones that pulled the Harry Houdini disappearing trick. MacArthur says we're to be home for Christmas."

"He didn't say which Christmas," Johnny said.

"I think that's enough of that, Private. What's your name? You new?"

"DaSilva, *sir*." Johnny's "sir" was loud. "I'm not new, *sir*. I wasn't new after the first day. And will never be new again."

"That's enough, DaSilva," the gunny whispered to him. "You trying to get the lieutenant killed with that 'sir' bit?" Then turning to Lieutenant Smith, the gunny said, "He's tired."

"I understand, Sergeant. The men get tired."

The gunny looked over his men . . . *Jesus . . . they've got runny noses . . . some . . . so young . . . some still twanging their banjos under the sheets . . .*

"OK, men, this is the Grand Hotel for the night. Set up," the new twenty-three-year-old company commander, now in charge of what was left of the 180 men of Dog, commanded.

After setting out their listening posts, their trips and boobies, and lining up their fields of fire, Dog and their dead slept side by side in the ditch on the side of the road, a road that was leading to the Yalu River and the Manchurian border.

"What do you figure we'll do when we get to China?" Righty asked no one in particular.

"Kick ass," Lace said.

"Why do you think we're heading to China," Righty asked, "for a chocolate, cream-filled Drake Cake or a stale fortune cookie that reads 'Woman who fly in plane upside down will have crack up'?"

"Man, that's an old one," Lace said.

"I heard we're heading to China cuz Chesty Puller wants to leave his laundry off," Quince said.

"If it's like mine," Johnny said, "they'll have to whack the hell out of his skivvies with an ax, just to loosen up the flotsam and jetsam that froze, and set up housekeeping there."

"The last time I had so many hash marks in my skivvies was when the NKPA dropped a few mortar rounds on us when we were at the mess tents back at battalion," Quince said. "I was letting a shit into the slit trench when that first round hit, and a piece of shrapnel boiled past my whizzer."

"Nothing would be lost there," Rhesus said, his crooked grin growing more and more crooked as mouth muscles dropped from exhaustion.

"Y'all weren't gonna tell if I let you touch my weapon of mass destruction, and now you done told," the tall Kentuckian said.

"So what's the poop scoop?" Pointer asked.

"Well," Quince drawled, "I said, as that explosion flapped my pecker in the wind like the tail of a farting hummingbird, pride goeth before a fall."

"So?"

"So this ol' boy, he just did a belly flop into a slit trench full of shit. Well, my skivvies honchos are the same today, although it took longer for today's menu down there."

"Wasn't that the mortar attack that cookie got a free ride home on?" the gunny asked.

"Yup. Seems that old boy, Cheek was his name, who was a short-order cook in civilian life, had hounded his company commander for six months to get transferred to cook at battalion. He had been in the thick of all the fightin', Seoul twice, Incheon, all the way up here toward China, without a scratch. Company commander got darn right tired of listening to Cheek's whining and sent him back to battalion to cook. His first day behind the lines, the North Koreans laid some mortars in just to fuck up chow down."

"Cheek got kilt?" Mulligan asked.

"Worse."

"What's worserer than gettin' kilt?"

"You know those GI cans with the boiling water you dunk your mess kits in? Well, a round landed in that, splattering Cheek. It burned the living-piss-be-Jesus out of his pecker and, worse, his balls. Oh, he howled worse than any tomcat sitting on a fence looking for love. It was pitiful."

The listeners took on looks of pain.

"What's the story on Pointer?" Scoff asked.

"Lieutenant's trying to figure out what to do with him, keep him because we're short of men, to throw him to the sharks, a court-martial, or what?" the gunny said.

"Gunny, he's gotta stay. I know him," Johnny said.

"You know we can't risk Dog for one runner."

"Runner? Jesus, that heavy stuff came right in on our heads."

"You should know, DaSilva, you called the shit in," Lace said.

"Look, you pickled asshole," Righty said, "that shit saved our asses."

"'Cept those that didn't get into their holes in time. Those fighting up on the deck."

"Knock off the Monday morning quarterback crap," the gunny said. "I don't know whether to kiss him or kill him, but we need every lick of experience we can get. Unless you want some porgy bait replacement. We all get that movin' on feeling when the dam burst and the dingle berries come swamping around our necks."

"Guess he's better than nothin', but that's only a guess and probably not a good one."

"What you got to say, Yanders?" Lace asked.

"I am not saying anything. If I was saying something, it would be what anyone with a brain and a pair of eyes would say. John is the best, and Pointer has some of his blood in his veins."

"That's what I'd expect from someone like you."

Johnny stood up. "Do you want to be more specific, Lace?"

"My good happy, holy, horse shit, I hope you guys save a little chutzpah, as the Jews say, for the Chinamen. They'll be plenty of them," Quince said.

"They're runnin' all the way back to Hong Kong or King Kong, or whatever in hell is the name of that city in China," Lace said.

"Something doesn't fit," Tim said.

And they felt something didn't fit as they headed north, into higher, colder weather.

Even the practically gourmet dinner all the front line troops enjoyed that November 23, 1950, Thanksgiving Day, didn't make sense, roasted turkey, yams, cranberry sauce, mince and apple pies, and not only olives, but stuffed olives.

"How in good happy goofus shit did they get this stuff up here?" Rhesus asked.

Quince, Johnny, Lace, Tim, Mulligan, and Pointer, who had won a reprieve when the gunny put in the good word, were on a ridge that reached out beyond the battalion perimeter. They had a light machine gun manned by Lace, with Mulligan, the belt feeder, Righty as the BAR man, with Pointer his assistant. Johnny had an old bolt action Enfield.

"Where in hell you get that antique?" Quince asked.

"Traded for it."

"What did you give, the Empire State Building and the Brooklyn Bridge?"

"Just some trinkets Scoff had confiscated."

"We used those suckers as sniper rifles in the islands," Quince said. "I heard a few made it to Korea, but I didn't believe it."

"Better believe it."

"Better not let Lieutenant Smith see it," Mulligan said. "He can be a stickler for the book. And that's a nonissue."

"What will he do, take away my good housekeeping merit badge?"

"I don't know what your hard-on for Lieutenant Smith is," Quince said, "but why don't you stow it? He's OK, a little bit chicken shit but OK. He's not chicken. He got to shit his pants with us and stood. He's one of us."

"Yah, I know," Johnny said, "but we have to have something to bitch about. Can't bitch about the Chinese—they seem like a pretty good bunch of guys, except when they're killing us. Mulligan likes 'em."

"I like that nearsighted one that looked down into my foxhole and smiled when he didn't see nothing."

"What's that, running down that valley, a deer?" Tim asked.

Quince brought up his binoculars. "It's a Chinaman, and he's setting the three-minute mile."

Johnny shouldered the Enfield.

"Forget it," Lace said, "too far and through the thick shit."

Johnny's shot echoed through the valley. The runner went down. Stayed down.

"How the fuck did you do that?" Lace said.

"Yah, are you some kind of squirrel hunter from Kentucky, or somethin'?" Quince said.

"When they're running downhill in the brush, you just have to pretend they're a bouncing tire in a sandpit."

"What the hell you talking about?" Lace asked. "Only us Kentucky windage boys can shoot like that."

Pointer smiled when he heard Johnny mention tire shooting. It seemed like a million years ago when the three of them, Johnny, Dink, and he, would go to the sandpit to shoot or ski. It was always hot when they went to the pits. They had made skis of barrel staves and tacked tin to the bottom and shushed downhill over the sand fast enough to bring tears to their eyes. Then after the skiing came the rolling tire shoots.

Pointer's smile was his first in some time. He hadn't talked or shown any emotion since the artillery barrage on the hill and his runaway.

"What you smiling at?" Lace challenged.

Pointer didn't answer; he just continued to smile.

"Probably that little feather of a cock is ingrown and tickling him some," Lace said.

"That reminds me, Quince," Johnny said, "I owe you an apology."

"What for? Eat your turkey before you answer."

They had all stuffed their dungaree pockets before setting up the flank.

"Seems everyone thought you were full of shit . . ."

"I am."

"Seems like everyone thought you were full of shit when you said that when you were first terrified, you got this great erection. Well, when that artillery was coming in on our heads, I got this fantastic erection the size and hardness of an Academy Award Oscar."

"I had a hard-on once," Righty said, "or I thought I did, then I remembered I had a roll of pennies I was taking to the bank to cash."

As the late afternoon cold and wind started their bone-terrifying Virginia reel through the high peaks, each struggled to cut out the draft, only to find that pulling the great coats around their necks allowed more wind to whip around their legs. That was only the preview of coming attractions; the night brought cold and chill factors down.

"Must be eighty below zero," Righty said.

"Did you stick that little thermometer that's between your legs in the snow?" Rhesus laughed.

"Did you see that?" It was Quince.

"I see it," Johnny said. "It was some kind of northern light or bolt of lightning or something, and there was that silver ribbon in the distance."

Almost solemnly, Quince said, "That's the Yellow River."

"God save us," Tim said.

"I wouldn't worry, Chesty talks to God," Lace said.

"Yah, but he pisses him off," Quince said.

"Rumor has it that some doggies from the Seventh Army are at the Yalu," Quince said.

"That was weird, that light," Tim said.

Guards and listening posts were set up, although there was little need, as none could sleep in the numbing cold, despite the exhaustion.

The sleep came the next day as they marched up the road or walked the steep sides of the mountain when it was their turn protecting the flank.

"Unless my map is wrong," Tim said, "we're moving through something called Funchilin Pass."

"Sounds like some of that good old South Boston Italian home cooking," Johnny said.

"And some little town called Koto, and there's a reservoir that would make our Quabbin Reservoir seem like a puddle," Johnny, who had fished the shore of the state reservoir with his father, said.

"That would be Chosen. Where'd you get that map?" Quince asked.

"I took it off one of those Chinese officers that got caught in our artillery. Looking at this map, it just makes sense why we're not even meeting sniper fire," Pointer said.

"I got some chow Scoff had swiped back in that village where they ate their dogs. What you got for chow? and it better not bark," Johnny asked.

"Not much. Nothing. Although I could give you a snow sandwich if I had bread."

They were too cold to laugh.

What they thought had been cold was downright balmy compared to the sudden shock of the weather that set in within minutes as the wind shifted and came down from Manchuria.

The temperature dropped to a wind chill factor that would freeze the gonads off a polar bear.

Several members of Dog went into what appeared to be shock and wept quietly, staring into the distance, not seeing. The gunny secreted with Quince, "I don't think we can fight in this cold. Anyone who took off a glove to pull a trigger would have his fingers freeze. I don't know if General Smith knows this."

"Old Oliver knows it," Quince said. "He's everywhere."

Lieutenant Smith, one scarf coming from under his helmet and over his ears and a second from behind his head and covering much of his face, yelled to the gunny, "Have those men keep their faces covered. They're breaking out in frostbite."

Not only were some being bitten by the bitter cold, but also some of the silver spots in the skin, body fluids, froze and blackened.

"I heard General Smith is building an airstrip some place behind us," Tim said.

"I hope not. That doesn't sound good," Quince said. "It could mean an evacuation strip at some vacation spot called Hagaru. Like he thinks the shit might hit the muzzle blast."

"Hey, if it hits, an emergency airstrip could be a good thing," the gunny said. "We've lost a lot of integrity here. Units are too far spread, especially the doggie troopers."

"Shit," Quince said.

"Next stop is Yudam, them's the orders," the gunny said, shaking his head.

"Yah, dam you too," Quince said.

"Jesus, Corporal, your head frostbit or what? Don't go giving me no shit," the older man said.

Rumor was the only hot thing around as temperatures continued to dip.

"Radio ears reports the ROKs have broken and run, and the Eighth Army is being overrun on our far flank, and we're gonna advance? Did some fat-ass general gorge himself on ape shit and pound on his chest or something?" Pointer asked.

"We're moving out," the gunny said. "General Smith is covering our rear and flanks. He only trusts us. Move those feet."

Rhesus said, "Unless some of us can swipe new feet, we're gonna have to issue them scooters. I saw a guy with frozen feet. They' were black. Looks like he's wearing a pair of CCM hockey boots without the blades. I don't know much, but it looks like they're gonna break off like a turkey drumstick."

"Don't rub your nose, Rhesus, it will fall off. From what I can see, it's frozen," Righty said.

"Let's melt some snow and drink some warm water," Rhesus said.

They lit a fire and stuffed a metal cup with snow, but because of the cold, it would not melt.

"DaSilva, Lace, Yanders, Gouveira, take point," the gunny said, his brain numbed by the cold. He turned to Quince. "What did I just say?"

"You told them to move out. I think."

"Yah, well, good. Lieutenant Smith got the word. We have to move toward some pass, Tonkin, or somethin' like that. We got some guys we left behind to protect our asses, and we have to get them out."

"What's happening, John?" Tim asked. "I thought we were chasing them."

"I dunno. I guess a whole shit load more of Chinese appeared from out of nowhere. Maybe millions!"

"Move it, or lose it," the gunny said, then turning to Quince, "Did I tell them to move out?"

The tall Kentuckian didn't answer. He couldn't hear through all the clothing covering his head. To have the ears in hearing order meant exposure. Exposure at sixty below meant they would wilt like old lettuce and fall the fuck off.

Johnny's point team moved out.

They appeared as piles of rags in their layers of clothing, barely moving but fast enough for the other ragbags that followed some hundred yards behind.

It was up to Tim to look behind to check for hand signals from the gunny or Lieutenant Smith far below.

The gunny pointed up the steep mountainside then moved his hand northward. He ended up by pumping his hand in the air.

Tim halted Johnny at the lead and whispered inside his hood to be heard.

Johnny looked at his friend, cocked his head sideways, his eyes blank . . . *Tim's breath . . . is . . . sweet . . .*

"Up the ridge. North. Double time," Tim said, relaying Lieutenant Smith's hand signals.

"Double time," Johnny mumbled . . . *Two times zero . . . is . . . zero . . . Keep them . . . shuffling . . . along . . .*

He stared up. He thought the wind was whispering his name. "John."

He turned. It was Pointer. The word was the first his cousin had spoken to him since the artillery barrage when they found him shivering in his foxhole.

Johnny looked at him. Everyone's eyes were sunken, but Pointer's had the look of the dead.

He took Pointer's gloved hand, wrapped it in a scarf that he had in his great coat, and tucked the hand in the back of his web coat belt and led him upward.

Lace spotted the lone Chinese soldier disappearing in the distance and brought his rifle up to his face. The corner of his lips immediately froze to the steel.

He tried to fire, but his glove finger would not fit in the M1 trigger guard.

He tried breathing out of the corner of his mouth to free the frozen flesh. His breath froze, locking his lips to the steel all the more.

Tim saw the giant marine with the rifle frozen to him in the offhand position and cupped his hands to warm his breath, keeping it protected from the terrifying cold, so he could blow on Lace's lip.

He saw Lace's eye widen as Tim approached him, then relaxed as Tim put his gloves against his lips and the rifle, and blew warm breath, unintercepted by the cold, on them, until they were free.

They looked into each other's eyes.

Lace tried to smile, but his lips split in several places. The blood that appeared froze immediately, leaving his lips looking like racing stripes on the nose of a souped-up Merc.

It was then that the snow in front of them appeared to move. It was an enemy soldier that had been frozen in the snow.

Johnny leveled his rifle at him and walked slowly forward. He could feel Pointer being pulled behind him.

The soldier had an old Enfield. Apparently, it had been taken from a dead marine. His right hand was frozen inside the trigger guard. He had been foolish enough to take off a glove to try and get a shot at them. His other hand was on the forehand stock, also frozen in the shooting position. The forward hand wrapped around the .03s forearm held something; it looked like a picture.

Johnny looked into the enemy's face. He was very young. Johnny's age at most. He checked out the padded clothing, the feet. He wore two toed sneakers . . . *Fucken' sneakers . . .*

They were frozen in solid blocks of ice.

The small group of marines read his eyes. They begged that they shoot him.

"We can't waste a bullet," Lace said.

"They'd hear a shot, John," Tim said.

Johnny took the photo out of the frozen hand. It was the young soldier, rice paddies behind him. On a warmer day. He had been a farmer. The old people had to be his parents. The young girl, perhaps his wife or a sister, was holding a baby. He placed the picture back in the hand and bent the frozen arm upward so he could see his family. The young Chinese soldier's eyes looked at Johnny for a brief moment, an eternity, and then shifted back to the picture, where they remained until Johnny's rifle shot, muffled by the snow, tore a hole in the middle of the chest; the blood that wanted to spurt out froze almost instantly.

The soldier did not fall to the ground, but froze in a crumpling position.

Johnny attempted to take the picture from the frozen hand. It tore, separating him from the young woman and baby.

Johnny took the two pieces and placed them inside the dead man's padded jacket.

He felt the hand on his shoulder.

"John. Down below," Tim said softly. "The gunny signaled us to move ahead."

They were several hundred feet above and ahead of the rest of Dog far below.

They moved forward. Zombies, their weapons carried in their arms like firewood, rather than at a high combat port ready to fire.

Johnny looked at the surrounding ridges, back at Lace and Tim. Their eyes all read the same. They walked into a perfect ambush site.

Johnny stepped into the slot, Pointer still tethered behind him.

The machine gun fire that greeted Johnny shattered both his legs below the knee, blew away the inside top of his thighs, and caused him to fall straight down, dragging Pointer down with him. The splinted shins jammed into the frozen ground.

The machine gun fire whipped the snow into a frenzy as a bitter high wind joined the action, causing the snow to swirl in a blinding maelstrom.

Johnny, his splintered shins stuck in the snow, could see his buddies hit the deck and roll, like tramps being kicked off a park bench by the cop on the beat, onto and into the snow, disappearing before his eyes.

Then the bugle and the cymbals came; they sounded so silly, especially with the strange little men, half frozen, coming toward them in slow motion looking like they were headed toward the rag pickers' ball rather than at Johnny and his fire team.

Johnny wasn't sure how long he had been unconscious. He was in a sitting position. The blood that wanted to pour from his wounds froze, serving better than tourniquets. He was alone.

Had Pointer and the others been killed?

"I'm so cold," he told the clouds . . . *It was so warm . . . when Pointer . . . Dink . . . and me . . . dug that hole to . . . the outhouse . . . to see if . . . if . . . a girl's . . . you know . . . was underneath . . . or in the front . . . Maybe . . . I'll never . . . know . . .*

He looked down at his shattered legs. He would surely bleed to death . . . *if I could . . . bleed . . . I guess I . . . will have to freeze . . . to death . . . Oh, Ma . . .* "Ma!"

No one was around. His friends. The zombies that had shot him that had gotten out of their graves and tried to claim him. No one.

The pain from the smashed legs fought with the bitter cold to claim him.

He tried to get the morphine out of his dungarees that Scoff had swiped from sick bay weeks before. He couldn't get his gloved hand into his pockets. He tried to get a glove off with his teeth. The cold froze his teeth . . . *If I only had some . . . hot wax . . . or tar . . . to chew . . . they would not . . . hurt . . . Yelena's mouth would keep . . . my mouth . . . warm . . . and they . . . would . . . stop . . . hurting . . .*

He wondered if the dead Chinese soldier he had helped to die could take a second out from death to do the same for him. He would have had anyone do it, but he was alone and realized no one would come for him. Not that they wouldn't. They couldn't.

"Johnny?"

"They're gone," Lace said. "Tim chased the bastards off with that fucken' Pointer right beside him. They chased a whole fucken' platoon. We thought you'd bought it. The big ticket. Your fucken' cousin insisted we bring your body back. Looks like we'll bring it back. But alive. You fucked up a good funeral. Blame Pointer, he insisted we reclaim your dead body."

Pointer picked up Johnny's rifle, shattered it on the frozen ground, then shattered his own.

He took the broken pieces and made splints for the two mangled legs.

Lace lifted Johnny, but Pointer claimed his cousin, who was put on his back. It was difficult to discover which way was down, as the blinding snow that had whipped up caused them to walk with their eyes closed. Righty tried to take a compass reading, but the alcohol in the compass froze.

They had to take turns carrying Johnny, taking over when one could no longer continue the carry.

They waited blinded in a whiteout. Then the driving snow stopped.

It restarted with renewed vigor, hissing as the chill factor changed from molten needles into needles of ice.

The wind cleared the snow, and they could finally see the ribbon of road far below.

Johnny, who passed in and out of consciousness, heard Pointer's voice through the fog, a sleepiness was coming over him. "Johnny, remember the time we took the Model A up to Fort Ticonderoga? And we saw all those bullets in the glass showcase with the teeth marks in them as the wounded bit into them to stand the pain? Well, you've got to bite it. Remember one bullet had a tooth stuck in it? You've got to bite it. You've got to bite it." Pointer placed a M1 shell casing in his teeth and grabbed under one shoulder, while Lace grabbed under the left shoulder and dragged him behind them, his eyes staring blankly at the sky.

Johnny's teeth sunk into the shell as his splintered legs thumped on the frozen, rocky ground . . . *For I cherish . . . the old rugged . . . cross . . .*

Their trail through the snow was marked by blood when his legs kept opening as the frozen snow tore at them.

Below, the marine lines were heading home. "Advancing in another direction," someone had said, as the enemy troops behind them became thicker than those in front.

The thin line of marines was still moving as they reached the road.

Pointer stopped a Jeep towing a trailer, its sides torn off so wounded marines could be laid side by side on a shelf of planks.

Johnny saw the Jeep driver look down . . . *staring at . . . staring at what? . . . Am I missing . . . missing . . . ?*

He heard the driver's voice; it sounded many miles away. "This poor bastard seems to have had his crotch pretty much shot away."

Johnny was placed between a young corporal, perhaps nineteen, who was missing the lower jaw, and an old-timer, a buck sergeant in his thirties, with a missing eye bandaged with a torn green T-shirt. All three stared at the sky.

Sleeping bags were spread over them, along with pieces of canvas.

"You OK, Johnny?" Pointer asked.

Johnny looked at his cousin then stared back at the sky, not answering.

"Johnny, don't do it. Don't you dare die. Don't quit," Tim said.

"Johnny," Pointer said, "you can't die. You can't die a fucken' virgin."

Pointer and Tim walked along holding on to the side of the Jeep.

The Chinese machine gun fire from a ridge above sent all the able bodied scurrying into the ditch.

Johnny heard the gunny's voice as the spasmodic fire continued, "Lay it on those pricks! Using us as a shooting gallery."

Johnny remembered the county fair coming to Lowell, with a Ferris wheel and merry-go-round, and he and Dink and Pointer walking there from the farm.

Dink would bet on which colored hole on the turning wheel the mouse would go into. Pointer and he would hang around the tent that cooked up the steaks and smothered them with fried onions and green peppers. Then they would shoot at the metal bears with the lights in their arms that lit up when you plinked one . . . *Now we're the fucken' . . . bears . . . fucken' polar bears . . . with ice bit tits . . . Jesus . . . let me escape this . . . let me die . . . don't do it . . .*

Johnny worked himself free of the mouthless and eyeless marines beside him, hung head first off the trailer, as Pointer and Righty lifted him and carried him into the ditch out of the Chinese fire from above.

Once in the relative safety of the ditch, Tim and Pointer lit up, which was interesting since neither smoked. Pointer and Johnny had puffed on straw cigs they made on the farm and on Prince Albert in the can rolled in toilet paper . . . *Mr. Druggist . . . you got Prince Albert in the can . . . You better let him out . . . Lord, that was . . . funny . . .*

"Nice, guys, not sharing your fags. Give me a puff."

Tim handed Johnny the quarter inch of smoldering cigarette.

"Where in hell did you get butts?" Johnny asked.

"Scoff's ditty bag. He had swiped them from some dentist in Boot Camp was treating him for a toothache," Pointer said.

The firing stopped.

Johnny was lifted out of the ditch and back onto the Jeep bed, and the convoy squirmed painfully along like a garter snake mangled by a lawn rake, fighting every inch of the way.

The long line of exhausted men and convoy stopped each time Chinese machine guns sizzled down from the ridge above and a fire team was sent out to hopefully still them. Tim and Lace were in the team, and Johnny knew he would never see them again.

The Chinese fire from the ridges above was stilled, and Lace and Tim struggled back down, out of ammunition, their faces frozen.

Johnny could see Lace as he went by. Saw his lips, shredded like a fillet of fish. Heard his bitch, "Why can't I keep my fucken' lips off this fucker of a rifle?"

It was a short while later, the sniper fire started up again.

The convoy stopped, and everyone who was able made it into a ditch, including Johnny, who was carried by Pointer as Tim lugged the one-eyed buck sergeant.

Each time Johnny was carried to the ditch when fire broke out, he appeared more exhausted, weaker. His eyes sunk deeper into his head, until he appeared to be a small raccoon peeping out of a dark, hollowed-out tree, only shiny little beads of eyes showing.

"He's not gonna make it," Pointer said. "He's quit."

"He just has no more left," Tim said.

"I know."

The fire poured down around them, continuing until it was answered. Sometimes machine gun fire sprayed ridgeward did the job; other times, mortar fire sufficed. Each time the overcast cleared, Corsairs dropped napalm on the ridges.

Heavy machine gun fire greeted them again. Everyone hit the ditch, except Tim and Pointer. They tried to get Johnny up; he wouldn't budge. He was playing with some sort of stick and told them to "get the fuck in the ditch"; his urging was accompanied by machine gun bursts that exploded over their heads.

"Come on, man," Pointer said.

"Go. I'm staying here. Those Chink pricks couldn't hit a bull in the ass with a git fiddle."

Another burst of machine gun fire sent the two friends on a beeline for the ditch.

"That was his last hurrah," Pointer said, the tears that wanted to spill out were foiled when the first ones froze immediately in their ducts.

The machine gun fire continued.

Then one burst was followed by laughter.

Then another burst.

More laughter from some of those in the ditch.

Another volley.

Laughter along the ditch.

"What the fuck?" Pointer said.

On the next burst, he popped his head up.

Johnny had fashioned a red Maggie's drawers flag on a pole, and after each burst from a Chinese machine gun, he waved the flag back and forth, signaling a complete miss, a signal used on all marine ranges.

"My asshole cousin is gonna make it!"

Rhesus, who caught up with his friends, greeted Pointer with a kiss, "I'm legal today," Pointer said.

"What are you talking about? You found out you have a father or somethin'?"

"It's my birthday. I'm eighteen. Now I can legally get killed, and the Marine Corps won't have to take a batch of shit in the newspapers."

The firing stopped, and the thin line continued on, beaten but not broken. Its movement was like that of a wounded warrior that declined to die.

"Think we're gonna make it?" Pointer asked.

"I dunno. But there's Hagaru. Sure as shit."

They watched as the old World War II mothballed R4Ds and R5Cs fishtailed through the muddy skies, found the emergency strip, and bumped into the cheers of the marines who had already arrived.

"This one," a blood-covered surgeon said, pointing at Johnny.

"You drew the brass ring, buddy," Righty said.

"You lucky piece of ape shit," Pointer said, taking his cousin by the hand.

"Hey," Johnny said, squeezing Pointer's hand, "I was smart enough to get spit out by a four-leaf clover eating goat and am going home."

"You're not as lucky as Mulligan—he could have got killed," Righty said, winking. "Look, say hello to everyone back in Rockledge. You'll get there first. Give my hello to Yelena. Or Bernadette."

"Load him up!" It was the doctor.

"Johnny, we'll write you from Koto," Tim said. "We'll vacation there."

But not immediately; it would take some time to advance in another direction to Koto and then the sea.

"Next stop, Itami," a corpsman playing train conductor said, as the plane door was closed. The idling engines were revved, expressing hope that they had the power to get airborne and, once airborne, get over that first ridge.

Johnny's frozen wounds started to thaw, and the blood came.

As did darkness.

CHAPTER 15

JAPAN

He wasn't strapped to the bed in the hospital ship where the wounded from Korea's battlefields lay, and he thought . . . *They don t have me strapped down . . . Thank God for . . . little favors . . .*

When the target rifle blew up in his face that day in the farm sandpit years earlier, leaving him with pieces of lead and metal from the bullet and casing in his eye, he didn't at first realize how seriously he was injured.

Even when he realized that he was immobilized by straps across his forehead, chest, and hips at the Boston Eye and Ear Infirmary of Massachusetts General Hospital, which gave him as little movement as a hermit crab shedding one shell and trying to wiggle into its next one, Johnny didn't understand the seriousness.

He was typical of a young teenager that rarely understands what the potential seriousness of a situation can be.

That's why the Marine Corps, Navy, Army, and Air Force wanted their Raiders, Seals, Rangers, fighter pilots, and tank crews to be young, as most young people just do not believe that it can happen to them.

But combat lets you know immediately that you are no longer young. It can happen to you. You can be tagged in a game of "it" and a tag tied to your toe telling your name, rank, and serial number. When you are killed or seriously wounded, you cannot just tag someone else, making them "it" and allowing you to be free again.

Johnny and his Dog Company mates did not discuss the fact that they could be tagged, as they continued whistling past the graveyard day after day, sometimes moment after moment.

Even when one on one in a foxhole, it was easier on the nerves to talk about other things happening around them. It was easier to talk about when they had copped a feel from a cheerleader, had collected a Babe Ruth rookie card, or how a little brother scored a touchdown but that little brother was a Wrong-Way Corrigan who had run in the wrong direction.

Johnny did not think of Jazz's touchdown, one he had never bragged about. It was Romola that told on their brother. Johnny did not think of the green grass of the football field, the ever-shifting multicolors of the ever-changing fans, the rah-rah royal blue of the Rockledge uniforms.

All he saw was white; everywhere he looked it was white, a stark, startling white . . . *like that satin . . . on the inside of a . . . casket . . .* and he called out, "If I'm inside a casket, why the fuck do I hear Bing Crosby singing with that usual mouthful of marshmallows?"

"Money in the bank, buddy?" It was Tim. He had his hospital johnny on backward, leaving his front wide open to the world rather than his rumble seat.

"What are you doing here?" Johnny asked . . . *Are you in the . . . casket . . . with me . . . ?*

"They sent me here to count my marbles. Seems the Chinks swiped a couple when they tossed that concussion grenade into my skivvies. Why would anyone want to set off an explosion down there? How sadistic can you be?"

Johnny didn't want to look down to see if his body line ended at the knees. "At least they don't itch. My legs, that is. They say if you lose your legs, it itches down there."

"Yes, even my brain itches."

"Not your brain, my legs."

"I'll tell you my brain itches," Tim said.

"You know your johnny is on backward? What happened?"

"I had jumped into a shell hole, and the Chinks charged, and one dropped a concussion grenade in with me."

"Why do you have your johnny on backward?"

"Let's say I'm investigating my options. Whether to go back to Korea when I'm better."

"You mean you are looking for a ticket home—a ticket called a 'Section Eight'?"

"I'm thinking about it. They just don't give those passes home away. You walk around with your johnny on backward, and your, Mr. Do-little, out, and you have a chance. I don't owe Cold-rea anything. Quite simply, I've paid my dues. Either a medical or a Section Eight. Preferably a medical."

Johnny said, "I understand wanting out. We had so many close calls, even our pubic hair was turning gray."

"Do you know, Johnny, that the pubic area is the last part of your body to turn gray? How do you figure?"

Johnny shrugged. "Maybe the pubic area worries the least, has the most fun."

"You could be right. I checked your medical charts. It should get your attention. You've been out cold since they wheeled you in several days ago, after they wheeled you out of surgery. You'll be happy to know you're not pregnant. And that you will keep your legs, somehow. But you won't be jumping center for the Celtics as they took a section of bone out of both."

"Can I play goalie for the Bruins? They could pin me up in the net. Take me out for a piss between periods."

"John?"

"Yah?"

"I'm not sure on a trip home or back to what's left of Dog. I'm just keeping my options open. You understand? By the way, I've collected all your missing mail, found it in Scoff's belongings being shipped home. I was looking for the pen my father gave me."

Johnny closed his eyes tight . . . *Mail* . . . yet the tear still escaped from his left eye. The right eye had always closed tighter. "Scoff had my mail?"

"Yah?"

"Thanks. The poor dead bastard. Perhaps he can swipe enough dirt piled over him to come back. That's not funny."

"He had swiped some strange stuff, including a butterfly net and a box of Kotex. By the way, you won't be on the plane going home with me, like I had hoped. You are scheduled for some more fancy knit one, pearl two, stitching, with some of Grandma's crewel work thrown in."

"Tim?"

"Yah."

"Thanks."

The first letter brought the second laugh of the day to Johnny. "Dear son, I'm so glad you're not getting shot at. The news is so bad. How did you ever get a job bagging groceries at the PX in Hawaii? God is looking out for you."

Jazz gave him the third laugh of the day.

"Deer Johnny, Ma makes me wash my face in water every day despite the fact it freezes on my face right away. Me and my friend Bobbie are going down to the tracks and call the engineer and coal men peckerheads so they will throw coal at me and Bobbie, and we can heat this fricken place. I can say fricken 'cause Ma isn't gonna read this. She doesn't let me swear at all. Sometimes I do good. When I'm with the guys, I practice not swearing and don't say 'you piss me off.' I say 'you urinate me off.' One of the train guys could pitch for the Sox as he hit me in the head with one of his chucks. Ma could buy some coal, except she puts all the money you send her in a bankbook for you. Rags died. I hate to tell you, so I won't. I wanted to cry, but I never saw you do it."

Johnny read on. "They are trying to learn me al-g-bra when I don't even know how to spell it.

"Some big guy picked on Roma, so I hit him in the bawls. He said he was gonna kill me, but he seems to walk big circles around me when he sees me. I keep my eye on him.

"Roma beat me up for hitting some other guy. She said she would never have no boyfriends if I kept that up. She beat me bad with a metal coat hanger. Said the next time she was going to heat the coat hanger up until it glowed and then would whack me. She won't do that cuz she loves me. But if she tries it, I'll whack her in the bawls too."

Johnny wasn't sure whether the tears that fell were as warm as the baby pee when he used to help change Jazz's diapers or were tears of lonely laughter.

I always liked . . . multi . . . multiple . . . choice . . .

Romola wrote, "Johnny, you have to speak to Jazz! He frightens away all my boyfriends. I'll never get a date with Clark Gable. I still have the cardboard doll you drew of him, and the cowboy outfit you drew and I colored.

"Back to Jazz, he's such a terror for such a small package. Do you think if I killed him, they would send me to jail? Maybe I should get him on tape and tape people he has terrorized just in case I have to defend myself in court. He should be in reform school. He'd be number one in the class.

"I've been reading a little bit about law, just in case I do kill him. I might have to defend myself unless I can get one of those free 'pro boner' lawyers. Love, your sister Roma."

Roma . . . you funny, funny girl . . . a boner is a woodie . . . a stiffy . . . a hard-on . . . not a free/pro bono lawyer . . . You would be asking for a lawyer . . . that was in favor of erections . . .

"PS Johnny—Ma was going to fix the two steps in the hallway, but didn't. I accused her of trying to save money. She puts all the money you send home in the bank, or buries it or something. She said the reason she doesn't want to fill in the missing stairs is she wants everything just the same as when you get home.

"PPS If that's the truth, why did she give away your stamp collection ⸱ball cards and your Ricardo Hall-burton and Edgar Rice Bureaus books? Huh? Why did she give those away? We need some stuff here. Please tell her to spend some of what you send her on us.

"PPPS You're going to have to talk to Jazz. He's real weird. Said he was going to crack my nuts. What in heaven's name is he talking about? He's the one that's nuts. Come home, quick. Ma told me not to tell you. Rags died. Jazz kept him in his bed for a full day cuz he didn't want no one tossing dirt on him. He actually cried. I know I beat him bad sometimes and couldn't make him cry. Oh, well, you gotta keep trying. Come home."

"My Dearest Johnny," his mother wrote, "If you love me, you'll make arrangements to come home to me fast. Talk to one of those nice sergeants and have him send you home right away!!!"

Yelena wrote, "A friend of mine, actually, the boy who was king at the carnival ball and had to escort me, told me it was really thoughtless of me to ask you to win a medal for me. Of course, he was right. I just don't like people telling me what to do. You never did anything like that. He was so assertive.

"So forget the medal. It was a childish and selfish little girl that asked for one. I am no longer a girl. I am a woman who wants her man to come home in one piece.

"Yes, I am a woman. I thought I knew myself, but college has made me search my soul.

"Which brings up the subject of what our future together is.

"You have not mentioned going to college or medical school. You did mention you might like to write. That would be nice, to get our name out there. But perhaps you should put off your Pulitzer Prize until you make your first million as a doctor—Ha-ha. Anyway, we are not getting any younger. And decisions must be made.

"I adore and miss you and think of you nearly every day. Till we meet again. Your adoring Yelena."

"John, this is Bernadette. Bernadette Clarkson? Remember? You hit our Rockledge fullback in the nose during the football game? When he said something about me. There are so many things I want to say to you. Real important. So very most important stuff. We had some snow.

"My little sister ran away from home. I want to find her and help her. I have my own apartment now with four other girls. I got a job in the box factory and see your mother sometimes. Especially after work. She walks so fast that lots of little kids wait outside the factory waiting to race her.

"I saw Yelena's picture in the paper. She was a queen. She is the most beautiful woman in the world. You are so lucky.

"I can hear the snowplow outside. When the blade hits the sewer cover, it scares me. I get scared easy. I don't know why.

"I read a lot. Because I have lots of time. I'm not interested in dating. Just sort of because one time I talked to Yelena. She treated me really nice. She always was the nicest girl in the class. Others weren't always as nice. She said you wanted to be a doctor! That is wonderful!! And that someday later, you wanted to write some stuff. She didn't say what. Maybe like in the movie star magazines. Or even a book or something. But later, much later, after college, she said. If you like to write, maybe you could write first, doctor later. Or both at the same time. It's your choice. If I knew you better, I'd say do what your heart tells you. But I don't know you better. So I'll shut my mouth and say no more. I know I have no right to ask you this, but would you take the very best care of yourself that you can, for me?"

"Your friend, Bernadette Clarkson.

"PS I'm your classmate that thinks Yelena is the greatest.

"PPS You are too. You deserve each other. Please take care. Pretty, pretty please, with sugar on it."

What is she trying to say? . . . and who gives a good toot about snowplows hitting . . . sewer covers . . . "Come on."

He put the letters under his pillow. He would read some of them several times. And more. His left ear itched . . . *itched . . .*

It was missing. Or most of it was. Johnny wasn't prepared for the letter that came from Righty. "Johnny, you old grunt, you. I know you're getting better and will be leaving the land of the Nippon real soon.

"I lucked out. I'm in an army hospital at Fort Devens, not all that far from home. Maybe you can get sent here too. My toes healed up real good. I mean the spot where the toes were healed up real good. They got black when they froze. Some medic snapped them off. Said they looked like wieners that got overcooked at a barbecue.

"Other good news too. I won't have to waste a lot of money on tap dancing lessons. So Fred Astaire lucked out.

"Some nurse here accused me of stealing her box of Kotex and some money from her locker. Does she think I am Scoff? I told her I'd take a lie detector test. Asked her if she was willing to take one. Things were bad for a while. Until I gave her this nice ring I found in the garbage disposal in the mess hall. I guess some guy got a 'Dear John.'

"Got a letter from Lace, of all people. He said him and Tim are due to get bronze stars for the bit on the mountaintop. Says he should have gotten the Silver Star. Neither got a scratch.

"Buckle your seat belt on this one. Lace said, but of course, he lies like all rebels, that your cousin was a nervous wreck and is getting sent home in the next padded cell they can put wheels on. They should have known better than sending Pointer there. They should have made him an MP or something, let him direct traffic at Lejeune at the BAM barracks. The broad-assed marines would love him.

"How much luck can you have? The lucky shit. He'll get a Section Eight or a medical. They'll give him the Purple Heart with an acorn on it so the squirrels around him won't go hungry.

"Then they'll hand him a job in the post office. Maybe they'll let him wear the mortar plate on his chest so the stamps won't stick to his shirt, or something.

"I get tons of visitors. They think I'm sort of a hero. But none of them know where or what Korea is. I might as well have gotten my toes caught in a nudist colony mousetrap, or something.

"I haven't told anyone the type of wound you got. It's no one's business. It's private business. Private business, get it?

"Hey, if you think you had to buckle up for the news on Pointer, have them strap you to the bed on this one.

"Nookie Clarkson is on the way to Japan to see you. I guess Yelena told her you were hurt. She's a whacko. She left Rockledge bumming across the country and without a pot to piss in or a window to toss it out. She'll have to do the dirty deed for every trucker that picks her up. Sort of a trucker fucker.

"And if she hitchhikes a ride on some sort of slow boat to China, every swab in the Merchant Marine will take a shot at her. With those jugs, she could outfit every jug band in Kentucky. Oh, yah, Quince bought the big one. Right between the eyes.

"Gunny was beside him. Gunny caught a round that went right into his helmet, got hung up on a centrifugal force ride around it, and went out the same hole, without messing up his hair. He'll be all set for the war that comes after this one. They'll have to put an arm stretcher on his shirt to fit all the stripes and hash marks on it.

"Let's see. Who else? As you know, Punderson and his panties got a free trip home. Can you believe it—they gave him the Silver Star. For what? Eating panties while the rest of us starved. The dirty little chow hound.

"Oh, yah, Mulligan used up all his free lifts. Guess some Chink mortar man, a good one, put one right down his stack. He had got sent back to battalion. Somehow, probably through my training, he lifted a case of beer and was returning back to what was left of Dog, when a Chinky-Chinky Chinaman with big binoculars, spotted him carrying the beer through a valley toward the company and thought he'd have a little fun.

"He laid one in front of him, behind him, and to both sides to bracket him out a safe distance. And then stopped firing. He had had his ha-has at Mulligan's expense."

"But Mulligan got pissed. Put down the case of beer, pulled out a .45 and started shooting in the general direction of the mountain the mortar rounds were coming from. Course, the .45 goes to sleep while in full flight and hits the ground out a long way from the gook, but the laundryman saw the puff of the .45 hit.

"And it did peeve that China fella. He put that next mortar round down his stack. No more Mulligan. A mulligan in golf is when you flub your shot and you get to take a second one without the first counting on your score card, but he didn't get a mulligan on that round. Too bad. He was a funny shit. Every time he told the story about the Chinaman peeking down in his foxhole, smiling, and walking off, well, I loved it. He was sort of like a black Ma Toots. The poor bastards."

Johnny thought of Bernadette traveling across the United States and the ocean to see how bad he was wounded. "She's crazier than a hoot owl out of hoots. What does she want to see me for? So she can go home and tell people where I got hurt?" . . . *No one will ever know where I got hurt . . . no one . . . I'll run away . . . Oh my Jesus Lord in heaven . . . please, God, protect her . . . What can she be thinking?* . . . "Oh god" . . .

CHAPTER 16

THE JOURNEY

The sounds were of giant beasts that roared, modern Jurassics that chewed up miles of pavement.

The tiny brain of the beast that drove it onward talked a language over a walkie-talkie to a second driver with words only their own species understood.

"Howdy, good buddy, glad you got your ears on. Don't you go putting the pedal to the metal. Y'all hear? Your old friend Long Eyes sees Brownie Bear up ahead, unmarked. See you in Kansas. Keep your finger on it, but keep an eye on the road too."

The truck stop was loaded with such beasts that had used up their government allotted time on the road for the day, although a few were making up a second set of books, a log they would show an officer that they had only been driving for ten hours.

Many of the trucks idled all night, and the parking area was smothered with diesel fumes that would choke a giant smokestack.

A lone figure made its way among the trucks, climbed up on the running board, and tapped on a door. The door opened, and an upside-down head appeared as the driver was unwinding in the bed behind and above the seats.

The driver shone his light into the face of the young woman who perched there, then down her dress. "You come right on in, honey. I just happen to have something looks mighty like a diploma in my hands from the finest teacher you ever learned you somethin'."

He reached out and tried to grab the woman's wrist, but she jumped backward off the high perch, losing her balance, causing her knees to crunch against the hard pavement.

She ran quickly between two trucks and hid behind one of the giant tires, trying to still her heaving chest. The last trucker had jumped out of the truck and followed her when she jumped away terrified.

She hid beneath the giant rig, terrified, as the trucker circled the area, taunting, "I ain't gonna hurt you, honey. Your nice ol' daddy just wants to give you a piece of candy, sugar candy for a little sugar."

The syrupy sweet voice was edged with a meanness that sent shivers down Bernadette's spine, causing the fine down on the back of her neck to stand on end . . . *No, Daddy . . . Please . . . Daddy . . . don't . . .*

She could see the cowboy boots with the pointed steel toes circling the truck. "I know you're under there in your underwear, so much fun to tear. I'm coming in. In more ways than one, little darlin'. So make way for big daddy and his sugar daddy under there."

She watched in utter terror as the knees belonging to the voice started to bend slowly. She could see the belt buckle—"Dishonor before death." The fly was open. She looked around frantically for anything to strike out with. Heard him say, "I'll just have Billy Joe start up his dragon and move its sixteen paws forward. Maybe you'll come out before you get run over, little miss."

She heard the starter of the truck clang like a giant meat grinder, stutter, and then catch. The engine roared like a wounded bull.

The truck did not move forward, and the motor was cut.

"Now you gotta come out from under, little sissy." She heard the snap, click of a switchblade. "Well, you're not coming out? We'll see about that, Ms. Suddenly Goody Two-shoes. Come out!"

"No!"

"It was plenty good enough for you to tap on my door, but, well, lady's choice. Here's a small something for you to remember me by," and he reached under the truck, swinging the knife blindly, and made a thin slit on her cheek, not deep, not long, yet it burned even in the bitter cold of night.

She didn't move, then screamed, "I'm not here!"

The cowboy boots disappeared and then stepped on the truck's running board. "Hum her up."

The driver switched the key on and revved the giant Mac motor several times, causing the entire bottom of the truck and trailer to shake and shudder like a beast, puking flames and fumes around her.

She froze as the truck started forward, brought her knees against her chest, bowed her head between them . . . *Please God . . .* It rolled slowly forward. She felt the sagging wiring brush her hair . . . *Don't turn . . . Please don't turn . . .*

If the truck went left or right, she would be ground into pulp by the tires. The trailer's rear axle passed within inches of her head. She felt a drop of grease land on her eyelid . . . *It's turning . . .*

The inside tire passed within inches of her body, and then it was gone. She saw the cowboy boots running toward a second truck, hop in, and drive off.

Bernadette lay on the oil-soaked tarmac in the pitch black that hung like a hangman's shroud over her, as other panting giants that could at any moment flatten her to road kill-size spewed their guttural fumes and voices.

She sat up and hugged her knees in complete helplessness. The hot tears rolled down her cheeks, free-falling from her cheeks onto her jacket.

The fear from the chase and the rolling wheels that had warmed her frigid body quickly left, leaving her shivering.

There was a small light on in the cab of a nearby truck. The motor was idling. The driver was reading while the cab warmed, and he seemed tucked in for the night.

She wasn't sure how much more cold she could take. The cold was even more fierce than the hunger that gnawed in her stomach like a rat on cheese. Johnny had told her that hunger was like a rat gnawing your stomach away. It was the only time they were ever alone together.

She had been sitting on a swing, humming, when Johnny took the swing beside her. Neither spoke at first. Then he asked, "You ever been hungry?."

And she said "Yes."

He had asked, "Did it feel like a rat was gnawing in there?"

And she said, "Yes, when I'm hungriest. When I'm just hungry, it only felt like a mouse."

He had laughed and said, "When I'm only just a little hungry, I drink water. It helps. That's in the winter or other times when there are no fruit trees to snitch from. Being hungry is the worst thing in the world, isn't it?"

She had looked into his eyes. Looked downward . . . *No . . . Daddy is something . . . much worse . . .*

Then they swung for a little while, not saying much until, and she didn't know where she found the courage, Bernadette said, "Your eyes are green."

"Yours are blue. A blue lighter, brighter than the feathers of a bluebird."

"You ought to be a poet or somethin'," she said.

One other time, she was alone with him, but not really. She had followed him down the railroad tracks at the Fellsway and stood in the dark of the trees, watching him carve initials on the smooth bark of a big tree, but that was a long time ago.

Now Bernadette walked slowly toward the truck with the driver in it, knocked just once on the door, and wished she could take it back.

The door opened slowly. "Hi, Miss, sorry, I can't help you. You're looking at a strange one who is happy as hell with my bride of twenty-seven years. And I'm not one of those *Homo sapiens* that likes other men. It's just that I like my wife. You shivering? You come in and warm up."

Bernadette stepped back.

"Don't you worry none. You're about the age of my daughter, Mindy, was when she died. I'll get out of the truck on the driver's side. You get in on the passenger side. Lock the doors. And when you're warm enough, you can go back to work. You look awful young for this kinda work. Don't be afraid. I talk too much. I'll go have a coffee."

Bernadette remained silent as she walked around the truck to the passenger side. He started to get out the other side. Just as he was about to close the door behind him, she shook her head no, and he returned to the driver's seat.

"When's the last time you ate anything, child?"

"I don't remember."

"That's a long time. Here's some stuff Mildred packed for me. Good home cooking." He handed her the open lunch pail.

"I can't. It's . . . it's . . . yours."

"No, now it's yours, child." She ate slowly, having a difficult time getting the food down and holding it down while shivering.

The driver opened his thermos and poured a cup. "Hot tea?"

"You'll be hungry."

"I'm an old dogface and got used to living on short rations during the big one, World War II, when I was airborne. Plus I'm putting on a little pot," he said, patting his stomach, which didn't show the slightest sign of a bulge. "My stomach used to be a six-pack, rows of muscle. Now I guess you would describe it as a twelve-pack, rows of chub."

"Weren't you too young to have been in World War I when Mr. Lindberg was president?"

"Are you saying in sort of a nice way that I was too old to fight in World War II? Well, I was, but I got in. Corny as it might seem, I felt I had to give my country somethin' small. Even it only was my life. Sort of like a patriot would. There aren't many, if any, patriots around these days."

"I'm going to see one, a patriot."

"Where?"

"In Japan."

"Child, that's a long way to go even to see a patriot. You can look at me if it will save you the trip."

"This patriot is special."

"Your boyfriend, huh?"

"No. Nothing like that. He has a girlfriend, the most beautiful girl in the world."

"I would have reserved that honor for you, child."

"Why do you call me child?"

"Well, I still miss my Mindy after all these years. Couldn't have one after that. Me and Mildred were shut out by our broken hearts, the head doctor said. Said we were a little crazy. To want a child at our age. Seems like he was right cuz we paid the $350 he charged to tell us we were too old. So why are you heading to Japan if this boy belongs to someone else?"

"Because I told Yelena, that's his girlfriend, that I would tell him she loves him and to come home safely. And that she would love his Purple Heart. I don't think he can have the beautiful babies she expects from him. It was suspected he was hurt real bad down there." She looked down at her feet. Her sneakers were covered with grease. The laces were badly frayed. "That's not entirely true. Maybe I want to say hello to him for myself. But I'll speak for Yelena."

"I know, dear, but perhaps I should play the part of Pocahontas and you could be John Smith, and I would say, 'Speak for yourself, John,' or somethin' like that."

She looked at the small smile wrinkles around the corners of his eyes, his mouth. "Mindy was lucky. You were a wonderful daddy."

"I know."

They both sat in silence until the young trucker that had chased and terrorized Bernadette pounded on the truck door—"Send the little tramp out," he said, waving a lead pipe in circles like an anxious baseball player waiting for his turn at bat.

The old trucker reached beneath his seat, pulled out a sawed-off, single-barrel pump shotgun and said to the pipe wielder, "Guess you'll best be saying good-bye, one way or another. Your choice."

The young trucker made the only choice a coward can make, "You'll get yours old man!" and then turned and ran into the dark.

And the old man and the young girl were alone again.

"I'm only goin' about halfway across the country. Take about two days, give or take a tidge," he said.

"That's a lot further than I traveled the last couple of days," she said.

"Where did you start from?"

"Near Boston."

"And this is only Pennsylvania, home of the whitetail deer. You musta hopped a ride on a snail and forgot to say 'giddy up,' child."

She smiled.

"That's the softest smile I've ever seen. Softer than a baby's cheek. I'd say, that boy you're gonna tell that Miss Yelena loves him, is one lucky fella to have such a 'message to Garcia' carrier. You couldn't have had a lot of luck hitching rides. I mean, you didn't come far. And not in a very straight line."

"I just want to get there."

"The truckers picked you up were mostly pretty good guys? Most are. Some is bums."

She shuddered remembering one bum ... *"Hop in, Miss ... Nothing to be afraid of here ... Your little hand must be getting a little tired ... thumbing rides and all that ... now hold and read this map for me ... My name is Gerald ..."*

Gerald tried to take her hand and place it on the bulge in his dungarees. "I can't."

"Sure, you can. It don't bite none."

She had looked away. "I can pull off the road. No one would ever know what we're doing in here. I could drive you a long ways out of my way."

She turned her head and stared out the window.

"Now don't go turning away. I won't hurt you. It's just that it gets awful lonely on the road. A man just wants someone to talk to. If you could just like sort of take it out of my pants and sorta put it in your mouth a bit. Some say it's good for your complexion. Others say it cures the common cold. No one ever says it can bite you. It don't got no teeth. I wouldn't be lonely if you could just help me just a little bit. You look like a nice girl. Could go a long, long way out of my way to get you where you're going."

They rode in silence for some time. "At least take it out and sort of work it with your hand."

She turned and looked into his eyes and shook her head.

"Then just show me your melons, and I'll drive you until I run out of gas."

She lifted her sweater, then her bra, and cried, "I have to go all the way across the country."

"Here, if you work your hand on it while I drive, I'll take you 'cross the country."

She felt his hand on her wrist, moving it onto him, "Now you just move it slowly."

She tried to remove her hand, but he held hers tightly, working it up and down. "Now that doesn't hurt no one, does it? Fact is, it probably feels as good for you as it does for me. My name's Gerald, or did I tell you that?"

Gerald had driven her just under fifty miles, forty-nine and nine-tenths, to be exact. He had forced her out about a mile from the truck stop with the words "It was put out or get out. Out! You made your own bed, now you can lie in it. Get out."

He had wiped his stickiness on the front of her blouse and told her, "Now you can paste the rips in your dress together."

She had wanted to slap his face and scratch out those mean little pig eyes. She wasn't afraid of him but was afraid she'd be arrested and couldn't continue her journey to Johnny.

Now she was in another truck, one that not only was going halfway across the country, but also when it arrived there, she would see the driver reach into his wallet and provide her with bus fare and food money the rest of the way. He had told her of stories he had read. That's how he had known about John Smith and *A Message from Garcia* and Mr. Henry Shakespeare and Mr. Henry Thoreau.

"What did you mean about the Pocahontas and John Smith thing?" she asked him.

"Not much. A man does best when he's minding his own business, but when that Indian maiden was listening to John Smith building up his buddy before her eyes, she said something like 'Speak for yourself, John.'"

"Johnny could never do that, tell me to speak for myself. And I couldn't do that anyway, tell him to speak for himself."

Bernadette kissed the old trucker's cheek when they said good-bye at the bus stop.

"Are you OK?" she asked him. He looked like he wanted to cry.

"Yah, guess I have to go to the little boys' room or somethin'."

She made it to San Francisco. At the bus stop, she had learned that all marines that came back into the country landed at Treasure Island, just across the Golden Gate Bridge, located sort of behind Alcatraz. It was there at Treasure Island that she learned this from a man named Gunny, who was sent home "with, of all things," a bad back that wouldn't unlock. "Sleeping on too much ground over the years. Yah, John DaSilva. Good Marine. Got hurt. Wished he had bought the farm."

She had talked to numerous other marines. None knew of PFC John DaSilva. Although one said he could get her all the information she needed if he could "get a little poo tang or ying yang yo' from her."

The Treasure Island marines took up a collection so she could fly safely home. One had called her "Sis," the one who had started the collection, passing his hat around and telling all to "fill this piss cutter till it overflows." And they did, but Bernadette had no intention of heading home.

A young marine passing by said, "I knew DaSilva. I was there when he backed his front into the fan, rather than backing his ass into it. Tell him Sal Galvas told him to keep a stiff upper lip. That's the only thing that will be stiff, unless they have helper wheels for peckers."

"Fuck off," the gunny who was passing by said to Galvas. Then turning to Bernadette said, "Excuse my language, it gets a little salty when you've been away from a human for a while. But DaSilva's injury is one that happens sometimes. The wop just meant that your boyfriend will have to take a lot of stiff drinks till the doctors fix him up."

"He's not my boyfriend, but Johnny's tough, very tough. And I love him. And don't you go writing him what I just said. I just want to tell him that Yelena loves him."

She thought for a moment of Capt. John Smith's words . . . *"Speak for yourself"* . . . *but Johnny . . . is Johnny . . . and Yelena is . . . Yelena . . . and I am only . . . Bernadette . . .*

CHAPTER 17

HOME

It took months to rebuild Johnny legs for walking. The plastic surgery ear repair was fine, except it was a little shiny in one spot . . . *Hadn't the doctor said . . . your new ear is fine . . . sure . . . except for the shine. The other part will take years . . . to build a new . . . like Hemmingway said . . . to build a new . . . the sun also rises . . . part . . .*

Only his mother knew where he was, so very close to home. She didn't understand why he didn't want anyone, *"anyone,* under *any* conditions!" to visit him. And he was so close to home; the Chelsea Naval Hospital was less than a rifle shot away from his home.

"Johnny, you look fine. Jazz and Roma are so close. Let them see you."

"When I walk out of here, Ma. It will be soon enough."

"I didn't fix the stairs for you. Roma says maybe I should? What do you think?"

"I think you're the greatest, but let the open stairs stay, please, and you'll remain the greatest thing since the pee cutter was invented."

"You never said nothing like that to me before. The greatest? Are you sure you feel OK? You know I'm angry with you. You didn't learn to lie from our family. It must be from the Catholic side. You and your 'I'm not getting shot at; I'm packing grocery bags at the Post Exchange.'"

"Well, the Fleet Marine Force sort of moves you around."

"Fleet Marine Force. I wondered what that meant on your mailing address, 'FMF.' Johnny?"

"Yes, Ma?"

"What's a pee cutter?"

"It's something you cut peas with when you have KP, kitchen patrol." . . .

Actually, Ma . . . it's a cap . . . with a sharp edge top to it . . . and you snatch it . . . off the head of the guy . . . at the urinal beside you . . . and you cut through his stream of piss . . . before he does it to you . . . cut your piss . . . but if I told you that . . . you'd probably . . . cross your heart Catholic-style . . . Catholics are lucky . . . getting a free call through to God . . . I can remember going to bat . . . time after time . . . against some pitcher who tossed . . . baseballs that looked as small . . . as the period at the end of a sentence . . . or a curve ball that looked like a strand of spaghetti coming . . . and wanting to cross . . . myself . . .

"You're still one of those—virgins, aren't you, Johnny?"

"Come on, Ma. Look. I'll be getting out of here soon. I'm walking pretty good, a little herky-jerky, but I'll move my shoulders from side to side and pretend I'm practicing feinting for a boxing match coming up, or keeping time to some real cool music. I won't embarrass anyone."

"You never did, never could, Johnny. Although I hope people won't think you've been drinking. If anyone says anything, I'll take the broom to them, or worse, I'll sic your brother Jazz on them. He's a holy terror. You'll come right to our house, first, won't you, when you get out?"

"Yes, Ma."

"Yelena asks about you. I tell her you want to be all better from your wounds before you see anyone. She said that yes, she wanted you all better before—well, you know what she means. She wants to talk to you about 'things.' She must be the most beautiful girl in the world, John. She says you're going to be a doctor, even if she wasn't there to help you. She talks to me in public. She's not ashamed of me working in a box factory, or nothing. She told me so. You're very lucky. I think your children would be beautiful."

There will be no children . . . Ma . . . not for a long while . . . after a lot of fixing . . . maybe I'll always be a . . . virgin . . . "Ma, don't fix the stairs. I want to bound up those fuc— I mean, bound up those steps, especially the missing ones."

"Johnny, you don't do no swearing, do you? I'd call the president and give him a piece of my mind. You didn't swear none when you went into the marines."

"I don't swear, Ma."

"Swear that you don't swear, Johnny. Or smoke. Or drink."

"I don't swear, Ma." . . . Goddamn it . . . I left my pipe in the . . . barroom . . . I'm practically innocent . . .

His second lie to his mother came a week later. The taxi that picked him up at the hospital left him off on Rockledge Heights, where the money lived. Where gardeners and servants tended lawns and tea parties.

He walked toward Yelena's house.

And past it. Van Holt the smug, and Yelena were playing croquet.

From the twenty-room Tudor mansion of somber stucco and dark-stained woods of English design, he entered the colorful six-room ranch section where boys played stickball and wrestled with a cross section of who's who pooches. Girls jumped rope and played hopscotch.

He looked down when he spotted one group playing "war," the boys with their dishpan helmets, the girls with their white armbands with red crosses.

The ranches ended, and the gray ghost, triple-deckers appeared. There were small three-room cottages, like dust balls strewn between huge five-deckers that stood like giant discarded vacuum cleaner bags full to the brim.

As he approached one cottage, the curtain opened again ever so slightly.

He tried to change his limp to a swagger. A swagger similar to the one when he wore that first set of dress greens on liberty.

The act failed when it took all his balancing skills to maneuver onto the steps-missing porch . . . on well . . . nine and four are thirteen . . .

He knocked on the door . . . *If she doesn't answer . . . I'll know why . . .*

It was two lifetimes before the door opened.

She looked into his hazel eyes, so young to be filled with pain, and softly asked, "Are you sure you want to see me?"

"I would like to see you very much. But I'm not sure you'll want to see me," he said to the woman standing there, the woman with the eyes as light and blue and beautiful as that of a bluebird.

"Oh, yes! Why not? You walk like a peg-legged pirate."

He looked deeper into her eyes . . . *She didn't pretend . . . that I wasn't . . . limping . . .*

And then Bernadette ran into his arms.

And stayed there. Forever more.

It was two years later that they climbed the Big Tree, where once-young Flash Gordons manned their spaceship's limbs; Tarzans swung on high; Flying Tiger fighters in squadrons downed Jap Zeros. They climbed the high masts of Admiral Perry's flagship against the English fleet on Lake Erie, and Johnny hollered down, "We have met the enemy, and they are ours!"

They climbed hand in hand to the Big Tree's largest limb.

And then, quick as an arrow, all the answers in life were theirs . . .

Johnny vowed that someday he would be rebuilt, that they would make love, have a child, that they would recover all the dreams of the Big Tree. Little did they realize that it was easier to dream than make them come true. That decisions would be forced to be made.

Made in the USA
Middletown, DE
17 December 2014